Charlotte Mary Yonge

The Long Vacation

Outlook

Charlotte Mary Yonge

The Long Vacation

1. Auflage | ISBN: 978-3-73261-920-7

Erscheinungsort: Paderborn, Deutschland

Erscheinungsjahr: 2018

Outlook Verlag GmbH, Paderborn.

Reproduction of the original.

THE LONG VACATION

By Charlotte M. Yonge

How the children leave us, and no traces
   Linger of that smiling angel-band,
Gone, for ever gone, and in their places
   Weary men and anxious women stand.
               ADELAIDE A. PROCTOR

PREFACE

If a book by an author who must call herself a veteran should be taken up by readers of a younger generation, they are begged to consider the first few chapters as a sort of prologue, introduced for the sake of those of elder years, who were kind enough to be interested in the domestic politics of the Mohuns and the Underwoods.

Continuations are proverbially failures, and yet it is perhaps a consequence of the writer's realization of characters that some seem as if they could not be parted with, and must be carried on in the mind, and not only have their after-fates described, but their minds and opinions under the modifications of advancing years and altered circumstances.

Turner and other artists have been known literally to see colours in absolutely different hues as they grew older, and so no doubt it is with thinkers. The outlines may be the same, the tints are insensibly modified and altered, and the effect thus far changed.

Thus it is with the writers of fiction. The young write in full sympathy with, as well as for, the young, they have a pensive satisfaction in feeling and depicting the full pathos of a tragedy, and on the other hand they delight in their own mirth, and fully share it with the beings of their imagination, or they work out great questions with the unhesitating decision of their youth.

But those who write in elder years look on at their young people, not with inner sympathy but from the outside. Their affections and comprehension are with the fathers, mothers, and aunts; they dread, rather than seek, piteous scenes, and they have learnt that there are two sides to a question, that there are many stages in human life, and that the success or failure of early enthusiasm leaves a good deal more yet to come.

Thus the vivid fancy passes away, which the young are carried along with, and the older feel refreshed by; there is still a sense of experience, and a pleasure in tracing the perspective from another point of sight, where what was once distant has become near at hand, the earnest of many a day-dream has been gained, and more than one ideal has been tried, and merits and demerits have become apparent.

And thus it is hoped that the Long Vacation may not be devoid of interest for readers who have sympathized in early days with Beechcroft, Stoneborough, and Vale Leston, when they were peopled with the outcome of a youthful mind, and that they may be ready to look with interest on the perplexities and successes attending on the matured characters in after years.

If they will feel as if they were on a visit to friends grown older, with their children about them, and if the young will forgive the seeing with elder eyes, and observing instead of participating, that is all the veteran author would ask.

C. M. YONGE.

Elderfield,

January 31, 1895.

THE LONG VACATION

CHAPTER I. — A CHAPTER OF RETROSPECT

"Ah! my Gerald boy! There you are! Quite well?"

Gerald Underwood, of slight delicate mould, with refined, transparent-looking features, and with hair and budding moustache too fair for his large dark eyes, came bounding up the broad stair, to the embrace of the aunt who stood at the top, a little lame lady supported by an ivory-headed staff. Her deep blue eyes, dark eyebrows, and sweet though piquant face were framed by the straight crape line of widowhood, whence a soft white veil hung on her shoulders.

"Cherie sweet! You are well? And the Vicar?"

"Getting on. How are they all at Vale Leston?"

"All right. Your mother got to church on Easter-day." This was to Anna Vanderkist, a young person of the plump partridge order, and fair, rosy countenance ever ready for smiles and laughter.

"Here are no end of flowers," as the butler brought a hamper.

"Daffodils! Oh!—and anemones! How delicious! I must take Clement a bunch of those dear white violets. I know where they came from," and she held them to her lips. "Some primroses too, I hope."

"A few; but the main body, tied up in tight bunches like cauliflowers, I dropped at Kensington Palace Gardens."

"A yellow primrose is much more than a yellow primrose at present," said Mrs. Grinstead, picking out the few spared from political purposes. "Clement will want his button-hole, to greet Lance."

"So he is advanced to button-holes! And Lance?"

"He is coming up for the Press dinner, and will sleep here, to be ready for Primrose-day."

"That's prime, whatever brings him."

"There, children, go and *do* the flowers, and drink tea. I am going to read to your uncle to keep him fresh for Lance."

"How bright she looks," said Gerald, as Anna began collecting vases from the tables in a drawing-room not professionally artistic, but entirely domestic, and full of grace and charm of taste, looking over a suburban garden fresh with budding spring to a church spire.

"The thought of Uncle Lance has cheered them both very much."

"So the Vicar is really recovering?"

"Since Cousin Marilda flew at the curates, and told them that if they came near him with their worries, they should never see a farthing of hers! And they are all well at home? Is anything going on?"

"Chiefly defence of the copses from primrose marauders. You know the great agitation. They want to set up a china clay factory on Penbeacon, and turn the Ewe, not to say the Leston, into milk and water."

"The wretches! But they can't. It is yours."

"Not the western quarry; but they cannot get the stream without a piece of the land which belongs to Hodnet's farm, for which they make astounding bids; but, any way, nothing can be done till I am of age, when the lease to Hodnet is out, except by Act of Parliament, which is hardly worth while, considering—"

"That you are near twenty. But surely you won't consent?"

"Well, I don't want to break all your hearts, Cherie's especially, but why should all that space be nothing but a playground for us Underwoods, instead of making work for the million?"

"And a horrid, nasty million it would be," retorted Anna. "You born Yankee! Don't worry Aunt Cherry about profaning the Ewe, just to spoil good calico with nasty yellow dust."

"I don't want to worry her, but there never were such groovy people as you are! I shall think it over, and make up my mind by the time I have the power."

"I wish you had to wait till five-and-twenty, so as to get more time and sense."

Gerald laughed, and sauntered away. He was not Yankee, except that he had been born at Boston. His father was English, his mother a Hungarian singer, who had divorced and deserted his father, the ne'er-do-weel second son of an old family. When Gerald was five years old his father was killed, and he himself severely injured, in a raid of the Indians far west, and he was brought home by an old friend of the family. His eldest uncle's death made him heir to the estate, but his life was a very frail one till his thirteenth year, when he seemed to have outgrown the shock to spine and nerves.

Much had befallen the house of Underwood since the days when we took leave of them, still sorrowing under the loss of the main pillar of their house, but sending forth the new founders with good hope.

Geraldine had made her home at St. Matthew's with her brother Clement and the little delicate orphan Gerald; but after three years she had yielded to the persevering constancy of Mr. Grinstead, a sculptor of considerable genius and repute, much older than herself, who was ready and willing to be a kind uncle to her little charge, and who introduced her to all at home or abroad that was refined, intellectual, or beautiful.

It was in the first summer after their marriage that he was charmed with the vivacity and musical talent of her young sister Angela, now upon the world again. Angela had grown up as the pet and plaything of the Sisters of St. Faith's at Dearport, which she regarded as another home, and when crushed by grief at her eldest brother's death had hurried thither for solace. Her family thought her safe there, not realizing how far life is from having its final crisis over at one-and-twenty. New Sisters came in, old ones went to found fresh branches; stricter rules grew, up, and were enforced by a Superior out of sympathy with the girl, who had always rebelled against what she thought dictation. It was decided that she could stay there no longer, and her brother Lancelot and his wife received her at Marshlands with indignant sympathy for her wrongs; but neither she nor her sister-in-law were made to suit one another. With liberty her spirit and audacity revived, and she showed so much attraction towards the Salvation Army, that her brother declared their music to have been the chief deterrent from her becoming a "Hallelujah lass." However, in a brief visit to London, she so much pleased Mr. Grinstead that he invited her to partake in the winter's journey to Italy. Poor man, he little knew what he undertook. Music, art, Roman Catholic services, and novelty conspired to intoxicate her, and her sister was thankful to carry her off northward before she had pledged herself to enter a convent.

Mountain air and scenery, however, proved equally dangerous. Her enterprises inspired the two quiet people with constant fears for her neck; but it was worse when they fell in with a party of very Bohemian artists, whom Mr. Grinstead knew just well enough not to be able to shake them off. The climax came when she started off with them in costume at daybreak on an expedition to play the zither and sing at a village fete. She came back safe and sound, but Geraldine was already packed up to take her to Munich, where Charles Audley and Stella now were, and to leave her under their charge before she had driven Mr. Grinstead distracted.

There was a worse trouble at home. Since the death of his good old mother and of Felix Underwood, Sir Adrian Vanderkist had been rapidly going downhill; as though he had thrown off all restraint, and as if the yearly birth of a daughter left him the more free to waste his patrimony. Little or nothing had been heard direct from poor Alda till Clement was summoned by a telegram from Ironbeam Park to find his sister in the utmost danger, with a new-born son by her side, and her husband in the paroxysms of the terrible Nemesis of indulgence in alcohol.

Sir Adrian had quarrelled with all the family in turn except Clement, and this fact, or else that gentleness towards a sufferer that had won on old Fulbert Underwood, led him in a lucid interval to direct and sign a hurried will, drawn up by his steward, leaving the Reverend Edward Clement Underwood sole guardian to his children, and executor, together with his lawyer. It was done without Clement's knowledge, or he would have remonstrated, for never was there a more trying bequest than the charge which in a few days he found laid on him.

He had of course already made acquaintance with the little girls. Poor children, they had hitherto led a life as dreary as was possible to children who had each other, and fresh air and open grounds. Their mother was more and more of an invalid, and dreaded that their father should take umbrage at the least expense that they caused; so that they were scrupulously kept out of his way, fed, dressed, and even educated as plainly as possible by a governess, cheap because she was passe, and made up for her deficiencies by strictness amounting to harshness, while they learnt to regard each new little sister's sex as a proof of naughtiness on her part or theirs.

The first time they ever heard a man's step in the school-room passage was in those days of undefined sorrow, alarm, and silence after the governess had despatched the message to the only relation whose address she knew. The step came nearer; there was a knock, the sweet, strong voice asked,

"Are the poor little girls here?" and the tall figure was on one knee among them, gathering as many as he could within his loving arms. Perhaps he recollected Sister Constance among the forlorn flock at Bexley; but these were even more desolate, for they had no past of love and loyalty. But with that embrace it seemed to the four elders that their worst days were over. What mattered it to them that they all eight of them—were almost destitute? the birth of the poor little male heir preventing the sale of the property, so terribly encumbered; and the only available maintenance being the £5000 that Mr. Thomas Underwood had settled securely upon their mother.

They began to know what love and kindness meant. Kind uncles and aunts gathered round them. Their mother seemed to be able to live when her twin-sister hung over her, and as soon as she could be moved, the whole party left the gloom of Ironbeam for Vale Leston, where a house was arranged for them.

Lady Vanderkist continued a chronic invalid, watched over by her sister Wilmet and her excellent young daughter Mary. Robina, who had only one girl, and had not forgotten her training as a teacher, undertook, with the assistance of Sophia, the second daughter, the education of the little ones; and the third and fourth, Emilia and Anna, were adopted into the childless homes of Mrs. Travis Underwood and Mrs. Grinstead, and lived there as daughters. Business cares of the most perplexing kind fell, however, on Clement Underwood's devoted and unaccustomed head, and in the midst arrived a telegram from Charles Audley, summoning him instantly to Munich.

Angela was in danger of fulfilling her childish design of marrying a Duke, or at least a Graf. Diplomates could not choose their society, and she had utterly disdained all restraints from "the babies," as she chose to call Mr. and Mrs. Audley, and thus the wunderschones madchen had fascinated the Count, an unbelieving Roman Catholic of evil repute, and had derided their remonstrances.

Clement hurried off, but to find the bird flown. She had come down in the morning, white and tear-stained, and had told Stella that she could stay no longer, kissed her, and was gone out of the house before even Charles could be called. Stella's anxiety, almost despair, had however been relieved just before her brother's arrival by an electric message from Vale Leston with the words, "Angela safe at home."

Letters followed, and told how Robina had found her sobbing upon her brother Felix's grave. Her explanation was, that on the very night before her proposed betrothal, she had dreamt that she was drifting down the Ewe in the little boat Miss Ullin, and saw Felix under the willow-tree holding out his bared arms to her. She said, "Is that the scar of the scald?" and his only answer was the call "Angela! Angela!" and with the voice still sounding in her ears, she awoke, and determined instantly to obey the call, coming to her, as she felt, from another world. If it were only from her own conscience, still it was a cause of great thankfulness to her family, and she soon made herself very valuable at Vale Leston in a course of epidemics which ran through the village, and were in some cases very severe. The doctors declared that two of the little Vanderkists owed their lives to her unremitting care.

Her destiny seemed to be fixed, and she went off radiant to be trained at a London hospital as a nurse. Her faculty in that line was undoubted. All the men in her ward were devoted to her, and so were almost all the young doctors; but the matron did not like her, and at the end of the three years, an act of independent treatment of a patient caused a tremendous commotion, all the greater because many outsiders declared that she was right. But it almost led to a general expulsion of lady nurses.

Of course she had to retire, and happily for her, Mother Constance was just at that time sentenced by her rheumatism to spend the winter in a warm climate. She eagerly claimed Angela's tendance, and just at the end of the year there came an urgent request for a Sister from England to form a foundation in one of the new cities of Australia on the model of St. Faith's; and thither Mother Constance proceeded, with one Sister and Angela, who had thenceforth gone on so well and quietly that her family hoped the time for Angela's periodical breaking out had passed.

The ensuing years had been tranquil as to family events, though the various troubles and perplexities that fell on Clement were endless, both those parochial and ritualistic, and those connected with the Vanderkist affairs, where his sister did not spare him her murmurs. Fulbert's death in Australia was a blow both to Lancelot and to him, though they had never had much hope of seeing this brother again. He had left the proceeds of his sheep-farm between Lancelot, Bernard, and Angela.

Thus had passed about fourteen years since the death of Felix, when kind old Mr. Grinstead died suddenly at a public meeting, leaving his widow well endowed, and the possessor of her pretty home at Brompton. When, soon after the blow, her sisters took her to the home at Vale Leston, she had seemed oppressed by the full tide of young life overflowing there, and as if she again felt the full force of the early sorrow in the loss that she had once said made Vale Leston to her a desolation. On her return to Brompton, she had still been in a passive state, as though the taste of life had gone from her, and there was nothing to call forth her interest or energy. The first thing that roused her was the dangerous illness of her brother Clement, the result of blood-poisoning during a mission week in a pestilential locality, after a long course of family worries and overwork in his parish. Low, lingering fever had threatened every organ in turn, till in the early days of January, a fatal time in the family, he was almost despaired of. However, Dr. Brownlow and Lancelot Underwood had strength of mind to run the risk, with the earnest co-operation of Professor Tom May, of a removal to Brompton, where he immediately began to mend, so that he was in April decidedly convalescent, though with doubts as to a return to real health, nor had he yet gone beyond his dressing-room, since any exertion was liable to cause fainting.

CHAPTER II. — A CHAPTER OF TWADDLE

When Mrs. Grinstead, on her nephew's arm, came into her drawing-room after dinner, she was almost as much dismayed as pleased to find a long black figure in a capacious arm-chair by the fire.

"You adventurous person," she said, "how came you here?"

"I could not help it, with the prospect of Lancey boy," he said in smiling excuse, holding out a hand in greeting to Gerald, and thanking Anna, who brought a cushion.

"Hark! there he is!" and Gerald and Anna sprang forward, but were only in time to open the room door, when there was a double cry of greeting, not only of the slender, bright-eyed, still youthful-looking uncle, but of the pleasant face of his wife. She exclaimed as Lancelot hung over his brother—

"Indeed, I would not have come but that I thought he was still in his room."

"That's a very bad compliment, Gertrude, when I have just made my escape."

"I shall be too much for you," said Gertrude. "Here, children, take me off somewhere."

"To have some dinner," said Geraldine, her hand on the bell.

"No, no, Marilda feasted me."

"Then don't go," entreated Clement. "It is a treat to look at you two sunny people."

"Let us efface ourselves, and be seen and not heard," returned Gertrude, sitting down between Gerald and Anna on a distant couch, whence she contemplated the trio—Clement, of course, with the extreme pallor, languor, and emaciation of long illness, with a brow gaining in dignity and expression by the loss of hair, and with a look of weary, placid enjoyment as he listened to the talk of the other two; Lance with bright, sweet animation and cheeriness, still young-looking, though his hair too was scantier and his musical tones subdued; and Geraldine, pensive in eye and lip, but often sparkling up with flashes of her inborn playfulness, and, like Clement, resting in the sunshine diffused by Lance. This last was the editor and proprietor of the 'Pursuivant', an important local paper, and had come up on journalistic business as well as for the fete. Gertrude meantime had been choosing carpets and curtains.

"For," said Lance, with a smack of exultation, "we are actually going back to our old quarters over the shop."

"Oh!" A responsive sound of satisfaction from Geraldine.

"Nothing amiss?" asked Clement.

"Far from it. We let Marshlands to great advantage, and there are many reasons for the flitting. I ought to be at head-quarters, and besides there are the Sundays. We are too many now for picnicking in the class-room, or sponging on the rectory."

"And," said Gertrude, "I dare not put his small family in competition with his organ."

"Besides," said Lance, "the 'Pursuivant' is more exacting, and the printing Will Harewood's books has brought in more business—"

"But how about space? We could squeeze, but can you?"

"We have devoured our two next-door neighbours. There's for you! You know Pratt the dentist had a swell hall-door and staircase, which we absorb, so we shall not eat in the back drawing-room, nor come up the flight which used to be so severe on you, Cherry."

"I can only remember the arms that helped me up. I have never left off dreaming of the dear old step springing up the stair after the day's work, and the whistle to Theodore."

"Ah, those were the jolly old days!" returned Lance, con amore.

"Unbroken," added Clement, in the same tone.

"Better than Vale Leston?" asked Gertrude.

"The five years there were, as Felix called those last hours of delight, halcyon days," said Geraldine; "but the real home was in the rough and the smooth, the contrivances, the achievements, the exultation at each step on the ladder, the flashes of Edgar, the crowded holiday times—all happier than we knew! I hope your children will care as much."

"Vale Leston is their present paradise," said Gertrude. "You should see Master Felix's face at the least hope of a visit, and even little Fulbert talks about boat and fish."

"What have you done with the Lambs?" demanded Clement.

"They have outgrown the old place in every direction, and have got a spick-and-span chess-board of a villa out on the Minsterham road."

"They have not more children than you have."

"Five Lambkins to our four, besides Gussy and Killy," said Lance; "though A—which is all that appears of the great Achilles' unlucky name—is articled to Shapcote, and as for Gussy, or rather Mr. Tanneguy, he is my right hand."

"We thought him a nice sort of youth when he was improving himself in London," said Clement.

"You both were very good to him," said Lance, "and those three years were not wasted. He is a far better sub-editor and reporter than I was at his age, with his French wit and cleverness. The only fault I find with him is that he longs for plate-glass and flummery instead of old Froggatt's respectable panes."

"He has become the London assistant, who was our bugbear," said Geraldine.

"I don't know how we should get on without him since we made 'Pur' daily," said Lance.

"How old ambitions get realized!" said Geraldine.

"Does his mother endure the retail work, or has she not higher views for him?" asked Clement.

"In fact, ever since the first Lambkin came on the stage any one would have thought those poor boys were her steps, not good old Lamb's; whereas Felix always made a point of noticing them. Gus was nine years old that last time he was there, while I was ill, and he left such an impression as to make him the hero model.—Aye, Gus is first-rate."

"I am glad you have not altered the old shop and office."

"Catch me! But we are enlarging the reading-room, and the new press demands space. Then there's a dining-room for the young men, and what do you think I've got? We (not Froggatt, Underwood, and Lamb, but the Church Committee) have bought St. Oswald's buildings for a coffee hotel and young men's lodging-house."

"Our own, old house. Oh! is Edgar's Great Achilles there still?"

"I rushed up to see. Alas! the barbarians have papered him out. But what do you think I've got? The old cupboard door where all our heights were marked on our birthdays."

"He set it up in his office," said Gertrude. "I think he danced round it. I know he brought me and all the children to adore it, and showed us, just like a weather record, where every one shot up after the measles, and where

Clement got above you, Cherry, and Lance remained a bonny shrimp."

"A great move, but it sounds comfortable," said Clement.

"Yes; for now Lance will get a proper luncheon, as he never has done since dear old Mrs. Froggatt died," said Gertrude, "and he is an animal that needs to be made to eat! Then the children want schooling of the new-fashioned kinds."

All this had become possible through Fulbert's legacy between his brothers and unmarried sister, resulting in about £4000 apiece; besides which the firm had gone on prospering. Clement asked what was the present circulation of the 'Pursuivant', and as Lance named it, exclaimed—

"What would old Froggatt have said, or even Felix?"

"It is his doing," said Lance, "the lines he traced out."

"My father says it is the writing with a conscience," said Gertrude.

"Yes, with life, faculty, and point, so as to hinder the conscience from being a dead weight," added Geraldine.

"No wonder," said Lance, "with such contributors as the Harewoods, and such a war-correspondent as Aubrey May."

Just then the door began to open, and a black silk personage disconsolately exclaimed—

"Master Clement! Master Clem! Wherever is the boy gone, when he ought to be in his bed?"

"Ha, Sibby!" cried Lance, catching both hands, and kissing the cheery, withered-apple cheeks of the old nurse. "You see your baby has begun to run alone."

"Ah, Master Lance, 'twas your doing. You always was the mischief."

"No indeed, Sibby, the long boy did it all by himself, before ever I was in the house; but I'll bring him back again."

"May I not stay a little longer, Sibby," said Clement, rather piteously, "to hear Lance sing? I have been looking forward to it all day."

"If ye'll take yer jelly, sir," said Sibby, "as it's fainting ye'll be, and bringing our hearts into our mouths."

So Sibby administered her jelly, and heard histories of Lance's children, then, after exacting a promise that Master Lance should only sing once, she withdrew, as peremptory and almost as happy as in her once crowded nursery.

"What shall that once be, Clem?" asked Lance.

"'Lead, kindly Light.'"

"Is it not too much?" he inquired, glancing towards his widowed sister.

"I want it as much as he does," she answered fervently.

At thirty-eight Lance's voice was, if possible, more perfect in sweetness, purity, and expression than it had been at twenty, and never had the poem, connected with all the crises of their joint lives, come more home to their hearts, filling them with aspiration as well as memory.

Then Lance helped his brother up, and was surprised, after those cheerful tones, to feel the weight so prone and feeble, that Gerald's support on the other side was welcome. Mrs. Grinstead followed to take Gertrude to her room and find her children's photographs.

The two young people began to smile as soon as they were left alone.

"Did you ever see Bexley?" asked Anna.

"Yes—an awful hole," and both indulged in a merry laugh.

"My mother mentions it with pious horror," said Anna.

"Life is much more interesting when it is from hand to mouth," said Gerald, with a yawn. "If I went in for sentiment, which I don't, it would be for Fiddler's Ranch; though it is now a great city called Violinia, with everything like everything else everywhere."

"Not Uncle Lance."

"Certainly not. For a man with that splendid talent to bury it behind a counter, mitigated by a common church organ, is as remarkable as absurd; though he seems to thrive on it. It is a treat to see such innocent rapture, all genuine too!"

"You worn-out old man!" laughed Anna. "Aunt Cherry has always said that self-abnegation is the secret of Uncle Lance's charm."

"All very well in that generation—ces bons jours quand nous etions si miserables," said Gerald, in his low, maundering voice. "Prosperity means the lack of object."

"Does it?"

"In these days when everything is used up."

"Not to those two—"

"Happy folk, never to lose the sense of achievement!"

"Poor old man! You talk as if you were twenty years older than Uncle Lance."

"I sometimes think I am, and that I left my youth at Fiddler's Ranch."

Wherewith he strolled to the piano, and began to improvise something so yearning and melancholy that Anna was not sorry when her uncle came back and mentioned the tune the old cow died of.

Was Gerald, the orphan of Fiddler's Ranch, to be always the spoilt child of prosperity and the creature of modern life, with more aspirations than he saw how to fulfil, hampered as he was by duties, scruples, and affections?

CHAPTER III. — DARBY AND JOAN

Lancelot saw his brother's doctors the next morning, and communicated to his wife the upshot of the interview when they were driving to their meeting in Mrs. Grinstead's victoria, each adorned with a big bunch of primroses.

"Two doctors! and not Tom," said Gertrude.

"Both Brownlows. Tom knows them well, and wrote. One lives at the East-end, and is sheet anchor to Whittingtonia. He began with Clement, but made the case over to the cousin, the fashionable one, when we made the great removal."

"So they consulted?"

"And fairly see the way out of the wood, though not by any means quit of it, poor Tina; but there's a great deal to be thankful for," said Lance, with a long breath.

"Indeed there is!" said the wife, with a squeeze of the hand. "But is there any more to be feared?"

"Everything," Lance answered; "heart chiefly, but the lungs are not safe. He has been whirling his unfortunate machine faster and faster, till no wonder the mainspring has all but broken down. His ideal always was working himself to death, and only Felix could withhold him, so now he has fairly run himself down. No rest from that tremendous parish work, with the bothers about curates, school boards and board schools, and the threatened ritual prosecution, which came to nothing, but worried him almost as much as if it had gone on, besides all the trouble about poor Alda, and the loss of Fulbert took a great deal out of him. When Somers got a living, there was no one to look after him, and he never took warning. So when in that Stinksmeech Mission he breathed pestiferous air and drank pestiferous water, he was finished up. They've got typhus down there—a very good thing too," he added vindictively.

"I put it further back than Mr. Somers' going," said Gertrude. "He never was properly looked after since Cherry married. What is he to do now?"

"Just nothing. If he wishes to live or have a chance of working again, he must go to the seaside and vegetate, attempt nothing for the next six months, nor even think about St. Matthew's for a year, and, as they told me afterwards, be only able to go on cautiously even then.”

“How did he take it?”

“He laid his head against Cherry, who was standing by his chair, put an arm round her, and said, ‘There!’ and she gave him such a smile as I would not have missed seeing on any account. ‘Mine now,’ she said. ‘Best!’ he said. He is too much tired and worn out to vex himself about anything.”

“Where are they to go? Not to Ewmouth, or all the family worries would come upon them. Alda would give him no peace.”

“Certainly not there. Brownlow advises Rockquay. His delicate brother is a curate there, and it agrees with him better than any other place. So I am to go and see for a house for them. It is the very best thing for Cherry.”

“Indeed it is. Was not she like herself last night? Anna says she has never brightened up so much before! I do believe that if Clement goes on mending, the dear person will have a good time yet; nay, all the better now that she is free to be a thorough-going Underwood again.”

“You Underwooder than Underwood!”

“Exactly! I never did like—Yes, Lance, I am going to have it out. I do think Clement would have done better to let her alone.”

“He did let her alone. He told me so.”

“Yes, but she let out to me the difference between that time and the one of the first offer when dear Felix could not keep back his delight at keeping her; whereas she could not help seeing that she was a burthen on Clement’s soul, between fear of neglecting her and that whirl of parish work, and that St. Wulstan’s Hall was wanted for the girls’ school. Besides, Wilmet persuaded her.”

“She did. But it turned out well. The old man worshipped her, and she was very fond of him.”

“Oh! very well in a way, but you know better, Lance.”

“Well, perhaps he did not begin young enough. He was a good, religious man, but Pro Ecclesia Dei had not been his war-cry from his youth, and he did not understand, and thought it clerical; good, but outside his life. Still, she was happy.”

“Petting, Society, Art, travels! I had rather have had our two first years of tiffs than all that sort of happiness.”

“Tiffs! I thought we might have gone in for the Dunmow flitch.”

"You might! Do you mean that you forget how fractious and nasty and abominable I was, and how many headaches I gave you?"

"Only what you had to put up with."

"You don't recollect that first visit of my father's, when I was so frightfully cross because you said we must ask the Lambs and Bruces to dinner? You came down in the morning white as a ghost, an owl in its blinkers, and though I know you would rather have died than have uttered a word, no sooner were you off than he fell upon me with, 'Mrs. Daisy, I give you to understand that you haven't a husband made of such tough commodity as you are used to at home, and if you worry him you will have to rue it.'"

"What an ass I must have looked! Did I really go playing the martyr?"

"A very smiling martyr, pretending to be awfully jolly. I believe I requited papa by being very cross."

"At his interfering, eh? No wonder."

"Chiefly to conceal my fright, but I did begin trying not to fly out as I used to do, and I was frightened whenever I did so."

"Poor Daisy! That is why you always seemed to think every headache your fault."

"The final effect—I won't say cure—was from that book on education which said that a child should never know a cross word or look between father and mother. So you really have forgotten how horrid I couldbe?"

"Or never felt it! But to return to our muttons. I can't believe otherwise than that Cherry liked her old man, and if their parallel lines did not meet, she never found it out."

"That is true. She liked him and leant on him, and was constantly pleased and amused as well as idolized, but I don't think the deep places in her heart were stirred. Then there were constraints. He could not stand Angela's freaks. And his politics—"

"He was not so very much advanced."

"Enough not to like the 'Pursuivant' to lie about, nor her writing for it, even about art or books; nor did his old bones enjoy the rivers at Vale Leston. Now you will see a rebound."

"Or will she be too tender of him to do what he disliked?"

"That will be the test. Now she has Clement, I expect an article will come on the first book they read together."

Lance laughed, but returned to defend his sister.

"Indeed she was attached to him. She was altogether drooping and crushed at Vale Leston in the autumn."

"It was too soon. She was overdone with the multitudes, and in fact it was more the renewal of the old sorrow than the new one. Anna tells me that when they returned there was the same objectless depression. She would not take up her painting again, she said it was of no use, there was no one to care. I remember her being asked once to do something for the Kyrle Society, and Mr. Grinstead did not like it, but now Clement's illness has made a break, and in a new place, with him to occupy her instead of only that dawdling boy, you will see what you shall see!"

"Ah! Gerald!" was the answer, in a doubtful, wistful tone, just as they arrived.

CHAPTER IV. — SLUM, SEA, OR SEASON

Mr. and Mrs. Lancelot Underwood had not long been gone to their meeting when there ran into the drawing-room a girl a year older than Anna, with a taller, better figure, but a less clear complexion, namely Emilia, the adopted child of Mr. Travis Underwood. She found Anna freshening up the flowers, and Gerald in an arm-chair reading a weekly paper.

"I knew I should find you," she cried, kissing Anna, while Gerald held out a finger or two without rising. "I thought you would not be gone primrosing."

"A perspicacity that does you credit," said Gerald, still behind his paper.

"Are the cousins gone?" asked Anna.

"Of course they are; Cousin Marilda, in a bonnet like a primrose bank, is to pick up Fernan somewhere, but I told her I was too true to my principles to let wild horses drag me there."

"Let alone fat tame ones," ejaculated Gerald.

"What did she say?" asked Anna.

"Oh, she opened her eyes, and said she never should ask any one to act against principles, but principles in her time were for Church and State. Is Aunt Cherry in the vortex?"

"No, she is reading to Uncle Clem, or about the house somewhere. I don't think she would go now at least."

"Uncle Grin's memory would forbid," muttered Gerald. "He saw a good many things, though he was a regular old-fashioned Whig, an Edinburgh Review man."

"You've got the 'Censor' there! Oh, let me see it. My respected cousins don't think it good for little girls. What are you going to do?"

"I believe the doctors want Uncle Clem to get a long leave of absence, and that we shall go to the seaside," replied Anna.

"Oh! then you will come to us for the season! We reckon on it."

"No, indeed, Emmie, I don't see how I can. Those two are not in the least fit to go without some one."

"But then mother is reckoning on our having a season together. You lost the last."

Gerald laughed a little and hummed—

"Don't be so disgusting, Gerald! My friends have too much sense," cried Anna.

"But it is true enough as regards 'my minnie,'" said Emilia.

"Well, eight daughters *are* serious—baronet's daughters!" observed Gerald in his teasing voice.

"Tocherless lasses without even the long pedigree," laughed Anna. "Poor mother."

"The pedigree is long enough to make her keep poor Vale Leston suitors at arm's length," mumbled Gerald; but the sisters did not hear him, for Emilia was exclaiming—

"I mean to be a worker. I shall make Marilda let me have hospital training, and either go out to Aunt Angela or have a hospital here. Come and help me, Annie."

"I have a hospital here," laughed Anna.

"But, Nan dear, do come! You know such lots of swells. You would get one into real society if one is to have it; Lady Rotherwood, Lady Caergwent, besides all your delightful artist friends; and that would pacify mother, and make it so much pleasanter for me. Oh, if you knew what the evenings are!"

"What an inducement!"

"It would not be so if Annie were there. We should go out, and miss the horrid aldermanic kind of dinners; and at home, when we had played the two old dears to sleep, as I have to do every night, while they nod over their piquet or backgammon, we could have some fun together! Now, Annie, you would like it. You do care for good society, now don't you?"

"I did enjoy it very much when Aunt Cherry went with me, but—"

"No buts, no buts. You would come to the laundry girls, and the cooking-class, and all the rest with me, and we should not have a dreary moment. Have you done fiddling over those flowers?"

"Not yet; Vale Leston flowers, you know. Besides, Aunt Cherry can't bear them not artistic."

"Tidy is enough for Marilda. She does them herself, or the housekeeper; I can't waste time worrying over them."

"That's the reason they always look like a gardener's prize bouquet at a country horticultural show," said Gerald.

"What does it signify? They are only a testimony to Sir Gorgias Midas' riches. I do hate orchids."

"I wish them on their native rocks, poor things," said Gerald. "But poor Fernan, you do him an injustice."

"Oh, yes, he does quantities of good works, and so does Marilda, till I am quite sick of hearing of them! The piles of begging letters they get! And then they want them read and explained, and answered sometimes."

"A means of good works," observed Gerald.

"How would you like it? Docketing the crumbs from Dives' table," exclaimed Emilia.

"A clerk or secretary could do it," said Anna.

"Of course. Now if you have finished those flowers, do come out with me. I want to go into Ponter's Court, and Fernan won't let me go alone."

"Have you any special object?" said Gerald lazily, "or is it to refresh yourself with the atmosphere?"

"That dear boy—that Silky—has been taken up, and they've sent him to a reformatory."

"What a good thing!"

"Yes, only I don't believe he did it! It was that nasty little Bill Nosey. I am sure that he got hold of the lady's parcel, and stuffed it into Silky's cap."

Emilia spoke with a vehemence that made them both laugh, and Gerald said—

"But if he is in a reformatory, what then? Are we to condole with his afflicted family, or bring Bill Nosey to confess?"

"I thought I would see about it," said Emilia vaguely.

"Well, I decline to walk in the steps of the police as an amateur! How about the Dicksons?"

"Drifted away no one knows where. That's the worst of it. Those poor things do shift about so."

"Yes. I thought we had got hold of those boys with the gymnasium. But work wants regulating."

"Oh, Gerald, I am glad you are coming. Now I am free! Just fancy, they had a horrid, stupid, slow dinner-party on Easter Monday, of all the burgomasters and great One-eyers, and would not let me go down and sing to the match-girls!"

"You had the pleasure of a study of the follies of wealth instead of the follies of poverty."

"Oh, to hear Mrs. Brown discourse on her troubles with her first, second, and third coachman!"

"Was the irresistible Ferdinand Brown there?"

"Yes, indeed, with diamond beetle studs and a fresh twist to his moustache. It has grown long enough to be waxed."

"How happy that fellow would be if he were obliged to dig! I should like to scatter his wardrobe over Ponter's Court."

"There, Nan, have you finished?" as Anna swept the scattered leaves into a basket. "Are you coming?"

"I don't think I shall. You would only talk treason—well—social treason all the way, and you don't want me, and Aunt Cherry would have to lunch alone, unless you wait till after."

"Oh no, I know a scrumptious place for lunch," said Gerald. "You are right, Annie, one lady is quite enough on one's hands in such regions. You have no jewellery, Emmie?"

"Do you see any verdure about me?" she retorted.

So when Gerald's tardy movements had been overcome, off they started to their beloved slum, Emilia looking as if she were setting forth for Elysium, and they were seen no more, even when five o'clock tea was spread, and Anna making it for her Uncle Lance and his wife, who had just returned, full of political news; and likewise Lance said that he had picked up some intelligence for his sister. He had met General Mohun and Sir Jasper Merrifield, both connections of the Underwoods.

General Mohun lived with his sister at Rockstone, Sir Jasper, his brother- in-law, at Clipstone, not far off, and they both recommended Rockquay and its bay "with as much praise," said Lance, "as the inhabitants ever give of a sea place."

"Very good, except for the visitors," said Geraldine.

"Exactly so. Over-built, over-everythinged, but still tolerable. The General lives there with his sister, and promises to write to me about houses, and Sir

Jasper in a house a few miles off."

"He is Bernard's father-in-law?"

"Yes," said Gertrude; "and my brother Harry married a sister of Lady Merrifield, a most delightful person as ever I saw. We tell my father that if she were not out in New Zealand we should all begin to be jealous, he is so enthusiastic about Phyllis."

"You have never told us how Dr. May is."

"It is not easy to persuade him that he is not as young as he was," said Gertrude.

"I should say he was," observed Lance.

"In heart—that's true," said Gertrude; "but he does get tired, and goes to sleep a good deal, but he likes to go and see his old patients, as much as they like to have him, and Ethel is always looking after him. It is just her life now that Cocksmoor has grown so big and wants her less. Things do settle themselves. If any one had told her twenty years ago that Richard would have a great woollen factory living, and Cocksmoor and Stoneborough meet, and a separate parish be made, with a disgusting paper-mill, two churches, and a clergyman's wife—(what's the female of whipper-snapper, Lance?)—who treats her as—"

"As an extinct volcano," murmured Lance.

"She would have thought her heart would be broken," pursued Gertrude. "Whereas now she owns that it is the best thing, and a great relief, for she could not attend to Cocksmoor and my father both. We want her to take a holiday, but she never will. Once she did when Blanche and Hector came to stay, but he was not happy, hardly well, and I don't think she will ever leave him again."

"Mrs. Rivers is working still in London?"

"Oh yes; I don't know what the charities of all kinds and descriptions would do without her."

"No," said Clement from his easy-chair. "She is a most valuable person. She has such good judgment."

"It has been her whole life ever since poor George Rivers' fatal accident," said Gertrude. "I hardly remember her before she was married, except a sense that I was naughty with her, and then she was terribly sad. But since she gave up Abbotstoke to young Dickie May she has been much brighter, and she can do more than any one at Cocksmoor. She manages Cocksmoor and London affairs in her own way, and has two houses and young Mrs. Dickie on her hands to boot."

"How many societies is she chairwoman of?" said Lance. "I counted twenty-four pigeon-holes in her cabinet one day, and I believe there was a society for each of them; but I must say she is quiet about them."

"It is fine to see the little hen-of-the-walk of Cocksmoor lower her crest to her!" said Gertrude, "when Ethel has not thought it worth while to assert herself, being conscious of being an old fogey."

"And your Bishop?"

"Norman? I do believe he is coming home next year. I think he really would if papa begged him, but that he—my father, I mean—said he would never do so; though I believe nothing would be such happiness to him as to have Norman and Meta at home again. You know they came home on George's death, but then those New Somersetas went and chose him Bishop, and there he is for good."

"For good indeed," said Clement; "he is a great power there."

"So are his books," added Geraldine. "Will Harewood sets great store by them. Ah! I hear our young folks—or is that a carriage?"

Emilia and Gerald came in simultaneously with Marilda, expanded into a portly matron, as good-humoured as ever, and better-looking than long ago.

She was already insisting on Gerald's coming to a party of hers and bringing his violin, and only interrupted her persuasions to greet and congratulate Clement.

Gerald, lying back on a sofa, and looking tired, only replied in a bantering, lazy manner.

"Ah! if I asked you to play to the chimney-sweeps," she said, "you would come fast enough, you idle boy. And you, Annie, do you know you are coming to me for the season when your uncle and aunt go out of town?"

"Indeed, Cousin Marilda, thank you, I don't know it, and I don't believe it."

"Ah, we'll see! You haven't thought of the dresses you two are to have for the Drawing-Room from Worth's, and Lady Caergwent to present you."

Anna shook her head laughingly, while Gerald muttered—

"Salmon are caught with gay flies."

They closed round the tea-table while Marilda sighed—

"Alda's daughters are not like herself."

"A different generation," said Geraldine.

"See the Beggars Opera," said Lance—

"Ah! your time has not come yet, Lance. Your little girls are at a comfortable age."

"There are different ways of throwing oneself away," said Clement. "Perhaps each generation says it of the next."

"Emmie is not throwing herself away, except her chances," said Marilda. "If she would only think of poor Ferdy Brown, who is as good a fellow as ever lived!"

"Not much chance of that," said Geraldine.

Their eyes all met as each had glanced at the tea-table, where Emilia and Gerald were looking over a report together, but Geraldine shook her head. She was sure that Gerald did not think of his cousins otherwise than as sisters, but she was by no means equally sure of Emilia, to whom he was certainly a hero.

Anna had not heard the last of the season. Her mother wrote to her, and also to Geraldine, whom she piteously entreated not to let Anna lose another chance, in the midst of her bloom, when she could get good introductions, and Marilda would do all she could for her.

But Anna was obdurate. She should never see any one in society like Uncle Clem. She had had a taste two years ago, and she wished for no more. She should see the best pictures at the studios before leaving town, and she neither could nor would leave her uncle and aunt to themselves. So the matter remained in abeyance till the place of sojourn had been selected and tried; and meantime Gerald spent what remained of the Easter vacation in a little of exhibitions with Anna, a little of slumming with Emilia, a little of society impartially with swells and artists, and a good deal of amiable lounging and of modern reading of all kinds. His aunt watched, enjoyed, yet could not understand, his uncle said, that he was an undeveloped creature.

CHAPTER V. — A HAPPY SPRITE

A retired soldier, living with his sister in a watering-place, is apt to form to himself regular habits, of which one of the most regular is the walking to the station in quest of his newspaper. Here, then, it was that the tall, grey-haired, white-moustached General Mohun beheld, emerging on the platform, a slight figure in a grey suit, bag in hand, accompanied by a pretty pink-cheeked, fair-haired, knicker-bockered little boy, whose air of content and elation at being father's companion made his sapphire eyes goodly to behold.

"Mr. Underwood! I am glad to see you."

"I thought I would run down and look at the house you were so good as to mention for my sister, and let this chap have a smell of the sea."

There was a contention between General Mohun's hospitality and Lancelot's intention of leaving his bag at the railway hotel, but the former gained the day, the more easily because there was an assurance that the nephew who slept at Miss Mohun's for the sake of his day-school would take little Felix Underwood under his protection, and show him his curiosities. The boy's eyes grew round, and he exclaimed—

"Foolish guillemots' eggs?"

"He is in the egg stage," said his father, smiling.

"I won't answer for guillemots," said the General, "but nothing seems to come amiss to Fergus, though his chief turn is for stones."

There was a connection between the families, Bernard Underwood, the youngest brother of Lance, having married the elder sister of the aforesaid Fergus Merrifield. Miss Mohun, the sister who made a home for the General, had looked out the house that Lance had come to inspect. As it was nearly half-past twelve o'clock, the party went round by the school, where, in the rear of the other rushing boys, came Fergus, in all the dignity of the senior form.

"Look at him," said the General, "those are honours one only gets once or twice in one's life, before beginning at the bottom again."

Fergus graciously received the introduction; and the next sound that was heard was, "Have you any good fossils about you?" in a tone as if he doubted whether so small a boy knew what a fossil meant; but little Felix was equal to the occasion.

"I once found a shepherd's crown, and father said it was a fossil sea-urchin, and that they are alive sometimes."

"Echini. Oh yes—recent, you mean. There are lots of them here. I don't go in for those mere recent things," said Fergus, in a pre-Adamite tone, "but my sister does. I can take you down to a fisherman who has always got some."

"Father, may I? I've got my eighteenpence," asked the boy, turning up his animated face, while Fergus, with an air of patronage, vouched for the honesty of Jacob Green, and undertook to bring his charge back in time for luncheon.

Lancelot Underwood had entirely got over that sense of being in a false position which had once rendered society distasteful to him. Many more men of family were in the like position with himself than had been the case when his brother had begun life; moreover, he had personally achieved some standing and distinction through the 'Pursuivant'.

General Mohun was delighted with his companion, whom he presented to his sister as the speedy consequence of her recommendation. She was rather surprised at the choice of an emissary, but her heart was won when she found Mr. Underwood as deep in the voluntary school struggle as she could be. Her brother held up his hands, and warned her that it was quite enough to be in the fray without going over it again, and that the breath of parish troubles would frighten away the invalid.

"I'll promise not to molest him," she said.

"Besides," said Lance, "one can look at other people's parishes more philosophically than at one's own."

He had begun to grow a little anxious about his boy, but presently from the garden, up from the cliff-path, the two bounded in—little Felix with the brightest of eyes and rosiest of cheeks, and a great ruddy, white-beaded sea-urchin held in triumph in his hands.

"Oh, please," he cried, "my hands are too dirty to shake; we've been digging in the sand. It's too splendid! And they ought to have spines. When they are alive they walk on them. There's a bay! Oh, do come down and look for them."

"And pray what would become of Aunt Cherry's house, sir? Miss Mohun, may I take him to make his paws presentable?"

"A jolly little kid," pronounced Fergus, lingering before performing the same operation, "but he has not got his mind opened to stratification, and only cares for recent rubbish. I wish it was a half-holiday, I would show him something!"

The General, who had a great turn for children, and for the chase in any form, was sufficiently pleased with little Felix's good manners and bright intelligence about bird, beast, and fish, as to volunteer to conduct him to the region most favourable to spouting razor-fish and ambulatory sea-urchins. The boy turned crimson and gasped—

"Oh, thank you!"

"Thank you indeed," said his father, when he had been carried off to inspect Fergus's museum in the lumber-room. "'To see a real General out of the wars' was one great delight in coming here, though I believe he would have been no more surprised to hear that you had been at Agincourt than in Afghanistan. 'It's in history,' he said with an awe-stricken voice."

When Fergus, after some shouting, was torn from his beloved museum, Felix came down in suppressed ecstasy, declaring it the loveliest and most delicious of places, all bones and stones, where his father must come and see what Fergus thought was a megatherium's tooth. The long word was pronounced with a triumphant delicacy of utterance, amid dancing bounds of the dainty, tightly-hosed little legs.

The General and his companion went their way, while the other two had a more weary search, resulting in the choice of not the most inviting of the houses, but the one soonest available within convenient distance of church and sea. When it came to practical details, Miss Mohun was struck by the contrast between her companion's business promptness and the rapt, musing look she had seen when she came on him listening to the measured cadence of the waves upon the cliffs, and the reverberations in the hollows beneath. And when he went to hire a piano she, albeit unmusical, was struck by what her ears told her, yet far more by the look of reverent admiration and wonder that his touch and his technical remarks brought out on the dealer's face.

"Has that man, a bookseller and journalist, missed his vocation?" she said to herself. "Yet he looks too strong and happy for that. Has he conquered something, and been the better for it?"

He made so many inquiries about Fergus and his school, that she began to think it must be with a view to his own pretty boy, who came back all sea-water and ecstasy, with a store of limpets, sea-weeds, scales, purses, and cuttle-fish's backbones for the delectation of his sisters. Above all, he was eloquent on the shell of a lacemaker crab, all over prickles, which he had seen hanging in the window of a little tobacconist. He had been so much fascinated by it that General Mohun regretted not having taken him to buy it, though it appeared to be displayed more for ornament than for sale.

"It is a disgusting den," added the General, "with 'Ici on parle Francais' in the window, and people hanging about among whom I did not fancy taking the boy."

"I know the place," said Miss Mohun. "Strange to say, it produces rather a nice girl, under the compulsion of the school officer. She is plainly half a foreigner, and when Mr. Flight got up those theatricals last winter she sung most sweetly, and showed such talent that I thought it quite dangerous."

"I remember," said her brother. "She was a fairy among the clods."

The next morning, to the amazement of Miss Mohun, who thought herself one of the earliest of risers, she not only met the father and son at early matins, but found that they had been out for two hours enjoying sea-side felicity, watching the boats come in, and delighting in the beauty of the fresh mackerel.

"If they had not all been dead!" sighed the tender-hearted little fellow. "But I've got my lacemaker for Audrey."

"'The carapace of a pagurus,' as Fergus translated it." Adding, "I don't know the species."

"I can find out when father has time to let us look at the big natural history book in the shop," said Felix. "We must not look at it unless he turns it over, so Pearl and I are saving up to buy it."

"For instance!" said his father, laughing.

"Oh, I could not help getting something for them all," pleaded the boy, "and pagurus was not dear. At least he is, in the other way."

"Take care, Fely—he won't stand caresses. I should think he was the first crab ever so embraced."

"I wonder you got entrance so early in the day," said Miss Mohun.

"The girl was sweeping out the shop, and singing the morning hymn, so sweetly and truly, that it would have attracted me anyway," said Lancelot. "No doubt the seafaring men want 'baccy at all hours. She was much amazed at our request, and called her mother, who came out in remarkable dishabille, and is plainly foreign. I can't think where I have seen such a pair of eyes— most likely in the head of some chorus-singer, indeed the voice had something of the quality. Anyway, she stared at me to the full extent of them."

So Lancelot departed, having put in hand negotiations for a tolerable house not far from St. Andrew's Church, and studied the accommodation available for horses, and the powers of the pianos on hire.

CHAPTER VI. — ST. ANDREW'S ROCK

"How does he seem now?" said Geraldine, as Lancelot came into the drawing-room of St. Andrew's Rock at Rockquay, in the full glare of a cold east windy May evening.

"Pretty well fagged out, but that does not greatly matter. I say, Cherry, how will you stand this? Till I saw you in this den, I had no notion how shabby, and dull, and ugly it is."

"My dear Lance, if you did but know how refreshing it is to see anything shabby, and dull, and ugly," Mrs. Grinstead answered with imitative inflections, which set Anna Vanderkist off into a fit of laughter, infecting both her uncle and aunt. The former gravely said—

"If you had only mentioned it in time, I could have gratified you more effectually."

"I suppose it is Aunt Cherry's charity," said Anna, recovering. "The reflection that but for her the poor natives would never have been able to go to their German baths."

"Oh, no such philanthropy, my dear. It is homeliness, or rather homeyness, that is dear to my bourgeoise mind. I was afraid of spick-and-span, sap-green aestheticism, but those curtains have done their own fading in pleasing shades, that good old sofa can be lain upon, and there's a real comfortable crack on that frame; while as to the chiffonier, is not it the marrow of the one Mrs. Froggatt left us, where Wilmet kept all the things in want of mending?"

"Ah! didn't you shudder when she turned the key?" said Lance.

"Not knowing what was good for me."

"But you will send for some of our things and make it nice," entreated Anna, "or Gerald will never stay here."

"Never fear; we'll have it presentable by the vacation. As for Uncle Clement, he would never see whether he was in a hermit's cell, if he only had one arm-chair and one print from Raffaelle."

There was a certain arch ring in her voice that had long been absent, and Anna looked joyous as she waited on them both.

"I am glad you brought her," said Lance, as she set off with Uncle Clement's tea.

"Yes, she would not hear of the charms of the season."

"So much the better for her. She is a good girl, and will be all the happier down here, as well as better. There's a whole hive of Merrifields to make merry with her; and, by the bye, Cherry, what should you think of housing a little chap for the school here where Fergus Merrifield is?"

"Your dear little Felix? Delightful!"

"*Ouf*! No, he is booked for our grammar school."

"The grammar school was not good for any of you, except the one whom nothing hurt."

"It is very different now. I have full confidence in the head, and the tone is improved throughout. Till my boys are ready for a public school I had rather they were among our own people. No, Cherry, I can't do it, I can't give up the delight of him yet; no, I can't, nor lose his little voice out of the choir, and have his music spoilt."

"I don't wonder."

"I don't think I spoil him. I really have flogged him once," said Lance, half wistfully, half playfully.

"How proud you are of it."

"It was for maltreating little Joan Vanderkist, though if it had only been her brother, I should have said, 'Go it, boys.' It was not till afterwards that it turned out that Joan was too loyal not to bear the penalty of having tied our little Audrey into a chair to be pelted with horse-chestnuts."

"At Adrian's bidding?"

"Of course. I fancy the Harewood boys set him on. And what I thought of was sending Adrian here to be schooled at Mrs. Edgar's, boarded by you, mothered by Anna, and altogether saved from being made utterly detestable, as he will inevitably be if he remains to tyrannize over Vale Leston."

"Would his mother consent?"

"You know he is entirely in Clement's power."

"It would only be another worry for Clement."

"He need not have much of him, and I believe he would prefer to have him under his own eye; and Anna will think it bliss to have him, though what it may prove is another question. She will keep you from being too much bothered."

"My dear Lance, will you never understand, that as furze and thistles are to a donkey, so are shabbiness and bother to me—a native element?"

In the morning Clement, raised on his pillows in bed, showed himself highly grateful for the proposal about his youngest ward.

"It is very good of you, Cherry," he said. "That poor boy has been very much on my mind. This is the way to profit by my enforced leisure."

"That's the way to make me dread him. You were to lie fallow."

"Not exactly. I have thirteen or fourteen years' reading and thinking to make up. I have done no more than get up a thing cursorily since I left Vale Leston."

"You are welcome to read and think, provided it is nothing more recent than St. Chrysostom."

"So here is the letter to Alda," giving it to her open.

"Short and to the purpose," she said.

"Alda submits to the inevitable," he said. "Don't appear as if she had a choice."

"Only mention the alleviations. No, you are not to get up yet. There's no place for you to sit in, and the east wind is not greatly mitigated by the sea air. Shall I send Anna to read to you?"

"In half-an-hour, if she is ready then; meantime, those two books, if you please."

She handed him his Greek Testament and Bishop Andrews, and repaired to the drawing-room, where she found Anna exulting in the decorations brought from home, and the flowers brought in from an itinerant barrow.

"I have been setting down what they must send us from home—your own chair and table, and the Liberty rugs, and the casts of St. Cecilia and little St. Cyrillus for those bare corners, and I am going out for a terra-cotta vase."

"Oh, my dear, the room is charming; but don't let us get too dependent on pretty things. They demoralize as much or more than ugly ones."

"Do you mean that they are a luxury? Is it not right to try to have everything beautiful?"

"I don't know, my dear."

"Don't know!" exclaimed Anna.

"Yes, my dear, I really get confused sometimes as to what is mere lust of the eye, and what is regard to whatever things are lovely. I believe the principle is really in each case to try whether the high object or the gratification of the senses should stand first."

"Well," said Anna, laughing, "I suppose it is a high object not to alienate Gerald, as would certainly be done by the culture of the ugly—"

"Or rather of that which pretends to be the reverse, and is only fashion," said her aunt, who meantime was moving about, adding nameless grace by her touch to all Anna's arrangements.

"May I send for the things then?" said Anna demurely.

"Oh yes, certainly; and you had better get the study arm-chair for your uncle. There is nothing so comfortable here. But I have news for you. What do you say to having little Adrian here, to go to school with the Merrifield boy?"

"What fun! what fun! How delicious!" cried the sister, springing about like a child.

"I suspected that the person to whom he would give most trouble would feel it most pleasure."

"You don't know what a funny, delightful child he is! You didn't see him driving all the little girls in a team four-in-hand."

It would be much to say that Mrs. Grinstead was enchanted by this proof of his charms; but they were interrupted by Marshall, the polite, patronizing butler, bringing in a card. Miss Mohun would be glad to know how Mr. Underwood was, and whether there was anything that she could do for Mrs. Grinstead.

Of course she was asked to come in, and thus they met, the quick, slim, active little spinster, whose whole life had been work, and the far younger widow, whose vocation had been chiefly home-making. Their first silent impressions were—

"I hope she is not going to be pathetic," and—

"She is enough to take one's breath away. But I think she has tact."

After a few exchanges of inquiry and answer, Miss Mohun said—

"My niece Gillian is burning to see you, after all your kindness to her."

"I shall be very glad. This is not quite a land of strangers."

"I told her I was sure you would not want her to-day."

"Thank you. My brother is hardly up to afternoon visitors yet, and we have not been able to arrange his refuge."

"You have transformed this room."

"Or Anna has."

On which Miss Mohun begged for Miss Vanderkist to meet her nieces by and by at tea. Gillian would call for her at four o'clock, and show her the way that it was hoped might soon be quite natural to her.

"Gillian's 'Aunt Jane,'" said Anna, when the visitor had tripped out. "I never quite understood her way of talking of her. I think she worried her."

"Your pronouns are confused, Annie. Which worried which? Or was it mutual?"

"On the whole," laughed Anna back, "I prefer an aunt to be waited on to one who pokes me up."

"Aunt Log to Aunt Stork? To be poked will be wholesome."

In due time there was a ring at the front door; Gillian Merrifield was indulged with a kiss and smile from the heroine of her worship, and Anna found herself in the midst of a garland of bright girls. She was a contrast to them, with her fair Underwood complexion, her short plump Vanderkist figure, and the mourning she still wore for the fatherly Uncle Grinstead; while the Merrifield party were all in different shades of the brunette, and wore bright spring raiment.

They had only just come down the steps when they were greeted by a young clergyman, who said he was on his way to inquire for Mr. Underwood, and as he looked as if he expected a reply from Miss Vanderkist, she said her uncle was better, and would be glad to see Mr. Brownlow when he had rested after his journey.

"I hope he will not bother him," she added; "I know who he is now. He was at Whittingtonia for a little while, but broke down. There's no remembering all the curates there. My aunt likes his mother. Does he belong to this St. Andrew's Church?"

"No, to the old one. You begin to see the tower."

"Is that where you go?"

"To the old one in the morning, but we have a dear little old chapel at Clipstone, where Mr. Brownlow comes for the afternoon. It is all a good deal mixed up together."

Then another voice—

"Do you think Mr. Underwood would preach to us? Mr. Brownlow says he never heard any one like him."

Anna stood still.

"Nobody is to dare to mention preaching to Uncle Clement for the next six months, or they will deserve never to hear another sermon in their lives."

"What an awful penalty!"

"For shame, Dolores! Now," as the short remainder of a steep street was surmounted, "here, as you may see, is the great hotel, and next beyond is Aunt Jane's, Beechcroft. On beyond, where you see that queer tower, is Cliff House, Mr. White's, who married our Aunt Adeline, only they are in Italy; and then comes Carrara, Captain Henderson's—"

"You are expected to rave about Mrs. Henderson's beauty," said the cousin, Dolores Mohun, as she opened Miss Mohun's gate, between two copper beeches, while Anna listened to the merry tongues, almost bewildered by the chatter, so unlike the seclusion and silent watching of the last month; but when Mysie Merrifield asked, "Is it not quite overwhelming?" she said—

"Oh no! it is like being among them all at Vale Leston. My sisters always tell me my tongue wants greasing when I come down."

Her tongue was to have exercise enough among the bevy of damsels who surrounded her in Miss Mohun's drawing-room—four Merrifields, ranging from twenty-two to twelve years old, and one cousin, Dolores Mohun, with a father in New Zealand.

"Won't you be in the Mouse-trap?" presently asked number three, by name Valetta.

"If I did not know that she would drag it in!" cried Dolores.

"What may it be?" asked Anna.

"An essay society and not an essay society," was the lucid answer. "Gillian said you would be sure to belong to it."

"I am afraid I can't if it takes much time," said Anna in a pleading tone. "My uncle is very far from well, and I have a good deal to do in the way of reading to him, and my little brother is coming to go to school with yours."

"Mr. Underwood brought his little boy," said Gillian. "Fergus said he was one of the jolliest little chaps he had ever seen."

"Uncle Reginald quite lost his heart to him," said Mysie, "and Aunt Jane says he is a charming little fellow."

"Oh, Felix Underwood!" said Anna. "Adrian is much more manly. You should see him ride and climb trees."

The comparative value of brothers and cousins was very apparent. However, it was fixed that Anna should attend the Mouse-trap, and hear and contribute as she could find time.

"I did the Erl King," said Valetta.

"'Who rideth so late in the forest so wild?
        It is the fond father and his loving child.'"

"Oh, spare us, Val," cried her sister Gillian. "Every one has done that."

"Gerald parodied mine," said Anna.

"'Who trampeth so late in a shocking bad hat?
        'Tis the tipsy old father a-hugging his brat."

"Oh, go on."

"I can't recollect any more, but the Erl King's daughter is a beggar-woman, and it ends with—

"I'll give thee a tanner and make him a bait,
        So in the gin palace was settled his fate."

Some of the party were scandalized, others laughed as much or more than the effusion deserved.

"We accept drawings," added another voice, "and if any one does anything extraordinarily good in that way, or in writing, it makes a little book."

"We have higher designs than that," said Gillian. "We want to print the cream."

"For the benefit of the school board—no, the board school."

"Oh! oh! Valetta!" cried the general voice.

"The thing is," explained Gillian, "that we must build a new school for the out-liers of St. Kenelm's, or 'my lords' will be down on us, and we shall be swamped by board schools."

"Aunt Jane is frantic about it," said Dolores Mohun.

"There's no escape from school board worries!" exclaimed Anna. "They helped to demolish Uncle Clement."

"There is to be a sale of work, and a concert, and all sorts of jolly larks," added Valetta.

"Larks! Oh, Val!"

"Larks aren't slang. They are in the dictionary," declared Valetta.

"By the bye, she has not heard the rules of the Mice," put in Mysie.

"I'll say them," volunteered Valetta the irrepressible. "Members of the Mouse-trap never utter slang expressions, never wear live birds—I mean dead ones—in their hats."

"Is an ostrich feather a live bird or a dead?" demanded Anna.

"And," said Dolores, "what of the feather screens that the old Miss Smiths have been making all the winter—circles of pheasants' feathers and peacocks' eyes outside a border of drakes' curls?"

"Oh, like ostriches they don't count, since peacocks don't die, and drakes and pheasants *must*," said Gillian.

"We have been getting ready for this sale ever so long," said Mysie. "Aunt Jane has a working party every Friday for it."

"The fit day," said Dolores, "for she is a perfect victim to other people's bad work, and spends the evening in stitching up and making presentable the wretched garments they turn out."

"The next rule—" began Valetta, but Gillian mercilessly cut her short.

"You know clever people, Anna. Do you know how to manage about our Mouse-trap book? Our bookseller here is a school-board man, all on the wrong side, and when I tried to feel our way, he made out that the printing and getting it up would cost a great deal more than we could risk."

"It is a pity that Uncle Lance is gone home," said Anna. "He could tell you all about it."

"Could you not write to him?"

"Oh, yes, but I know he will want to see a specimen before he can make any estimate."

It was agreed that the specimen should be forthcoming on the next occasion, and Miss Mohun coming home, and tea coming in, the conference was ended. Anna began to unravel the relationships.

Dolores Mohun was a niece of Lady Merrifield. She had lost her own mother early, and after living with the Merrifields for a year, had been taken by her father to New Zealand, where he had an appointment. He was a man of science, and she had been with him at Rotaruna during the terrible volcanic eruption, when there had been danger and terror enough to bring out her real character, and at the same time to cause an amount of intimacy with a young lady visitor little older than herself, which had suddenly developed into a second marriage of her father. In this state of things she had gladly availed herself of the home offered her at Clipstone, and had gone home under the escort of her Aunt Phyllis (Mrs. Harry May), who was going with her husband to spend a year in England. Dolores had greatly improved in all ways during her two years' absence, and had become an affectionate, companionable, and thoughtful member of the Merrifield household, though still taking a line of her own.

The Kalliope whom Gillian had befriended, to her own detriment, was now the very beautiful Mrs. Henderson, wife to the managing partner in the marble works. She continued to take a great interest in the young women employed in designing and mosaics, and had a class of them for reading and working. Dolores had been asked to tell first Aunt Jane's G. F. S. (Girl's Friendly Society) girls, and afterwards Mrs. Henderson's, about her New Zealand experiences and the earthquake, and this developed into regular weekly lectures on volcanoes and on colonies. She did these so well, that she was begged to repeat them for the girls at the High School, and she had begun to get them up very carefully, studying the best scientific books she could get, and thinking she saw her vocation.

Mrs. Henderson was quite a power in the place. Her brother Alexis was an undergraduate, but had been promised a tutorship for the vacation. He seldom appeared at Carrara, shrinking from what recalled the pain and shame that he had suffered; while Petros worked under Captain Henderson, and Theodore was still in the choir at St. Matthew's. Maura had become the darling of Mr. White, and was much beloved by Mrs. White, though there had been a little alarm the previous year, when Lord Rotherwood and his son came down to open a public park or garden on the top of the cliffs, where Lord Rotherwood's accident had occurred. Lord Ivinghoe, a young Guardsman, had shown himself enough disposed to flirt with the pretty little Greek to make the prudent very glad that her home was on the Italian mountains.

Gillian was always Mrs. Henderson's friend, but Gillian's mind was full of other things. For her father had reluctantly promised, that if one of her little brothers got a scholarship at one of the public schools, Gillian might fulfil her ardent desire of going to a ladies' college. Wilfred was a hopeless subject. It might be doubted if he could have succeeded. He had apparently less brain power than some of the family, and he certainly would not exert what he had. His mother had dragged him through holiday tasks; but nobody else could attempt to make him work when at home, and Gillian's offers had been received with mockery or violence. So all her hopes centred on Fergus, who, thanks to Aunt Jane's evening influence over his lessons, stood foremost in Mrs. Edgar's school, and was to go up to try for election at Winchester College at the end of the term. Were Gillian's hopes to be ruined by his devotion to the underground world?

CHAPTER VII. — THE HOPE OF VANDERKIST

There had been some curiosity as to who would be thought worthy to bring the precious little baronet to Rockquay, and there was some diversion, as well as joy, when it proved that no one was to be entrusted with him but his eldest aunt, Mrs. Harewood, who was to bring him in Whitsun week, so that he might begin with a half-term.

The arrival was a pretty sight, as the aunt rejoiced at seeing both her hosts at the front door to greet her, and as Anna held out her glad arms to the little brother who was the pride of the family.

"Ha, Adrian, boy!" said the Vicar, only greeting with the hand, at sight of the impatient wriggle out of the embrace.

It was an open, sunburnt, ruddy face, and wide, fearless grey eyes that looked up to him, the bullet head in stiff, curly flaxen hair held aloft with an air of "I am monarch of all I survey," and there was a tone of equality in the "Holloa, Uncle Clement," to the tall clergyman who towered so far above the sturdy little figure.

Presently on the family inquiries there broke—

"I say, Annie, where's the school?"

"At the foot of this hill."

"I want to see it" (imperiously).

"You must have some tea first."

"Then you are glad to come, Adrian?" said Mrs. Grinstead.

"Yes, Aunt Cherry. It is high time I was away from such a lot of women-folk," he replied, with his hands in his pockets, and his legs set like a little colossus.

Anna had no peace till, after the boy had swallowed a tolerable amount of bread-and-butter and cake, she took him out, and then Mrs. Harewood had to explain his mother's urgent entreaties that the regime at Vale Leston should be followed up, and the boy see only such habits as would be those of total abstainers.

Poor woman! as her brother and sisters knew, there was reason to believe that the vice which had been fatal to her happiness and her husband's life, had descended to him from Dutch forefathers, and there was the less cause for wonder at the passionate desire to guard her son from it. Almost all her family had been water-drinkers from infancy, and though Major Harewood called teetotalism a superstitious contempt of Heaven's good gifts, and disapproved of supplementing the baptismal vow, his brother the Rector had found it expedient, for the sake of the parish, to embrace formally the temperance movement, and thus there had been little difficulty in giving way to Alda's desire that, at the luncheon-table, Adrian should never see wine or beer, and she insisted that the same rule should prevail at Rockquay.

Clement had taken the pledge when a lad of sixteen, and there were those who thought that, save for his persistence under warnings of failing strength, much of his present illness might have been averted, with all the consequent treatment. He believed in total abstinence as safer for his ward, but he thought that the time had come for training, in seeing without partaking. Wilmet agreed, and said she had tried to persuade her sister; but she had only caused an hysterical agitation, so that weakness as usual gained the victory, and she had all but promised to bring the boy home again unless she could exact an engagement.

"To follow the Vale Leston practice at his early dinner," said Geraldine.

"That may be," said Clement; "but I do not engage not to have the matter out with him if I see that it is expedient."

"I am only doubtful how Gerald will take it," said his sister.

"Gerald has always been used to it at Vale Leston," said Wilmet.

"True, but there he is your guest. Here he will regard himself as at home. However, he is a good boy, and will only grumble a little for appearance sake."

"I should hope so," said Wilmet severely.

"How is the Penbeacon affair going on?" asked Clement.

"Oh, Clem, I did not think you had heard of it."

"I had a letter in the middle of the mission, but I could not answer it then, and it seems to have been lost."

Geraldine pronounced it the straw that broke the camel's back, when she heard of the company that only waited to dig china clay out of Penbeacon and wash it in the Ewe till they could purchase a slice of the hill pertaining to the Vale Leston estate. Major Harewood had replied that his fellow-trustee was too ill to attend to business, and that the matter had better be let alone till the heir attained his majority.

"Shelved for the present," said Mrs. Grinstead. "Fancy Ewe and Leston contaminated!"

"John talks to the young engineer, Mr. Bramshaw, and thinks that may be prevented; but that is not the worst," said Wilmet; "it would change the whole face of the parish, and bring an influx of new people."

"Break up Penbeacon and cover it with horrible little new houses. Men like Walsh never see a beautiful place but they begin to think how to destroy it."

"Well, Cherry, you have the most influence with Gerald, but he talks to the girls of our having no right to keep the treasures of the hills for our exclusive pleasure."

"It is not exclusive. Half the country disports itself there. It is the great place for excursions."

"Then he declares that it is a grave matter to hinder an industry that would put bread into so many mouths, and that fresh outlets would be good for the place; something too about being an obstruction, and the rights of labour."

"Oh, I know what that means. It is only teasing the cousinhood when they fall on him open-mouthed," said Geraldine, with a laugh, though with a qualm of misgiving at her heart, while Clement sat listening and thinking.

Mrs. Harewood farther explained, that she hoped either that Gerald would marry, or that her sister would make a home for him at the Priory. It then appeared that Major Harewood thought it would be wise to leave the young man to manage the property for himself without interference; and that the uncle to whom the Major had become heir was anxious to have the family at hand, even offering to arrange a house for Lady Vanderkist.

"A year of changes," sighed Geraldine; "but this waiting time seems intended to let one gather one's breath."

But Wilmet looked careworn, partly, no doubt, with the harass of continual attention to her sister Alda, who, though subdued and improved in many important ways, was unavoidably fretful from ill-health, and disposed to be very miserable over her straitened means, and the future lot of her eight daughters, especially as the two of the most favourable age seemed to resign their immediate chances of marrying. Moreover, though all began life as pretty little girls, they had a propensity to turn into Dutchwomen as they grew up, and Franceska, the fifth in age, was the only one who renewed the beauty of the twin sisters.

Alda was not, however, Wilmet's chief care, though of that she did not speak. She was not happy at heart about her two boys. Kester was a soldier in India, not actually unsteady, but not what her own brothers had been, and Edward was a midshipman, too much of the careless, wild sailor. Easy-going John Harewood's lax discipline had not been successful with them in early youth, and still less had later severity and indignation been effectual.

"I am glad you kept Anna," said Mrs. Harewood, "though Alda is very much disappointed that she is not having a season in London."

"She will not take it," said Geraldine. "She insists that she prefers Uncle Clem to all the fine folk she might meet; and after all, poor Marilda's acquaintance are not exactly the upper ten thousand."

"Poor Marilda! You know that she is greatly vexed that Emilia is bent on being a hospital nurse, or something like it, and only half yields to go out with her this summer in very unwilling obedience."

"Yes, I know. She wants to come here, and I mean to have her before the long vacation for a little while. We heard various outpourings, and I cannot quite think Miss Emilia a grateful person, though I can believe that she does not find it lively at home."

"She seems to be allowed plenty of slum work, as it is the fashion to call it, and no one can be more good and useful than Fernan and Marilda, so that I call it sheer discontent and ingratitude not to put up with them!"

"Only modernishness, my dear Wilmet. It is the spirit of the times, and the young things can't help it."

"You don't seem to suffer in that way—at least with Anna."

"No; Anna is a dear good girl, and Uncle Clem is her hero, but I am very glad she has nice young companions in the Merrifields, and an excitement in prospect in this bazaar."

"I thought a bazaar quite out of your line."

"There seems to be no other chance of saving this place from board schools. Two thousand pounds have to be raised, and though Lord Rotherwood and Mr. White, the chief owners of property, have done, and will do, much, there still remains greater need than a fleeting population like this can be expected to supply, and Clement thinks that a bazaar is quite justifiable in such a case."

"If there is nothing undesirable," said Mrs. Harewood, in her original "what it may lead to" voice.

"Trust Lady Merrifield and Jane Mohun for that! I am going to take you to call upon Lilias Merrifield."

"Yea; I shall wish to see the mother of Bernard's wife."

Clement, who went with them, explained to his somewhat wondering elder sister that he thought safeguards to Christian education so needful, that he was quite willing that, even in this brief stay, all the aid in their power should be given to the cause at Rockquay. Nay, as he afterwards added to Wilmet, he was very glad to see how much it interested Geraldine, and that the work for the Church and the congenial friends were rousing her from her listless state of dejection.

Lady Merrifield and Mrs. Harewood were mutually charmed, perhaps all the more because the former was not impassioned about the bazaar. She said she had been importuned on such subjects wherever she had gone, and had learnt to be passive; but her sister Jane was all eagerness, and her younger young people, as she called the present half of her family, were in the greatest excitement over their first experience of the kind.

"Well is it for all undertakings that there should always be somebody to whom all is new, and who can be zealous and full of delight."

"By no means surtout point de zele," returned Geraldine.

"As well say no fermentation," said Lady Merrifield.

"A dangerous thing," said Clement.

"But sourness comes without it, or at least deadness," returned his sister.

Wherewith they returned to talk of their common relations.

It was like a joke to the brother and sisters, that their Bernard should be a responsible husband and father, whereas Lady Merrifield's notion of him was as a grave, grand-looking man with a splendid beard.

Fergus Merrifield was asked to become the protector of Adrian, whereat he looked sheepish; but after the round of pets had been made he informed his two youngest sisters, Valetta and Primrose, that it was the cheekiest little fellow he had ever seen, who would never know if he was bullied within an inch of his life; not that he (Fergus) should let the fellows do it.

So though until Monday morning Anna was the slave of her brother, doing her best to supply the place of the six devoted sisters at home, the young gentleman ungratefully announced at breakfast—

"I don't want gy-arls after me," with a peculiarly contemptuous twirl at the beginning of the word; "Merrifield is to call for me."

Anna, who had brought down her hat, looked mortified.

"Never mind, Annie," said her uncle, "he will know better one of these days."

"No, I shan't," said Adrian, turning round defiantly. "If she comes bothering after me at dinner-time I shall throw my books at her—that's all! There's Merrifield," and he banged out of the room.

"Never mind," again said his uncle, "he has had a large dose of the feminine element, and this is his swing out of it."

Hopes, which Anna thought cruel, were entertained by her elders that the varlet would return somewhat crestfallen, but there were no such symptoms; the boy re-appeared in high spirits, having been placed well for his years, but not too well for popularity, and in the playground he had found himself in his natural element. The boys were mostly of his own size, or a little bigger, and bullying was not the fashion. He had heard enough school stories to be wary of boasting of his title, and as long as he did not flaunt it before their eyes, it was regarded as rather a credit to the school.

Merrifield was elated at the success of his protege, and patronized him more than he knew, accepting his devotion in a droll, contemptuous manner, so that the pair were never willingly apart. As Fergus slept at his aunt's during the week, the long summer evenings afforded splendid opportunities for what Fergus called scientific researches in the quarries and cliffs. It was as well for Lady Vanderkist's peace of mind that she did not realize them, though Fergus was certified by his family to be cautious and experienced enough to be a safe guide. Perhaps people were less nervous about sixth sons than only ones.

There was, indeed, a certain undeveloped idea held out that some of the duplicates of Fergus's precious collection might be arranged as a sample of the specimens of minerals and fossils of Rockquay at the long-talked-of sale of work.

CHAPTER VIII. — THE MOUSE-TRAP

If a talent be a claw, look how he claws him with a talent.
Love's Labour's Lost.

The young ladies were truly in an intense state of excitement about the sale of work, especially about the authorship; and Uncle Lancelot having promised to send an estimate, a meeting of the Mouse-trap was convened to consider of the materials, and certainly the mass of manuscript contributed at different times to the Mouse-trap magazine was appalling to all but Anna, who knew what was the shrinkage in the press.

She, however, held herself bound not to inflict on her busy uncle the reading of anything entirely impracticable, so she sat with a stern and critical eye as the party mustered in Miss Mohun's drawing-room, and Gillian took the chair.

"The great design," said she impressively, "is that the Mouse-trap should collect and print and publish a selection for the benefit of the school."

The Mice vehemently applauded, only Miss Norton, the oldest of the party, asked humbly—

"Would any one think it worth buying?"

"Oh, yes," cried Valetta. "Lots of translations!"

"The Erl King, for instance," put in Dolores Mohun.

"If Anna would append the parody," suggested Gillian.

"Oh, parodies are—are horrid," said Mysie.

"Many people feel them so," said Gillian, "but to others I think they are almost a proof of love, that they can make sport with what they admire so much."

"Then," said Mysie, "there's Dolores' Eruption!"

"What a nice subject," laughed Gillian. "However, it will do beautifully, being the description of the pink terraces of that place with the tremendous name in New Zealand."

"Were you there?" cried Anna.

"Yes. I always wonder how she can look the same after such adventures," said Mysie.

"You know it is much the same as my father's paper in the Scientific

World," said Dolores.

"Nobody over reads that, so it won't signify," was the uncomplimentary verdict.

"And," added Mysie, "Mr. Brownlow would do a history of Rockquay, and that would be worth having."

"Oh yes, the dear ghost and all!" cried Valetta.

The acclamation was general, for the Reverend Armine Brownlow was the cynosure curate of the lady Church-helpers, and Mysie produced as a precious loan, to show what could be done, the volume containing the choicest morceaux of the family magazine of his youth, the Traveller's Joy, in white parchment binding adorned with clematis, and emblazoned with the Evelyn arms on one side, the Brownlow on the other, and full of photographs and reproductions of drawings.

"Much too costly," said the prudent.

"It was not for sale," said Mysie, obviously uneasy while it was being handed round.

"Half-a-crown should be our outside price," said Gillian.

"Or a shilling without photographs, half-a-crown with," was added.

"Shall I ask Uncle Lance what can be done for how much?" asked Anna, and this was accepted with acclamation, but, as Gillian observed, they had yet got no further than Dolores' Eruption and the unwritten history.

"There are lots of stories," said Kitty Varley; "the one about Bayard and all the knights in Italy."

"The one," said Gillian, "where Padua got into the kingdom of Naples, and the lady of the house lighted a lucifer match, besides the horse who drained a goblet of red wine."

"You know that was only the pronouns," suggested the author.

"Then there's another," added Valetta, "called Monrepos—such a beauty, when the husband was wounded, and died at his wife's feet just as the sun gilded the tops of the pines, and she died when the moon set, and the little daughter went in and was found dead at their feet."

"No, no, Val," said Gillian. "Here is a story that Bessie has sent us—really worth having."

"Mesa! Oh, of course," was the acclamation.

"And here's a little thing of mine," Gillian added modestly, "about the development of the brain."

At this there was a shout.

"A little thing! Isn't it on the differential calculus?"

"Really, I don't see why Rockquay should not have a little rational study!"

"Ah! but the present question is what Rockquay will buy; to further future development it may be, but I am afraid their brains are not yet developed enough," said Emma Norton.

"Well then, here is the comparison between Euripides and Shakespeare."

"That's what you read papa and everybody to sleep with," said Valetta pertly.

"Except Aunt Lily, and she said she had read something very like it in Schlegel," added Dolores.

"You must not be too deep for ordinary intellects, Gillian," said Emma Norton good-naturedly. "Surely there is that pretty history you made out of Count Baldwin the Pretender."

"That! Oh, that is a childish concern."

"The better fitted for our understandings," said Emma, disinterring it, and handing it over to Anna, while Mysie breathed out—

"Oh! I did like it! And, Gill, where is Phyllis's account of the Jubilee gaieties and procession last year?"

"That would make the fortune of any paper," said Anna.

"Yes, if Lady Rotherwood will let it be used," said Gillian. "It is really delightful and full of fun, but I am quite sure that her name could not appear, and I do not expect leave to use it."

"Shall I write and ask?" said Mysie.

"Oh yes, do; if Cousin Rotherwood is always gracious, it is specially to you."

"I wrote to my cousin, Gerald Underwood," said Anna, "to ask if he had anything to spare us, though I knew he would laugh at the whole concern, and he has sent down this. I don't quite know whether he was in earnest or in mischief."

And she read aloud—

```
"Dreaming of her laurels green,
        The learned Girton girl is seen,
        Or under the trapeze neat
```

        Figuring as an athlete.

        Never at the kitchen door
        Will she scrub or polish more;
        No metaphoric dirt she eats,
        Literal dirt may form her treats.

        Mary never idle sits,
        Home lessons can't be learnt by fits;
        Hard she studies all the week,
        Answers with undaunted cheek.

        When to exam Mary goes,
        Smartly dressed in stunning clothes,
        Expert in algebraic rule,
        Best pupil-teacher of her school.

        Oh, how clever we are found
        Who live on England's happy ground,
        Where rich and poor and wretched may
        Be drilled in Whitehall's favoured way."

There was a good deal of laughter at this parody of Jane Taylor's Village Girl, though Mysie was inclined to be shocked as at something profane.

"Then what will you think of this?" said Anna, beginning gravely to read aloud The Inspector's Tour.

It was very clever, so clever that Valetta and Kitty Varley both listened as in sober earnest, never discovering, or only in flashes like Mysie, that it was really a satire on all the social state of the different European nations, under the denomination of schools. One being depicted as highly orthodox, but much given to sentence insubordination to dark cold closets; another as given to severe drill, but neglecting manners; a third as repudiating religious teaching, and now and then preparing explosions for the masters—no, teachers. The various conversations were exceedingly bright and comical; and there were brilliant hits at existing circumstances, all a little in a socialistic spirit, which made Anna pause as she read. She really had not perceived till she heard it in her own voice and with other ears how audacious it was, especially for a school bazaar.

Dolores applauded with her whole heart, but owned that it might be too good for the Mouse-trap, it would be too like catching a monkey! Gillian, more doubtfully, questioned whether it would "quite do"; and Mysie, when she understood the allusions, thought it would not. Emma Norton was more decided, and it ended by deciding that the paper should be read to the elders at Clipstone, and their decision taken before sending it to Uncle Lance.

The spirits of the Muscipula party rose as they discussed the remaining MSS., but these were not of the highest order of merit; and Anna thought that the really good would be sufficient; and all the Underwood kith and kin had sufficient knowledge of the Press through their connection with the

'Pursuivant' to be authorities on the subject.

"Fergus has some splendid duplicate ammonites for me and bits of crystal," said Mysie.

"Oh, do let Fergus alone," entreated Gillian. "He is almost a petrifaction already, and you know what depends on it."

"My sister is coming next week for a few days," said Anna. "She is very clever, and may help us."

Emilia was accordingly introduced to the Mice, but she was not very tolerant of them. Essay societies, she said, were out of date, and she thought the Rockquay young ladies a very country-town set.

"You don't know them, Emmie," said Anna. "Gillian and Dolores are very remarkable girls, only—"

"Only they are kept down by their mothers, I suppose. Is that the reason they don't do anything but potter after essay societies and Sunday-schools like our little girls at Vale Leston? Why, I asked Gillian, as you call her, what they were doing about the Penitents' Home, and she said her mother and Aunt Jane went to look after it, but never talked about it."

"You know they are all very young."

"Young indeed! How is one ever to be of any use if mothers and people are always fussing about one's being young?"

"One won't always be so—"

"They would think so, like the woman of a hundred years old, who said on her daughter's death at eighty, 'Ah, poor girl, I knew I never should rear her!' How shall I get to see the Infirmary here?"

"Miss Mohun would take you."

"Can't I go without a fidgety old maid after me?"

"I'll tell you what I wish you would do, Emmie. Write an account of one of your hospital visits, or of the match-girls, for the Mouse-trap. Do! You know Gerald has written something for it."

"He! Why he has too much sense to write for your voluntary schools. Or it would be too clever and incisive for you. Ah! I see it was so by your face! What did he send you? Have you got it still?"

"We have really a parody of his which is going in—The Girton Girl. Now, Emmie, won't you? You have told me such funny things about your match-girls."

"I do not mean to let them be turned into ridicule by your prim, decorous swells. Why, I unfortunately told Fernan Brown one story—about their mocking old Miss Bruce with putting on imitation spectacles—and it has served him for a cheval de bataille ever since! Oh, my dear Anna, he gets more hateful than ever. I wish you would come back and divert his attention."

"Thank you."

"Don't you think we could change? You could go and let Marilda fuss with you, now that Uncle Clem and Aunt Cherry are so well, and I could look after Adrian, and go to the Infirmary, and the penitents, and all that these people neglect; maybe I would write for the Mouse-trap, if Gerald does when he comes home."

Anna did not like the proposal, but she pitied Emilia, and cared for her enough to carry the scheme to her aunt. But Geraldine shook her head. The one thing she did not wish was to have Emmie riding, walking, singing, and expanding into philanthropy with Gerald, and besides, she knew that Emilia would never have patience to read to her uncle, or help Adrian in his preparation.

"Do you really wish this, my dear?" she asked.

"N—no, not at all; but Emmie does. Could you not try her?"

"Annie dear, if you wish to have a fortnight or more in town—"

"Oh no, no, auntie, indeed!"

"We could get on now without you. Or we would keep Emmie till the room is wanted; but I had far rather be alone than have the responsibility of Emmie."

"No, no, indeed; I don't think Adrian would be good long with her. I had much rather stay—only Emmie did wish, and she hates the—"

"Oh, my dear, you need not tell me; I only know that I cannot have her after next week; the room will be wanted for Gerald."

"She could sleep with me."

"No, Annie, I must disappoint you. There is not room for her, and her flights when Gerald comes would never do for your uncle. You know it yourself."

Anna could not but own the wisdom of the decision, and Emmie, after grumbling at Aunt Cherry, took herself off. She had visited the Infirmary and the Convalescent Home, and even persuaded Mrs. Hablot to show her the Union Workhouse, but she never sent her contribution to the Mouse-trap.

CHAPTER IX. — OUT BEYOND

"Drawing? Well done, Cherie! That's a jolly little beggar; quite masterly, as old Renville would say," exclaimed Gerald Underwood, looking at a charming water-colour of a little fisher-boy, which Mrs. Grinstead was just completing.

"'The Faithful Henchman,' it ought to be called," said Anna. "That little being has attached himself to Fergus Merrifield, and follows him and Adrian everywhere on what they are pleased to call their scientific expeditions."

"The science of larks?"

"Oh dear, no. Fergus is wild after fossils, and has made Adrian the same, and he really knows an immense deal. They are always after fossils and stones when they are out of school."

"The precious darling!"

"Miss Mohun says Fergus is quite to be trusted not to take him into dangerous places."

"An unlooked-for blessing. Ha!" as he turned over his aunt's portfolio, "that's a stunner! You should work it up for the Academy."

"This kind of thing is better for the purpose," Mrs. Grinstead said.

"Throw away such work upon a twopenny halfpenny bazaar! Heaven forefend!"

"Don't be tiresome, Gerald," entreated Anna. "You are going to do all sorts of things for it, and we shall have no end of fun."

"For the sake of stopping the course of the current," returned Gerald, proceeding to demonstrate in true nineteenth-century style the hopelessness of subjecting education to what he was pleased to call clericalism. "You'll never reach the masses while you insist on using an Apostle spoon."

"Masses are made up of atoms," replied his aunt.

"And we shall be lost if you don't help," added Anna.

"I would help readily enough if it were free dinners, or anything to equalize the existence of the classes, instead of feeding the artificial wants of the one at the expense of the toil and wretchedness of the other."

He proceeded to mention some of the miseries that he had learnt through the Oxford House—dilating on them with much enthusiasm—till presently his uncle came in, and ere long a parlour-maid announced luncheon, just as there was a rush into the house. Adrian was caught by his sister, and submitted, without more than a "Bother!" to be made respectable, and only communicating in spasmodic gasps facts about Merrifield and hockey.

"Where's Marshall?" asked Gerald at the first opportunity, on the maid leaving the room.

"Marshall could not stand it," said his aunt. "He can't exist without London, and doing the honours of a studio."

"Left you!"

"Most politely he informed me that this place does not agree with his health; and there did not seem sufficient scope for his services since the Reverend Underwood had become so much more independent. So we were thankful to dispose of him to Lord de Vigny."

"He was a great plague," interpolated Adrian, "always jawing about the hall-door."

"Are you really without a man-servant?" demanded Gerald.

"In the house. Lomax comes up from the stables to take some of the work. Some lemonade, Gerald?"

Gerald gazed round in search of unutterable requirements; but only met imploring eyes from aunt and sister, and restraining ones from his uncle. He subsided and submitted to the lemonade, while Anna diverted attention by recurring rather nervously to the former subject.

"And I have got rid of Porter, she kept me in far too good order."

"As if Sibby did not," said Clement.

"Aye, and you too! But that comes naturally, and began in babyhood!"

"What have you done with the house at Brompton?"

"Martha is taking care of it—Mrs. Lightfoot, don't you know? One of our old interminable little Lightfoots, who went to be a printer in London, married, and lost his wife; then in our break-up actually married Martha to take care of his children! Now he is dead, and I am thankful to have her in the house."

"To frighten loafers with her awful squint."

"You forgive the rejection of 'The Inspector's Tour'? Indeed I think you expected it."

"I wanted to see whether the young ladies would find it out."

"No compliment to our genius," said his aunt.

"I assure you, like Mrs. Bennet, 'there is plenty of that sort of thing,'" said Anna. "Some of them were mystified, but Gillian and Dolores Mohun were in ecstasies."

"Ecstasies from that cheerful name?"

"She is the New Zealand niece—Mr. Maurice Mohun's daughter. They carried it home to their seniors, and of course the verdict was 'too strong for Rockquay atmosphere,'" said his aunt.

"So it did not even go to Uncle Lance," said Anna. "Shall you try the 'Pursuivant'?"

"On the contrary, I shall put in the pepper and salt I regretted, and try the 'Censor'."

"Indeed?" observed his uncle, in a tone of surprise.

"Oh," said Gerald coolly, "I have sent little things to the 'Censor' before, which they seem to regard in the light of pickles and laver."

The 'Censor' was an able paper on the side of philosophical politics, and success in that quarter was a feather in the young man's cap, though not quite the kind of feather his elders might have desired.

"Journalism is a kind of native air to us," said Mrs. Grinstead, "but from 'Pur.'"

"'Pur' is the element of your dear old world, Cherie," said Gerald, "and here am I come to do your bidding in its precincts, for a whole long vacation."

He spoke lightly, and with a pretty little graceful bow to his aunt, but there was something in his eyes and smile that conveyed to her a dread that he meant that he only resigned himself for the time and looked beyond.

"Uncle Lance is coming," volunteered Adrian.

"Yes," said Geraldine. "Chorister that he was, and champion of Church teaching that he is, he makes the cause of Christian education everywhere his own, and is coming down to see what he can do inexpensively with native talent for concert, or masque, or something—'Robin Hood' perhaps."

"Ending in character with a rush on the audience?" said Gerald. "Otherwise 'Robin Hood' is stale."

"Tennyson has spoilt that for public use," said Mrs. Grinstead. "But was not something else in hand?"

"Only rehearsed. It never came off," said Gerald.

"The most awful rot," said Adrian. "I would have nothing to do with it."

"In consequence it was a failure," laughed Gerald.

"It was 'The Tempest', wasn't it?" said Anna.

"Not really!" exclaimed Mrs. Grinstead.

"About as like as a wren to an eagle," said Gerald.

"We had it at the festival last winter. The authors adapted the plot, that was all."

"The authors being—

"The present company," said Gerald, "and Uncle Bill, with Uncle Lance supplying or adapting music, for we were not original, I assure you."

"It was when Uncle Clem was ill," put in Anna, "and somehow I don't think we took in the accounts of it."

"No," said Gerald, "and nobody did it con amore, though we could not put it off. I should like to see it better done."

"Such rot!" exclaimed Adrian. "There's an old man, he was Uncle Lance with the great white beard made out of Kit's white bear's skin, and he lived in a desert island, where there was a shipwreck—very jolly if you could see it, only you can't—and the savages—no, the wreckers all came down."

"What, in a desert island?"

"It was not exactly desert. Gerald, I say, do let there be savages. It would be such a lark to have them all black, and then I'd act."

"What an inducement!"

"Then somebody turned out to be somebody's enemy, and the old chap frightened them all with squibs and crackers and fog-horns, till somebody turned out to be somebody else's son, and married the daughter."

"If you trace 'The Tempest' through that version you are clever," said Gerald.

"I told you it was awful rot," said Adrian.

"There's Merrifield! Excuse me, Cherie." And off he went.

"The sentiments of the actors somewhat resembled Adrian's. It was too new, and needed more learning and more pains, so they beg to revert to 'Robin Hood'. However, I should like to see it well got up for once, if only by amateurs. Miranda has a capital song by Uncle Bill, made for Francie's soprano. She cuts you all out, Anna."

"That she does, in looks and voice, but she could not act here in public. However, we will lay it before the Mouse-trap. Was it printed?"

"Lance had enough for the performers struck off. Francie could send some up."

"After all," said Cherie, "the desert island full of savages and wreckers is not more remarkable than the 'still-vex'd Bermoothes' getting between Argiers and Sicily."

"It *really was* one of the Outer Hebrides," said Gerald, with the eagerness that belonged to authorship, "so that there could be any amount of Scottish songs. Prospero is an old Highland chief, who has been set adrift with his daughter—Francie Vanderkist to wit—and floated up there, obtaining control over the local elves and brownies. Little Fely was a most dainty sprite."

"I am glad you did not make Ariel an electric telegraph," said his aunt.

"Tempting, but such profanity in the face of Vale Leston was forbidden, and so was the comic element, as bad for the teetotallers."

"But who were the wreckers?" asked Anna.

"Buccaneers, my dear, singing songs out of the 'Pirate'—schoolmaster, organist, and choir generally. They had captured Prospero's supplanter (he was a Highland chief in league with the Whigs) by the leg, while the exiled fellow was Jacobite, so as to have the songs dear to the feminine mind. They get wrecked on the island, and are terrified by the elves into releasing Alonso, etc. Meantime Ferdinand carries logs, forgathers with Miranda and Prospero —and ends—" He flourished his hands.

"And it wasn't acted!"

"No, we were getting it up before Christmas," said Gerald, "and then—"

He looked towards Clement, whose illness had then been at the crisis.

"Very inconsiderate of me," said Clement, smiling, "as the old woman said when her husband did not die before the funeral cakes were stale. But could it not come off at the festival?"

"Now," said Gerald, "that the boy is gone, I may be allowed a glass of beer.

Is that absurdity to last on here?"

"Adrian's mother would not let him come on any other terms," said Mrs. Grinstead.

"Did she also stipulate that he was never to see a horse? Quite as fatal to his father."

"You need not point the unreason, but consider how she has suffered."

"You go the way to make him indulge on the sly."

"True, perhaps," said Clement, "but I mean to take the matter up when I know the poor little fellow better."

Gerald gave a little shrug, a relic of his foreign ancestry, and Anna proposed a ride to Clipstone to tell Gillian Merrifield of the idea.

"Eh, the dogmatic damsel that came with you the year we had 'Midsummer Night's Dream'?"

"Yes, sister to Uncle Bernard's wife. Do you know Jasper Merrifield? Clever man. Always photographing."

So off they went, Gerald apparently in a resigned state of mind, and came upon dogs and girls in an old quarry, where Mysie had dragged them to look for pretty stones and young ferns to make little rockeries for the sale of work. 'The Tempest' was propounded, and received with acclamation, though the Merrifields declared that they could not sing, and their father would not allow them to do so in public if they could!

Dolores looked on in a sort of silent scorn at a young man who could talk so eagerly about "a trumpery raree-show," especially for an object that she did not care about. None of them knew how far it was the pride of authorship and the desire of pastime. Only Jasper said when he heard their report—

"Underwood is a queer fellow! One never knows where to have him. Socialist one minute, old Tory the next."

"A dreamer?" asked Dolores.

"If you like to call him so. I believe he will dawdle and dream all his life, and never do any good!"

"Perhaps he is waiting."

"I don't believe in waiting," said Jasper, wiping the dust off his photographic glasses. "Why, he has a lovely moor of his own, and does not know how to use it!"

"Conclusive," said Gillian.

CHAPTER X. — NOBLESSE OBLIGE

"I say, Aunt Cherry," said Adrian, "the fossil forest is to be uncovered to-morrow, and Merrifield is going to stay for it, and I'm going down with him."

"Fossil forest? What, in the Museum?"

"No, indeed. In Anscombe Cove, they call it. There's a forest buried there, and bits come up sometimes. To-morrow there's to be a tremendous low tide that will leave a lot of it uncovered, and Merrifield and I mean to dig it out, and if there are some duplicate bits they may be had for the bazaar."

"Yes, they have been begging Fergus's duplicates for a collection of fossils," said Anna. "But can it be safe? A low tide means a high tide, you know."

"Bosh!" returned Adrian.

"Miss Mohun is sure to know all about the tides, I suppose," said Clement; "if her nephew goes with her consent I suppose it is safe."

"If—" said Mrs. Grinstead.

Adrian looked contemptuous, and muttered something, on which Anna undertook to see Miss Mohun betimes, and judge how the land, or rather the sea, lay, and whether Fergus was to be trusted.

It would be a Saturday, a whole holiday, on which he generally went home for Sunday, and Adrian spent the day with him, but the boys' present scheme was, to take their luncheon with them and spend the whole day in Anscombe Cove. This was on the further side of the bay from the marble works, shut in by big cliffs, which ran out into long chains of rocks on either side, but retreated in the midst, where a little stream from the village of Anscombe, or rather from the moorland beyond, made its way to the sea.

The almanacks avouched that on this Saturday there would be an unusually low tide, soon after twelve o'clock, and Fergus had set his heart on investigating the buried forest that there was no doubt had been choked by the combined forces of river and sea. So Anna found that notice had been sent to Clipstone of his intention of devoting himself to the cove and not coming home till the evening, and that his uncle and aunt did not think there was any danger, especially as his constant henchman, Davie Blake, was going with him, and all the fisher-boys of the place were endowed with a certain instinct for their own tides. The only accident Jane Mohun had ever known was with a stranger.

Anna had no choice but to subside, and the boys started as soon as the morning's tide would have gone down sufficiently, carrying baskets for their treasures containing their luncheon, and apparently expecting to find the forest growing upright under the mud, like a wood full of bushes.

The cove for which they were bound was on the further side of the chain of rocks, nearly two miles from Rockquay, and one of the roads ran along the top of the red cliffs that shut it in, with no opening except where the stream emerged, and even that a very scanty bank of shingle.

In spite of all assurances, Anna could not be easy about her darling, and when afternoon came, and the horses were brought to the door, she coaxed Gerald into riding along the cliffs in the Anscombe direction, where there was a good road, from whence they could turn down a steep hill into the village, and thence go up a wild moor beyond, or else continue along the coast for a considerable distance.

As they went out she could see nothing of the boys, only rocks rising through an expanse of mud, and the sea breaking beyond. She would have preferred continuing the cliff road, but Gerald had a turn for the moor, and carried her off through the village of Anscombe, up and up, till they had had a lively canter on the moor, and looked far out at sea. When they turned back and had reached the cliff road, what had been a sheet of mud before had been almost entirely covered with sparkling waves, and there was white foam beating against some of the rocks.

"I hope Adrian is gone home," sighed Anna.

"Long ago, depend on it," returned Gerald carelessly; but the next moment his tone changed. "By Jove!" he exclaimed, and pointed with his whip to a rock, or island, at the end of the range of rocks.

He was much the more long-sighted of the two, and she could only first discern that there was something alive upon the rock.

"Oh!" she cried, "is it the boys—I can't see?"

"I can't tell. It is boys, maybe fishers. I must get out to them," he replied. "Now, Anna, be quiet—use your senses. It is somebody, anyway. I saw the opening of a path down the rock just now," and he threw himself off his horse, and threw her the bridle. "You ride to the first house; find where there is a Coast-guard station, or any fisherman to put out a boat. No time to be lost."

"Oh, is it, is it—" cried the bewildered girl, with no hand to feel for her eyeglass. "Where shall I go?"

"I tell you I can't tell," he shouted in answer to both questions, half angrily, already on his way. "Don't dawdle," and he disappeared.

Poor Anna, she had no inclination to dawdle, but the two horses were a sore impediment, and she went on some way without seeing any houses. Should she turn back to the little road leading down from Anscombe? but that was rough and difficult, and could not be undertaken quickly with a led horse; or should she make the best of her way to the nearest villas, outskirts of Rockquay? However, after a moment the swish of bicycles was heard, and up came two young men, clerks apparently, let loose by Saturday. They halted, and in answer to her agitated question where there was a house, pointed to a path which they said led down to the Preventive station, and asked whether there had been an accident, and whether they could be of use. They were more able to decide what was best to be done than she could be, and they grew more keenly interested when they understood for whom she feared. Petros White, brother to Mrs. Henderson, and nephew to Aunt Adeline's husband, was one of them, the other, a youth also employed at the marble works. This latter took the horses off her hands, while Petros showed her the way to the Coast-guard station by a steep path, leading to a sort of ledge in the side of the cliff, scooped out partly by nature and partly by art, where stood the little houses covered with slate.

There the mistress was looking out anxiously with a glass; while below, the Preventive man was unlocking the boat-house, having already observed the peril of the boys, but lamenting the absence of his mate. Petros ran down at speed to offer his help, and Anna could only borrow the glass, through which she plainly saw the three boys, bare-legged, sitting huddled up on the top of the rock, but with the waves still a good way from them, and their faces all turned hopefully towards the promontory of rock along which she could see Gerald picking his way; but there was evidently a terrible and fast-diminishing space between its final point and the rock of refuge.

Anna was about to rush down, and give her help with an oar; but the woman withheld her, saying that she would only crowd the boat and retard the rescue, for which the two were quite sufficient, only the danger was that the current of the stream might make the tide rise rapidly in the bay. There were besides so many rocks and shoals, that it was impossible to proceed straight across, but it was needful absolutely to pass the rock and then turn back on it from the open sea. It was agonizing for the sister to watch the devious course, and she turned the glass upon the poor boys, plainly making out Adrian's scared, restless look, as he clung to the fisher-lad, and Fergus nursing his bag of specimens with his knees drawn up. By and by Gerald was wading, and with difficulty preventing himself from being washed off the rocks. He paused, saw her, and waved encouragement. Then he plunged along, not off his feet, and reached the island where the boys were holding out their arms to him. There ensued a few moments of apparently hot debate, and she saw, to her horror and amazement, that he was thrusting back one boy, who struggled and almost fell off the rock in his passion, as Gerald lifted down the little fisher-boy. Of course she could not hear the words, "Come, boy. No, Adrian. Noblesse oblige. I will come back, never fear. I can take but one, don't I tell you. I will come back."

Those were Gerald's words, while Adrian threw himself on the rock, sobbing and screaming, while Fergus sat still, hugging his bag. Anna could have screamed with her brother, for the boat seemed to have overshot the mark, and to be going quite aloof, when all depended upon a few minutes. She could hardly hear the words of the Preventive woman, who had found a second glass: "Never you fear, miss, the boat will be up in time."

She could not speak. Her heart was in wild rebellion as she thought of the comparative value of her widowed mother's only son with that of the fisher-boy, or even of Fergus, one of so large a family. She could not or would not look to see what Gerald was doing with the wretched little coast boy; but she heard her companion say that the gentleman had put the boy down to scramble among the rocks, and he himself was going back to the pair on the rock, quite swimming now.

She durst look again, and saw that he had scrambled up to the boys' perch, and had lifted Adrian up, but there was white spray dashing round now. She could not see the boat.

"They have to keep to the other side," explained the woman. "God keep them! It will be a near shave. The gentleman is taking off his coat!"

Again there was a leap of foam—over! over! Then all was blotted out, but the woman exclaimed—

"There they are!"

"Oh! where?"

"One swimming! He is floating the other."

Anna could see no longer. She dashed aside the telescope, then begged to be told, then looked again. No prayer would come but "Save him! save him!"

There was a call quite close.

"Mr. Norris, sir, put off your boat! Master Fergus—Oh! is he off?" and, drenched and breathless, Davy sank down on the ground at their feet, quite spent, unable at first to get out a word after those panting ones; but in a minute he spoke in answer to the agonized "Which? Who?"

"Master Fergus is swimming. The young sir couldn't."

Anna recollected how her mother's fears and entreaties had prevented Mr. Harewood from teaching Adrian to swim.

"Gent is floating him," added the boy. "He took me first, because I could get over the rocks and get help soonest. He is a real gentleman, he is."

Anna could not listen to anything but "The boat is coming!"

"Oh, but they don't see! They are going away from it!"

"That's the current," said Mrs. Norris. "My man knows what he is about, and so does the gentleman, never fear."

There was another terrible interval, and then boat and swimmers began to approach, though in what condition could not be made out. A dark little head, no doubt that of Fergus, was lifted in, then another figure was raised and taken into the boat; Gerald swam with a hand on it for a short distance, then was helped in, and almost at once took an oar.

"That's right," said Mrs. Norris. "It will keep out the cold."

"They are not coming here," exclaimed Anna. "They are going round the point."

"All right," was the answer. "'Tis more direct, you see, no shoals, and the young gentlemen will get to their own homes and beds all the quicker. Now, miss, you will come in and take a cup of tea, I am sure you want it, and I had just made it when Norris saw the little lads."

"Oh, thank you, I must get back at once. My little brother—"

"Yes, yes, miss, but you'll be able to ride the faster for a bit of bread and cup of tea! You are all of a tremble."

It was true, and to pacify her, Mrs. Norris sent a child up to bid Petros have the horses ready, and Anna was persuaded to swallow a little too, which happily had cooled enough for her haste, but she hurried off, leaving Mrs. Norris to expend her hospitality on Davy, who endured his drenching like a fish, and could hardly wait even to swallow thick bread-and-butter till he could rush off to hear of his dear Master Fergus.

The horses were ready. Petros had been joined by other spectators, and was able to entrust the bicycles to one of them, while he himself undertook to lead Mr. Underwood's horse to the stable. Anna rode off at as much speed or more than was safe downhill among the stones. She had to cross the broad parade above the quay, and indeed she believed she had come faster than the boat, which had to skirt round the side of the promontory between Anscombe Cove and Rockquay. In fact, when she came above the town she could see a crowd on the quay and pier, all looking out to sea, and she now beheld two boats making for the harbour.

Then she had to ride between walls and villas, and lost sight of all till she emerged on the parade, and thought she saw Uncle Clement's hat above the crowd as she looked over their heads.

She gave her horse to a bystander, who evidently knew her, for a murmur went through the crowd of "Little chap's sister," and way was made for her to get forward, while several rough voices said, "All right"; "Coast-guard boat"; "Not this one."

Her uncle and Miss Mohun wore standing together. General Mohun could be seen in the foremost boat, and they could hear him call out, with a wave of his arm—

"All right! All safe!"

"You hero! Where's Gerald?" Miss Mohun exclaimed, as Anna came up to her.

"There!" and she pointed to the Coast-guard boat. "We saw the boys from Anscombe Cliff, and he went out to them."

"Gerald," exclaimed his uncle, with a ring of gladness in his voice, all the more that it was plain that the rower was indeed Gerald, and he began to hail those on shore, while Fergus's head rose up from the bottom of the boat.

In a few moments they were close to the quay, and the little sodden mass that purported to be Fergus was calling out—

"Aunt Jane! Oh, I've lost such a bit of aralia. Where's Davy?"

"Here, take care. He is all right," were Gerald's words.

He meant Adrian, whom his cousin lifted out, with eyes open and conscious, but with limp hands and white exhausted looks, to be carried to the fly that stood in waiting.

"Is the other boy safe?" asked Gerald anxiously.

"Oh yes; but how could you?" were the first words that came to Anna; but she felt rebuked by a strange look of utter surprise, and instead of answering her he replied to General Mohun—

"Thanks, no, I'll walk up!" as a rough coat was thrown over his dripping and scanty garments.

"The wisest way," said the General. "Can you, Fergus?"

"Yes, quite well. Oh, my aralia!"

"He has been half crying all the way home about his fossils," said Gerald. "Never mind, Fergus; look out for the next spring-tide. Uncle Clem, you ought to drive up."

Clement submitted, clearly unable to resist, and sat down by Anna, who had her brother in her arms, rubbing his hands and warming them, caressing him, and asking him how he felt, to which the only answer she got was—

"It was beastly. I have my mouth awfully full of water still."

Clement made a low murmur of thanksgiving, and Anna, looking up, was startled to see how white and helpless he was. The way was happily very short, but he had so nearly fainted that Gerald, hurrying on faster uphill than the horse to reassure his aunt, lifted him out, not far from insensible, and carried him with Sibby's help to his bed in the room on the ground-floor, where the remedies were close at hand, Geraldine and nurse anxiously administering them; when the first sign of revival he gave was pointing to Gerald's dripping condition, and signing to him to go and take care of himself.

"All right, yes, boys and all! All right Cherie."

And he went, swallowing down the glass of stimulant which his aunt turned from her other patient for a moment to administer, but she was much too anxious about Clement to have thought for any one else, for truly it did seem likely that he would be the chief sufferer from the catastrophe.

Little Davy's adventure, as he had lost no clothes, made no more impression on his parents than if he had been an amphibious animal or a water dog, and when Fergus came out of Beechwood Cottage after having changed the few clothes he had retained, and had a good meal, to be driven home with his uncle in the dog-cart, his constant henchman was found watching for news of him at the gate.

"Please, sir, I think we'll find your aralia next spring-tide."

Whereupon General Mohun told him he was a good little chap, and presented him with a half-crown, the largest sum he had ever possessed in his life.

Fergus did not come off quite so well, for when the story had been told, though his mother had trembled and shed tears of thankfulness as she kissed him, and his sisters sprang at him and devoured him, while all the time he bemoaned his piece of the stump of an aralia, and a bit of cone of a pinus, and other treasures to which imaginative regret lent such an aid, that no doubt he would believe the lost contents of his bag to have been the most precious articles that he had ever collected; his father, however, took him into his study.

"Fergus," he said gravely, "this is the second time your ardour upon your pursuits has caused danger and inconvenience to other people, this time to yourself too."

Fergus hung his head, and faltered something about—"Never saw."

"No, that is the point. Now I say nothing about your pursuits. I am very glad you should have them, and be an intelligent lad; but they must not be taken up exclusively, so as to drive out all heed to anything else. Remember, there is a great difference between courage and foolhardiness, and that you are especially warned to be careful if your venturesomeness endangers other people's lives."

So Fergus went off under a sense of his father's displeasure, while Adrian lay in his bed, kicking about, admired and petted by his sister, who thought every one very unkind and indifferent to him; and when he went to sleep, began a letter to her eldest sister describing the adventure and his heroism in naming terms, such as on second thoughts she suppressed, as likely to frighten her mother, and lead to his immediate recall.

CHAPTER XI. — HEROES AND HERO-WORSHIP

Sunday morning found Anna in a different frame of mind from that of the evening before. Uncle Clement had been very ill all night, and the house was to be kept as quiet as possible. When Anna came in from early Celebration, Aunt Cherry came out looking like a ghost, and very anxious, and gave a sigh of relief on Adrian being reported still sound asleep. Gerald presently came down, pale and languid, but calling himself all right, and loitering over his breakfast till after the boy appeared, so rosy and ravenous as to cause no apprehension, except that he should devour too much apricot jam, and use his new boots too noisily on the stairs.

Anna devised walking him to Beechcroft to hear if there were any news of Fergus, and though he observed, with a certain sound of contemptuous rivalship, that there was no need, for "Merrifield was as right as a trivet," he was glad enough to get out of doors a little sooner, and though he affected to be bored by the kind inquiries of the people they met, he carried his head all the higher for them.

Nobody was at home except General Mohun, but he verified Adrian's impression of his nephew's soundness, whatever the mysterious comparison might mean; and asked rather solicitously not only after Mr. Underwood but after Gerald, who, he said, was a delicate subject to have made such exertions.

"It really was very gallant and very sensible behaviour," he said, as he took his hat to walk to St. Andrew's with the brother and sister, but Anna was conscious of a little pouting in Adrian's expression, and displeasure in his stumping steps.

Gerald came to church, but went to sleep in the sermon, and had altogether such a worn-out look that no one could help remembering that he had never been very strong, and had gone through much exertion the day before, nor could he eat much of the mid-day meal. Mrs. Grinstead, who was more at ease about her brother, looked anxiously at him, and with a kind of smile the word "Apres" passed between them. The Sunday custom was for Clement to take Adrian to say his Catechism, and have a little instruction before going out walking, but as this could not be on this day, Anna and he were to go out for a longer walk than usual, so as to remove disturbance from the household. Gerald declined, of course, and was left extended on the sofa; but just as

Anna and Adrian had made a few steps along the street, and the boy had prevailed not to walk to Clipstone, as she wished, but to go to the cliffs, that she might hear the adventure related in sight of the scene of action, he discovered that he had left a glove. He was very particular about Sunday walking in gloves in any public place, and rushed back to find it, leaving his sister waiting. Presently he came tearing back and laughing.

"Did you find it?"

"Oh yes; it was in the drawing-room. And what else do you think I found? Why, Cherie administering"—and he pointed down his throat, and made a gulp with a wild grimace of triumph. "On the sly! Ha! ha!"

Anna felt as if the ground had opened under her feet, but she answered gravely—

"Poor Gerald went through a great deal yesterday, and is quite knocked up, so no wonder he needs some strengthening medicine."

"Strengthening grandmother! Don't you think I know better than that?" he cried, with a caper and a grin.

"Of course you had to have some cordial when you were taken out of the water."

"And don't you know what it was?"

"I know the fisher-people carry stuff about with them in case of accidents."

"That's the way with girls—just to think one knows nothing at all."

"What do you know, Adrian?"

"Know? Why, I haven't been about with Kit and Ted Harewood for nothing! Jolly good larks it is to see how all of you take for granted that a fellow never knew the taste of anything but tea and milk-and-water."

"But what do you know the taste of?" she asked, with an earnestness that provoked the boy to tease and put on a boasting manner, so that she could not tell how much he was pretending for the sake of amazing and tormenting her, in which he certainly succeeded.

However, his attention was diverted by coming round the corner to where there was a view of Anscombe Bay, when he immediately began to fight his battles o'er again, and show where they had been groping in the mud and seaweed in pursuit of sea-urchins, and stranded star-fish, and crabs.

"And it wasn't a forest after all, it was just a sell—nothing but mud and weed, only Fergus would go and poke in it, and there were horrid great rough stones and rocks too, and I tumbled over one."

Anna here became conscious that the whole place was the resort of the afternoon promenaders of Rockquay, great and small, of all ranks and degrees, belonging to the "middle class" or below it, and that they might themselves become the object of attention; and she begged her brother to turn back and wait till they could have the place to themselves.

"These are a disgusting lot of cads," he agreed, "but there won't be such a jolly tide another time. I declare I see the very rock where I saw the sea-mouse—out there! red and shiny at the top."

Here a well-dressed man, who had just come up the Coast-guard path, put aside his pipe, and taking off his hat, deferentially asked—

"Have I the honour of addressing Sir Adrian Vanderkist?"

Adrian replied with a gracious nod and gesture towards his straw hat, and in another moment Anna found him answering questions, and giving his own account of the adventure to the inquirer, who, she had little doubt, was a reporter, and carrying his head, if possible, higher in consequence as he told how Fergus Merrifield had lingered over his stones, and all the rest after his own version. She did not hear the whole, having had to answer the inquiries of one of the bicycle friends of the previous day, but when her attention was free she heard—

"And the young lady, Sir Adrian?"

"Young lady! Thank goodness, we were not bothered with any of that sort."

"Indeed, Sir Adrian, I understood that there was a young lady, Miss Aurelia, that Master Merrifield was lamenting, as if she had met with a watery grave."

"Ha! ha! Aralia was only the name of a bit of fossil kind of a stick that Merrifield had us down there to find in the fossil forest. I'm sure I saw no forest, only bits of mud and stuff! But he found a bit, sure enough, and was ready to break his heart when he had to leave his bag behind him on the rock. Aralia a young lady! That's a good one."

He forgathered with a school-fellow on the way home, and Anna heard little more.

The next day, however, there arrived the daily local paper, addressed to Sir Adrian Vanderkist, Bart., and it was opened by him at breakfast-time.

"I say! Look here! 'Dangerous Accident in Anscombe. A Youthful Baronet in peril!' What asses people are!" he added, with an odd access of the gratified shame of seeing himself for the first time in print. But he did not proceed to read aloud; there evidently was something he did not like, and he was very near pocketing it and rushing off headlong to school with it, if his aunt and Anna had not entreated or commanded for it, when he threw it over with an uncomplimentary epithet.

"Just what I was afraid of when I saw the man talking to him!" exclaimed Anna. "Oh, listen!

"'The young Sir Adrian Vanderkist, at present residing at St. Andrew's Rock with his aunt, Mrs. Grinstead, and the Rev. E. C. Underwood, and who is a pupil at Mrs. Edgar's academy for young gentlemen, was, we are informed, involved in the most imminent danger, together with a son of General Sir Jasper Merrifield, K.G.C., a young gentleman whose remarkable scientific talent and taste appear to have occasioned the peril of the youthful party, from whence they were rescued by Gerald F. Underwood, Esq., of Vale Leston.'"

"What's all that?" said Gerald F. Underwood, Esquire, sauntering in and kissing his aunt. "Good-morning. How is Uncle Clement this morning?"

"Much better; I think he will be up by and by," answered Mrs. Grinstead.

"What bosh have you got there? The reporters seized on their prey, eh?"

"There's Sir Jasper!" exclaimed Anna, who could see through the blinds from where she sat.

Sir Jasper had driven over with his little son, and, after leaving him at school, had come to inquire for Mr. Underwood, and to obtain a fuller account of the accident, having already picked up a paper and glanced at it.

"I am afraid my little scamp led them into the danger," he said. "Scientific taste forsooth! Science is as good a reason as anything else for getting into scrapes."

"Really," said Gerald, "I can't say I think your boy came out the worst in it, though I must own the Rockquay Advertiser bestows most of the honours of the affair on the youthful baronet! You say he blew his own trumpet," added Gerald, turning to Anna.

"The reporter came and beset us," said Anna, in a displeased voice. "I did not hear all that passed, but of course Adrian told him what he told me, only those people make things sound ridiculous."

"To begin with," said Gerald, "I don't think Fergus, or at any rate Davy Blake, was in fault. They tried to go home in good time, having an instinct for tides, but Adrian was chasing a sea-mouse or some such game, and could not be brought back, and then he fell over a slippery rock, and had to be dragged out of a hole, and by that time the channel of the Anscombe stream was too deep, at least for him, who has been only too carefully guarded from being amphibious.”

“Oh! that did not transpire at home,” said Sir Jasper. “Boys are so reserved.”

Mrs. Grinstead and Anna looked rather surprised. Anna even ventured—

“I thought Fergus got too absorbed.”

“So did I,” said his father dryly. “And he did not justify himself.”

“M—m—m,” went on Gerald, skimming the article.

“Read it,” cried Anna. “You know none of us have seen it.”

Gerald continued—

“‘Their perilous position having been observed from Anscombe cliffs, Mr. G. F. Underwood of Vale Leston heroically’ (i.e. humbugically) ‘made his way out to their assistance, while a boat was put off by the Coast-guard, and that of Mr. Carter, fisherman, from Rockquay was launched somewhat later.’ We could not see either of them, you know. My eye, this is coming it strong! ‘The young baronet generously insisted that the little fisher-boy, DavidBlake, who had accompanied them, should first be placed in safety—’”

“Didn’t he?” exclaimed Anna. “I saw, and I wondered, but I thought it was his doing.”

“You saw?”

“Yes, in the Coast-guard’s telescope.”

“Oh! That is a new feature in the case!”

“Then he did not insist?” said Mrs. Grinstead.

“It was with the wrong side of his mouth.”

“But why did you send the fisher-boy first, when after all his life was less important?” exclaimed Anna, breaking forth at last.

“First, for the reason that I strove to impress on ‘the youthful baronet,’ Noblesse oblige. Secondly, that Davy knew how to make his way along the rocks, and also knew where to find the Preventive station. I could leave him to get on, as I could not have done with the precious Adrian, and that gave a much better chance for us all. It was swimming work by the time I got back, and by that time I thought the best alternative for any of us was to keep hold as long as we could, and then keep afloat as best we might till we were picked up. Your boy was the hero of it all. Adrian was so angry with me for my disrespect that I could hardly have got him to listen to me if Fergus had not made him understand, that to let himself be passive and be floated by me till the boats came up was the only thing to be done. There was one howl when he had to let go his beloved aralia, but he showed his soldier blood, and behaved most manfully."

"I am most thankful to hear it," said his father, "and especially thankful to you."

"Oh! there was not much real danger," said Gerald lightly, "to any one who could swim."

"But Adrian could not," said Anna. "Oh! Gerald, what do we not owe to you?"

"I must be off," said Sir Jasper; "I must see about a new jacket for my boy. By the bye, do you know how the little Davy fared in the matter of clothes?"

"Better than any of us," said Gerald. "He was far too sharp to go mud-larking in anything that would be damaged, and had his boots safe laid up in a corner. I wish mine were equally safe."

Sir Jasper's purchases were not confined to boots and jacket, but as compensation for his hard words included a certain cabinet full of drawers that had long been Fergus's cynosure.

Anna and her aunt were much concerned at what was said of Adrian, and still more at the boastful account that he seemed to have given; but then something, as Mrs. Grinstead observed, must be allowed for the reporter's satisfaction in having interviewed a live baronet. Each of the parties concerned had one hero, and if the Merrifields' was Fergus, to their own great surprise and satisfaction, Aunt Cherry was very happy over her own especial boy, Gerald, and certainly it was an easier task than to accept "the youthful baronet" at his own valuation or that of the reporter.

Mrs. Grinstead considered whether to try to make him less conceited about it, and show him his want of truth. She consulted his uncle about it, showing the newspaper, and telling, and causing Gerald to tell, the history of the accident, which Clement had not been fit to hear all the day before.

He was still in bed, but quite ready to attend to anything, and he laughed over the account, which she illustrated by the discoveries she had made from the united witnesses.

"And is it not delightful to see for once what Gerald really is?" she said.

"Yes, he seems to have behaved gallantly," said his uncle; "and I won't say just what might have been expected."

"One does expect something of an Underwood," she said.

"Little Merrifield too, who saw the danger coming, deserves more honour than he seems to have taken to himself."

"Yes, he accepted severity from that stern father of his, who seems very sorry for it now. It is curious how those boys' blood comes out in the matter— chasser de race."

"You must allow something for breeding. Fergus had not been the idol of a mother and sisters, and Gerald remembered his father in danger."

"Oh, I can never be glad enough that he has that remembrance of him! How like him he grows! That unconscious imitation is so curious."

"Yes, the other day, when I had been dozing, I caught myself calling out that he was whistling 'Johnny Cope' so loud that he would be heard in the shop."

"He seems to be settling down more happily here than I expected. I sometimes wonder if there is any attraction at Clipstone."

"No harm if there were, except—"

"Except what? Early marriage might be the very best thing."

"Perhaps, though sometimes I doubt whether it is well for a man to have gone through the chief hopes and crises of life so soon. He looks out for fresh excitement."

"There are so many stages in life," said Geraldine, sighing. "And with all his likenesses, Gerald is quite different from any of you."

"So I suppose each generation feels with those who succeed it. Nor do I feel as if I understood the Universities to-day as I did Cambridge thought of old. We can do nothing but wait and pray, and put out a hand where we see cause."

"Where we see! It is the not seeing that is so trying. The being sure that there is more going on within than is allowed to meet one's eye, and that one is only patronized as an old grandmother—quite out of it."

"I think the conditions of life and thought are less simple than in our day."

"And to come to the present. What is to be done about Adrian—the one who was not a hero, though he made himself out so?"

"Probably he really thought so. He is a mere child, you know, and it was his first adventure, before he has outgrown the days of cowardice."

"He need not have told stories."

"Depend upon it, he hardly knew that he did so."

"He had the reporter to help him certainly, and the 'Rockquay Advertiser' may not keep to the stern veracity and simplicity of the 'Pursuivant'."

"And was proud to interview a live baronet."

"Then what shall we do—Anna and I, I mean?"

"Write the simple facts to Vale Leston, and then let it alone."

"To him?"

"Certainly. He would think your speaking mere nagging. Preserve an ominous silence if he speaks. His school-fellows will be his best cure."

"Well, he did seem ashamed!"

Clement was right. The boy's only mention of the paragraph was once as "that beastly thing"; and Anna discovered from Valetta Merrifield, that whatever satisfaction he might have derived from it had been effectually driven out of him by the "fellows" at Mrs. Edgar's, who had beset him with all their force of derision, called him nothing but the "youthful Bart.," and made him ashamed as none of the opposite sex or of maturer years could ever have succeeded in doing. Valetta said Fergus had tried to stop it, but there had certainly been one effect, namely, that Adrian was less disposed to be "Merry's" shadow than heretofore, and seemed inclined instead to take up with the other seniors.

One thing, however, was certain. Gerald enjoyed a good deal more consideration among the Clipstone damsels than before. True, as Jasper said, it was only what any one would have done; but he had done it, and proved himself by no means inferior to "any one," and Fergus regarded him as a true hero, which had a considerable effect on his sisters, the more perhaps because Jasper derided their admiration.

They were doubly bent on securing him for a contributor to the Mouse-trap. They almost thought of inviting him to their Browning afternoons, but decided that he would not appreciate the feminine company, though he did so often have a number of the 'Censor' to discuss it with Dolores, whenever they met him.

CHAPTER XII. — THE LITTLE BUTTERFLY

The Matrons, otherwise denominated lady patronesses, met in committee, Miss Mohun being of course the soul and spirit of all, though Mrs. Ellesmere, as the wife of the rector of old Rockstone Church, was the president, Lady Flight, one of the most interested, was there, also Lady Merrifield, dragged in to secure that there was nothing decided on contrary to old-world instincts, Mrs. Grinstead, in right of the musical element that her brother promised, the beautiful Mrs. Henderson, to represent the marble works, Mrs. Simmonds of the Cliff Hotel, the Mayoress, and other notables.

The time was fixed for the first week in August, the only one when engagements would permit the Rotherwood family to be present for the opening, and when the regatta was apt to fill Rockquay with visitors. The place was to be the top of the cliffs of Rockstone, where the gardens of the Cliff Hotel, of Beechcroft Cottage, Rocca Marina, and Carrara, belonging respectively to Miss Mohun, Mr. White, and Captain Henderson, lay close together separated by low walls, and each with a private door opening on a path along the top of the cliffs. They could easily be made to communicate together, by planks laid over the boundaries, and they had lawns adapted for tents, etc., and Rocca Marina rejoiced in a shrubbery and conservatories that were a show in themselves, and would be kindly lent by Mr. and Mrs. White, though health compelled them to be absent and to resort to Gastein. The hotel likewise had a large well-kept garden, where what Mrs. Simmonds called a pavilion, "quite mediaeval," was in course of erection, and could be thrown open on the great day.

It was rather "tea-gardenish," but it could be made available for the representation of The Outlaw's Isle. Lancelot made a hurried visit to study the place, and review the forces, and decided that it was practicable. There could be a gallery at one end for the spectators, and the outer end toward the bay could be transformed into a stage, with room for the orchestra, and if the weather were favourable the real sea could be shown in the background. The scenes had been painted by the clever fingers at Vale Leston. It remained to cast the parts. Lancelot himself would be Prospero, otherwise Alaster Maclan, and likewise conductor, bringing with him the school-master of Vale Leston, who could supply his part as conductor when he was on the stage. His little boy Felix would be Ariel, the other elves could be selected from the school-children, and the local Choral Society would supply the wreckers and the wrecked. But the demur was over Briggs, a retired purser, who had always had a monopoly of sea-songs, and who looked on the boatswain as his right, and was likely to roar every one down. Ferdinand would be Gerald, under the name of Angus, but the difficulty was his Miranda—Mona as she was called. The Vanderkists could not be asked to perform in public, nor would Sir Jasper Merrifield have consented to his daughters doing so, even if they could have sung, and it had been privately agreed that none of the other young ladies of Rockquay could be brought forward, especially as there was no other grown-up female character.

"My wife might undertake it," said Lancelot, "but her voice is not her strong point, and she would be rather substantial for a Miranda."

"It would be rather like finding a mother instead of a wife—with all respect to my Aunt Daisy," laughed Gerald.

"By the bye, I'm sure I once heard a voice, somewhere down by the sea, that would be perfect," exclaimed Lance. "Sweet and powerful, fresh and young, just what is essential. I heard it when I was in quest of crabs with my boy."

"I know!" exclaimed Gerald, "the Little Butterfly, as they call her!"

"At a cigar-shop," said Lance.

"Mrs. Schnetterling's. Not very respectable," put in Lady Flight.

"Decidedly attractive to the little boys, though," said Gerald. "Sweets, fishing-tackle, foreign stamps, cigars. I went in once to see whether Adrian was up to mischief there, and the Mother Butterfly looked at me as if I had seven heads; but I just got a glimpse of the girl, and, as my uncle says, she would make an ideal Mona, or Miranda."

"Lydia Schnetterling," exclaimed Mr. Flight. "She is a very pretty girl with a nice voice. You remember her, Miss Mohun, at our concerts? A lovely fairy."

"I remember her well. I thought she was foreign, and a Roman Catholic."

"So her mother professes—a Hungarian. The school officer sent her to school, and she did very well there, Sunday-school and all, and was a monitor. She was even confirmed. Her name is really Ludmilla, and Lida is the correct contraction. But when I wanted her to be apprenticed as a pupil-teacher, the mother suddenly objected that she is a Roman Catholic, but I very much doubt the woman's having any religion at all. I wrote to the priest about her, but I believe he could make nothing of her. Still, Lydia is a very nice girl— comes to church, and has not given up the Choral Society."

"She is a remarkably nice good girl," added Mrs. Henderson. "She came to me, and entreated that I would speak for her to be taken on at the marble works."

"You have her there?"

"Yes; but I am much afraid that her talents do not lie in the way of high promotion, and I think if she does not get wages enough to satisfy her mother, she is in dread of being made to sing at public-houses and music-halls."

"That nice refined girl!"

"Yes; I am sure the idea is dreadful to her."

"Could you not put her in the way of getting trained?" asked Gerald of his uncle.

"I must hear her first."

"I will bring her up to the Choral Society tonight," said Mr. Flight.

"What did you call her?" said Geraldine.

"Some German or foreign name, Schnetterling, and the school calls her Lydia."

At that moment the council was invaded, as it sat in Miss Mohun's drawing-room, upon rugs and wicker chairs, to be refreshed with tea. In burst a whole army of Merrifields, headed by little Primrose, now a tall girl of twelve years old, more the pet of the family than any of her elders had been allowed to be. Her cry was—

"Oh, mamma, mamma, here's the very one for the captain of the buccaneers!"

The startling announcement was followed by the appearance of a tall, stalwart, handsome young man of a certain naval aspect, whom Lady Merrifield introduced as Captain Armytage.

"We must congratulate him, Gillian," she said. "I see you are gazetted as commander."

Primrose, who had something of the licence of the youngest, observed—

"We have been telling him all about it. He used to be Oliver Cromwell in 'How Do You Like It?' and now he will be a buccaneer!"

"Oliver Cromwell, you silly child!" burst out Gillian, with a little shake, while the rest fell into fits of laughing.

"I fear it was a less distinguished part," said Captain Armytage.

"May I understand that you will help us?" said Lancelot. "I heard of you at Devereux Castle."

"I don't think you heard much of my capabilities, especially musical ones. I was the stick of the party," said Captain Armytage.

It was explained that Captain Armytage had actually arrived that afternoon at the Cliff Hotel, and had walked over to call at Clipstone, whence he found the young ladies setting out to walk to Rockstone. He could not deny that he had acted and sung, though, as he said, his performance in both cases was vile. Little Miss Primrose had most comically taken upon her to patronize him, and to offer him as buccaneer captain had been a freak of her own, hardly to be accounted for, except that Purser Briggs's unsuitableness had been discussed in her presence.

"Primrose is getting to be a horrid little forward thing," observed Gillian to her aunt.

"A child of the present," said Miss Mohun. "Infant England! But her suggestion seems to be highly opportune."

"I don't believe he can sing," growled Gillian, "and it will be just an excuse for his hanging about here."

There was something in Gillian's "savagery" which gave Aunt Jane a curious impression, but she kept it to herself.

Late in the evening Lance appeared in his sister's drawing-room with—

"I have more hopes of it. I did not think it was feasible when Anna wrote to me, but I see my way better now. That parson, Flight, has a good notion of drilling, and that recruit of the little Merrifield girl, Captain Armytage, is worth having."

"If he roared like a sucking dove we would have him, only to silence that awful boatswain," said Gerald; "and as to the little Cigaretta, she is a born prima donna."

"Your Miranda? Are you content with her?" said his aunt.

"She is to the manner born. Lovely voice, acts like a dragon, and has an instinct how to stand and how to hold her hands."

"Coming in drolly with her prim dress and bearing. Though she was dreadfully frightened," said Lance. "Being half-foreign accounts for something, I suppose, but it is odd how she reminds me of some one. No doubt it is of some singer at a concert. What did they say was her name?"

"Ludmilla Schnetterling, the Little Butterfly they call her. Foreign on both sides apparently," said Gerald. "Those dainty ankles never were bred on English clods."

"I wonder what her mother is," said Mrs. Grinstead.

"By the bye, I think it must have been her mother that I saw that morning when little Felix dragged me to a cigar-shop in quest of an ornamental crab— a handsome, slatternly hag sort of woman, who might have been on the stage," said Lance.

"Sells fishing-tackle, twine, all sorts," came from Adrian.

"Have you been there?" asked his sister, rather disturbed.

"Of course! All the fellows go! It is the jolliest place for"—he paused a moment—"candies and ginger-beer."

"I should have thought there were nicer places!" sighed Anna.

"You have yet to learn that there is a period of life when it is a joy to slip out of as much civilization as possible," said Lance, putting his sentence in involved form so as to be the less understood by the boys.

"Did you say that Flight had got hold of them?" asked Clement.

"Hardly. They are R.C.'s, it seems; and as to the Mother Butterfly, I should think there was not much to get hold of in her; but Mrs. Henderson takes interest in her marble-workers, and the girl is the sort of refined, impressible creature that one longs to save, if possible. To-morrow I am going to put you all through your parts, Master Gerald, so don't you be out of the way."

"One submits to one's fate," said Gerald, "hoping that virtue may be its own reward, as it is in the matter of 'The Inspector's Tour', which the 'Censor' accepts, really enthusiastically for a paper, though the Mouse-trap would have found it—what shall I say?—a weasel in their snare."

"Does it indeed?" cried Anna, delighted. "I saw there was a letter by this last post."

"Aye—invites more from the same pen," he replied lazily.

"Too much of weasel for the 'Pursuivant' even?" said Geraldine.

"Yes," said Lance; "these young things are apt to tear our old traps and flags to pieces. By the bye, who is this Captain Armytage, who happily will limit Purser Briggs to 'We split, we split, we split,' or something analogous?"

"I believe," said Gerald, "that he joined the Wills-of-the-Wisp, that company which was got up by Sir Lewis Willingham, and played at Devereux Castle a year or two ago. Some one told me they were wonderfully effective for amateurs."

"That explains the acquaintance with Lady Merrifield," said Mrs. Grinstead.

"Oh, yes," said Anna. "Mysie told me all about it; and how Mr. David Merrifield married the nicest of them all, and how much they liked this Captain Armytage."

"Was not Mysie there when he arrived?"

"No, she was gone to see the Henderson children, but Gillian looked a whole sheaf of daggers at him. You know what black brows Gillian has, and she drew them down like thunder," and Anna imitated as well as her fair open brows would permit, "turning as red as fire all the time."

"That certainly means something," said Geraldine, laughing.

"I should like to see Gillian in love," laughed Anna; "and I really think she is afraid of it, she looked so fierce."

The next evening there was time for a grand review in the parish school-room of all possible performers on the spot. In the midst, however, a sudden fancy flashed across Lancelot that there was something curiously similar between those two young people who occupied the stage, or what was meant to be such. Their gestures corresponded to one another, their voices had the same ring, and their eyes wore almost of the same dark colour. Now Gerald's eyes had always been the only part of him that was not Underwood, and had never quite accorded with his fair complexion.

"Hungarian, I suppose," said Lance to himself, but he was not quite satisfied.

What struck him as strange was that though dreadfully shy and frightened when off the stage, as soon as she appeared upon it, though not yet in costume, she seemed to lose all consciousness that she was not Mona.

Perhaps Mrs. Henderson could have told him. Her husband being manager and partner at Mr. White's marble works, she had always taken great interest in the young women employed, had actually attended to their instruction, assisted in judging of their designs, and used these business relations to bring them into inner contact with her, so that her influence had become very valuable. She was at the little room which she still kept at the office, when there was a knock at the door, and "Miss Schnetterling" begged to speak to her. She felt particularly tender towards the girl, who was evidently doing her best in a trying and dangerous position, and after the first words it came out—

"Oh, Mrs. Henderson, do you think I must be Mona?"

"Have you any real objection, Lydia? Mr. Flight and all of them seem to wish it."

"Yes, and I can't bear not to oblige Mr. Flight, who has been so good, so good!" cried Lydia, with a foreign gesture, clasping her hands. "Indeed, perhaps my mother would not let me off. That is what frightens me. But if you or some real lady could put me aside they could not object."

"I do not understand you, my dear. You would meet with no unpleasantness from any one concerned, and you can be with the fairy children. Are you shy? You were not so in the fairy scenes last winter—you acted very nicely."

"Oh yes, I liked it then. It carries me away; but—oh! I am afraid!"

"Please tell me, my dear."

Lydia lowered her voice.

"I must tell you, Mrs. Henderson, mother was a singer in public once, and a dancer; and oh! they were so cruel to her, beat her, and starved her, and ill-used her. She used to tell me about it when I was very little, but now I have grown older, and the people like my voice, she is quite changed. She wants me to go and sing at the Herring-and-a-Half, but I won't, I won't—among all the tipsy men. That was why she would not let me be a pupil-teacher, and why she will not see a priest. And now—now I am sure she has a plan in her head. If I do well at this operetta, and people like me, I am sure she will get the man at the circus to take me, by force perhaps, and then it would be all her life over again, and I know that was terrible."

Poor Ludmilla burst into tears.

"Nay, if she suffered so much she would not wish to expose you to the same."

"I don't know. She is in trouble about the shop—the cigars. Oh! I should not have told! You won't—you won't—Mrs. Henderson?"

"No, you need not fear, I have nothing to do with that."

"I don't think," Lydia whispered again, "that she cares for me as she used to do when I was a little thing. Now that I care for my duty, and all that you and Mr. Flight have taught me, she is angry, and laughs at English notions. I was in hopes when I came to work here that my earnings would have satisfied her, but they don't, and I don't seem to get on."

Mrs. Henderson could not say that her success was great, but she ventured as much as to tell her that Captain Henderson could prevent any attempt to send her away without her consent.

“Oh! but if my mother went too you could not hinder it.”

“Are you sixteen, my dear? Then you could not be taken against your will.”

“Not till December. And oh! that gentleman, the conductor, he knew all about it, I could see, and by and by I saw him lingering about the shop, as if he wanted to watch me.”

“Mr. Lancelot Underwood! Oh, my dear, you need not be afraid of him, he is a brother of Mrs. Grinstead’s, a connection of Miss Mohun’s; and though he is such a musician, it is quite as an amateur. But, Lydia, I do think that if you sing your best, he may very likely be able to put you in a way to make your talent available so as to satisfy your mother, without leading to anything so undesirable and dangerous as a circus.”

“Then you think I ought—”

“It is a dangerous thing to give advice, but really, my dear, I do think more good is likely to come of this than harm.”

CHAPTER XIII. — TWO SIDES OF A SHIELD AGAIN

The earlier proofs of the Mouse-trap were brought by Lance, who had spent more time in getting them into shape than his wife approved, and they were hailed with rapture by the young ladies on seeing themselves for the first time in print. As to Gerald, he had so long been bred—as it were—to journalism that, young as he was, he had caught the trick, and 'The Inspector's Tour' had not only been welcomed by the 'Censor', but portions had been copied into other papers, and there was a proposal of publishing it in a separate brochure. It would have made the fortune of the Mouse-trap, if it had not been so contrary to its principles, and it had really been sent to them in mischief, together with The 'Girton Girl', of which some were proud, though when she saw it in print, with a lyre and wreath on the page, sober Mysie looked grave.

"Do you think it profane to parody Jane Taylor?" said Gerald.

"No, but I thought it might hurt some people's feelings, and discourage them, if we laugh at the High School."

"Why, Dolores goes to give lectures there," exclaimed Valetta.

"Nobody is discouraged by a little good-humoured banter," said Gillian. "Nobody with any stuff in them."

"There must be some training in chaff though," said Gerald, "or they don't know how to take it."

"And in point of fact," said Dolores, "the upper tradesmen's daughters come off with greater honours in the High School than do the young gentlewomen."

"Very wholesome for the young Philistines," said Gerald. "The daughters of self-made men may well surpass in energy those settled on their lees."

Gerald and Dolores were standing with their backs to the wall of Anscombe Church, which Jasper Merrifield and Mysie were zealously photographing, the others helping—or hindering.

"I thought upper tradesfolk were the essence of Philistines," returned Dolores.

"The elder generation—especially if he is the son of the energetic man. The younger are more open to ideas."

"The stolid Conservative is the one who has grown up while his father was making his fortune, the third generation used to be the gentleman, now he is the man who is tired of it."

"Tired of it, aye!" with a sigh.

"Why you are a man with a pedigree!" she returned.

"Pedigrees don't hinder—what shall I call it?—the sense of being fettered."

"One lives in fetters," she exclaimed. "And the better one likes one's home, the harder it is to shake them off."

He turned and looked full at her, then exclaimed, "Exactly," and paused, adding, "I wonder what you want. Has it a form?"

"Oh yes, I mean to give lectures. I should like to see the world, and study physical science in every place, then tell the next about it. I read all I can, and I think I shall get consent to give some elementary lectures at the High School, though Uncle Jasper does not half like it, but I must get some more training to do the thing rightly. I thought of University College. Could you get me any information about it?"

"Easily; but you'll have to conquer the horror of the elders."

"I know. They think one must learn atheism and all sorts of things there."

"You might go in for physical science at Oxford or Cambridge."

"I expect that is all my father would allow. In spite of the colonies, he has all the old notions about women, and would do nothing Aunt Lily really protested against."

"You are lucky to have a definite plan and notion to work for. Now fate was so unkind as to make me a country squire, and not only that, but one bound down, like Gulliver among the Liliputians, with all manner of cords by all the dear good excellent folks, who look on that old mediaeval den with a kind of fetish-worship, sprung of their having been kept out of it so long, and it would be an utter smash of all their hearts if I uttered a profane word against it. I would as soon be an ancient Egyptian drowning a cat as move a stone of it. It is a lovely sort of ancient Pompeii, good to look at now and then, but not to be bound down to."

"Like Beechcroft Court, a fossil. It is very well there are such places."

"Yes, but not to be the hope of them. It is my luck. If my eldest uncle, who had toiled in a bookseller's shop all his youth and reigned like a little king, had not gone and got killed in a boating accident, there he would be the ruling Sir Roger de Coverley of the county, a pillar of Church and State, and I should be a free man.”

“Won’t they let you go about, and see everything?”

“Oh yes, I am welcome to do a little globe-trotting. They are no fools; if they were I should not care half so much; but wherever I went, there would be a series of jerks from my string, and not having an integument of rhinoceros hide, I could not disregard them without a sore more raw than I care to carry about. After all, it is only a globe, and one gets back to the same place again.”

“Men have so many openings.”

“I’m not rich enough for Parliament, and if I were, maybe it would be worse for their hearts,” he said, with a sigh.

“There’s journalism, a great power.”

“Yes, but to put my name to all I could—and long to say—would be an equal horror to the dear folks.”

“Yet you are helping on this concern.”

“True, but partly pour passer le temps, partly because I really want to hear ‘The Outlaws Isle’ performed, and all under protest that the windmill will soon be swept away by the stream.”

“Indeed, yes,” cried Dolores. “They hope to regulate the stream. They might as well hope to regulate Mississippi.”

“Well-chosen simile! The current is slow and sluggish, but irresistible.”

“Better than stagnating or sticking fast in the mud.”

“Though the mud may be full of fair blossoms and sweet survivals,” said Gerald sadly.

“Oh yes, people in the old grooves are delightful,” said Dolores, “but one can’t live, like them, with a heart in G. F. S., like my Aunt Jane, really the cleverest of any of us! Or like Mysie, not stupid, but wrapped up in her classes, just scratching the surface. Now, if I went in for good works I would go to the bottom—down to the slums.”

“Slums are one’s chief interest,” said Gerald; “but no doubt it will soon be the same story over and over, and only make one wish—”

“What?”

“That there could be a revolution before I am of age.”

“What’s that?” cried Primrose, coming up as he spoke. “A revolution?”

“Yes, guillotines and all, to cut off your head in Rotherwood Park,” said

Gerald lightly.

"Oh! you don't really mean it."

"Not that sort," said Dolores. "Only the coming of the coquecigrues."

"They are in 'The Water Babies'," said Primrose, mystified.

Each of those two liked to talk to the other as a sort of fellow-captive, solacing themselves with discussions over the 'Censor' and its fellows. Love is not often the first thought, even where it lurks in modern intellectual intercourse between man and maid; and though Kitty Varley might giggle, the others thought the idea only worthy of her. Aunt Jane, however, smelt out the notion, and could not but communicate it to her sister, though adding—

"I don't believe in it: Dolores is in love with Physiology, and the boy with what Jasper calls Socialist maggots, but not with each other, unless they work round in some queer fashion."

However, Lady Merrifield, feeling herself accountable for Dolores, was anxious to gather ideas about Gerald from his aunt, with whom she was becoming more and more intimate. She was more than twenty years the senior, and the thread of connection was very slender, but they suited one another so well that they had become Lilias and Geraldine to one another. Lady Merrifield had preserved her youthfulness chiefly from having had a happy home, unbroken by family sorrows or carking cares, and with a husband who had always taken his full share of responsibility.

"Your nephew's production has made a stir," said she, when they found themselves alone together.

"Yes, poor boy." Then answering the tone rather than the words, "I suppose it is the lot of one generation to be startled by the next. There is a good deal of change in the outlook."

"Yes," said Lady Merrifield. "The young ones, especially the youngest, seem to have a set of notions of their own that I cannot always follow."

"Exactly," said Geraldine eagerly.

"You feel the same? To begin with, the laws of young ladyhood— maidenliness—are a good deal relaxed—"

"There I am not much of a judge. I never had any young ladyhood, but I own that the few times I went out with Anna I have been surprised, and more surprised at what I heard from her sister Emily."

"What we should have thought simply shocking being tolerated now."

"Just so; and we are viewed as old duennas for not liking it. I should say, however, that it is not, or has not, been a personal trouble with me. Anna's passion is for her Uncle Clement, and she has given up the season on his account, though Lady Travis Underwood was most anxious to have her; and as to Emily, though she is obliged to go out sometimes, she hates it, and has a soul set on slums and nursing."

"You mean that the style of gaieties revolts a nice-minded girl?"

"Partly. Perhaps such as the Travis Underwoods used to take part in, rather against their own likings, poor things, are much less restrained for the young people than what would come in your daughters' way."

"Perhaps; though Lady Rotherwood has once or twice in country-houses had to protect her daughter, to the great disgust of the other young people. That is one development that it is hard to meet, for it is difficult to know where old-fashioned distaste is the motive, and where the real principle of modesty. Though to me the question is made easy, for Sir Jasper would never hear of cricket for his daughters, scarcely of hunting, and we have taken away Valetta and Primrose from the dancing-classes since skirt-dancing has come in; but I fear Val thinks it hard."

"Such things puzzle my sisters at Vale Leston. They are part of the same spirit of independence that sends girls to hospitals or medical schools."

"Or colleges, or lecturing. Dolores is wild to lecture, and I see no harm in her trying her wings at the High School on some safe subject, if her father in New Zealand does not object, though I am glad it has not occurred to any of my own girls."

"Sir Jasper would not like it?"

"Certainly not; but if my brother consents he will not mind it for Dolores. She is a good girl in the main, but even mine have very different ideals from what we had."

"Please tell me. I see it a little, and I have been thinking about it."

"Well, perhaps you will laugh, but my ideal work was Sunday-schools."

"Are not they Miss Mohun's ideal still?"

"Oh yes, infinitely developed, and so they are my cousin Florence's—Lady Florence Devereux; but the young ones think them behind the times. I remember when every girl believed her children the prettiest and cleverest in nature, showed off her Sunday-school as her pride and treasure, and composed small pink books about them, where the catastrophe was either being killed by accident, or going to live in the clergyman's nursery. Now, those that teach do so simply as a duty and not a romance."

"And the difficulty is to find those who will teach," said Geraldine. "One thing is, that the children really require better teaching."

"That is quite true. My girls show me their preparation work, and I see much that I should not have thought of teaching the Beechcroft children. But all the excitement of the matter has gone off."

"I know. The Vale Leston girls do it as their needful work, not with their hearts and enthusiasm. I expect an enthusiasm cannot be expected to last above a generation and perhaps a half."

"Very likely. A more indifferent thing; you will laugh, but my enthusiasm was for chivalry, Christian chivalry, half symbolic. History was delightful to me for the search for true knights. I had lists of them, drawings if possible, but I never could indoctrinate anybody with my affection. Either history is only a lesson, or they know a great deal too much, and will prove to you that the Cid was a ruffian, and the Black Prince not much better."

"And are you allowed the 'Idylls of the King'?"

"Under protest, now that the Mouse-trap has adopted Browning for weekly reading and discussion. Tennyson is almost put on the same shelf with Scott, whom I love better than ever. Is it progress?"

"Well, I suppose it is, in a way."

"But is it the right way?"

"That's what I want to see."

"Now listen. When our young men, my brothers—especially my very dear brother Claude and his contemporaries, Rotherwood is the only one left— were at Oxford, they got raised into a higher atmosphere, and came home with beautiful plans and hopes for the Church, and drew us up with them; but now the University seems just an ordeal for faith to go through."

"I should think there was less of outward temptation, but more of subtle trial. And then the whole system has altered since the times you are speaking of, when the old rules prevailed, and the great giants of Church renewal were there!" said Geraldine.

"You belong to the generation whom they trained, and who are now passing away. My father was one who grew up then."

"We live on their spirit still."

"I hope so. I never knew much about Cambridge till Clement went there, but it had the same influence on him. Indeed, all our home had that one thought ever since I can remember. Clement and Lance grew up in it."

"But you will forgive me. These younger men either go very, very much further than we older ones dreamt of, or they have flaws in their faith, and sometimes—which is the strangest difficulty—the vehement observance and ritual with flaws beneath in their faith perhaps, or their loyalty—Socialist fancies."

"There is impatience," said Geraldine. "The Church progress has not conquered all the guilt and misery in the world."

"Who said it would?"

"None of us; but these younger ones fancy it is the Church's fault, instead of that of her members' failures, and so they try to walk in the light of the sparks that they have kindled."

"Altruism as they call it—love of the neighbour without love of God."

"It may lead that way."

"Does it?"

"Perhaps we are the impatient ones now," said Geraldine, "in disliking the young ones' experiments, and wanting to bind them to our own views."

"Then you look on with toleration but with distrust."

"Distrust of myself as well as of the young ones, and trying not to forget that 'one good custom may corrupt the world,' so it may be as well that the pendulum should swing."

"The pendulum, but not its axis—faith!"

"No; and of my boy's mainspring of faith I *do* feel sure, and of his real upright steadiness."

Lady Merrifield asked no more, but could wait.

But is not each generation a terra incognita to the last? A question which those feel most decidedly who stand on the border-land of both, with love and sympathy divided between the old and the new, clinging to the one, and fearing to alienate the other.

CHAPTER XIV. — BUTTERFLY'S NECTAR

Clement Underwood was so much better as to be arrived at taking solitary rides and walks, these suiting him better than having companions, as he liked to go his own pace, and preferred silence. His sister had become much engrossed with her painting, and saw likewise that in this matter of exercise it was better to let him go his own way, and he declared that this time of thought and reading was an immense help to him, restoring that balance of life which he seemed to himself to have lost in the whirl of duties at St. Matthew's after Felix's death.

The shore, with the fresh, monotonous plash of the waves, when the tide served, was his favourite resort. He could stand still and look out over the expanse of ripples, or wander on, as he pleased, watching the sea-gulls float along—

There had been a somewhat noisy luncheon, for Edward Harewood, a midshipman in the Channel Fleet, which was hovering in the offing, had come over on a day's leave with Horner, a messmate whose parents lived in the town. He was a big lad, a year older than Gerald, and as soon as a little awe of Uncle Clement and Aunt Cherry had worn off, he showed himself of the original Harewood type, directing himself chiefly to what he meant to be teasing Gerald about Vale Leston and Penbeacon.

"All the grouse there were on the bit of moor are snapped up."

"Very likely," said Gerald coolly.

"Those precious surveyors and engineers that Walsh brings down can give an account of them! As soon as you come of age, you'll have to double your staff of keepers, I can tell you."

"Guardians of ferae naturae," said Gerald.

"I thought your father did all that was required in that line," said Clement.

"Not since duffers and land-lubbers have been marauding over Penbeacon —aye, and elsewhere. What would you say to an engineer poaching away one of the august house of Vanderkist?"

"The awful cad! I'd soon show him what I thought of his cheek," cried

Adrian, with a flourish of his knife.

"Ha, ha! I bet that he will be shooting over Ironbeam Park long before you are of age."

"I shall shoot him, then," cried Adrian.

"Not improbably there will be nothing else to shoot by that time," quietly said Gerald.

"I shall have a keeper in every lodge, and bring up four or five hundred pheasants every year," boasted the little baronet, quite alive to the pride of possession, though he had never seen Ironbeam in his life.

Edward laughed a "Don't you wish you may get it," and the others, who knew very well the futility of the poor boy's expectations, even if Gerald's augury were not fulfilled, hastened to turn away the conversation to plans for the afternoon. Anna asked the visitor if he would ride out with her and Gerald to Clipstone or to the moor, and was relieved when he declined, saying he had promised to meet Horner.

"You will come in to tea at five?" said his aunt, "and bring him if you like."

"Thanks awfully, but we hardly can. We have to start from the quay at six sharp."

All had gone their several ways, and Clement, after the heat of the day, was pacing towards a secluded cove out of an inner bay which lay nearer than Anscombe Cove, but was not much frequented. However, he smelt tobacco, and heard sounds of boyish glee, and presently saw Adrian and Fergus Merrifield, bare-legged, digging in the mud.

"Ha! youngsters! Do you know the tide has turned? I thought you had had enough of that."

"I thought I might find my aralia!" sighed Fergus. "The tide was almost as low."

Just then there resounded from behind a projecting rock a peal of undesirable singing, a shout of laughter, and an oath, with—

"Holloa, those little beasts of teetotallers have hooked it."

There were confused cries—"Haul 'em back! Drench 'em. Give 'em a roll in the mud!" and Adrian shrank behind his uncle, taking hold of his coat, as there burst from behind the rock a party of boys, headed by the two cadets, all shouting loudly, till brought to a sudden standstill by the sight of "Parson! By Jove!" as the Horner mid muttered, taking out his pipe, while Edward Harewood mumbled something about "Horner's brother's tuck-out." One or two other boys were picking up the remains of the feast, which had been on lobsters, jam tarts, clotted cream, and the like delicacies dear to the juvenile mind. The two biggest school-boys came forward, one voluble and thick of speech about Horner's tuck-out, and "I assure you, sir, it is nothing—not a taste. Never thought of such—" Just then the other lad, staggering about, had almost lurched over into the deepening channel; but Clement caught him by the collar and held him fast, demanding in a low voice, very terrible to his hearers—

"Where does this poor boy live?"

It was Adrian who answered.

"Devereux Buildings."

"You two, Adrian and Fergus, run to the quay and fetch a cab as near this place as it can come," said Clement. "You little fellows, you had better run home at once. I hope you will take warning by the shame and disgrace of this spectacle."

The boys were glad enough to disperse, being terrified by the condition of the prisoner, as well as by the detection; but the two who were encumbered with the baskets containing the bottles, jam-pots, and tin of cream remained, and so did the two young sailors, Horner saying civilly—

"You'll not be hard on the kids, sir, for just a spree carried a little too far."

"I certainly shall not be hard on the children, whom you seem to have tempted," was the answer as they moved along; and as the younger Horner turned towards a little shop near the end of the steps to restore the goods, he asked—"Were you supplied from hence?"

"Yes," said Horner, who was perhaps hardly sober enough for caution. "Mother Butterfly is a jolly old soul."

Looking up. Clement saw no licence to sell spirituous liquors under the name of Sarah Schnetterling, tobacconist. The window had the placard 'Ici on parle Francais', and was adorned in a tasteful manner with ornamental pipes, fishing-rods and flies, jars of sweets, sheets of foreign stamps, pictorial advertisements of innocuous beverages. A woman with black grizzling hair, fashionably dressed, flashing dark eyes, long gold ear-rings, gold beads and gaudy attire, came out to reclaim her property. A word or two passed about payment, during which Clement had a strange thrill of puzzled recollection. The bottles bore the labels of raspberry vinegar and lemonade, but he had seen too much not to say—

"You drive a dangerous trade."

"Ah, sir, young people will be gourmands," she said, with a foreign accent. "Ah, that poor young gentleman is very ill. Will he not come in and lie down to recover?"

"No, thank you," said Clement. "A carriage is coming to take him home."

Something about the fat in the fire was passing between the cadets, and the younger of them began to repeat that he had come for his brother's birthday, and that he feared they had brought the youngsters into a scrape by carrying the joke too far.

"I have nothing to say to you, sir," said the Vicar of St. Matthew's, looking very majestic, "except that it is time you were returning to your ship. As to you," turning to Edward Harewood, "I can only say that if you are aware of the peculiar circumstances of Adrian Vanderkist, your conduct can only be called fiendish."

Fergus and Adrian came running up with tidings that the cab was waiting. Edward Harewood stood sullen, but the other lad said—

"Unlucky. We are sorry to have got the little fellows into trouble."

He held out his hand, and Clement did not refuse it, as he did that of his own nephew. Still, there was a certain satisfaction at his heart as he beheld the clear, honest young faces of the other two boys, and he bade Adrian run home and wait for him, saying to Fergus—

"You seem to have been a good friend to my little nephew. Thank you."

Fergus coloured up, speechless between pleasure at the warm tone of commendation and the obligations of school-boy honour, nor, with young Campbell on their hands, was there space for questions. That youth subsided into a heavy doze in the cab, and so continued till the arrival at No. 7, Devereux Buildings, where a capable-looking maid-servant opened the door, and he was deposited into her hands, the Vicar leaving his card with his present address, but feeling equal to nothing more, and hardly able to speak.

He drove home, finding his nephew in the doorway. Signing to the maid to pay the driver, and to the boy to follow him, he reached his study, and sank into his easy-chair, Adrian opening frightened eyes and saying—

"I'll call Sibby."

"No—that bottle—drop to there," signing to the mark on the glass with his nail.

After a pause, while he held fast the boy, so to speak, with his eyes, he said—

"Thank you, dear lad."

"Uncle Clement," said Adrian then, "we weren't doing anything. Merrifield thought his old bit of auralia, or whatever he calls it, was there."

"I saw—I saw, my boy. To find you—as you were, made me most thankful. You must have resisted. Tell me, were you of this party, or did you come on them by accident?"

"Horner asked me," said Adrian, twisting from one leg to another.

Clement saw the crisis was come which he had long expected, and rejoiced at the form it had taken, though he knew he should suffer from pursuing the subject.

"Adrian," he said, "I am much pleased with you. I don't want to get you into a row, but I should be much obliged if you would tell me how all this happened."

"It wouldn't," returned Adrian, "but for that Ted and the other chap."

"Do you mean that there would have been none of this—drinking—but for them? Don't be afraid to tell me all. Was the stuff all got from that Mrs. Schnetter—?"

"Mother Butterfly's? Oh yes. She keeps bottles of grog with those labels, and it is such a lark for her to be even with the gangers that our fellows generally get some after cricket, or for a tuck-out."

"Not Fergus Merrifield?"

"Oh no; he's captain, you know, but he is two years younger than Campbell and Horner, and they can't bear him, and when he made a jaw about it—he can jaw awfully, you know—and he is stuck up, and Horner major swore he would make him know his bearings—"

"I wonder he was there at all."

"Well, Horner asked him, and he can't get those fossils that were lost out of his head, and he thought they might be washed up. He said too, he knew they would be up to something if he wasn't there."

"Oh!" said Clement, with an odd recollection, "but I suppose he did not know about these cadets?"

"No, the big Horner sent up to Mother Butterfly's for some more stuff, not so mild, and then Ted set upon me, and said it was all because of me that Vale Leston had to live like a boiling of teetotal frogs and toads, just to please the little baronet's lady mamma, but I was a Dutchman all the same, and should sell them yet—I sucked it in so well, and they talked of seeing how much I could stand. Something about my governor, and here—that word in the Catechism."

"Ah!" gasped Clement, fairly clutching his arm, "and what spared you?"

"Horner came down, and Sweetie Bob, that's the errand-boy, and there was a bother about the money, for Bob wasn't to leave anything without being paid, and while they were jawing about that, Merry laid hold of me and said, 'Come and look for the aralia.' They got to shouting and singing, and I don't think they saw what was doing. They were nasty songs, and Merry touched me and said, 'Let us go after the aralia.' We got away without their missing us at first, but they ran after us when they found it out, and if you had not been there, Uncle Clem—"

"Thank God I was! Now, Adrian, first tell me, did you taste this stuff? You said you sucked it in."

"Well, I did, a little. You know, uncle, one cannot always be made a baby. Women don't understand, you know, and don't know what a fool it makes a man to have them always after him, and have everything put out of his way like a precious infant, and people drinking it on the sly like Gerald, or—"

"Or me, eh, Adrian? I can tell you that I never tasted it for thirty years, and now only as a medicine. Lance, never."

"But they did not treat you like a baby, and never let you see so much as a glass of beer."

"Well, I am going to treat you like a man, but it is a sorrowful history that I have to tell you. You know that your mother and Aunt Wilmet are twin sisters?"

"Oh yes, though Aunt Wilmet is stout and jolly, and mother ever so much prettier and more delicate and nice."

"Yes, from ill-health. She is never free from suffering."

"I know. Old Dr. May said there was no help for it."

"Do you know what caused that ill-health? My boy, they spoke of your father to-day—brutes that they were," he could not help muttering.

"Yes, he died when I was a week old."

"He had ruined himself when quite a young man, body, soul, and estate— and you too, beforehand, in estate, and broken your mother's heart and health by being given up to that miserable habit from which we want to save you."

"I thought it was only poor men that got drunk and beat their wives" (more knowledge, by the bye, than he was supposed to possess). "He did not beat her?"

"Oh no, no," said Clement, "but he as surely destroyed all her happiness, and made you and your sisters very poor for your station in life, so that it is really hard to educate you, and you will have to work for yourself and them. And at only thirty-six years old his life was cut off."

"Was that what D. T. meant? I heard Ted whisper something about that."

"It was well," thought Clement, "that he had grace enough to whisper. Yes, my poor boy, it is only too true. I was sent for to find your father dying of delirium tremens—you just born, your mother nearly dead, the desolation of your sisters unspeakable. He was only thirty-six, and that vice, together with racing, had devoured him and all the property that should have come to his children. I think he tried to repent at the very last, but there was little time, little power, only he put you and your sisters in my charge, and begged me to save you from being like him."

"Did they mean that I was sure to be like that? Like a pointer puppy, pointing."

"They meant it. And, Adrian, it is so far true that there is an inheritance— with some more, with some less—of our forefathers' nature. Some have tendencies harder to repress than others. But, my dear boy, you know that we all have had a force given us wherewith to repress and conquer those tendencies, and that we can."

"When we were baptized, God the Holy Spirit," said Adrian, under his breath.

"You know it, you can believe now. Your uncle Lance and I prayed that the old nature might be put down, the new raised up. We pray, your mother and sisters have prayed ever since, that so it may be, that you may conquer any evil tendencies that may be in you; but, Adrian, no one can save you from the outside if you do not strive yourself. Now you see why your poor mother has been so anxious to keep all temptation out of your reach."

"But I'm growing a man now. I can't always go on so."

"No, you can't. You shall be treated as a man while you are with me. But I do very seriously advise you—nay, I entreat of you, not to begin taking any kind of liquor, for it would incite the taste to grow upon you, till it might become uncontrollable, and be your tyrant. If you have reason to think the pledge would be a protection to you, come to me, or to Uncle Bill."

He was interrupted by Sibby coming in with his cup of tea, and—

"Now, Mr. Clement, whatever have you been after now? Up to your antics the minute Miss Cherry is out of the way. Aye, ye needn't go to palavering me. I hear it in your breath," and she darted at the stimulant.

"I've had some, Sibby, since I came in."

"More reason you should have it now. Get off with you, Sir Adrian, don't be worriting him. Now, drink that, sir, and don't speak another word."

He was glad to obey. He wanted to think, in much thankfulness for the present, and in faith and love which brought hope for the future.

CHAPTER XV. — A POOR FOREIGN WIDOW

Early in the day General Mohun received a note from Clement Underwood, begging him to look in at St. Andrew's Rock as soon as might be convenient.

"Ah," said his sister, "I strongly suspect something wrong about the boys. Fergus was very odd and silent last night when I asked him about Jem Horner's picnic, and he said something about that Harewood cousin being an unmitigated brute."

"I hope Fergus was not in a scrape."

"Oh no, it is not his way. His geology is a great safeguard. If it had been Wilfred I might have been afraid."

"His head is full—at least as much room as the lost aralia leaves—of the examination for the Winchester College election."

"Yes, you know Jasper has actually promised Gillian that if either of her brothers gets a scholarship, she may be allowed a year at Lady Margaret Hall."

"Yes, it incited her to worry Wilfred beyond sufferance in his holidays. I know if you or Lily had been always at me I should have kicked as hard as he does."

"Lily herself can hardly cram him with his holiday task; but Fergus is a good little fellow."

"You have kept him at it in a more judgmatical way. But won't Armytage come in between the damsel and her college?"

"Poor Mr. Armytage—Captain, I believe, for he has got his commandership. Gill snubs him desperately. I believe she is afraid of herself and her heart."

"I hope she won't be a goose. Jasper told me that he is an excellent fellow, and it will be an absolute misfortune if the girl is besotted enough to refuse him."

"Girls have set up a foolish prejudice against matrimony."

"Well, I am off. Clement Underwood is a reasonable man, and would not send for me without cause."

General Mohun came to that opinion when he heard of the scene on the beach, and of the absolute certainty that the contraband goods had been procured at Mrs. Schnetterling's. Before his visit was over, a note came down on gold-edged, cyphered pink paper, informing the Reverend E. C. Underwood that Mrs. Campbell was much obliged to him for his attention to her son, who was very unwell, entirely from the effects of clotted cream. And while they were still laughing over the scored words, Anna knocked at the door with a message from her aunt, to ask whether they could come and speak to poor Mrs. Edgar, who was in a dreadful state.

"It is not about Adrian, I hope?" said she.

"Oh no, no, my dear; Adrian is all right, thanks to Fergus again," said her uncle. "He is the boy's great protector; I only wish they could be always together."

Poor Mrs. Edgar! Rumours had not been slow in reaching her of the condition in which her scholars had been found, very odd rumours too. One that James Campbell had been brought home insensible, and the two sailors carried on board in the like state; and an opposite report, that the poor dear boys had only made themselves sick with dainties out of Mrs. Schnetterling's, and it was all a cruel notion of that teetotal ritualist clergyman. Some boys would not speak, others were vague and contradictory, and many knew nothing, Horner and Campbell were absent. Clement much relieved her by giving an account of the matter, and declaring that he feared his own elder nephew was the cause of all the scandal, though he believed that some of her bigger pupils were guilty of obtaining a smaller quantity, knowingly, of the Schnetterling's illicit wares, chiefly so far for the fun of doing something forbidden—"Stolen waters are sweet."

"A wicked woman! Surely she should not be allowed to go on."

"I am going, on the spot, to see what can be done," said General Mohun; "but indeed I should have thought young Campbell rather too old for your precincts."

"Ah! yes. He is troublesome, but he is so backward, and is so delicate, that his mother has implored me to keep him on, that he may have sea-bathing. But this shall be the final stroke!"

"It will be the ruin of your school otherwise," said the General.

"Ah! it might. And yet Mrs. Campbell will never be persuaded of the fact! And she is a person of much influence! However, I cannot have my poor dear little fellows led astray."

Then, with some decided praises of dear little Sir Adrian, and regrets at losing Fergus Merrifield, whom she declared, on the authority of her gentleman assistant, to be certain of success, she departed; and Clement resumed his task of writing letters, which he believed to be useless, but which he felt to be right—one a grave warning to Edward Harewood, and one to his father, whose indulgence he could not but hold accountable.

Reginald Mohun meanwhile went his way to the officer of Inland Revenue, who already had his suspicions as to Mrs. Schnetterling, and was glad of positive evidence. He returned with the General to hear from Mr. Underwood the condition in which he had found the boys, and the cause he had for attributing it to the supplies from Mother Butterfly, and this was thought sufficient evidence to authorize the sending a constable with a search-warrant to the shop. The two gentlemen were glad that the detection should be possible without either sending a spy, or forcing evidence from the boys, who had much better be kept out of the matter altogether. No lack of illicit stores was found when the policemen made their descent, and a summons was accordingly served on its mistress to appear at the next Petty Sessions.

Reginald Mohun, used to the justice of county magistrates, and the unflinching dealings of courts-martial, was determined to see the affair through, so he went to the magistrates' meeting, and returned with the tidings that the possession of smuggled tobacco ready for sale had been proved against Mrs. Schnetterling, and she had been fined twenty-five pounds, to be paid at the next Petty Sessions. Otherwise goods would be seized to that value, or she would have a short term of imprisonment. There was no doubt that contraband spirits were also found, but it was not thought expedient to press this charge.

He said the poor woman had been in a great passion of despair, wringing her hands and weeping demonstratively.

"Quite theatrical," he said. "I am sure she has been an actress."

"It did not prejudice your hard-headed town-councillors in her favour," said Gerald.

"Far from it! In fact old Simmonds observed that she was a painted foreign Jezebel."

"Not to her face!" said Gerald.

"We are not quite brutes, whatever you may think us, my boy," said the General good-humouredly.

"Well," said Gerald, in the same tone, "how could I tell how it might be when the Philistines conspired to hunt down a poor foreign widow trying to pick up a scanty livelihood?"

"If the poor foreign widow had been content without corrupting the boys," said Clement, "she would have been let alone."

"It was not for corrupting the boys. That was done—or not done—by my amiable cousin Ted. What harm did her 'baccy do to living soul?"

"It is a risky thing, to say the least of it, for a living soul to defraud the revenue," said Clement.

"Of which probably she never heard."

"She must have seen the terms of her licence," said the General.

"Aye, a way of increasing the revenue by burthens on the chief solace of poverty," said Gerald hotly.

"You'll come to your senses by and by, young man," imperturbably answered the General.

"Is she likely to be able to pay?" asked Gerald in return.

"Oh yes, the policeman said she drove a very thriving trade, both with the boys and with the sailors, and that there was no doubt that she could pay."

Clement was very glad to hear it, for it not only obviated any sense of harshness in his mind, but he thought Gerald, in his present mood of compassion—or opposition, whichever it was—capable of offering to undertake to pay the fine for her.

Poor little Ludmilla was found the next day by Mrs. Henderson, crying softly over her work at the mosaic department—work which was only the mechanical arrangement from patterns provided, for she had no originality, and would never attain to any promotion in the profession.

Mrs. Henderson took the poor girl to her own little office, to try to comfort her, and bring her into condition for the rehearsal of the scene with Ferdinand, which she was to go through in Mr. Flight's parlour chaperoned by his mother. She was so choked with sobs that it did not seem probable that she would have any voice; for she had been struggling with her tears all day, and now, in the presence of her friend, she gave them a free course. She thought it so cruel— so very cruel of the gentlemen; how could they do such a thing to a poor helpless stranger? And that tall one—to be a clergyman—how could he?

Mrs. Henderson tried to represent that, having accepted the licence on certain terms, it was wrong to break them; and that the gentlemen must be right to hinder harm to their nephews.

It seemed all past the poor girl's understanding, since the nephews had taken no harm; and indeed the other boys had only touched the spirits by way of joke and doing something forbidden: it had all come of those horrid young midshipmen, who had come down and worried and bothered her mother into giving them the bottles of spirits which had not been mixed. It was very hard.

"Ah, Lydia, one sin leads no one knows where! Those little boys, think of their first learning the taste for alcohol in secret!"

Lydia did see this, but after all, she said, it was not the spirits, but the tobacco, which the Dutch and American sailors were glad enough to exchange for her mother's commodities. She had never perceived any harm in the arrangement, and hardly comprehended when the saying, "Custom to whom custom," was pointed out to her.

Kalliope asked whether the fine would fall heavily on her mother.

"Oh, that is worst of all. Mother is gone to Avoncester to raise the money. She won't tell me how. And I do believe O'Leary's circus is there."

Then came another sobbing fit.

"But how—what do you mean, my dear?"

"O'Leary was our clown when my father—my dear father—was alive. He was a coarse horrid man, as cruel to the poor dear horses as he dared. And now he has set up for himself, and has been going about all over the county. Mother has been quite different ever since she met him one day in Avoncester, and I fear—oh, I fear he will advance her this money, and make her give me up to him; and my dear father made her promise that I would never be on the boards."

This was in an agony of crying, and it appeared that Schnetterling had really been a very decent, amiable person, who had been passionately fond of his little daughter. Her recollection dated from the time when the family had come from America, and he had become partner in a circus, intending to collect means enough to retire to a home in Germany, but he had died five years ago, at Avoncester, of fever, and his wife had used his savings to set up this little shop at Rockquay, choosing that place because it was the resort of foreign trading-vessels, with whom her knowledge of languages would be available. She had suffered from the same illness, and her voice had been affected at the time, and she was altogether subdued and altered, and had allowed her daughter to receive a good National school training; but with the recovery of health, activity, and voice, a new temper, or rather the old one renewed, had seized her, and since she had met her former companion, Ludmilla foreboded that the impulse of wandering had come upon her, and that if the interference of the authorities pressed upon her and endangered her traffic, she would throw it up altogether, and drag her daughter into the profession so dreadful to all the poor child's feelings.

No wonder that the girl cried till she had no voice, and took but partial comfort from repeated assurances that her friends would do their utmost on her behalf. Mrs. Henderson tried to compose and cheer her, walking with her herself to St. Kenelm's Parsonage, and trying to keep up her earnest desire to please Mr. Flight, the special object of her veneration. But wishes were ineffectual to prevent her from breaking down in the first line of her first song, and when Mr. Flight blamed, and Lady Flight turned round on the music-stool to say severely—"Command yourself, Lydia," she became almost hysterical.

"Wait a minute," said Gerald. "Give her a glass of wine, and she will be better."

"Oh no, no; please, I'm temp—" and a sob.

The five o'clock tea was still standing on a little table, and Gerald poured out a cup and took it to her, then set her down in an arm-chair, and said—

"I'll go through Angus' part, and she will be better," and as she tried to say "Thank you," and "So kind," he held up his hand, and told her to be silent. In fact, his encouragement, and the little delay he had made, enabled her to recover herself enough to get through her part, though nothing like as well as would have been expected of her.

"Never mind," said Gerald, "she will be all right when my uncle comes. Won't you, Mona?"

"I should have expected—" began Lady Flight.

Gerald held up his hand in entreaty.

"People's voices can't be always the same," he said cheerily. "I know our Mona will do us credit yet! Won't you, Mona? You know how to pity me with my logs!"

"You had better go and have some tea in the kitchen, Lydia," said Lady Flight repressively; and Ludmilla curtsied herself off, with a look of gratitude out of her swollen eyelids at Gerald.

"Poor little mortal," he said, as she went. "I am afraid that in her case summum jus was summa injuria."

"It was quite right to prosecute that mischievous woman," said Mr. Flight.

"Maybe," said Gerald; "but wheat will grow alongside of tares."

"I hope the girl is wheat," half ironically and severely said the lady.

Gerald shrugged his shoulders and took his leave.

CHAPTER XVI. — "SEE, THE CONQUERING HERO COMES"

A telegram from Sir Jasper brought the good news that Fergus's name was high on the Winchester roll, and that he was sure of entering college after the holidays. Gillian alone was allowed to go up to the station with her uncle Reginald to meet the travellers, lest the whole family should be too demonstrative in their welcome. And at the same time there emerged from the train not only Captain Armytage, but also Lancelot Underwood and his little boy. All the rest of his family were gone to Stoneborough to delight the hearts of Dr. May and his daughter Ethel.

Gillian was in such training that she durst not embrace her brother when he tumbled out of the carriage, though she could hardly keep her feet from dancing, but she only demurely said—

"Mamma and all of them are at Aunt Jane's."

"Come then," said Sir Jasper to Captain Armytage, for which Gillian was not grateful, or thought herself not, for she made a wry face.

There was a good deal of luggage—theatrical appliances to be sent to the pavilion.

"This may as well go too," said Captain Armytage.

"Oh! oh! It is the buccaneer's sword!" cried little Felix. "How lovely! Last time we only had Uncle Jack's, and this is ever so much longer!"

"Do let me draw it!" cried Fergus.

"Not here, my boy, or they would think a conspiracy was breaking out. Ha!" as a sudden blare of trumpets broke out as they reached the station gate.

"Oh, is it for him?" cried Felix, who had been instructed in Fergus's triumph.

said the General.

Fergus actually coloured crimson, but the colour was deepened as he muttered "Bosh!" while two piebald ponies, drawing the drummers and trumpeters in fantastic raiment, preceded an elephant shrouded in scarlet and gold trappings, with two or three figures making contortions on his back, and followed by a crowned and sceptred dame in blue, white, and gold, perched aloft on a car drawn by four steeds in glittering caparisons.

"Will you mount it, Fergus?" asked his uncle. "You did not expect such a demonstration."

Fergus bit his lip. It was hard to be teased instead of exalted; but Fely and he were absorbed in the pink broadsides that the lady in the car was scattering.

```
CIRCUS—THIS NIGHT—ROTHERWOOD PARK.

                The Sepoy's Revenge!
               Thrilling Incidents!
               Sagacious Elephant!
             Dance of Arab Coursers!!
            Acrobatic Feats!! &c., &c.
```

"Oh, daddy! daddy! do take me to see it!"

"Father, I should like to see it very much indeed," were the exclamations of the two little boys. "You know I have never seen any acrobatic feats."

"A long word enough to please you," said Uncle Reginald. "He deserves something. I'll take you, master."

"I should think this was not of the first quality," said Sir Jasper.

"Never mind. Novelty is the charm that one can have only once in one's life," said the General.

"Some of those van fellows are very decent folk," said Lancelot. "I have seen a great deal of them at Bexley Fair times. You would be astonished to know how grateful they are for a little treatment as if they were not out of humanity's reach."

Gillian was trying to make Fergus tell her what his questions had been, and how he had answered them.

"I declare, Gill, you are as bad as some of the boys' horrid governors. There was one whose father walked him up and down and wouldn't let him play cricket, and went over all the old questions with him. I should never have got in, if papa hadn't had more sense than to badger me out of my life."

At the gate between the copper beeches the Underwoods and Merrifields parted, with an engagement to meet at the circus on the part of the boys and their conductors.

Fergus was greeted with open-mouthed, open-armed delight by all the assembled multitude, very little checked by the presence of Captain Armytage. Only Lady Merrifield did not say much, but there was a dew in her eyes as she held fast the little active fingers, and whispered—

"My good industrious boy."

Sir Jasper, in his grand and gracious manner, turned to his sister-in-law, saying—

"We could not but come first to you, Jane, for it is to you that he is indebted, as we all are, primarily for his success."

"That is the greatest compliment I ever had, Jasper," she answered, smiling but almost tearful, and laughing it off. "I feel ready to mount yonder elephant lady's triumphal car."

The General refrained from any more teasing of Fergus on his first impression; and at seven that evening the younger Merrifield boys with their uncle, and the two from St. Andrew's Rock with Lance, set off in high spirits.

They re-appeared much sooner than they were expected at Beechcroft Cottage, where the Underwoods were spending the long twilight evening.

"A low concern!" was the General's verdict.

"We fled simultaneously from the concluding ballet," said Lance. "There had been quite as much as we could bear for ingenuous youth."

"We stood the Sepoy's Death Song," said the General, "but the poster of the Bleeding Bride was enough for us."

"They had only one elephant!" cried Adrian.

"A regular swindle," said Wilfred.

"No lions!" added Fely, "nothing to see but that poor old elephant! I wish he would have turned round and spouted water at them, as that one did to the tailor."

"Water would be uncommonly good for them," said the General, laughing, "they are not much acquainted therewith."

"And such an atmosphere!" said Lance.

"I see it on your forehead, poor boy," said Geraldine.

"I should like to set on the Society against cruelty to animals," said the General; "I saw galls on the horses' necks, and they were all half starved."

"Then to see the poor old elephant pretend to be drunk!" added Fergus, "stagger about, and led off by the policeman, drunk and disorderly!"

"Was that being drunk?" asked Adrian, with wide-open eyes. "It was like Campbell that day." Everybody laughed.

Wilfred did so now.

"You green kid, you."

"Happy verdure," said the General, "to be unaware that some people can laugh when they ought to weep."

"Weep!" exclaimed Wilfred, "every time one sees a fellow screwy in the street."

"Perhaps the angels do," murmured Clement.

"Come, Master Wilfred, you have expressed your opinions sufficiently to-night," said the General. "Suppose you and Fergus walk home together. A nasty low place as ever I saw. I have a mind to tell the Mayor about it."

Gerald said—

"Is not that making yourself very unpopular?"

"That is no great matter," said the General, rather surprised.

"I should have thought it better to refine the people's tastes than to thwart their present ones."

"The improper must be stopped before the taste for the proper can be promoted," said Clement.

"With all the opposition and ill-blood that you cause?" said Gerald. "Why, if I were an errand-boy, the suppression would send me direct to the circus. Would it not do the same by you, Uncle Lance?"

"Discouragement might, prohibition would prevent wholly, and I should be thankful," said Lance.

"Ah! you are of the old loyal nature," said Gerald. "You of the old school can never see things by modern lights."

"I am thankful to say—not," responded Reginald Mohun, in a tone that made some laugh, and Gerald sigh in Anna's ear—

"Happy those who see only one side of a question."

There was another great day for the boys, namely, the speech or closing day at the school, when Fergus was the undoubted hero, and was so exalted that his parents thought it would be very bad for him, and were chiefly consoled by his strong and genuine dislike to having to declaim with Clement Varley the quarrel of Brutus and Cassius. He insisted on always calling the former "Old Brute," and all the efforts of mother and aunt never got him beyond the dogged repetition of a lesson learnt by heart, whereas little Varley threw himself into the part with spirit that gained all the applause. Fergus carried off a pile of prizes too, but despised them. "Stupid old poetry!" said he, "what should I do with that? Do let me change it, father, for the Handbook of Paleontology, or something worth having."

Adrian had three prizes too, filling Anna with infinite delight. He was not to go home immediately on the break-up of the school, but was to wait for his sisters, who were coming in a few days more with Lady Travis Underwood to the bazaar and masque, so that he would go home with them.

Neither the prospect nor the company of little Fely greatly reconciled him to the delay, but his mother could not believe that her darling could travel alone, and his only satisfaction was in helping Fergus to arrange his spare specimens for sale.

CHAPTER XVII. — EXCLUDED

The ladies' committee could not but meet over and over again, wandering about the gardens, which were now trimmed into order, to place the stalls and decide on what should and should not be.

There was to be an art stall, over which Mrs. Henderson was to preside. Here were to be the very graceful and beautiful articles of sculpture and Italian bijouterie that the Whites had sent home, and that were spared from the marble works; also Mrs. Grinstead's drawings, Captain Henderson's, those of others, screens and scrap-books and photographs. Jasper and a coadjutor or two undertook to photograph any one who wished it; and there too were displayed the Mouse-traps. Mrs. Henderson, sure to look beautiful, quite Madonna-like in her costume, would have the charge of the stall, with Gillian and two other girls, in Italian peasant-dresses, sent home by Aunt Ada.

Gillian was resolved on standing by her. "Kalliope wants some one to give her courage," she said. "Besides, I am the mother of the Mouse-trap, and I must see how it goes off."

Lady Flight and a bevy of young ladies of her selection were to preside over the flowers; Mrs. Yarley undertook the refreshments; Lady Merrifield the more ordinary bazaar stall. Her name was prized, and Anna was glad to shelter herself under her wing. The care of Valetta and Primrose, to say nothing of Dolores, was enough inducement to overcome any reluctance, and she was glad to be on the committee when vexed questions came on, such as Miss Pettifer's offer of a skirt-dance, which could not be so summarily dismissed as it had been at Beechcroft, for Lady Flight and Mrs. Varley wished for it, and even Mrs. Harper was ready to endure anything to raise the much-needed money, and almost thought Lady Merrifield too particular when she discontinued the dancing-class for Valetta and Primrose.

"That speaks for itself," said Mrs. Grinstead.

"I can fancy seeing no harm in it for little girls," said Lady Merrifield, "but I don't like giving them a talent the use of which seems to be to enable them to show off."

"And I know that Lady Rotherwood would not approve," said Miss Mohun, aware that this settled the matter. "And here's another outsider, Miss Penfeather, who offers to interpret handwriting at two-and-sixpence a head."

"By all means," was the cry. "We will build her a bower somewhere near the photography."

"I am only afraid," added Jane, "of her offering to do palmistry. Do you know, I dabbled a little in that once, and I came to the conclusion that it was not a safe study for oneself or any one else."

"Quite right," said Geraldine.

"Do you believe in it then?"

"Not so as to practise it, or accept it so far as the future is concerned, and to play at it as a parody of fortune-telling seems to me utterly inadmissible."

"And to be squashed with Lord Rotherwood's mighty name," said her sister, laughing.

Lady Rotherwood would do so effectively. Wherewith came on the question of raffles, an inexhaustible one, since some maintained that they were contrary to English law, and were absolutely immoral, while others held that it was the only way of disposing of really expensive articles. These were two statues sent by Mrs. White, and an exquisite little picture by Mrs. Grinstead, worth more than any one could be expected to give. It was one that she had nearly finished at the time of Mr. Grinstead's illness—John Inglesant arriving in his armour of light on his wedding morning—and the associations were so painful that she said she never wished to see it again.

There were likewise a good many charming sketches of figures and scenery, over which Gerald and Anna grieved, though she had let them keep all they could show cause for; but drawing had become as much her resource as in the good old days. She was always throwing off little outlines, and she had even begun a grand study, which she called "Safe Home," a vessel showing signs of storm and struggle just at the verge of a harbour lost in golden light.

And the helmsman's face?

Clement and Lance neither of them said in words whose it was, as they both stood looking at it, and owned to themselves the steadfast face of their eldest brother, but Clement said, with a sigh—

"Ah! we are a long way as yet from that."

"I'm very glad to hear you say so," exclaimed Lance; then laughing at himself, "You are ever so much better."

"Oh yes, I suppose I am to start again, going softly all my days, perhaps, and it is well, for I don't think the young generation can spare me yet."

"Nor Cherry."

"How thankful I am to have Cherry restored to me I cannot say, and I do not feel convinced that there may not be care at hand with Gerald. The boy is in a reserved mood, very civil and amiable, but clearly holding back from confidence."

"Does she see it?"

"Yes; but she fancies he bestows his confidence on Dolores Mohun, the girl from New Zealand, and resigns herself to be set aside. It is pretty well time that we went to meet her."

For there was to be a dress rehearsal in the pavilion, to which certain spectators were to be admitted, chiefly as critics.

"Do you walk up the hill, Clem?"

"Yes, as long as I don't go too fast. Go on if you are wanted, and I will follow. Cherry has sent the carriage for an invalid who cannot venture to be there all the day."

"Let them wait. A walk with you is not to be wasted. Run on, Fely, tell them we are coming," he added to his little Ariel, who had got lost in Jungle Beasts.

As they went up the hill together, Clement not sorry to lean on his brother's arm, a dark woman of striking figure and countenance, though far from young, came up with them, accompanied by a stout, over-dressed man.

"That's the cigar-shop woman," said Lance, "the mother of our pretty little Miranda."

"I wonder she chooses to show herself after her conviction," said Clement.

"And if I am not much mistaken, that is the villain of The Sepoy's Revenge," said Lance. "Poor little Butterfly, it is a bad omen for her future fate."

As they reached the doors of the great hotel, they found the pair in altercation with the porter before the iron gate that gave admittance to the gardens. "Mother Butterfly" was pleading that she was the mother of Miss Schnetterling, who was singing, and the porter replying that his orders were strict.

"No, not on any consideration," he repeated, as the man was evidently showing him the glance of silver, and a policeman, who was marching about, showed signs of meaning to interfere.

At the same moment Gerald's quick steps came up from the inside.

"That's right, Lance; every one is crying out for you. Vicar, Cherie is keeping a capital place for you."

The gate opened to admit them, and therewith Mrs. Schnetterling, trying to push in, made a vehement appeal—

"Mr. Underwood, sir, surely the prima donna's own mother should not be excluded."

"Her mother!" said Gerald. "Well, perhaps so, but hardly this—person," as his native fastidiousness rose at the sight.

"No, sir," said the porter. "Captain Henderson and Mr. Simmonds, they have specially cautioned me who I lets in."

The man grumbled something about swells and insolence, and Lance, with his usual instinct of courtesy, lingered to say—

"This is quite a private rehearsal—only the persons concerned!"

"And if I'm come on business," said the man confidentially. "You are something in our line."

"Scarcely," said Lance, rather amused. "At any rate, I don't make the regulations."

He sped away at the summons of his impatient son and Gerald.

They met Captain Henderson on the way, and after a hasty greeting, he said—

"So you have let in the Schnetterling woman?"

"One could not well keep out the mother," returned Lance.

"Well, no, but did she bring a man with her? My wife says the poor little Mona is in mortal terror lest he is come to inspect her for a circus company."

"Quite according to his looks," said Lance. "Poor child, it may be her fate, but she ought to be in safe hands, but I suppose the woman wants to sacrifice her to present gain."

They went on their way, and Lance and Gerald were soon absorbed in their cares of arrangement, while Clement was conducted to the seat reserved for him between his sister and Lady Merrifield. The pavilion had been fitted with stages of seats on the inner side, but the back—behind the stage—was so contrived that in case of favourable weather the real sea-view could be let in upon occasion, though the curtain and adjuncts, which had been painted by some of the deft fingers at Vale Leston, represented the cavern; also there was a first scene, with a real sail and mast.

It was a kind of semi-dress rehearsal, beginning with pirate songs by the school-master and choir, who had little difficulty in arranging themselves as buccaneers. The sail was agitated, then reefed, stormy songs were heard, where Captain Armytage did his part fairly well; the boatswain was gratified by roaring out his part characteristically, and the curtain fell on "We split, we split, we split."

Then came a song of Prospero, not much disguised by a plaid and Highland bonnet, interrupted by the pretty, graceful Miranda, very shy and ill-assured at first, but gathering strength from his gentle encouraging ways, while he told what was needful in the recitative that he alone could undertake. Then the elves and fairies, led by little Felix, in a charming cap like Puck, danced on and sang, making the prettiest of tableaux, lulling Miranda to sleep, and then Ariel conversing in a most dainty manner with Prospero.

Next Ferdinand and Miranda had their scene, almost all songs and duets. Both sang very sweetly, and she had evidently gained in courage, and threw herself into her part.

The shipwrecked party then came on the scene, performed their songs, and were led about Puck-fashion by the fairies, and put to sleep by the lament over Ferdinand. The buccaneers in like manner were deluded by more mischievous songs and antics, till bogged and crying out behind the scenes.

Their intended victims were then awakened, to find themselves in the presence of Prospero; sing themselves into the reconciliation, then mourn for Ferdinand, until the disclosure of the two lovers, and the final release of Ariel and the sprites, all singing Jacobite songs.

To those who were not au fait with the 'Tempest' and felt no indignation or jealousy at the travesty, it was charming; and though the audience at the rehearsal numbered few of these, the refined sweetness and power of the performers made it delightful and memorable. Every one was in raptures with the fairies, who had been beautifully drilled, and above all with their graceful little leader, with his twinkling feet and arch lively manner, especially in the parts with his father.

Ferdinand and Miranda—or rather Angus and Mona—were quite ideal in looks, voices, and gestures.

"Almost dangerously so," said Jane Mohun; "and the odd thing is that they are just alike enough for first cousins, as they are here, though Shakespeare was not guilty of making them such."

"The odd thing is," said Geraldine, as she drove home with Clement, "that this brought me back so strangely to that wonderful concert at home, with all of you standing up in a row, and the choir from Minsterham, and poor Edgar's star."

"An evil star!" sighed Clement.

CHAPTER XVIII. — THE EVIL STAR

It was on the night before the final bustle and fury, so to speak, of preparation were to set in, when arrivals were expected, and the sellers were in commotion, and he had been all day putting the singers one by one through their parts, that as he went to his room at night, there was a knock at Lancelot's door, and Gerald came in, looking deadly white. He had been silent and effaced all the evening, and his aunt had thought him tired, but he had rather petulantly eluded inquiry, and now he came in with—

"Lance, I must have it out with some one."

"An Oxford scrape?" said Lance.

"Oh no, I wish it was only that." Then a silence, while Lance looked at him, thinking, "What trouble could it be?" He had been very kind and gentle with the little Miranda, but the manner had not struck Lance as lover-like.

There was a gasp again—

"That person, that woman at the gate, do you remember?"

Therewith a flash came over Lance.

"My poor boy! You don't mean to say—"

Neither could bring himself to say the word so sacred to Lancelot, and which might have been so sacred to his nephew.

"How did you guess?" said Gerald, lifting up the face that he had hidden on the table.

"I saw the likeness between you and the girl. She reminded me of some one I had once seen."

"Had you seen her?"

"Once, at a concert, twenty odd years ago. Your aunt, too, was strangely carried back to that scene, by the girl's voice, I suppose."

"Poor child!" said Gerald, still laying down his head and seeming terribly oppressed, as Lance felt he well might be.

"It is a sad business for you," said the uncle, with a kind hand on his shoulder. "How was it she did not claim you before?—not that she has any real claim."

"She did not know my real name. My father called himself Wood. I never knew the rest of it till after I came home. That fellow bribed the gardener, got in over the wall, or somehow, and when she saw you, and heard you and me and all three of us, it gave her the clue."

"Well, Gerald, I do not think she can dare to—"

"Oh!" interrupted Gerald, "there's worse to come."

"What?" said Lance, aghast.

"She says," and a sort of dry sob cut him short, "she says she had a husband when she married my father," and down went his head again.

"Impossible," was Lance's first cry; "your father's first care was to tell Travis all was right with you. Travis has the certificates."

"Oh yes, it was no fault of my father—my father, my dear father—no, but she deceived him, and I am an impostor—nobody."

"Gently, gently, Gerald. We have no certainty that this is true. Your father had known her for years. Tell me, how did it come out—what evidence did she adduce?"

Gerald nerved himself to sit up and speak collectedly.

"I believe it is half that circus fellow's doing. I think she is going to marry him, if she hasn't already. She followed me, and just at the turn down this road, as I was bidding the Mona girl goodnight, she came up with me, and said I little thought that the child was my sister, and how delightful it was to see us acting together. Well then, I can't say but a horror came over me. I couldn't for the life of me do anything but draw back, there was something so intolerable in the look of her eyes, and her caressing manner," and he shuddered, glad of his uncle's kind hand on his shoulder. "Somehow, I let her get me out upon the high ground, and there she said, 'So you are too great a swell to have word or look for your mother. No wonder, you always were un vilain petit misérable; but I won't trouble you—I wouldn't be bound to live your dull ennuyant ladies' life for millions. I'll bargain to keep out of your way; but O'Leary and I want a couple of hundred pounds, and you'll not grudge it to us.' I had no notion of being blackmailed, besides I haven't got it, and I told her she might know that I am not of age, and had no such sum ready to hand. She was urgent, and I began to think whether I could do anything to save that poor little sister, when she evidently got some fresh impulse from the man, and began to ask me how I should like to have it all disclosed to my nobs of friends. Well, I wasn't going to be bullied, and I answered that my friends knew already, and she might do her worst. 'Oh, may I?' she said; 'you wouldn't like, my fine young squire, to have it come out that I never was your father's wife at all, and that you are no more than that gutter-child.' I could not understand her at first, and said I would not be threatened, but that made her worse, and that rascal O'Leary came to her help. They raised their demands somehow to five hundred, and declared if they had not it paid down, they should tell the whole story and turn me out. Of course I said they were welcome. Either I am my father's lawful son, or I am not, and if not, the sooner it is all up with me the better, for whatever I am, I am no thief and robber. So I set off and came down the hill; but the brute kept pace with me to this very door, trying to wheedle me, I believe. And now what's to be done? I would go off at once, and let Uncle Clem come into his rights, only I don't want to be the death of him and Cherie."

"No," said Lance, "my dear fellow! You have stood it wisely and bravely so far, go on to do so. I don't feel the least certain that this is not mere bullying. She did not tell you any particulars?"

"No, certainly not."

"Not the name of this supposed predecessor of Edgar's? Where she may have been married, or how? How she parted from him, or how she knows he was alive? It sounds to me a bogus notion, got up to put the screw on you, by surprise. I'll tell you what I'll do. I'll go down to the shop tomorrow morning, see the woman, and extract the truth if possible, and I fully expect that the story will shrink up to nothing."

"'Tis not the estate I care for," said Gerald, looking somewhat cheered. "It is my father's honour and name. If that can be cleared—"

"Do not I care?" said Lance. "My dear brother Edgar, my model of all that was noble and brilliant—whom Felix loved above all! Nay, and you, Gerald, our hope! I would give anything and everything to free you from this stain, though I trust it will prove only mud that will not stick. Anyway you have shown your true, faithful Underwood blood. Now go to bed and sleep if you can. Don't say a word, nor look more like a ghost than you can help—or we shall have to rouge ourselves for our parts. My boy, my boy! You are Edgar's boy, anyway."

And Lancelot kissed the young pale cheek as he had done when the little wounded orphan clung to him fourteen years ago, or as he kissed his own Felix.

Whatever the night was to Gerald, long was the night, and long the light hours of the morning to the ever sleepless Lance before he could rise and make his way to the shop with any hope of gaining admission, and many were the sighs and prayers that this tale might be confuted, and that the matter might be to the blessing of the youth to whom he felt more warmly now than since those winning baby days had given place to more ordinary boyhood. He had a long time to pace up and down watching the sparkling water, and feeling the fresh wind on the brow, which was as capable as ever of aching over trouble and perplexity, and dreading above all the effect on the sister, whose consolation and darling Gerald had always been. How little he had thought, when he had stood staunch against his brother Edgar's persuasions, that Zoraya was to be the bane of that life which had begun so gaily!

When at last the door was unfastened, and, as before, by Ludmilla, he greeted her kindly, and as she evidently expected some fresh idea about the masque, he gave her his card, and asked her to beg her mother to come and speak to him. She started at the name and said—

"Oh, sir, you will do nothing to hurt him—Mr. Underwood?"

"It is the last thing I wish," he said earnestly, and Ludmilla showed him into a little parlour, full of the fumes of tobacco, and sped away, but he had a long time to wait, for probably Mother Butterfly's entire toilette had to be taken in hand.

Before she appeared Lancelot heard a man's voice, somewhere in the entry, saying—

"Oh! the young ass has been fool enough to let it out, has he? I suppose this is the chap that will profit? You'll have your wits about you."

Lance was still his old self enough to receive the lady with—

"I beg to observe that I am not the 'chap who will profit' if this miserable allegation holds water. I am come to understand the truth."

The woman looked frightened, and the man came to her rescue, having evidently heard, and this Lance preferred, for he always liked to deal with mankind rather than womankind. Having gone so far there was not room for reticence, and the man took up the word.

"Madame cannot be expected to disclose anything to the prejudice of her son and herself, unless it was made worth her while."

"Perhaps not," said Lance, as he looked her over in irony, and drew the conclusion that the marriage was a fact accomplished; "but she has demanded two hundred pounds from her son, on peril of exposure, and if the facts are not substantiated, there is such a thing as an action for conspiracy, and obtaining money on false pretences."

"Nothing has been obtained!" said the woman, beginning to cry. "He was very hard on his poor mother."

"Who forsook him as an infant, cast off his father, and only claims him in order to keep a disgraceful, ruinous secret hanging over his life for ever, in order to extort money."

"Come now, this is tall talk, sir," said O'Leary; "the long and short of it is, what will the cove, yourself, or whoever it is that you speak for, come down for one way or another?"

"Nothing," responded Lance.

Neither of the estimable couple spoke or moved under an announcement so incredible to them, and he went on—

"Gerald Underwood would rather lose everything than give hush-money to enable him to be a robber, and my elder brother would certainly give no reward for what would be the greatest grief in his life."

O'Leary grinned as if he wanted to say, "Have you asked him?"

"The priest," she muttered.

"Ay, the meddling parson who has done for you! He would have to come down pretty handsomely."

Lancelot went on as if he had not heard these asides.

"I am a magistrate; I can give you in charge at once to the police, and have you brought before the Mayor for conspiracy, when you will have to prove your words, or confess them to be a lie."

He was not in the least certain that where there was no threatening letter, this could succeed, but he knew that the preliminaries would be alarming enough to elicit something, and accordingly Mrs. O'Leary began to sob out—

"It was when I was a mere child, a bambina, and he used me so cruelly."

There was the first thread, and on the whole, the couple were angry enough with Gerald, his refined appearance and air of careless prosperity, to be willing that he should have a fall, and Lance thus extracted that the "he" who had been cruel was a Neapolitan impresario in a small way, who had detected that Zoraya, when a very little child, had a charming voice, of which indeed she still spoke with pride, saying Lida would never equal it. Her parents were semi-gipsies, Hungarian, and had wandered all over the Austrian empire, acting, singing, and bringing up their children to the like. They had actually sold her to the impresario, who had sealed the compact, and hoped to secure the valuable commodity by making her his wife. In his security he had trained her in the severest mode, and visited the smallest want of success with violence and harshness, so that her life was utterly miserable, and on meeting her brother, who had become a member of a German band, she had contrived to make her escape with him, and having really considerable proficiency, the brother and sister had prospered, and through sundry vicissitudes had arrived at being "stars" in Allen's troupe, where Edgar Underwood, or, as he was there known, Tom Wood, had unfortunately joined them; and the sequel was known to Lancelot, but he could not but listen and gather up the details, disgusted as he was—how the prima donna had accepted his attention as her right, till her jealousy was excited by his evident attraction to "the little English doll, for whom he killed his man"; how she resolved to win him, and how scandalous reports at last had brought him to offer marriage, unknowing, it was plain, of her past. It was not possible to guess how much she was still keeping back, speaking under terror and compulsion as she did. But she declared that he had never loved her, and was always wanting her to be like ces Anglaises fades, and as to her child, he so tormented her about it, and the ways of his absurd mother and sisters, and so expected her to sacrifice her art and her prospects to the little wretch, that she was ready to strangle it! "Maternal love, bah! she was not going to be like a bird or a beast," she said, with a strange wild glance in her eyes that made Lance shudder, and think how much more he respected the bird or beast. Then at Chicago, when Wood's own folly and imprudence had brought on an illness that destroyed his voice, and she knew there would be only starvation, or she should have to toil for the whole of them, Schnetterling, manager of a circus, fell in love with her, and made her good offers to sing in Canada, and Chicago was a place where few questions were asked, so she freed herself.

She had made her rounds with Schnetterling, a prudent German, and in process of time had come to England, where, at Avoncester, both had been attacked by influenza; he died, and she only recovered with a total loss of voice; but he had been prudent and frugal enough to save a sufficient sum to set her up at Rockquay with the tobacco-shop. She had chosen that place on account of American trading-vessels putting in there, as well as those of various foreign nations, with whom her knowledge of languages was available, and no doubt there were some opportunities of dealing in smuggled goods. Just, however, as the smuggling was beginning to be suspected, the circus of O'Leary came in her way, and the old instincts were renewed. Then came the detection and prosecution, and the need of raising the fine. She had recourse to O'Leary, who had before been Schnetterling's underling, and now was a partner in Jellicoe's circus, who knew her capabilities as a manager and actress, and perceived the probabilities of poor little Lida's powers. The discovery that the deserted baby that she had left at Chicago was a young handsome squire, well connected, and, in her eyes, of unlimited means, had of course incited both to make the utmost profit of him. That he should not wish to hush the suspicion up, but should go straight to his uncles, was to them a quite unexpected contingency.

All this was not exactly told to Lancelot, but he extracted it, or gathered it before he was able to arrive at what was really important, the name of Zoraya's first husband, where she was married, and by whom, and where she had parted from him. She was so unwilling to give particulars that he began almost to hope to make her confess that the whole was a myth, but at last she owned that the man's name was Giovanni Benista, and that the marriage had taken place at Messina; she knew not in what church, nor in what year, only it was before the end of the old regime, for she recollected the uniforms of the Bomba soldiers, though she could not remember the name of the priest. Benista was old, very old—the tyrant and assassin that he was, no doubt he was dead. She often thought he would have killed her—and the history of his ill-treatment had to be gone through before it appeared that she had fled from him at Trieste with her brother, in an English trading-vessel, where their dexterity and brilliancy gained them concealment and a passage. This was certainly in the summer of 1865. Of Benista she knew nothing since, but she believed him to have come from Piedmont.

Lance found Gerald walking up and down anxiously watching for him, and receiving him with a "Well!" that had in it volumes of suspense.

"Well, Gerald, I do not think there can be any blame attached to your father, whatever comes of it. He was deceived as much as any one else, and his attachment to you seems to have been his great offence."

"Thank Heaven! Then he was deceived?"

"I am afraid there was some previous ceremony. But stay, Gerald! There is no certainty that it was valid in the first place, and in the next, nothing is known of Benista since 1865, when he was an old man, so that there is a full chance that he was dead before—"

"Before April 1868. I say, Uncle Lance, they want to make no end of a bear-fight for my coming of age. I must be out of the way first."

"Don't cry out too soon. Even if the worst came to the worst, as the property was left to you by will individually, I doubt whether this discovery, if real, would make any difference in law. I do not know."

"But would I take it on those terms? It would be simply defrauding Clement, and all of you—"

"Perhaps, long before, we may be satisfied," said Lance. "For the present, I think nothing can be done but endeavour to ascertain the facts."

"One comfort is," said Gerald, "I have gained a sister. I have walked with her to the corner of her place—the marble works, you know—and she really is a jolly little thing, quite innocent of all her mother's tricks, thinking Mrs.

Henderson the first of human beings, except perhaps Flight, the aesthetic parson. I should not have selected him, you know, but between them they have kept her quite a white sheet—a Miranda any Ferdinand might be glad to find, and dreading nothing so much as falling into the hands of that awful brute. Caliban himself couldn't have been worse! I have promised her to do what I can to save her—buy her off—anything."

"Poor child," said Lance. "But, Gerald, nothing of this must be said these next few days. We can't put ourselves out of condition for this same raree-show."

"I'm sure it's a mere abomination to me," said Gerald disconsolately. "I can't think why we should be dragged into all this nuisance for what is not even our own concern."

"I'm sure I thought you the rope that dragged me! At any rate much higher up on it."

"Well, I never thought you would respond—you, who have enough on your hands at Bexley."

"One stroke even on the outskirts is a stroke for all the cause."

"The cause! I don't believe in the cause, whatever it is. What a concatenation now, that you and I should make fools of ourselves in order to stave off the establishment of national education, as if we could, or as if it was worth doing."

"Then why did you undertake it?"

"Oh, ah! Why, one wants something to do down here, and the Merrifield lot are gone upon it; and I did want to go through the thing again, but now it seems all rot."

"Nevertheless, having pledged ourselves to the performance, we cannot cry off, and the present duty is to pack dull care away, put all this out of our heads, and regard it as a mere mare's nest as long as possible, and above all not upset Cherry. Remember, let this turn out as it will, you are yourself still, and her own boy, beloved for your father's sake, the joy of our dear brother, and her great comforter. A wretched mistake can never change that."

Lance's voice was quivering, and Gerald's face worked. Lance gave his hand a squeeze, and found voice to say—

"'Hold thee still in the Lord, and abide patiently upon Him.' And meantime be a man over it. It can be done. I have often had to forget."

CHAPTER XIX. — SHOP-DRESSING

It was not a day when any one could afford to be upset. It was chiefly spent in welcoming arrivals or in rushing about: on the part of Lance and Gerald in freshly rehearsing each performer, in superintending their stage arrangements, reviewing the dresses, and preparing for one grand final rehearsal; and in the multifarious occupations and anxieties, and above all in the music, Gerald did really forget, or only now and then recollect, that a nightmare was hanging on him, and that his little Mona need not shrink from him in maidenly shyness, but that he might well return her pretty appealing look of confidence.

The only quiet place in the town apparently was Clement Underwood's room, for even Cherry had been whirled off, at first to arrange her own pictures and drawings; and then her wonderful touch made such a difference in the whole appearance of the stall, and her dainty devices were so graceful and effective, that Gillian and Mysie implored her to come and tell them what to do with theirs, where they were struggling with cushions, shawls, and bags, with the somewhat futile assistance of Mr. Armine Brownlow and Captain Armytage, whenever the latter could be spared from the theatrical arrangements, where, as he said, it was a case of parmi les borgnes—for his small experience with the Wills-of-the-Wisp made him valuable.

The stalls were each in what was supposed to represent by turns a Highland bothie or a cave. The art stall was a cave, that the back (really a tool-house) might serve the photographers, and the front was decorated with handsome bits of rock and spar, even ammonites. Poor Fergus could not recover his horror and contempt when his collection of specimens, named and arranged, was very nearly seized upon to fill up interstices, and he was infinitely indebted to Mrs. Grinstead for finding a place where their scientific merits could be appreciated without letting his dirty stones, as Valetta called them, disturb the general effect.

"And my fern-gardens! Oh, Mrs. Grinstead," cried Mysie, "please don't send them away to the flower place which Miss Simmonds and the gardeners are making like a nursery garden! They'll snub my poor dear pterises."

"Certainly we'll make the most of your pterises. Look here. There's an elegant doll, let her lead the family party to survey them. That's right. Oh no, not that giantess! There's a dainty little Dutch lady."

"Charming. Oh! and here's her boy in a sailor's dress."

"He is big enough to be her husband, my dear. You had better observe proportions, and put that family nearer the eye."

"Those dolls!" cried Valetta, "they were our despair."

"Make them tell a story, don't you see. Where's that fat red cushion?"

"Oh, that cushion! I put it out of sight because it is such a monster."

"Yes; it is just like brick-dust enlivened by half-boiled cauliflowers! Never mind, it will be all the better background. Now, I saw a majestic lady reposing somewhere. There, let her sit against it. Oh, she mustn't flop over. Here, that match-box, is it? I pity the person deluded enough to use it! Prop her up with it. Now then, let us have a presentation of ladies—she's a governor's wife in the colonies, you see. Never mind costumes, they may be queer. All that will stand or kneel—that's right. Those that can only sit must hide behind, like poor Marie Antoinette's ladies on the giggling occasion."

So she went on, full of fun, which made the work doubly delightful to the girls, who darted about while she put the finishing touches, transforming the draperies from the aspect of a rag-and-bone shop, as Jasper had called it, to a wonderful quaint and pretty fairy bower, backed by the Indian scenes sent by Mr. and Mrs. Bernard Underwood, and that other lovely one of Primrose's pasture. There the merry musical laugh of her youth was to be heard, as General Mohun came out with Lancelot to make a raid, order the whole party to come and eat luncheon at Beechcroft Cottage, and not let Mrs. Grinstead come out again.

"Oh, but I must finish up Bernard's clay costume figures. Look at the expression of that delightful dollie! I'm sure he is watching the khitmutgars.

'Above on tallest trees remote
        Green Ayahs perched alone;
    And all night long the Mussah moaned
        In melancholy tone.'

Oh, don't you know Lear's poem? Can't we illustrate it?"

"Cherry, Cherry, you'll be half dead to-morrow."

"Well, if I am, this is the real fun. I shan't see the destruction."

Lance had her arm in his grip to take her over the bridge over the wall, when up rushed Kitty Varley.

"Oh, if Mrs. Grinstead would come and look at our stall and set it right! Miss Vanderkist gave us hopes."

"Perhaps—"

"Now, Cherry, don't you know that you are not to be knocked up! There are the Travises going to bring unlimited Vanderkists.”

“Oh yes, I know; but there’s renovation in breaths from Vale Leston, and I really am of some use here.” Her voice really had a gay ring in it. “It is such fun too! Where’s Gerald?”

“Having a smoke with the buccaneer captain. Oh, Miss Mohun, here’s my sister, so enamoured of the bazaar I could hardly get her in.”

“And oh! she is so clever and delightful. She has made our stall the most enchanting place,” cried Primrose, dancing round. “Mamma, you must come and have it all explained to you.”

“The very sight is supposed to be worth a shilling extra,” said General Mohun, while Lady Merrifield and Miss Mohun, taking possession of her, hoped she was not tired; and Gillian, who had been wont to consider her as her private property, began to reprove her sisters for having engrossed her while she herself was occupied in helping the Hendersons with their art stall.

“The truth is,” said Lance, “that this is my sister’s first bazaar, and so dear is the work to the female mind, that she can’t help being sucked into the vortex.”

“Is it really?” demanded Mysie, in a voice that made Mrs. Grinstead laugh and say—

“Such is my woeful lack of experience.”

“We have fallen on a bazaar wherever we went,” said Lady Merrifield.

“But this is our first grown-up one, mamma,” said Valetta. “There was only a sale of work before.”

They all laughed, and Lance said—

“To Stoneborough they seem like revenues—at least sales of work, for I can’t say I understand the distinction.”

“Recurring brigandages,” said General Mohun.

“Ah! Uncle Reggie has never forgotten his getting a Noah’s ark in a raffle,” said Mysie.

So went the merry talk, while one and another came in at Miss Mohun’s verandah windows to be sustained with food and rest, and then darted forth again to renew their labours until the evening, Miss Mohun flying about everywhere on all sorts of needs, and her brother the General waiting by the dining-room to do the duties of hospitality to the strays of the families who dropped in, chattering and laughing, and exhausted.

Lady Merrifield was authorized to detain Mrs. Grinstead to the last moment possible to either, and they fell into a talk on the morality of bazaars, which, as Lady Merrifield said, had been a worry to her everywhere, while Geraldine had been out of their reach; since the Underwoods had done everything without begging, and Clement disapproved of them without the most urgent need; but, as Lance had said, his wife had grown up to them, and had gone through all the stages from delighting, acquiescing, and being bored, and they had so advanced since their early days, from being simply sales to the grand period of ornaments, costumes, and anything to attract.

"Clement consents," said Geraldine; "as, first, it is not a church, and then, though it does seem absurd to think that singing through the murdered Tempest should be aiding the cause of the Church, yet anything to keep our children to learning faith and truth is worthy work."

"Alas, it is working against the stream! How things are changed when school was our romance and our domain."

"Yes, you should hear Lance tell the story of his sister-in-law Ethel, how she began at Cocksmoor, with seven children and fifteen shillings, and thought her fortune made when she got ten pounds a year for the school- mistress; and now it is all Mrs. Rivers can do to keep out the School-board, because they had not a separate room for the hat-pegs!"

"We never had those struggles. We had enough to do to live at all in our dear old home days, except that my brother always taught Sunday classes. But anyway, this is very amusing. Those young people's characters come out so much. Ah, Gerald, what is it?"

For Gerald was coming up to the verandah with a very pretty, dark-eyed, modest-looking girl in a sailor hat, who shrank back as he said—

"I am come to ask for some luncheon for my—my Mona. She has had nothing to eat all day, and we still have the grand recognition scene to come."

At which the girl blushed so furiously that the notion crossed Geraldine that he must have been flirting with the poor little tobacconist's daughter; but Lady Merrifield was exclaiming that he too had had nothing to eat, and General Mohun came forth to draw them into the dining-room, where he helped Ludmilla to cold lamb, salad, etc., and she sat down at Gerald's signal, very timidly, so that she gave the idea of only partaking because she was afraid to refuse.

Gerald ate hurriedly and nervously, and drank claret cup. He said they were getting on famously, his uncle's chief strength being expended in drawing out the voice of the buccaneer captain, and mitigating the boatswain. Where were the little boys? Happily disposed of. Little Felix had gone through his part, and then Fergus had carried him and Adrian off together to Clipstone to see his animals, antediluvian and otherwise.

Then in rushed Gillian, followed by Dolores.

"Oh, mother!" cried Gillian, "there's a fresh instalment of pots and pans come in, such horrid things some of them! There's a statue in terra-cotta, half as large as life, of the Dirty Boy. Geraldine, do pray come and see what can be done with him. Kalliope is in utter despair, for they come from Craydon's, and to offend them would be fatal."

"Kalliope and the Dirty Boy," said Mrs. Grinstead, laughing. "A dreadful conjunction; I must go and see if it is possible to establish the line between the sublime and the ridiculous."

"Shall I ask your nephew's leave to let you go," said Lady Merrifield, "after all the orders I have received?"

"Oh, no—" she began, but Gerald had jumped up.

"I'll steer you over the drawbridge, Cherie, if go you must. Yes,"—to the young ladies—"I appreciate your needs. Nobody has the same faculty in her fingers as this aunt of mine. Come along, Mona, it is Mrs. Henderson's stall, you know."

Ludmilla came, chiefly because she was afraid to be left, and Lady Merrifield could not but come too, meeting on the way Anna, come to implore help in arranging the Dirty Boy, before Captain Henderson knocked his head off, as he was much disposed to do.

Gillian had bounded on before with a handful of sandwiches, but Dolores tarried behind, having let the General help her to the leg of a chicken, which she seemed in no haste to dissect. Her uncle went off on some other call before she had finished, eating and drinking with the bitter sauce of reflection on the fleeting nature of young men's attentions and even confidences, and how easily everything was overthrown at sight of a pretty face, especially in the half-and-half class. She had only just come out into the verandah, wearily to return to the preparations, which had lost whatever taste they had for her, when she saw Gerald Underwood springing over the partition wall. Her impulse was to escape him, but it was too late; he came eagerly up to her, saying—

"She is safe with Mrs. Henderson. I am to go back for her when our duet comes on."

Dolores did not want to lower herself by showing jealousy or offence, but she could not help turning decidedly away, saying—

"I am wanted."

"Are you? I wanted to tell you why I am so interested in her. Dolores, can you hear me now?—she is my sister."

"Your sister!" in utter amaze.

"Every one says they see it in the colour of our eyes."

"Every one"—she seemed able to do nothing but repeat his words.

"Well, my uncle Lancelot, and—and my mother. No one else knows yet. They want to spare my aunt till this concern is over."

"But how can it be?"

"It is a horrid business altogether!" he said, taking her down to the unfrequented parts of the lower end of the garden, where they could walk up and down hidden by the bushes and shrubs. "You knew that my father was an artist and musician, who fled from over patronage."

"I think I have heard so."

"He married a singing-woman, and she grew tired of him, and of me, deserted and divorced him in Chicago, when I was ten months old. He was the dearest, most devoted of fathers, till he and I were devoured by the Indians. If they had completed their operations on my scalp, it would have been all the better for me. Instead of which Travis picked me up, brought me home, and they made me as much of an heir of all the traditions as nature would permit, all ignoring that not only was my father Bohemian ingrain, but that my mother was—in short—one of the gipsies of civilization. They never expected to hear of her again, but behold, the rapturous discovery has taken place. She recognised Lance, the only one of the family she had ever seen before, and then the voice of blood—more truly the voice of £ s. d.—exerted itself."

"How was it she did not find you out before?"

"My father seems to have concealed his full name; I remember his being called Tom Wood. She married in her own line after casting him off, and this pretty little thing is her child—the only tolerable part of it."

"But she cannot have any claim on you," said Dolores, with a more shocked look and tone than the words conveyed.

"Not she—in reason; but the worst of it is, Dolores, that the wretched woman avers that she deceived my father, and had an old rascally tyrant of an Italian husband, who might have been alive when she married."

"Gerald!"

Dolores stood still and looked at him with her eyes opened in horror.

"Yes, you may well say Gerald. 'Tis the only name I have a right to if this is true."

"But you are still yourself," and she held out her hand.

He did not take it, however, only saying—

"You know what this means?"

"Of course I do, but that does not alter you—yourself in yourself."

"If you say that, Dolores, it will only alter me to make me—more—more myself."

She held out her hand again, and this time he did take it and press it, but he started, dropped it, and said—

"It is not fair."

"Oh yes, it is. I know what it means," she repeated, "and it makes no difference," and this time it was she who took his hand.

"It means that unless this marriage is disproved, or the man's death proved, I am an outcast, dependent on myself, instead of the curled darling the Grinsteads—blessings on them!—have brought me up."

"I don't know whether I don't like you better so," exclaimed she, looking into his clear eyes and fine open face, full of resolution, not of shame.

"While you say so—" He broke off. "Yes, thus I can bear it better. The estate is almost an oppression to me. The Bohemian nature is in me, I suppose. I had rather carve out life for myself than have the landlord business loaded on my shoulders. Clement and Lance will make the model parson and squire far better than I. 'The Inspector's Tour' was a success—between that and the Underwood music there's no fear but I shall get an independent career."

"Oh! that is noble! You will be much more than your old self—as you said."

"The breaking of Cherie's heart is all that I care about," said he. "To her I was comfort, almost compensation for those brothers. I don't know how—" He paused. "We'll let her alone till all this is over; so, Dolores, not one word to any one."

"No, no, no!" she exclaimed. "I will—I will be true to you through everything, Gerald; I will wait till you have seen your way, and be proud of you through all."

"Then I can bear it—I have my incentive," he said. "First, you see, I must try to rescue my sister. I do not think it will be hard, for the maternal heart seems to be denied to that woman. Then proofs must be sought, and according as they are found or not—"

Loud calls of "Gerald" and "Mr. Underwood" began to resound. He finished—

"Must be *the* future."

"*Our* future," repeated Dolores.

CHAPTER XX. — FRENCH LEAVE

The evening of that day was a scene of welcomes, dinners, and confusion. The Rotherwoods had arrived that evening at the Cliff Hotel just in time for dinner, of which they considerately partook where they were, to save Jane Mohun trouble; but all four of the party came the instant it was over to hear and see all that was going on, and were fervently received by Gillian and Mysie, who were sleeping at their aunt's to be ready for the morrow, and in spite of all fatigue, had legs wherewith to walk Lord Ivinghoe and Lady Phyllis round the stalls, now closed up by canvas and guarded by police. Phyllis was only mournful not to have assisted in the preparations, and heard all the fun that Mrs. Grinstead had made. But over the wall of Carrara a sight was seen for which no one was prepared—no other than Maura White's pretty classical face!

"Yes," she said, "how could I be away from such an occasion? I made Uncle White bring me to London—he had business there, you know—and then I descended on Kalliope, and wasn't she surprised! But I have a lovely Italian dress!"

Kalliope Henderson looked more alarmed than gratified on the whole. She knew that there had been no idea of Maura's coming till after it had been known that the Rotherwoods were to open the bazaar, and "made Uncle White" was so unlike their former relations that all were startled, Gillian asking in a tone of reproof how Aunt Adeline spared Maura.

"Oh, we shall be back at Gastein in less than a week. I could not miss such an occasion."

"I only had her telegram half-an-hour ago," said Kalliope, in an apologetic tone; and Lord Ivinghoe was to be dimly seen handing Maura over the fence. Moonlight gardens and moonlight sea! What was to be done? And Ivinghoe, who had begun life by being as exclusive as the Marchioness herself! "People take the bit between their teeth nowadays," as Jane observed to Lady Rotherwood when the news reached her, and neither said, though each felt, that Adeline would not have promoted this expedition, even for the child whom she and Mr. White had conspired to spoil. Each was secretly afraid of the attraction for Ivinghoe.

At St. Andrew's Rock there was a glad meeting with the Travis Underwoods, who had disposed of themselves at the Marine Hotel, while they came up with a select party of three Vanderkists to spend the evening with Clement, Geraldine, and Lancelot, not to mention Adrian, who had been allowed to sit up to dinner to see his sisters, and was almost devoured by them. His growth, and the improved looks of both his uncle and aunt, so delighted Marilda, that Lancelot declared the Rockquay people would do well to have them photographed "Then" and "Now," as an advertisement of the place! But he was not without dread of the effect of the disclosure that had yet to be made, though Gerald had apparently forgotten all about it as he sat chaffing Emilia Vanderkist about the hospital, whither she was really going for a year; Sophy about the engineer who had surveyed the Penbeacon intended works, and Francie about her Miranda-Mona in strange hands.

The Vanderkists all began life as very pretty little girls, but showed more or less of the Hollander ancestry as they grow up. Only Franceska, content with her Dutch name, had shot up into a beautiful figure, together with the fine features and complexion of the Underwood twins, and the profuse golden flax hair of her aunt Angela, so that she took them all by surprise in the pretty dress presented by Cousin Marilda, and chosen by Emilia. Sophy was round and short, as nearly plain as one with the family likeness could be, but bright and joyous, and very proud of her young sister. It was a merry evening.

In fact, Lance himself was so much carried away by the spirit of the thing, and so anxious about the performance, that he made all the rest, including Clement, join in singing Autolycus's song, which was to precede the procession, to a new setting of his own, before they dispersed.

But Lance was beginning to dress in the morning when a knock came to his door.

"A note from Mr. Flight, please, sir."

The note was—"Circus and Schnetterlings gone off in the night! Shop closed! Must performance be given up?"

The town was all over red and blue posters! But Lance felt a wild hope for the future, and a not ill-founded one for the present. He rushed into his clothes, first pencilling a note—

```
"Never say die.  L. O. U."
```

Then he hurried off, and sent up a message to Miss Franceska Vanderkist, to come and speak to him, and he walked up and down the sitting-room where breakfast was being spread, like a panther, humming Prospero's songs, or murmuring vituperations, till Franceska appeared, a perfect picture of loveliness in her morning youthful freshness.

"Francie, there's no help for it. You must take Mona! She has absconded!"

"Uncle Lance!"

"Yes, gone off in the night; left us lamenting."

"The horrible girl!"

"Probably not her fault, poor thing! But that's neither here nor there. I wish it was!"

"But I thought—"

"It is past thinking now, my dear. Here we are, pledged. Can't draw back, and you are the only being who can save us! You know the part."

"Yes, in a way."

"You did it with me at home."

"Oh yes; but, Uncle Lance, it would be too dreadful before all these people."

"Never mind the people. Be Mona, and only think of Alaster and Angus."

"But what would mamma say, or Aunt Wilmet? And Uncle Clem?" each in a more awe-stricken voice.

"I'll tackle them."

"I know I shall be frightened and fail, and that will be worse."

"No, it won't, and you won't. Look here, Francie, this is not a self-willed freak for our own amusement. The keeping up the Church schools here depends upon what we can raise. I hate bazaars. I hate to have to obtain help for the Church through these people's idle amusement, but you and I have not two or three thousands to give away to a strange place in a lump; but we have our voices. 'Such as I have give I thee,' and this ridiculous entertainment may bring in fifty or maybe a hundred. I don't feel it right to let it collapse for the sake of our own dislikes."

"Very well, Uncle Lance, I'll do as you tell me."

"That's the way to do it, my dear. At least, when you make ready, recollect, not that you are facing a multitude, but that you are saving a child's Christian faith; when you prepare, that you have to do with nobody but Gerald and me; when it comes to 'One, two, three, and away,' mind nothing but your music and your cue."

"But the dress, uncle?"

"The dress is all safe at the pavilion. You must come up and rehearse as soon as you have eaten your breakfast. Oh, you don't know where. Well, one of us will come and fetch you. Good girl, Francie! Keep up your heart. By the bye, which is Fernan's dressing-room? I must prepare him."

That question was answered, for Sir Ferdinand's door into the corridor was opened.

"Lance! I thought I heard your voice."

"Yes, here's a pretty kettle of fish! Our Miranda has absconded, poor child. Happy thing you brought down Francie; nobody else could take the part at such short notice. You must pacify Marilda, silence scruples, say it is her duty to Church, country, and family. Can't stop!"

"Lance, explain—do! Music-mad as usual!" cried Sir Ferdinand, pursuing him down-stairs in despair.

"I *must* be music-mad; the only chance of keeping sane just now. There's an awful predicament! Can't go into it now, but you shall hear all when this is over."

Wherewith Lance was lost to view, and presently burst into St. Kenelm's Vicarage, to the relief of poor Mr. Flight, who had tried to solace himself with those three words as best he might.

"All right. My niece, Franceska Vanderkist, who took the part before, and who has a very good soprano, will do it better as to voice, if not so well as to acting, as the Little Butterfly."

"Is she here?"

"Yes, by good luck. I shall have her up to the pavilion to rehearse her for the afternoon."

"Mr. Underwood, no words can say what we owe you. You are the saving of our Church education."

Lance laughed at the magniloquent thanks, and asked how the intimation had been received.

It appeared that on the previous evening O'Leary had come to him, and, in swaggering fashion, had demanded twenty pounds as payment for his step-daughter's performance at the masque. Mr. Flight had replied that she had freely promised her services gratuitously for the benefit of the object in view. At this the man had scoffed, talked big about her value and the meanness of parsons, and threatened to withdraw her. Rather weakly the clergyman had said the question should be considered, but that he could do nothing without the committee, and O'Leary had departed, uttering abuse.

This morning "Sweetie Bob," the errand-boy, had arrived crying, with tidings that the shop and house were shut up; nobody answered his knock; Mother Butterfly had "cut" in the night, gone off, he believed, with the circus, and Miss Lydia too; and there was two-and-ninepence owing to him, besides his—his—his character!

He knew that Mother Butterfly had gone to the magistrates' meeting the day before, and paid her fine of twenty-five pounds, and he also believed that she had paid up her rent, and sold her shop to a neighbouring pastry-cook, but he had never expected her to depart in this sudden way, and then he began to shed fresh tears over his two-and-ninepence and his character.

Mr. Flight began to reassure him, with promises to speak for him as an honest lad, while Lance bethought himself of the old organist's description of that wandering star, "Without home, without country, without morals, without religion, without anything," and recollected with a shudder that turning-point in his life when Edgar had made him show off his musical talent, and when Felix had been sharp with him, and the office of the 'Pursuivant' looked shabby, dull, and dreary.

Nothing more could be done, except to make bold assurances to Mr. Flight that Mona's place should be supplied, and then to hurry home, meeting on his way a policeman, who told him that the circus was certainly gone away, and promised to let him know whither.

He was glad to find that Gerald had not come down-stairs, having overslept himself in the morning after a wakeful night. He was dressing when his uncle knocked at his door.

"Here is a shock, Gerald! I hope it is chiefly to our masque. These people have absconded, and carried off our poor little Mona."

"What? Absconded? My sister! I must be after them instantly," cried Gerald, wildly snatching at his coat.

"What good would that do? you can't carry her off vi et armis."

"Send the police."

"No possibility. The fine is paid, the rent and all. They have gone, it seems, with the circus."

"Ah! Depend upon it that fellow has paid the fine, and bought the poor child into slavery with it. Carried her off in spite of our demurring, and the Vicar's prosecution. I must save her. I'll go after and outbid."

"No hurry, Gerald. A circus is not such a microscopical object but that it can be easily traced. A policeman has promised to find out where, and meanwhile we must attend to our present undertaking."

Gerald strode up and down the room in a fiery fit of impatience and indignation, muttering furious things, quite transformed from the listless, ironical youth hitherto known to his family.

"Come," Lancelot said, "our first duty is to do justice to our part; Francie Vanderkist will take Mona."

"Hang Mona! you care for nothing on earth but your fiddling and songs."

"I do not see that being frantic will make any difference to the situation. All in our power is being done. Meanwhile, we must attend to what we have undertaken."

Gerald rushed about a little more, but finally listened to his uncle's representation that the engrossing employment was good to prevent the peril of disturbing the two whom they were so anxious to spare. Fely came running up with a message that Aunt Cherie and Anna had been sent for to see about the decorations of the art stall, and that they would have to eat their breakfast without them.

Appetite for breakfast was lacking, but Lance forced himself to swallow, as one aware of the consequences of fasting for agitation's sake, and he nearly crammed Gerald; so that Adrian and Fely laughed, and he excused himself by declaring that he wanted his turkey-cock to gobble and not pipe. For which bit of pleasantry he encountered a glare from Gerald's Hungarian eyes. He was afraid on one side to lose sight of his nephew, on the other he did not feel equal to encounter a scolding from Marilda, so he sent Adrian and Fely down to the Marine Hotel to fetch Franceska, while he stole a moment or two for greeting Clement, who was much better, and only wanted more conversation than he durst give him.

CHAPTER XXI. — THE MASQUE

Poor Franceska! First she encountered Cousin Marilda's wonder and displeasure, and the declaration that Uncle Lance went absolutely crazy over his musical mania. She had seen it before in poor Edgar, and knew what it came to. She wanted to telegraph at once to Alda to ask her consent or refusal to Franceska's appearance; but Sir Ferdinand stopped this on the ground that the circumstances could not be explained, and told her to content herself with Clement's opinion.

This she sent Sophy and Emilia to ascertain, before she would let them and the boys escort Francie to her destination. Clement, not yet up, had to hold a lit de justice, and pronounce that Uncle Lance was to be fully trusted to ask nothing unbecoming or unnecessary, and that Francie would have nothing to do with any one except him and Gerald.

"Besides," said Emilia, as they walked up, "nobody will find it out. The posters are all over the town, 'Mona, Miss Ludmilla Schnetterling.'"

So the sisters were received with a murmur on their delay. The pretty dress prepared for Mona was found to be too small for the tall shapely Franceska, and Sophy undertook to alter it, while poor Francie's troubles began.

Whether it was that Uncle Lance and Gerald were in a secret state of turmoil, or that their requirements were a good deal higher than for the Vale Leston audience, or perhaps that she had no inheritance of actress traditions, they certainly were a great deal sharper with her than they had been ever before or with Ludmilla.

Gerald derided her efforts sarcastically, and Uncle Lance found fault good-humouredly but seriously, and she was nearly in tears by eleven o'clock, when the procession was to take place. She was quite surprised when Lance turned to her and said—

"Thank you, my dear, you are doing capitally. I shall be proud of my daughter Mona."

Quite in spirits again, she was sewn by Sophy into her still unfinished dress, her beautiful light golden flax tresses were snooded, her Highland scarf pinned on her shoulder, and she hurried to her uncle, now be-robed and be- wigged, with Gerald in full Highland garb, looking very much disgusted, especially when her uncle said—

"Well done, Francie. You'll cut that poor little thing out in looks and voice, if not in acting."

"Oh, uncle, I sang so horridly."

"You can do better if you try; I wish there was time to train you. We'll do the 'logs duet' once more after this tomfoolery. Ha! Captain Armytage. You are an awful pirate, and no mistake. Where did you get that splendid horse-pistol?"

"From my native home, as well as my sword; but I wrote to Willingham for the rest. This will be an uncommonly pretty march-past. The girls look so well, and all out of doors too."

This was decidedly a great advantage, the trees, grass, and blue sky lending a great grace to the scene. The procession started from the garden entrance of the hotel, headed by the town band in uniform, and the fire brigade likewise, very proud of themselves, especially the little terrier whom nothing would detach from one of the firemen. Then came the four seasons belonging to the flower stall, appropriately decked with flowers, the Italian peasants with flat veils, bright aprons, and white sleeves, Maura White's beauty conspicuous in the midst, but with unnecessary nods and becks. Then came the "mediaeval" damsels in ruffs and high hats, the Highland maidens, with Valetta and Primrose giggling unmanageably; and Aunt Jane's troop of the various costumes of charity children, from the green frocks, long mittens, and tall white caps, and the Jemima Placid flat hats and long waists, down to the red cloaks, poke straw bonnets, and blue frocks of the Lady Bountiful age. These were followed by the merry fairies and elves; then by the buccaneers and the captive prisoners; and the rear was brought up by MacProspero, as Lord Rotherwood called him, with his niece on his arm and his nephew by his side.

When the central stall, or bothie, in the Carrara grounds was reached, after passing in full state and order over two of the bridges, the procession halted before a group of the Rotherwood family, Sir Jasper and Lady Merrifield, Lady Flight, and other local grandees, with the clergy, who had declined to walk in procession. There the performers spread themselves out, singing Autolycus's song, led of course by MacProspero; Lady Rotherwood, with as much dignity as the occasion permitted, declared the bazaar open, and the Marquis hoped every one was going to ruin themselves in the cause of Christian education.

The first idea of "every one" was luncheon, except that Lance laid hands on his unfortunate Angus and Mona for their duet, in the midst of which Lord Rotherwood made a raid on them.

"There! I'm sure Prospero never was so cruel as to starve what's-his-name!

Come in and have some food—it is just by."

They found themselves in a dining-room, in the presence of Lady Rotherwood, her son and daughter, and a sprinkling of Merrifields and actors, in full swing of joyous chatter; Mysie and Lady Phyllis telling all that was specially to be admired, and Lord Rotherwood teasing them about the prices, and their wicked extortions in the name of goodness, Gillian snubbing poor Captain Armytage in his splendid buccaneer dress, Ivinghoe making himself agreeable to Franceska, whose heightened carnation tints made her doubly lovely through her shyness. Gerald and Dolores in the less lively vicinity of the Marchioness carrying on a low-toned conversation, which, however, enabled Gerald to sustain nature with food better than he had done at breakfast.

It did not last long. The sellers had to rush off to relieve those who had begun the sale, and the performance was to commence at three o'clock, so that the final preparations had to be hurried through.

Geraldine had made the tour of the stalls on the arm of Anna, to admire them in their first freshness, and put finishing touches wherever solicited. The Rocca Marina conservatories were in rare glory, orchids in weird beauty, lovely lilies of all hues, fabulously exquisite ipomoeas, all that heart could wish. Before them a fountain played in the midst of blue, pink, and white lotus lilies, and in a flower-decked house the Seasons dispensed pot-flowers, bouquets, and button-holes; the Miss Simmondses and their friends with simpering graces, that made Geraldine glad to escape and leave them to the young men who were strolling up. At Carrara was the stall in which she was chiefly interested, and which had been arranged with a certain likeness to Italian gardens, the statues and other devices disposed among flowers; the Dirty Boy judiciously veiled by the Puzzle Monkey, and the front of the summer-house prolonged by pillars, sham but artistic. Jasper was zealously photographing group after group, handing his performances over to his assistant for printing off. Kalliope looked in her costume most beautiful and dignified. Her sister, grown to almost equal beauty, was hurrying off to see the masque, flushed and eager, while Gillian and one or two others were assisting in sales that would be rather slack till after the performance. Here Geraldine purchased only a couple of Mouse-traps, leaving further choice to be made after the stranger purchasers. Here Sir Jasper and General Mohun came up, and gave her a good deal of curious information about Bernard's bevy of figures in Indian costumes; and having the offer of such a strong arm as the General's, she dispensed with Anna, who was really wanted to help with the very popular photographs.

They passed the refreshments, at present chiefly haunted by Mrs. Edgar's boys, ready to eat at any time of day; they looked civilly at the Varley Elizabethans, and found Lady Merrifield in the midst of her bothie, made charming with fresh green branches and purple heather, imported by the Vanderkists.

"That's Penbeacon ling. I know that red tint in the mauve," said Geraldine; "I'll give you half-a-crown, if your decorations can spare that spiring spray!" And she put it in her bosom, after touching it with her lips. "You have a bower for the Lady of the Lake," she added.

"I'm afraid I'm only Roderick Dhu's mother," laughed Lady Merrifield; "but I shall have more ladies when the masque is done. Now I have only Mysie."

"And oh!" cried Mysie, "please set up the nurse in the nursery gardens right. Wilfred knocked her over, and she won't stand right for me."

"Perverse woman. There! No, I shall not buy anything now, I shall wait for Primrose and the refuse. How pretty it does all look! Ah, Mr. Brownlow," as she shook hands with the curate.

"I left my brother John at your house," he said; "I persuaded him to run down this morning with my mother and see our doings, and he was glad of the opportunity of looking in upon the Vicar."

"How very kind of him. We were wishing to know what he thought!"

"No doubt he will be here presently. My mother is at the masque. There was not a seat for us, so I took him down to St. Andrew's Rock."

"Not a seat! The five-shilling seats?"

"Not the fraction of one. Numbers standing outside! Pity there can't be a second performance."

"Four hundred seats! That's a hundred pounds! We shall beat the School-board yet!"

So, with the General politely expressing that there was no saying what Rockquay owed to the hearty co-operation of such birds of passage as herself and her brothers, she travelled on to the charity stall, which Miss Mohun had quaintly dressed in the likeness of an old-fashioned school, with big alphabet and samplers, flourished copies, and a stuffed figure of a 'cont-rare-y' naughty boy, with a magnificent fool's cap. She herself sat behind it, the very image of the Shenstone school-mistress, with wide white cap, black poke- bonnet, crossed kerchief, red cloak, and formidable rod; and her myrmidons were in costume to match. It was very attractive, and took every one by surprise, but Geraldine had had enough by this time, and listened to Miss

Mohun's invitation and entreaty that she would preside over tea-cups for the weary, in the drawing-room. The privacy of the houses had been secured by ropes extending from the stalls to the rails of the garden, and Geraldine was conducted by her two generals to the verandah, where they installed her, and lingered, as was usual with her squires, always won by her spirited talk, till messages came to each of them from below that some grandee was come, who must be talked to and entertained.

Already, however, Armine Brownlow had brought up his brother, the doctor—John or Jock, an old friend—over, first Clement's district and then his bed.

"Well, Mrs. Grinstead, I can compliment you much on your brother. He is very materially better, and his heart is recovering tone."

"I am very glad and thankful! I only wish you had seen him last week. He was better then, but he had a worry about our little nephew, which threw him back."

"So he told me. The more quiescent and amused you can keep him, the more chance of a fair recovery there will be. I am glad he thinks of dining with the party to-night."

"I am glad he still thinks. I had to come away early, when he had still left it doubtful."

"I encouraged the idea with all my might."

"Do you think he will be able to go back to his parish?"

"Most assuredly not while every worry tells on him in this manner. You must, if possible, take him abroad for the winter, before he begins to think about it."

"He has leave of absence for a year."

"Dating from Easter, I think. Keep him in warm climates as long as you can. Find some country to interest him without over-fatigue, and you will, I hope, be able to bring him home fit to consider the matter."

"That is all you promise?"

"All I dare—not even to promise—but to let you hope for."

An interruption came; one of the young ladies had had her skirt trodden on, and wanted it to be stitched up. Then came Jane Mohun to deposit a handkerchief which some one had dropped. "I can stay a moment," she said; "no one will come to buy till the masque is ended. Oh, this red cloak will be the death of me!"

"You look highly respectable without it."

"I shall only put it on for the coup d'oeil at first. Oh, Geraldine, what is to be done with that horrid little Maura?"

"The pretty little Greek girl—Mrs. Henderson's sister?"

"Oh! it is not Mrs. Henderson's fault, nor my sister Ada's either, except that the little wretch must have come round her. I know Ada meant to stay away on that very account."

"What account?"

"Ivinghoe's, to be sure! Oh! I forgot. You are so much one of us that I did not remember that you did not know how the foolish boy was attracted—no, that's too strong a word—but she thought he was, when they were here to open Rotherwood Park. He did flirt, and Victoria—his mother, I mean—did not like it at all. She would never have come this time, but that I assured her that Maura was safe at Gastein!"

"Is it so very undesirable?"

"My dear! Their father was old White's brother, a stone-mason. He was raised from the ranks, but his wife was a Greek peasant—and if you had seen her, when the Merrifield children called her the Queen of the White Ants! Ivinghoe is naturally as stiff and formal as his mother, I am not much afraid for him, except that no one knows what that fever will make of a young man, and I don't want him to get his father into a scrape. There, I have exhaled it to you, and there is a crowd as if the masque was done with."

It was, and the four hundred auditors were beginning to throng about the stalls, strays coming up from time to time, and reporting with absolute enthusiasm on the music and acting. Marilda was one of these.

"Well, Cherry, I saw no great harm in it after all, and Francie looked sweetly pretty, just as poor Alda did when she first came to us. Lance must make his own excuses to Alda. But Gerald looked horridly ill! He sang very well, but he had such red spots on his cheeks! I'd get Clement's doctor to sound him. Lord Rotherwood was quite complimentary. Now I must go and buy something—I hear there is the Dirty Boy—I think I shall get it for Fernan's new baths and wash-houses. Then isn't there something of yours, Cherry?"

"Not to compete with the Dirty Boy."

"Ah! now you are laughing at me, Cherry. Quite right, I am glad to hear you do it again."

The next visitor was Lance.

"Oh, Cherry, how cool you look! Give me a cup of tea—not refreshment-stall tea. That's right. Little Francie is a perfect gem—looks and voice—not acting—no time for that. Heigh-ho!"

"Where's Gerald?"

"Somewhere about after that Merrifield niece with the doleful name, I fancy. He did very well when it came to the scratch."

"Have you seen Dr. Brownlow? He has been to see Clement."

"That's first-rate! Where shall I find him?"

"Somewhere about, according to your lucid direction, I suppose."

"What does he think of old Tina?"

Geraldine told him, and was rather surprised, when he whistled as though perplexed, and as Fergus rushed in, glorious with the news that Sir Ferdinand had bought his collection of specimens for the Bexley museum, he rose up, looking perturbed, to find Dr. Brownlow.

Next came Gillian with news that the Dirty Boy was sold to Lady Travis Underwood.

"And mayn't I stay a moment or two?" said she. "Now the masque is over, that Captain Armytage is besetting me again."

"Poor Captain Armytage."

"Why do you pity him? He is going to join his ship, the Sparrow Hawk, next week, and that ought to content him."

"Ships do not always fill a man's heart."

"Then they ought. I don't like it," she added, in a petulant tone. "I have so much to learn and to do, I don't want to be tormented about a tiresome man."

"Well, he will be out of your way to-morrow."

"Geraldine, that is a horrid tone."

"If you choose to put meaning in it, I cannot help it."

"And that horrid little Maura! She is in the most awful flutter, standing on tiptoe, and craning out her foolish little neck. I know it is all after Ivinghoe, and he never has come to our counter! Kalliope has been trying to keep her in order, but I'm sure the Queen of the White Ants must have been just like that when she got poor Captain White to marry her. Kalliope is so much vexed, I can see. She never meant to have her here. And Aunt Ada stayed away on purpose."

"Has she seen much of him?"

"Hardly anything; but he did admire her, and she never was like Kalliope. But what would Aunt Ada do? Oh dear! there's that man! He has no business at Aunt Jane's charity stall. I shall go and tell him so."

Geraldine had her little private laugh before Adrian came up to her with a great ship in his arms—

"Take care of this, Aunt Cherry. She is going to sail on the Ewe. I bought her with the sovereign Uncle Fernan gave me."

Geraldine gave the ship her due admiration, and asked after the masque.

"Oh, that went off pretty well. I wouldn't have been Fely! All the ladies went and said 'Pretty dear!' when he sang his song about the bat's back. Disgusting! But then he has not been a fellow at school, so he made his bow and looked as if he didn't mind it."

"And Francie?"

"Francie looked perfectly stunning. Everybody said so, and she sang— well, she sang better than she did at home; but she was in an awful funk, though I kept on looking at her, and shouting bravo to encourage her; and she must have heard my voice, for I was just in front."

"I hope she was encouraged."

"But she is very stupid. I wanted to take her round to all the stalls, and show her what to buy with the five Jubilee sovereigns Uncle Fernan gave her, for you know she has never been anywhere, or seen anything. I thought she would like it, and besides, all our fellows say they never saw such an awfully pretty girl, and they can't believe all that hair is her own—she had it all down her back, you know—so I told them I would let them have a pull to try."

"Poor Francie! She declined, I suppose?"

"Well, there was that ridiculous swell, Fergus's cousin, Ivinghoe, and he has taken her off to see the stupid flowers in the conservatory. I told Sophy I wondered she permitted such flirting, but of course Francie knew no better."

"Oh! and you couldn't stop it?"

"Not I, though I called her over and over again to look at things, but Lord Ivinghoe always hung about and gave one no peace. So I just told Sophy to look after her, and came off to tell you. Oh my! here is old Miss Mohun coming up. I shall be off. I want some chocolate creams. Mrs. Simmonds has got some splendid ones."

Miss Mohun was coming, in fact.

"Well, Geraldine, the masque was a great success. People beg to have it repeated, so many could not get in. And it is worth at least a hundred pounds to us. People whose opinion is worth having were quite struck. They say your brother really ought to have been a great composer and singer."

"I think he might have been if he had not given up his real passion to come to the help of my dear eldest brother. And he is really happier as he is."

"I knew there was conquest in his face. And that dear little elf of a boy— what a voice! So bright and so arch too. Then the Miranda—she took all by surprise. I believe half the spectators took her for the Little Butterfly."

"Ah, the poor Little Butterfly is flown. There was nothing for it but to make Francie act, as she had taken the part once before."

"Her acting was no great things, they say—ladylike, but frightened. Her voice is lovely, and as to her looks—people rave about them. Tell me, she is not Lady Travis Underwood's daughter?"

"Oh no; she is Anna's sister, Adrian's sister."

"So I told Lady Rotherwood, I was sure it was so."

"The Travis Underwoods have no children, but they adopted Emilia when I took Anna, and they have brought three Vanderkists to this affair. Francie has never been from home before, it is all quite new to her." Then recollecting what Adrian had repeated, she thought it fair to add, "My sister was left very badly off, and all these eight girls will have nothing of their own."

"Well, I don't suppose anything will come of it. I hope it will put no folly into her head; but at any rate it effaces that poor silly little Maura. I hope too, as you say your niece is so innocent, it will do her no harm."

"I don't suppose any possibilities have occurred to the child."

Lord Rotherwood here came on the scene.

"Jenny, there's an offer for your boy in the fool's cap, and Mysie doubts if she ought to let him go. Well, Mrs. Grinstead, I think you have the best of it. Lookers on, etc."

"Looking on has always been my trade."

"You heard the rehearsal of the masque, I believe, but you did not hear that charming Mona?"

"No; she had to take the part suddenly. Her uncle had to tyrannize over her, to save the whole thing."

"We are much indebted to him, and to her," said Lord Rotherwood courteously. "She looked as if she hated it all in the first scene, though she warmed up afterwards. I must say I liked her the better for her shyness."

"Her little brother thinks she recovered in consequence of his applause," said Geraldine, smiling.

"Ah! I saw him. And heard. A little square fellow—very sturdy."

"Yes, the Dutchman comes out in him, and he has droll similitudes, very curious in one who never saw his father, nor any but his Underwood relations."

"So much the better for him perhaps; I have, and ought to have, great faith in uncles' breeding. I am glad to meet Sir Ferdinand Travis Underwood. I have often come across him about London good works."

"Yes, he is an excellent man."

"Not wholly English is he, judging by the depth of colour in those eyes?"

"No; his mother was a Mexican, partly Indian. We used to call him the Cacique;" and Geraldine had the pleasure of telling his story to an earnest listener, but interruption came in the shape of Sir Ferdinand himself who announced that he had hired a steam-yacht wherein to view the regatta, and begged Lord Rotherwood to join the party.

This was impossible, as the Marquis was due at an agricultural dinner at Clarebridge, but in return, in the openness of his heart, he invited the Travis Underwoods to their dinner that evening at the hotel, where the Merrifields and the Underwoods were already engaged, little boys and all.

"Thank you, my lord, but we are too large a party. We have three Vanderkist girls with us, and Anna and her brother are to join them to be with their sister."

"Never mind, never mind. The great hall will have room for all."

Still Fernan demurred, knowing that Marilda had ordered dinner at the Quay Hotel, and that even liberal payment would not atone for missing the feasting of the millionaires; so the matter was compounded by his promise to bring all his party, who were not ready for bed, up to spend the evening.

And Geraldine perceived from Lady Rotherwood's ceremonious politeness that she did not like it at all, though she never said so even to Lady Merrifield.

However, it was a very bright evening. Gerald had sung himself into spirits, and then found Dolores, and retreated into the depths of the garden with her, explaining to her all about his sister, and declaring that his first object must be to rescue her; and then, unless his name was cleared, and he had to resume all his obligations, the new life would be open to him, and he had no fear of not succeeding as a journalist, or if not, a musical career was possible to him, as Dolores had now the opportunity of fully perceiving. His sweet voice had indeed filled her with double enthusiasm. She had her plan for lecturing, and that very morning she had received from her father permission to enter a ladies' college, and the wherewithal. She would qualify herself for lecturing by the time he had fixed his career; and they built their airy castles, not on earth, but on railroads and cycles, and revelled on them as happily as is common to lovers, whether in castle or in cottage. Certainly if the prospect held out to her had been Vale Leston Priory, it would not have had the same zest; and when in the evening they joined the dinner-party, there was a wonderful look of purpose and of brightness on both their faces. And Emilia, who had been looking for him all the afternoon to tell him, "Gerald, I am really going to be a nurse," only got for answer an absent "Indeed!"

"Yes, at St. Roque's."

"I hope I shall never be a patient there," he said, in his half-mocking tone. "You'll look jolly in the cap and apron."

"I'm to be there all the time they are in America, and—"

"Well, I wonder you don't go and study the institutions."

"But, Gerald—"

His eye was wandering, and he sprang forward to give Dolores a flower that she had dropped.

Lancelot, knowing what was before Gerald, and having always regarded Vale Leston with something of the honours of Paradise, could not understand that joyous look of life, so unlike Gerald's usual weary, passive expression. He himself felt something of the depression that was apt to follow on musical enjoyment; he saw all the failures decidedly enough not to be gratified with the compliments he met on all sides, and "he bitterly thought on the morrow," when he saw how Clement was getting animated over a discussion on Church matters, and how Geraldine was enjoying herself. And as to that pretty Franceska, who had blossomed into the flower of the flock, he foresaw heart-break for her when he watched the Marchioness's countenance on hearing that her son had accepted Sir Ferdinand's invitation to cruise to-morrow in the yacht.

Vainly was Ivinghoe reminded of the agricultural dinner. He was only too glad to escape it, and besides, he thought he could be there in time.

Nevertheless, the present was delightful, and after dinner the young people all went off to the great assembly-room, whence Anna came back to coax

Uncle Lance to play for them. All the elders jumped up from their several discussions. Even Lady Rotherwood moved on, looking as benign as her feelings would permit. Jane squeezed Geraldine's arm, exceedingly amused. Lance struck up, by request, an old-fashioned country dance; Lord Rotherwood insisted that "Lily" should dance with him, as the remnant of forty good years ago or more, and with Sir Roger de Coverley the day ended.

Poor little Maura, making an excuse to wander about the gardens in the moonlight, saw the golden locks shining through the open windows, and Lord Ivinghoe standing over them, went home, and cried herself to sleep over the fickleness of the nobility, when she had better have cried over her own unjustified romance, excited by a few kindly speeches and a cup of tea.

And Emilia! What was Gerald's one laughing turn with her, compared with his long talk with Dolores in the moonlight?

CHAPTER XXII. — THE REGATTA

Such of the party as were not wanted for the second day of the bazaar, and were not afraid of mal de mer, had accepted the yachting invitation, except the three elders at St. Andrew's Rock. Even Adrian and Felix were suffered to go, under Sophy's charge, on the promise to go nowhere without express permission, and not to be troublesome to any one.

"Sophy can say, 'Now, boys,' as effectively as Wilmet," said Geraldine, when she met Lance, who had been to the quay to see them off.

"She did not say so to much advantage with her own boys," said Clement.

"We weren't Harewoods," returned Lance, "and John never could bear to see a tight hand over them; but there's good in them that will come out some day."

Clement gave an emphatic "Humph!" as he sat down to the second breakfast after Anna had gone to the cliff to resume her toils.

"Who are gone?" asked Geraldine.

"Poor Marilda, smilingly declaring she shall be in misery in the cabin all the time, Fernan, and four Vanderkists, General Mohun, Sir Jasper, and some of his progeny; but others stay to help Miss Mohun finish up the sales."

"Does Lord Ivinghoe go?"

"Oh yes, he came rushing down just in time. Francie was looking like a morning rose off the cloister at Vale Leston."

"I am sorry they have another day of it. I don't see how it can come to good," said Geraldine.

"Perhaps her roses may fade at sea," said Clement, "and disenchantment may ensue."

"At least I hope Alda may not hear of it, or she will be in an agony of expectation as long as hope lasts. Gerald is gone, of course?"

"Oh yes!" said Lance, who had had a farewell from him with the words, "Get it over while I am out of the way, and tell them I don't mind."

Cursory and incomprehensible, but conclusive; and Lance, who minded enough to have lost sleep and gained a headache, marvelled over young men's lightness and buoyancy. He had seen Dr. Brownlow, and arranged that there should be a call, as a friend, in due time after the communication, in case it should hurt Clement, and when Geraldine observed merrily that now they were quit of all the young ones they could feel like old times, he was quite grieved to disturb her pleasure.

Clement, however, began by taking out a letter and saying—

"Here is a remarkable missive left for me yesterday—'If the Rev. Underwood wishes to hear of something to his advantage, he should communicate with Mr. O'L., care of Mr. John Bast, van proprietor, Whitechapel.' An impostor?" said he.

"I am afraid not," said Lance. "Clement, I fear there is no doubt that she is that singing Hungarian woman who was the ruin of Edgar's life."

"Gerald's mother!" exclaimed Geraldine.

"Even so."

"But she is gone! She gave up all rights. She can't claim anything. Has she worried him?"

"Yes, poor boy! She has declared that she had actually a living husband at the time she married our poor Edgar."

Of course both broke out into exclamations that it was impossible, and Lance had to tell them of his interview with the woman at Gerald's entreaty. They were neither of them so overcome by the disclosure as he had feared during his long delay.

"I believe it is only an attempt at extortion," said Clement.

"Very cruel," said Geraldine. "How—how did my poor boy bear it all this time?"

"He was very much knocked down at first, quite overwhelmed, but less by the loss than by the shame, and the imputation on his father."

"It was no fault of dear Edgar's."

"No, indeed. I am glad Fernan is here to go over again what Edgar told him. We may be quite satisfied so far."

"And is it needful to take it up?" asked Geraldine wistfully. "If we don't believe it, the horrid story would get quashed."

"No, Cherry," said Clement. "If you think it over you will see that we must investigate. I should be relieved indeed to let it alone, but it would not be fair towards Lance there and his boys."

Lance made a strange noise of horror and deprecation, then added—

"I don't believe Gerald would consent to let it alone."

"No, now he knows, of course. He is a right-minded, generous boy," said Geraldine. "I was wrong. Did you say he was very much upset?"

"Just at first, when he came to me at night. I was obliged to dragoon him, and myself too, to throw it off enough to be able to get through our performance yesterday. How thankful I am to the regatta that it is not our duty to the country to go through it again to-day! However, he seems to have rebounded a good deal. He was about all the latter part of the day with Miss Mohun."

"I saw him dancing and laughing with some of them."

"And he parted from me very cheerfully, telling me to assure you 'he did not mind,' whatever that may mean."

"He knows that nothing can disturb our love for him, Edgar's little comfort, passed on to bear us up," said Cherry tearfully. "Oh yes, I know what he meant—Felix's delight, my darling always."

"It strikes me," said Lance, "that if he can save his sister—"

Geraldine started.

"Oh, the cigar-girl! Only by that mother's side."

"That is true, but she is his half-sister, and he is evidently much drawn towards her. She is a nice little thing, and I believe he made much of her on the rehearsal day. I saw they got on much better together, and I think she was aware of the relationship."

"Yes, it is quite right of him," said Geraldine, "but she will be a drag on him all his life. Now what ought we to do? Shall you answer this letter to the care of the van-man, Clem?"

"I shall think, and wait till I have seen Gerald and Travis. This letter is evidently written simply in the hope of raising money from me, not in any friendly spirit."

"Certainly not," said Lance. "Having failed to black-mail Gerald, and discovered that you are the heir, they begin on you, but not from any gratitude to you. Sweetie Bob, as they call the ex-errand-boy, gives a fine account of their denunciations of the tall parson who brought the bobbies down on them."

Lance felt much reassured by Clement's tone, and all the more when he had seen Dr. Brownlow, who made a thorough examination, and came to the conclusion that Clement had recovered tone, so that the shock, whatever it was, that his brother dreaded had done no present damage, but that he was by no means fit for any strain of work or exertion, should be kept from anxiety as much as possible, and had better spend the winter in a warm climate. It was not likely—Jock Brownlow said it with grief and pain—that he would ever be able to return to the charge of St. Matthew's, but as he had a year's holiday, there was no need to enter on that subject yet, and in a quiet country place, with a curate, he might live to the age of man in tolerable health if he took care of himself, or his sister took care of him for some time to come.

So much relieved was Lance that he recollected that he had laid in no stock of presents for those at home, and went up to profit by the second day's reductions, when he secured Geraldine's portrait of Davy Blake for his wife, and a statuette of St. Cecilia for Dr. May, some charming water-colours for Robina and Ethel, besides various lesser delights for the small fry, his own and the flock at Vale Leston, besides a cushion for Alda's sofa. John Inglesant had been bought by a connoisseur by special commission. He heard at every stall triumphant accounts of the grand outlay of the Travis Underwoods and Rotherwoods, and just the contrary of Mrs. Pettifer, whom he encountered going about in search of bargains, and heard haggling for a handsome table-cover, because it was quite aesthetic, and would not do except in a large house, so of course it had not sold.

The Mouse-traps had been a great success, and there were very few left of them. They really owed as much to Lance as did the play, for he had not only printed them at as small a cost as possible, but had edited, pruned, and got them into shape more than any of the young lady authors suspected. The interpretation of handwriting had likewise succeeded in obtaining many clients, and a large pile of silver coins. Anna, who was hovering near, was delighted to show him that her sister Sophy's writing had been declared to indicate homely tastes, an affectionate disposition, great perspicuity of perception, much force of character; and Franceska's, scarcely yet formed, showed that she was affectionate, romantic, and, of all things in the world, fond of horses and of boating. Emilia's was held as a great blunder, for she was said to have an eye devoted to temporal advantages, also volatile, yet of great determination, triumphing over every obstacle, and in much danger of self-deception.

"The triumph at least is true," said Anna, "now she has her way about the nursing."

"Has she? I did not know it."

"Yes, she is to try it for a year, while Cousins Fernan and Marilda go out to their farm in the Rocky Mountains."

Just then there was a little commotion, and a report came up that a boat had been run down and some one drowned. Somebody said, "One of those acting last night—a buccaneer." Somebody else, "A naval man." Then it was "The Buccaneer Captain," and Mrs. Pettifer was exclaiming, "Poor Captain Armytage! He was in our theatricals, I remember, but they thought him rather high. But he was a fine young man! Poor Captain Armytage!"

Lance had sufficient interests in those at sea to be anxious, and turned his steps to the gates to ascertain the facts, when he was overtaken by Gillian, with a hat hastily thrown over her snooded hair and Highland garb, hurrying along, and looking very white.

"Mr. Underwood! Oh! did you hear who it was?"

"No certainty. I was going down to find out. You," as he saw her purpose, "had better not come. There will be a great crowd. I will come back and tell you."

"Oh no, I must. This is the short way."

Her hands trembled so that she could hardly undo the private fastening of Miss Mohun's garden, and she began to dash down the cliff steps. Just at the turn, where the stair-way was narrowest, Lance heard her exclaim, and saw that she had met face to face no other than Captain Armytage himself.

"Oh! is it?" and she so tottered on the rocky step that the hand he had put out in greeting became a support, and a tender one, as Lance said (perhaps with a little *malice*)—

"We heard that the Buccaneer Captain had come to grief."

"I?" he laughed; and Gillian shook herself up, asking—

"Weren't you run down?" seeing even as she spoke that not a drop of wet was traceable.

"Me! What! did you think I was going to peril my life in a 'longshore concern like this?" said he, with a merry laugh, betraying infinite pleasure.

"But did nothing happen? Nobody drowned?" she asked, half disappointed.

"Not a mouse! A little chap, one of the fairies yesterday, tumbled off the sea-wall where he had no business to be, but he swam like a cork. We threw him a rope and hauled him up."

Wherewith he gave his arm to Gillian, who was still trembling, and clasped it so warmly that Lance thought it expedient to pass them as soon as possible and continue his journey on the staircase, giving a low whistle of amusement, and pausing to look out on the beautiful blue bay, crowded with the white sails of yachts and pleasure-boats, with brilliant festoons of little flags, and here and there the feather of steam from a launch. He could look, for he was feeling lighter of heart now that the communication was over.

Perhaps Lance would have been edified could he have heard the colloquy

—

"Gillian! you do care for me after all?"

Gillian tried to take her arm away and to say, "Common humanity," but she did not get the words out.

"No, no!" he said. "Confess that if it had been that fisher-boy, you would not be here now!" and he kept tight the arm that she was going to take away. Her face was in a flame.

"Well, well; and if—if it wasn't, you need not make such a fuss about it."

"Not when it is the first ray of hope you have afforded me, for the only joy of my life?"

"I never meant to afford—"

"But you could not help."

"Oh, don't! I never meant it. Oh dear! I never meant to be worried about troublesome things like this till I had got older, and learnt a great deal more; and now you want to upset it all. It is very—very disagreeable."

"But you need not be upset!" poor Ernley Armytage pleaded. "Remember, I am going away for three years. May I not take hope with me?"

Gillian paused.

"Well," again she said, "I do like you—I mean, I don't mind you as much as most people; you have done something, and you have some sense."

His look of rapture at these very moderate words quite overpowered her, and the tears welled up into her eyes, while she made a sudden change of tone.

"There, there—of course it is all right. I'm a nasty creature, and if you like me, it is more than I deserve, only, whatever you do, don't make me cry. I've got all the horrid dolls and pen-wipers, and bags and rags to get rid of."

"May I talk to your mother?"

"Oh yes, if you can catch her. She will be ever so much more good to you than I; and I only hope she will warn you what a Tartar I am."

Wherewith Gillian threw off her hat, swung open the gate, and dashed like a hunted hare up to her mother's stall, where in truth she had been wanted, since only two helpers had remained to assist in the cheapening and final disposal of the remnants. Lady Merrifield read something in those wild eyes and cheeks burning, but the exigencies of the moment obliged her to hold her peace, and apply herself to estimating the half-price of the cushions and table-cloths she rejoiced to see departing, as well as to preserve wits enough not to let Gillian sell the Indian screen for two shillings and sixpence, under the impression that this was the half of five pounds. Mysie was the only one who kept her senses fairly undisturbed, and could balance between her duty to the schools and her desire to gratify a child, happy in that she never saw more than one thing at a time. Valetta and Primrose were yachting, so that the distraction was less, and Captain Armytage lingered round, taking messages, and looking in wistful earnestness for some one to be disengaged. Yet there was something in his eyes that spoke of the calmness of an attained object, and Miss Mohun, who had sold off all her remaining frocks and pinafores at a valuation to Marilda for some institution, and was free to help her sister, saw in a moment that his mind was settled.

Yet speech was scarcely possible till the clearance was finally effected by a Dutch auction, when Captain Armytage distinguished himself unexpectedly as auctioneer, and made an end even of the last sachet, though it smelt so strongly of lip-salve that he declared that a bearer must be paid to take it away. But the purchaser was a big sailor, who evidently thought it an elegant gift for his sweetheart.

By the time it was gone the yachters had come home. Captain Armytage seized on Sir Jasper, who already know his purpose, and wished him success, though withheld from saying a word to urge the suit by Lady Merrifield's assurances, that to hurry Gillian's decision would be fatal to success, and that a reproof for petulance would be worse. She did not know whether to wish for the engagement or not; Gillian was her very dear and sufficient companion, more completely so than Mysie, who was far less clever; and she had sometimes doubted whether common domestic life beginning early was for the girl's happiness and full development; but she knew that her husband would scout these doubts as nonsense, and both really liked Ernley Armytage, and had heard nothing but what was to his advantage in every way, when they had been in his own county, and had seen his neighbours and his family. However, she could only keep quiet, and let her heart rise in a continual aspiration at every silent moment for her child's guidance.

Before she had had her moment of speech with either, she heard her husband calling Gillian, and she knew that he was the one person with whom his daughter never hid her true self in petulance or sarcasm. So Gillian met him in the General's sitting-room, gasping as she turned the handle of the door. He set a chair for her, and spoke gravely.

"My dear," he said, "I find you have gained the heart of a good man."

"I am sure I never meant it," half whispered Gillian.

"What is that—you never meant it? I never supposed you capable of such an unladylike design. You mean that you were taken by surprise?"

"No; I did see what he was at," and she hung her head.

"You guessed his intentions?"

"Yes, papa; but I didn't want—"

"Try to explain yourself," said Sir Jasper as she broke off.

"I—I did wish to go on improving myself and being useful. Surely it was not wrong, papa. Don't you see, I did not want to let myself be worried into letting myself go out, and spoiling all my happiness and improvement and work, and getting to care for somebody else?"

"But you have consented."

"Well, when I was frightened for him I found I did care, and he got hold of me, and made me allow that I did; and now I suppose nobody will give me any peace."

"Stay, Gillian—keep yourself from this impatient mood. I think I understand your unwillingness to overthrow old associations and admit a new overmastering feeling."

"That's just it, papa," said Gillian, looking up. "I can't bear that overmastering feeling, nor the being told every one must come to it. It seems such folly."

"Folly that Eve was given to be a helpmeet, and as the bride, the Church to her Bridegroom? Look high enough, Gillian, and the popular chatter will not confuse your mind. You own that you really love him."

"Oh, papa, not half so much as mamma, or Mysie, or Jasper, but—but I think I might."

"Is that all, Gillian? No one would coerce you. Shall I send him away, and tell him not to think of it? Remember, it is a serious thing—nay, an unworthy thing to trifle with a right-minded man."

Gillian sat clasping the elbow of her chair, her dark eyes fixed. At last she said—

"Papa, I do feel a sort of trust in him, a sort of feeling as if my life and all goodness and all that would be safe with him; and I couldn't bear him to go quite away and hear no more of him, only I do wish it wouldn't happen now; and if there is a fuss about it, I shall get cross and savage, and be as nasty as possible, I know I shall."

"You can't exercise enough self-command to remember what is due—I would say kind and considerate—to a man who has loved you through all your petulance and discouragement, and now is going to a life not without peril for three years? Suppose a mishap, Gillian—how would you feel as to your treatment of him on this last evening?"

"Oh, papa! if you talk in that way I must, I must," and she burst into tears.

Sir Jasper bent over her and gave her a kiss—a kiss that from him was something to remember. It was late, and summonses to a hurried meal were ringing through Beechcroft Cottage, where the Clipstone party waited to see the illuminations.

Talk was eager between the sellers and the sailors as Valetta described the two parties, the fate of the Indian screen, and the misconduct of Cockneys in their launches were discussed by many a voice, but Gillian was unwontedly silent. Her mother had no time for more than a kiss before the shouts of Wilfred, Fergus, and Primrose warned them that the illuminations were beginning. She could only catch Mysie, and beg her to keep the younger ones away from Gillian and the Captain. Mysie opened her brown eyes wide and said—

"Oh!" Then, "Is it really?"

"Really, my dear, and remember that it is his last evening!"

"Oh!" said Mysie again. "I never thought it of Gill! May I tell Valetta?"

"Better not, my dear, if it can be helped."

A screaming for Gill was heard, and Mysie hastened to answer it. Lady Merrifield was too much tired to do anything but sit in the garden with Miss Mohun and look out at the ships, glittering with festoons of coloured lamps, reflected in the sea, but the young people went further afield, out on the cliff path to Rotherwood Park. The populace were mainly collected on the quay, and this formed a more select promenade, though by no means absolute solitude. Sir Jasper really did keep guard over the path along which Gillian allowed her Captain to conduct her, not exactly knowing which way they were going, and quite away from the bay and all its attractions.

She heard him out without any of the sharp, impatient answers in which her maiden coyness was wont to disguise itself, as he told her of his hopes and plans for the time when his three years of the Mediterranean should be over.

"And you see you can go on studying all the time, if you must be so clever."

"I think one ought to make the most of oneself, just as you want to rise in your profession! No, indeed, I could not bear you if you wanted me to sit down and idle, or to dawdle yourself."

"Don't grow too clever for me."

"Mother always says that a real man has stuff in him that is quite different from cleverness, and yet I could not bear to give that up. I am so glad you don't mind."

"Mind! I mind nothing but to know you are caring for me. And you will write to me?"

"I shan't know what to say. You will tell of volcanoes, and Athens, and Constantinople, and Egypt, and the Holy Land, and I shall have nothing to say but who lectures in college."

"Little you know what that will be to me."

It was a curious sensation all the time to Gillian, with a dawning sense that was hardly yet love—she was afraid of that—but of something good and brave and worthy that had become hers. She had felt something analogous when the big deer-hound at Stokesley came and put his head upon her lap. But the hound showed himself grateful for caresses, and so did her present giant when the road grew rough, and she let him draw her arm into his and talk to her.

It was the parting, for he had to go to London and to his own family the next day early. Gillian spoke not a word all through the dark drive to Clipstone, but when the party emerged into the light her eyes were full of tears. Lady Merrifield followed her to her room, and her words half choked were—

"Mamma, I never knew what a great, solemn, holy thing *it* is. Will you look me out a prayer to help me to get worthy?"

CHAPTER XXIII. — ILLUMINATIONS

That moon and sparkling lights did not shine alone for Gerald and Dolores. There were multitudes on the cliffs and the beach, and Sir Ferdinand and Lady Travis Underwood with their party had come to an irregular sort of dinner-supper at St. Andrew's Rock. With them, or rather before them, came Mr. Bramshaw, the engineer, who sent in his card to Mr. Clement Underwood, and entered with a leathern bag, betraying the designs on Penbeacon.

Not that these were more than an introduction. Indeed, under the present circumstances, a definite answer was impossible; but there was another question, namely, that which regarded Sophia Vanderkist. She had indeed long been of age, but of course her suitor could not but look to her former guardian for consent and influence. He was a very bearded man, pleasant- spoken and gentlemanlike, and Lancelot had prepared his brother by saying that he knew all about the family, and they were highly respectable solicitors at Minsterham, one son a master in the school at Stoneborough. So Clement listened favourably, liked the young man, and though his fortunes at present depended on his work, and Lady Vanderkist was no friend to his suit, gave him fair encouragement, and invited him to join the meal, though the party was already likely to be too numerous for the dining-room.

That mattered the less when all the young and noisy ones could be placed, to their great delight, under the verandah outside, where they could talk and laugh to their utmost content, without incommoding Uncle Clement, or being awed by Cousin Fernan's black beard and Cacique-like gravity. How they discussed and made fun over the humours of the bazaar; nor was Gerald's wit the slackest, nor his mirth the most lagging. He was very far from depressed now that the first shock was over. He knew himself to be as much loved or better than ever by those whose affection he valued, and he was sure of Dolores' heart as he had never yet been. The latent Bohemianism in his nature woke with the prospect of having his own way to make, and being free from the responsibilities of an estate, and his chivalry was excited by the pleasure of protecting his little half-sister, in pursuit of whom he intended to go.

So, light-hearted enough to amaze the elders who knew the secret, he jumped up to go with the rest of the party to the cliff walk, where the brilliant ships could best be seen. Lance, though his headache was, as Geraldine said, visible on his brow, declared that night air and sea-breeze were the best remedy, and went in charge of the two boys, lest his dainty Ariel should make an excursion over the rocks; and the four young ladies were escorted by Gerald and the engineer.

The elders were much too tired for further adventures, and Geraldine and Marilda were too intimate to feel bound to talk. Only a few words dropped now and then about Emilia and her hospital, where she was to be left for a year, while Fernan with Marilda visited his American establishments, and on their return would decide whether she would return, or whether they would take Franceska, or a younger one, in her stead. The desertion put Marilda out of heart, and she sighed what a pity it was that the girl would not listen to young Brown.

Meanwhile, Clement was making Ferdinand go over with him Edgar's words about his marriage. They had all been written down immediately after his death, and had been given to Felix with the certificates of the marriage and birth and of the divorce, and they were now no doubt with other documents and deeds in the strong-box at Vale Leston Priory. Fernan could only repeat the words which had been burnt in on his memory, and promise to hunt up the evidence of the form and manner of the dissolution of the marriage at Chicago. Like Clement himself, he very much doubted whether the allegation would not break down in some important point, but he wished Gerald to be assured that if the worst came to the worst, he would never be left destitute, since that first meeting—the baptism, and the receiving him from the dying father— amounted to an adoption sacred in his eyes.

Then, seeing how worn-out Clement looked, he abetted Sibby and Geraldine, in shutting their patient safe up in his bedroom, not to be "mislested" any more that night, said Sibby. So he missed the rush of the return. First came the two sober sisters, Anna and Emilia, only sorry that Aunt Cherry had not seen the lovely sea, the exquisite twinkle of silvered waves as the moon rose, and then the outburst of coloured lights, taking many forms, and the brilliant fireworks darting to and fro, describing curves, bursting and scattering their sparks. Emilia had, however, begun by the anxious question—

"Nan, what is it with Gerald?"

"I don't quite know. I suspect Dolores has somehow teased him, though it is not like her."

"Then there is something in it?"

"I can't help believing so, but I don't believe it has come to anything."

"And is she not a most disagreeable girl! Those black eyebrows do look so sullen and thunderous.”

“Oh no, Emmie, I thought so at first, but she can’t help her eyebrows; and when you come to know her there is a vast deal in her—thought, and originality, and purpose. I am sure it has been good for Gerald. He has seemed more definite and in earnest lately, less as if he were playing with everything, with all views all round.”

“But his spirits are so odd!—so merry and then so grave.”

“That is only during these last few days, and I fancy there must be some hitch—perhaps about Dolores’ father, and we are all in such haste.”

Emilia did not pursue the subject. She had never indulged in the folly of expecting any signs of actual love from her cousin. She had always known that the family regarded any closer bond as impossible; but she had been always used to be his chief confidante, and she missed his attention, but she would not own this even to herself, go she talked of her hospital schemes with much zest, and how she should spend her outings at a favourite sisterhood.

“For,” said she, “I am tired of luxury.”

It had been a delightful walk to Anna, with her companion sister, discussing Adrian, or Emily’s plans, or Sophy’s prospects. They had come home the sooner, for Emily had to pack, as she was to spend a little while with her mother at Vale Leston. Where was Franceska? They were somewhat dismayed not to find her, but it was one of the nights when everybody loses everybody, and no doubt she was with Uncle Lance, or with Sophy, or Gerald.

No such thing. Here was Uncle Lance with his two boys in varying kinds of delight, Adrian pronouncing that “it was very jolly, the most ripping sight he ever saw,” then eating voraciously, with his eyes half shut, and tumbling off to bed “like a veritable Dutchman,” said Lance, who had his own son in a very different mood, with glowing cheeks, sparkling eyes, appetite gone for very excitement, as he sprang about and waved his hands to describe the beautiful course of the rockets, and the fall of the stars from the Roman candles.

“Oh, such as I never—never saw! How shall I get Pearl and Audrey to get even a notion of it? Grandpapa will guess in a moment! Oh, and the sea, all shine with a path of—of glory! Oh, daddy, there are things more beautiful than anybody could ever dream of!”

“Go and dream then, my sprite. Try to be as still as you can, even if you do go on feeling the yacht, and seeing the sparks when you shut your eyes. For you see my head is bad, and I do want a chance of sleep.”

“Poor daddy! I’ll try, even if the music goes on in my head. Good-night.”

"That will keep him quieter than anything," said Lance; "but I would not give much for the chance of his not seeing the dawn."

"Or you either, I fear," said Geraldine. "Have you slept since the discovery?"

"I shall make my sleep up at home, now I have had the whole out. Who comes now?"

It was Sophy, with her look of

Mr. Bramshaw had brought her to the door, and no doubt she and he had had a quiet, restful time of patient planning; but the not finding Francie soon filled her with great alarm and self-reproach for having let herself be drawn away from the party, when all had stood together on Miss Mohun's lawn. She wanted to start off at once in search of her sister, and was hardly pacified by finding that Gerald was still to come. Then, however, Gerald did come, and alone. He said he had just seen the Clipstone party off. No, he had not seen Francie there; but he added, rather as if recovering from a bewilderment, as Sophy was asking him to come out with her again, "Oh, never fear. Lord Ivinghoe was there somewhere!"

"I thought he was gone."

"No, he said the yacht got in too late for the train. Never mind, Sophy, depend upon it she is all right."

None of the ladies present felt equally pleased, but in a minute or two more in came a creature, bright, lovely, and flushed, with two starry eyes, gleaming like the blue lights on the ships.

"Oh, Cousin Marilda, have I kept you waiting? I am so sorry!"

"Where have you been?"

"Only on the cliff walk. Lord Ivinghoe took me to see the place where his father had the accident, and we watched the fireworks from there. Oh, it was so nice, and still more beautiful when the strange lights were out and the people gone, and only the lovely quiet moon shining on the sea, and a path of light from Venus."

"I should think so," muttered Gerald, and Marilda began—

"Pretty well, miss."

"I am very sorry to bo so late," began Francie, and Geraldine caught an opportunity while shawling Marilda to say—

"Dear, good Marilda, I implore you to say nothing to put it into her head or Alda's. I don't think any harm is done yet, but it can't be anything. It can't come to good, and it would only be unhappiness to them all."

"Oh, ah! well, I'll try. But what a chance it would be, and how happy it would make poor Alda!"

"It can't be. The boy's mother would never let him look at her! Don't, don't, don't!"

"Well, I'll try not." She kissed her fondly.

Gerald's walk had been with Dolores of course, a quiet, grave, earnest talk and walk, making them feel how much they belonged to one another, and building schemes in which they were to learn the nature of the poor and hard-worked, by veritably belonging to them, and being thus able to be of real benefit. In truth, neither of them, in their brave youthfulness, really regretted Vale Leston, and the responsibilities; and, as Gerald declared, he would give it up tomorrow gladly if he could save his name and his father's from shame, but, alas! the things went together.

Dolores wished to write fully to her father, and that Gerald should do the same, but she did not wish to have the matter discussed in the family at once, before his answer came, and Gerald had agreed to silence, as indeed they would not call themselves engaged till that time. Indeed, Dolores said there was so much excitement about Captain Armytage that no one was thinking of her.

CHAPTER XXIV. — COUNSELS OF PATIENCE

If Sibby hoped to keep her "long boy" from being "mislested," she was mistaken. He knew too well what was to come, and when she knocked at his door with his cup of tea, he came to it half dressed, to her extreme indignation, calling for his shaving water.

"Now, Master Clem, if you would only be insinsed enough to keep to your bed, you might have Miss Sophy to speak to you there, if nothing else will serve you."

"Is she there?"

"In coorse, and Miss Francie too. What should they do else, after colloguing with their young men all night? Ah, 'tis a proud woman poor Miss Alda would be if she could have seen the young lord! And the real beauty is Miss Francie, such as my own babbies were before her, bless them!"

"Stop," cried Clement in consternation. "It is only a bit of passing admiration. Don't say a word about it to the others."

"As if I would demane myself to the like of them! Me that has been forty-seven years with you and yours, and had every one of you in my arms the first thing, except the blessed eldest that is gone to a better place."

"Would that he were here now!" sighed Clement, almost as he had sighed that first morning of his loss. "Where are those girls?"

"Rampaging over the house with Sir Adrian, and his packing of all his rubbish, enough to break the heart of a coal-heaver! I'd not let them in to bother their aunt, and Mr. Gerald is asleep like a blessed baby."

"And Lance?"

"Oh! it is down to the sea he is with that child that looks as if he was made of air, and lived on live larks! And Master Lance, he's no better—eats like a sparrow, and sits up half the night writing for his paper."

Clement got rid of Sibby at last, but he was hardly out of his room before Sophy descended on him, anxious and blushing, though he could give her much sympathy and kindly hope of his influence, only he had to preach patience. It had been no hasty fancy, but there had long been growing esteem and affection, and he could assure her of all the aid the family could give with her mother, though Penbeacon works would be a very insecure foundation for hope.

"I think Gerald would consent," said Sophy, "and he will soon be of age."

Clement could only say "Humph!"

"One thing I hope is not wrong," said Sophy, "but I do trust that no one will tell mother about Lord Ivinghoe. It is not jealousy, I hope, but I cannot see that there is anything in it, only the very sound would set mother more against Philip than ever."

"You do not suppose that Francie is—is touched?"

"No," said Sophy, gravely as an elder, "she is such a child. She was very much pleased and entertained, and went on chattering, till I begged her to let us say our prayers in peace. We never talk after that, and she went to sleep directly, and was smiling when she woke, but I do not fancy she will dwell on it, or fancy there is more to come, unless some one puts it into her head."

It was sagely said, and Clement knew pretty well who was the one person from whom Sophy had fears. Poor Alda, improved and altered as she was, if such a hope occurred to her, would she be able to help imparting it to her daughter and looking out for the fulfilment?

Loud calls for Sophy rang through the house, and Clement had only time to add—

"Patience, dear child, and submission. They not only win the day, but are the best preparation for it when it is won."

That family of girls had grown up to be a care to one who had trusted that his calling would be a shield from worldly concerns; but he accepted it as providential, and as a trust imposed on him as certainly as Felix had felt the headship of the orphaned house.

He was rejoiced to find on coming down-stairs that Lance had decided on giving another day to family counsels, sending off little Felix with his cousins, who would drop him at the junction to Stoneborough, whence he would be proud to travel alone. Clement took another resolution, in virtue of which he knocked at his sister's door before she went down.

"Cherry," said he, "would it be inconvenient to keep Francie here just for the present?"

"Not at all; it would be only too pleasant for Anna now that she loses her brother. But why?"

"I want to hinder her from hearing the conclusions that her mother may draw from the diversions of yesterday."

"I see. It might soon be,

"And Sophy will keep her counsel as to those moonlight wanderings. When were they to go?"

"By the 11.30 train. Marilda is coming up first."

So the plan was propounded. Franceska was only too much charmed to stay in what had indeed been an enchanted coast to her, and Sophy was sure that mamma would not mind; so the matter was settled, and the explanatory notes written.

The party set off, with each little boy hugging a ship in full sail, and the two young sisters were disposed of by a walk to Clipstone to talk over their adventures. Mrs. Grinstead felt certain of the good manners and reticence prevailing there to prevent any banter about Lord Ivinghoe, and she secured the matter further by a hint to Anna.

However, Miss Mohun was announced almost as they left the house. She too was full of the bazaar, which seemed so long ago to her hearers, but with the result of which she was exceedingly delighted. The voluntary schools were secured for the present, and the gratitude of the Church folk was unbounded, especially to the Vale Leston family, who had contributed so greatly to the success of the whole.

Jane too had watched the evening manoeuvres, and perceived, with her sharp eyes, all that was avowed and not avowed under that rising moon. The pair of whom she had first to speak were "Ivanhoe and Rowena," as she called them, and she was glad to find that the "fair Saxon" had grown up at Vale Leston, educated by her aunt and sister, and imbibing no outside habits or impressions.

"Poor child," said Jane, "she looks like a flower; one is sorry it should be meddled with."

"So did my sister Stella, and there, contrary to all our fears, the course of true love did run smooth."

"If it depended entirely on Rotherwood himself, I think it would," said Jane, "but—" She paused and went on, "Ivinghoe is, I fear, really volage, and he is the mark of a good many London mammas."

"Is it true about Mrs. Henderson's sister?"

"There's nothing in it. I believe he danced with her a few times, and the silly little thing put her own construction on it, but her sister made her confess that he had never said a word to her, nor made love in any sense. Indeed, my sister Adeline would never have consented to her coming here if she had believed in it, but Maura has a Greek nature and turns the Whites round her fingers. Well, I hope all will go well with your pretty Franceska. I should not like her lovely bloom to be faded by Ivinghoe. He is Rotherwood's own boy, though rather a prig, and a man in London. Oh, you know what that means!"

"We have done *notre possible* to keep our interpretation from the poor child, or any hint of it from reaching her mother."

"That's right. Poor Rowena, I hope the spark will be blown out, or remain only a pleasant recollection. As to little Maura, she had her lesson when she was reduced to hanging on Captain Henderson's other arm! She is off to-day to meet Mr. White in London. That purpose has been served."

"And have you not a nearer interest?"

"Oh, Gillian! Well, Captain Armytage did get hold of her, in what we must now call the Lover's Walk! Yes, she has yielded, to her father's great satisfaction and perhaps to her mother's, for she will be more comfortable in looking forward to a commonplace life for her than in the dread of modern aberrations. But Gillian is very funny, very much ashamed of having given in, and perfectly determined to go to her college and finish her education, which she may as well do while the Sparrow Hawk is at sea. He is off to-day, and she says she is very glad to be rid of him. She sat down at once to her dynamite, as Primrose calls it, having bound over Mysie and Valetta never to mention the subject! I tell them that to obey in silence is the way to serve the poor man best."

Miss Mohun was interrupted by the announcement of Lady Flight and Mr. Flight, who came equally eager with delight and gratitude to thank the House of Underwood for the triumph. The rest of the clergy of Rockquay and half the ladies might be expected, and in despair at last of a "lucid interval," Geraldine ordered the carriage for a long drive into the country, so as to escape all visitors. Even then, they could not got up the hill without being stopped four or five times to receive the thanks and compliments which nearly drove Gerald crazy, so much did he want to hear what his family had to say to his plans, that he had actually consented to partake of a dowager-drive in a landau!

He and his uncle had discovered from the police in the course of the morning that Ludmilla and her mother had not gone with the circus, but had been seen embarking in the Alice Jane, a vessel bound for London. His idea had been to hurry thither and endeavour to search out his half-sister, and rescue her; but Lance had assured him not only that it would probably be a vain quest, but that there would be full time to meet the Alice Jane by land before she could get there by sea.

To this he had yielded, but not so readily to the representation that the wisest way would be to keep out of sight; but to let Lance, as a less interested party, go and interview the van proprietor, whose direction had been sent to Clement, try to see O'Leary, and do his best to bargain for Ludmilla's release, a matter on which all were decided, whatever might be the upshot of the question respecting Gerald. To leave a poor girl to circus training, even if there were no interest in her, would have been shocking to right-minded people; but when it was such a circus as O'Leary's, and the maiden was so good, sweet, and modest as Lida, the thought would have been intolerable even without the connection with Gerald, who had been much taken with all he had seen of her.

"That is fixed, even if we have to bid high for our Mona," said Lance.

"By all means," said Geraldine. "It will be another question what will be good for her when we have got her."

"I will take care of that!" said Gerald.

"Next," Lance went on, "we must see what proofs, or if there be any, of this person's story. I expect one of you will have to pay well for them, but I had better take a lawyer with me."

Clement named the solicitor who had the charge of the Vanderkist affairs.

"Better than Staples, or Bramshaw & Anderson. Yes, it would be best to have no previous knowledge of the family, and no neighbourly acquaintance. Moreover, I am not exactly an interested party, so I may be better attended to."

"Still I very much doubt, even if you do get any statement from the woman, whether it can be depended upon without verification," said Clement.

"From the registers, if there are any at these places?"

"Exactly, and there must be personal inquiry. The first husband, Gian Benista, will have to be hunted down, dead or alive."

"Yes; and another thing," said Lance, "if the Italian marriage were before the revolution in Sicily, I expect the ecclesiastical ceremony would be valid, but after that, the civil marriage would be required."

"Oh!" groaned Gerald, "if you would let me throw it all up without these wretched quibbles."

"Not your father's honour," said his aunt.

"Nor our honesty," said Clement. "It is galling enough to have your whole position in life depend on the word of a worthless woman, but there are things that must be taken patiently, as the will of One who knows."

"It is so hard to accept it as God's will when it comes of human sin," said Geraldine.

"Human thoughtlessness," said Clement; "but as long as it is not by our own fault we can take it as providential, and above all, guard against impatience, the real ruin and destruction."

"Yes," said Lance, "sit on a horse's head when he is down to keep him from kicking."

"So you all are sitting on my head," said Gerald; "I shall get out and walk —a good rush on the moors."

"Wait at least to allow your head to take in my scheme," said Clement.

"Provided it is not sitting still," said Gerald.

"Far from it. Only it partly depends on my lady and mistress here—"

"I guess," said Geraldine. "You know I am disposed that way by Dr. Brownlow's verdict."

"And 'that way' is that we go ourselves to try to trace out this strange allegation—you coming too, Gerald, so that we shall not quite be sitting on your head."

"But my sister?"

"We will see when we have recovered her," said Mrs. Grinstead.

"I would begin with a visit to Stella and her husband," said Clement; "Charlie could put us in the way of dealing with consuls and vice-consuls."

"Excellent," cried his sister; "Anna goes of course, and I should like to take Francie. It would be such an education for her."

"Well, why not?"

"And what is to become of Adrian?"

"Well, we should not have been here more than six months of course."

"I could take him," said Lance, "unless Alda holds poor old Froggatt & Underwood beneath his dignity."

"That can be considered," said Clement; "it approves itself best to me, except that he is getting on so well here that I don't like to disturb him."

"And when can you come up to town with me?" demanded Gerald; "tomorrow?"

"To-morrow being Saturday, it would be of little use to go. No, if you will not kick, master, I must go home to-morrow, and look up poor 'Pur,' also the organ on Sunday. Come with me, and renew your acquaintance. We will make an appointment with your attorney, Clem, and run up on Monday evening, see him on Tuesday."

Gerald sighed, submitting perforce, and they let him out to exhale as much impatience as he could in a tramp over the hills, while they sat and pitied him from their very hearts.

CHAPTER XXV. — DESDICHADO

Lancelot and Gerald did not obtain much by their journey to London. Gerald wanted to begin with Mr. Bast, van proprietor, but Lance insisted on having the lawyer's counsel first, and the advice amounted to exhortations not to commit themselves, or to make offers such as to excite cupidity, especially in the matter of Ludmilla, but to dwell on the fact of her being so close to the age of emancipation, and the illegality of tyrannical training.

This, however, proved to be wasted advice. Mr. Bast was impervious. He undertook to forward a letter to Mr. O'Leary, but would not tell where, nor whether wife and daughter were with him. The letter was written, and in due time was answered, but with an intimation that the information desired could only be given upon the terms already mentioned; and refusing all transactions respecting the young lady mentioned, who was with her natural guardians and in no need of intervention.

They were baffled at all points, and the lawyer did not encourage any idea of holding out a lure for information, which might easily be trumped up. Since Lancelot had discovered so much as that the first marriage had taken place at Messina, and the desertion at Trieste, as well as that the husband was said to have been a native of Piedmont, he much recommended personal investigation at all these points, especially as Mr. Underwood could obtain the assistance and interest of consuls. It was likely that if neither uncle nor nephew made further demonstration, the O'Learys would attempt further communication, which he and Lance could follow up. This might be a clue to finding "the young lady"— to him a secondary matter, to Gerald a vital one, but for the present nothing could be done for her, poor child.

So they could only return to Rockquay to make immediate preparations for the journey. Matters were simplified by Miss Mohun, who, hearing that Clement's doctors ordered him abroad for the winter, came to the rescue, saying that she should miss Fergus and his lessons greatly, and she thought it would be a pity for Mrs. Edgar to lose their little baronet, just after having given offence to certain inhabitants by a modified expulsion of Campbell and Horner, and therefore volunteering to take Adrian for a few terms, look after his health, his morals, and his lessons, and treat him in fact like a nephew, "to keep her hand in," she said, "till the infants began to appear from India."

This was gratefully accepted, and Alda liked the plan better than placing him at Bexley, which she continued to regard as an unwholesome place. The proposal to take Franceska was likewise welcome, and the damsel herself was in transports of delight. Various arrangements had to be made, and it was far on in August that the farewells were exchanged with Clipstone and Beechcroft Cottage, where each member of the party felt that a real friend had been acquired. The elders, ladies who had grown up in an enthusiastic age, were even more devoted to one another than were Anna and Mysie. Gillian stood a little aloof, resolved against "foolish" confidences, and devoting herself to studies for college life, in which she tried to swallow up all the feelings excited by those ship letters.

Dolores had her secret, which was to be no longer a secret when she had heard from her father, and in the meantime, with Gerald's full concurrence, she was about to work hard to qualify herself for lecturing or giving lessons on physical science. She could not enter the college that she wished for till the winter term, and meant to spend the autumn in severe study.

"We will work," was the substance of those last words between them, and their parting tokens were characteristic, each giving the other a little case of mathematical instruments, "We will work, and we will hope."

"And what for?" said Dolores.

"I should say for toil, if it could be with untarnished name," said Gerald.

"Name and fame are our own to make," said Dolores, with sparkling eyes.

This was their parting. Indeed they expected to meet at Christmas or before it, so soon as Mr. Maurice Mohun should have written. Gerald was, by the unanimous wish of his uncles, to finish his terms at Oxford. Whatever might be his fate, a degree would help him in life.

He had accepted the decision, though he had rather have employed the time in a restless search for his mother and sister; but after vainly pursuing two or three entertainments at fairs, he became amenable to the conviction that they were more likely to hear something if they gave up the search and kept quiet, and both Dolores and Mrs. Henderson promised to be on the watch.

The state of suspense proved an admirable tonic to the whole being of the young man. His listlessness had departed, and he did everything with an energy he had never shown before. Only nothing would induce him to go near Vale Leston, and he made it understood that his twenty-first birthday was to be unnoticed. Not a word passed between Gerald and his aunt as to the cause of the journey, and the doubt that hung over him, but nothing could be more assiduous and tender than his whole conduct to her and his uncle throughout the journey, as though he had no object in life but to save them trouble and make them comfortable.

The party started in August, travelled very slowly, and he was the kindest squire to the two girls, taking them to see everything, and being altogether, as Geraldine said, the most admirable courier in the world, with a wonderful intuition as to what she individually would like to see, and how she could see it without fatigue. Moreover, on the Sunday that occurred at a little German town, it was the greatest joy to her that he sought no outside gaiety, but rather seemed to cling to his uncle's home ministrations, and even to her readings of hymns. They had a quiet walk together, and it was a day of peace when his gentle kindness put her in mind of his father, yet with a regretful depth she had always missed in Edgar.

Nor was there any of that old dreary, half-contemptuous tone and manner which had often made her think he was only conforming to please her, and shrinking from coming to close quarters, where he might confess opinions that would grieve her. He was manifestly in earnest, listening and joining in the services as if they had a new force to him. Perhaps they had the more from the very absence of the ordinary externals, and with nothing to disturb the individual personality of Clement's low, earnest, and reverent tones. There were tears on his eyelashes as he rose up, bent over, and kissed his Cherie. And that evening, while Clement and the two nieces walked farther, and listened to the Benediction in the little Austrian church, Gerald sat under a linden-tree with his aunt, and in the fullness of his heart told her how things stood between him and Dolores.

Geraldine had never been as much attracted by Dolores as by Gillian and Mysie, but she was greatly touched by hearing that the meeting and opening of affection had been on the discovery that Gerald was probably nameless and landless, and that the maiden was bent on casting in her lot with him whatever his fate might be.

He murmured to himself the old lines, with a slight alteration—

```
"I could not love thee, dear, so much,
        Loved I not justice more."
```

"Yes, indeed, Cherie, our affection is a very different and better thing than it would be if I were only the rich young squire sure of my position."

"I am sure it is, my dear. I honour and love her for being my boy's brave comforter—comforter in the true sense. I see now what has helped you to be so brave and cheery. But what will her father say?"

"He will probably be startled, and—and will object, but it would be a matter of waiting anyway, the patience that the Vicar preaches, and we have made up our minds. I'll fight my own way; she to prepare by her Cambridge course to come and work with me, as we can do so much better among the people—among them in reality, and by no pretence."

"Ah! don't speak as if you gave up your cause."

"Well, I won't, if you don't like to hear it, Cherie," he said, smiling; "but anyway you will be good to Dolores."

"Indeed I will do my best, my dear. I am sure you and she, whatever happens, have the earnest purpose and soul to do all the good you can, whether from above or on the same level, and that makes the oneness of love."

"Thank you, Cherie carissima. You see the secret of our true bond."

"One bond to make it deeper must be there. The love of God beneath the love of man."

CHAPTER XXVI. — THE SILENT STAR

And so they came to Buda, where Charles Audley represented English diplomatic interests on the banks of the Danube. When the quaint old semi-oriental-looking city came in sight and the train stopped, the neat English-looking carriage, with gay Hungarian postillions, could be seen drawn up to meet them outside the station.

Charles and his father, now Sir Robert, were receiving them with outstretched hands and joyous words, and in a few seconds more they were with their little Stella! Yes, their little Stella still, as Clement and Cherry had time to see, when Gerald and the two girls had insisted on walking, however far it might be, with the two Audleys, though Charlie told them that no one ever walked in Hungary who could help it, and that he should be stared at for bringing such strange animals.

Geraldine had stayed with Stella once before, and Clement had made one hurried and distressful rush in the trouble about Angela; but that was at Munich, and nearly nine years ago, before the many changes and chances of life had come to them. To Stella those years had brought two little boys, whose appearance in the world had been delayed till the Audley family had begun to get anxious for an heir, but while the Underwoods thought it was well that their parents, especially their father, should have time to grow a little older.

And Stella looked as daintily, delicately pretty as ever, at first sight like a china shepherdess to be put under a glass shade, but on a second view, with a thoughtful sweetness and depth in her face that made her not merely pretty but lovely. How happy she was, gazing at her brother and sister, and now and then putting a question to bring out the overflow of home news, so dear to her. For she was still their silent star, making very few words evince her intense interest and sympathy.

Even when they were at home, in the house that looked outside like a castle in a romance, but which was so truly English within, and the two little fellows of four and three came toddling to meet her, shrinking into her skirts at sight of the new uncle and aunt, there was a quiet gentle firmness—all the old Stella—in her dealings with them, as she drew them to kiss and greet the strangers. Robbie and Theodore were sturdy, rosy beings, full of life, but perfectly amenable to that sweet low voice. Their father and grandfather might romp with them to screaming pitch, and idolize them almost to spoiling, yet they too were under that gentle check which the young wife exercised on all around.

She was only thirty-one, and so small, so fair and young in looks, that to her elder sister her pretty matronly rule *would* at first seem like the management of a dolls' house, even though her servants, English, German, or Magyar, obeyed her implicitly; and for that matter, as Charlie and Sir Robert freely and merrily avowed, so did they. The young secretary was her bounden slave, and held her as the ideal woman, though there came to be a little swerving of his allegiance towards the tall and beautiful Franceska, who had insensibly improved greatly in grace and readiness on her travels, and quite dazzled the Hungarians; while Anna was immensely exultant, and used to come to her aunt's room every night to talk of her lovely Francie as a safety- valve from discussing the matter with Francie herself, who remained perfectly simple and unconscious of her own charms. Geraldine could not think them quite equal to the more exquisite and delicately-finished, as well as more matured, beauty of little Stella, but that was a matter of taste.

The household was more English than Hungarian, or even German, and there were curious similitudes to the Vale Leston Priory arrangements, which kept Stella's Underwood heart in mind. There had to be receptions, and it was plain that when she put Fernan's diamonds on, Mrs. Audley was quite at home and at perfect ease in German and Hungarian society, speaking the languages without hesitation when she *did* speak, while in her quiet way keeping every one entertained, showing the art de tenir un salon, and moreover, preserving Francie from obtrusive admiration in a way perhaps learnt by experience on that more perilous subject, Angela, who had invited what Francie shrank from. The two girls were supremely happy, and Francie seemed to have a fountain of joy that diffused a rose-coloured spray over everything.

One of the famous concerts of Hungarian gipsies was given, and in that Clement and Geraldine were alike startled by tones recalling those of the memorable concert at Bexley, all the more because they seemed to have a curious fascination for Gerald. Moreover, those peculiar eyes and eyelashes, the first link observed between him and the Little Butterfly, were so often repeated in the gipsy band that it was plain whence they were derived. Charles Audley thought it worth while to find means of inquiry among the gipsies as to whether anything was known of Zoraya Prebel or her brother Sebastian; but after some delay and various excitements nothing was discovered, but that there had been a family, who were esteemed recreants to their race, and had sold their children to the managers of German or Italian bands of musicians. One brother had come back a broken man, who had learnt vices and ruined himself, though he talked largely of his wonderful success in company with his sister, who had made grand marriages. What had become of her he did not know; and when Gerald went with Mr. Audley to a little mountain valley to visit him, he had been dead for a week or more.

All this had made some delay, and it was almost the end of the long vacation. Charles Audley undertook to go to Trieste with the travellers, and make inquiries about Zoraya and her first husband. Sir Robert, the Skipper, as the family still termed him, had written for his yacht to meet him there, and be ready for him to convey the party to Sicily. He professed that he could not lose sight of Franceska, with whom he declared himself nearly as much smitten as ever he had been with his daughter-in-law.

They left that pretty creature in her happy home, and arrived at Trieste, where Charles Audley set various agencies to work, and arrived at a remembrance of Giovanni Benista, an impresario, having been in a state of great fury at his wife, his most able performer, having fled from him just as he had been at the expense of training and making her valuable. He tried to have her pursued, but there was reason to think that she had been smuggled away in an English or American ship, and nothing could be done.

Thus much of the story then was confirmed, and Gerald had little or no doubt of the rest of it, but he was obliged to leave the pursuit of the quest to his uncle and aunt, being somewhat consoled for having to return to England by the expectation of hearing from Mr. Maurice Mohun.

Twice he returned for his aunt's last kiss, nay, even a third time, and then with the half-choked words, "My true, my dearest mother!"

And he absolutely bent his knee as he asked for his uncle Clement's blessing.

CHAPTER XXVII. — THE RED MANTLE

Dolores was waiting till the Christmas term to go to her college. The fame of her volcanic lectures had reached Avoncester, and she was entreated to repeat them at the High School there. The Mouse-trap had naturally been sent to Miss Vincent, the former governess, who had become head-mistress of the High School at Silverton, and she wrote an urgent request that her pupils might have the advantage of the lectures. Would Dolores come and give her course there, and stay a few days with her, reviving old times?

Dolores consented, being always glad of an opportunity of trying her wings, though she had not the pleasantest recollections connected with Silverton, but she would be really glad to see Miss Vincent, who had been always kind to her. So she travelled up to Silverton, and found the head- mistress living in cheerful rooms, with another of the teachers in the same house, all boarding together, but with separate sitting-rooms.

Dolores' first walk was to see Miss Hackett. It was quite startling to find the good old lady looking exactly the same as when she had come to luncheon at Silverfold, and arranged for G. F. S., and weakly stood up for her sister nine years previously, those years which seemed ages long ago to the maiden who had made the round of the world since, while the lady had only lived in her Casement Cottage, and done almost the same things day by day.

There was one exception, however, Constance had married a union doctor in the neighbourhood. She came into Silverton to see her old acquaintance, and looked older and more commonplace than Dolores could have thought possible, and her talk was no longer of books and romances, but of smoking chimneys, cross landlords, and troublesome cooks, and the wicked neglects of her vicar's and her squire's wife. As Dolores walked back to Silverton, she heard drums and trumpets, and was nearly swept away by a rushing stream of little boys and girls. Then came before her an elephant, with ornamental housing and howdah, and a train of cars, meant to be very fine, but way-worn and battered, with white and piebald steeds, and gaudy tinselly drivers, and dames in scarlet and blue, much needing a washing, distributing coloured sheets about the grand performance to take place that night at eight o'clock, of the Sepoy's Death Song and the Bleeding Bride.

Miss Vincent had asked Miss Hackett to supper, and prepared herself and her fellow-teacher, Miss Calton, for a pleasant evening of talk, but to her great surprise, Dolores expressed her intention of going to the performance at the circus.

"My dear," said Miss Vincent, "this is a very low affair—not Sanger's, nor anything so respectable. They have been here before, and the lodging-house people went and were quite shocked."

"Yes," said Dolores, "but that is all the more reason I want to go. There is a girl with them in whom we are very much interested. She was kidnapped from Rockquay at the time this circus was there. At least I am almost sure it is the same, and I must see if she is there."

"But if she is you cannot do anything."

"Yes, I can; I can let her brother know. It must be done, Miss Vincent. I have promised, and it is of fearful consequence."

"Should you know her?"

"Oh yes. I have often talked to her in Mrs. Henderson's class. I could not mistake her."

Miss Hackett was so much horrified at the notion of a G. F. S. "business girl" being in bondage to a circus, that she gallantly volunteered to go with Miss Mohun, and Miss Vincent could only consent.

The place of the circus was an open piece of ground lying between Silverton and Silverfold, and thither they betook themselves—Miss Hackett in an old bonnet and waterproof that might have belonged to any woman, and Dolores wearing a certain crimson ulster, which she had bought in Auckland for her homeward voyage, and which her cousins had chosen to dub as "the Maori." After a good deal of jostling and much scent of beer and bad tobacco they achieved an entrance, and sat upon a hard bench, half stifled with the odours, to which were added those of human and equine nature and of paraffin. As to the performance, Dolores was too much absorbed in looking out for Ludmilla, together with the fear that Miss Hackett might either faint or grow desperate, and come away, to attend much to it; and she only was aware that there was a general scurrying, in which the horses and the elephant took their part; and that men and scantily dressed females put themselves in unnatural positions; that there was a firing of pistols and singing of vulgar songs, and finally the hero and heroine made their bows on the elephant's back.

Miss Hackett wanted to depart before the Bleeding Bride came on, but Dolores entreated her to stay, and she heroically endured a little longer. This seemed, consciously or not, to be a parody of the ballad of Lord Thomas and Fair Annet, but of course it began with an abduction on horseback and a wild chase, in which even the elephant did his part, and plenty more firing. Then the future bride came on, supposed to be hawking, during which pastime she sang a song standing upright on horseback, and the faithless Lord Thomas appeared and courted her with the most remarkable antics of himself and his piebald steed.

The forsaken Annet consoled herself with careering about, taking a last leave of her beloved steed—a mangy-looking pony—and performing various freaks with it, then singing a truculent song of revenge, in pursuance of which she hid herself to await the bridal procession. And as the bride came on, among her attendants Dolores detected unmistakably those eyes of Gerald's! She squeezed Miss Hackett's hand, and saw little more of the final catastrophe. Somehow the bride was stabbed, and fell screaming, while the fair Annet executed a war dance, but what became of her was uncertain. All Dolores knew was, that Ludmilla was there! She had recognized not only the eyes, but the air and figure.

When they got free of the crowd, which was a great distress to poor Miss Hackett, Dolores said—

"Yes, it is that poor girl! She must be saved!"

"How? What can you do?"

"I shall telegraph to her brother. You will help me, Miss Hackett?"

"But—what—who is her brother?" said Miss Hackett, expecting to hear he was a carpenter perhaps, or at least a clerk.

"Mr. Underwood of Vale Leston—Gerald Underwood," answered Dolores. "His father made an unfortunate marriage with a singer. She really is his half-sister, and I promised to do all I could to help him to find her and save her. He is at Oxford. I shall telegraph to him the first thing to-morrow."

There was nothing in this to object to, and Miss Hackett would not be persuaded not to see her to the door of Miss Vincent's lodgings, though lengthening her own walk—alone, a thing more terrible to her old-fashioned mind than to that of her companion.

Dolores wrote her telegram—

"Dolores Mohun, Valentia, Silverton, to Gerald Underwood, Trinity College, Oxford. Ludmilla here. Circus. Come."

She sent it with the more confidence that she had received a letter from her father with a sort of conditional consent to her engagement to Gerald, so that she could, if needful, avow herself betrothed to him; though her usual reticence made her unwilling to put the matter forward in the present condition of affairs. She went out to the post-office at the first moment when she could hope to find the telegraph office at work, and just as she had turned from it, she met a girl in a dark, long, ill-fitting jacket and black hat, with a basket in her hand.

"Lydia!" exclaimed Dolores, using the old Rockquay name.

"Miss Dolores!" she cried.

"Yes, yes. You are here! I saw you last night."

"Me! Me! Oh, I am ashamed that you did. Don't tell Mr. Flight."

There were tears starting to her eyes.

"Can I do anything for you?"

"No—no. Oh, if you could! But they have apprenticed me."

"Who have?"

"My mother and Mr. O'Leary."

"Are they here?"

"Yes. They wanted money—apprenticed me to this Jellicoe! I must make haste. They sent me out to take something to the wash, and buy some fresh butter. They must not guess that I have met any one."

"I will walk with you. I have been telegraphing to your brother that I have found you."

"Oh, he was so good to me! And Mr. Flight, I was so grieved to fail him. They made me get up and dress in the night, and before I knew what I was about I was on the quay—carried out to the ship. I had no paper—no means of writing; I was watched. And now it is too dreadful! Oh, Miss Dolores! if Mrs. Henderson could see the cruel positions they try to force on me, the ways they handle me—they hurt so; and what is worse, no modest girl could bear the way they go on, and want me to do the same. I could when I was little, but I am stiffer now, and oh! ashamed. If I can't—they starve me—yes, and beat me, and hurt me with their things. It is bondage like the Israelites, and I don't want to get to like it, as they say I shall, for then—then there are those terrible songs to be sung, and that shocking dress to be shown off in. My mother will not help. She says it is what she went through, and all have to do, and that I shall soon leave off minding; but oh, I often think I had rather die than grow like— like Miss Bellamour. I hope I shall (they often frighten me with that horse), only somehow I can't wish to be killed at the moment, and try to save myself. And once I thought I would let myself fall, rather than go on with it, but I thought it would be wicked, and I couldn't. But I have prayed to God to help me and spare me; and now He has heard. And will my brother be able—or will he choose to help me?"

"I am sure of it, my poor dear girl. He wishes nothing more."

"Please turn this way. They must not see me speak to any one."

"One word more. How long is the circus to be here?"

"We never know; it depends on the receipts—may go to-morrow. Oh, there —"

She hurried on without another word, and Dolores slowly returned to Miss Vincent's lodgings. Her lecture was to be given at three o'clock, but she knew that she should have to be shown the school and class-rooms in the forenoon. Gerald, as she calculated the trains, might arrive either by half-past twelve or a quarter past four.

Nervously she endured her survey of the school, replying to the comments as if in a dream, and hurrying it over, so as must have vexed those who expected her to be interested. She dashed off to the station, and reached it just in time to see the train come in. Was it—yes, it was Gerald who sprang out and came towards her.

"Dolores! My gallant Dolores! You have found her!"

"Yes, but in cruel slavery—apprenticed."

"That can be upset. Her mother—is she here?"

"Yes, and O'Leary. They sold her, apprenticed her, and these people use her brutally. She told me this morning. No, I don't think you can get at her now."

"I will see her mother at any rate. I may be able to buy her off. Where shall I find you?"

Dolores told him, but advised him to meet her at Miss Hackett's, whom she thought more able to help, and more willing than Miss Vincent, in case he was able to bring Ludmilla away with him.

"Have you heard from my father?"

"Yes—what I expected."

"But it will make no difference in the long run."

"Dearest, do I not trust your brave words? From Trieste I hear that the endeavour of Benista to recover his wife is proved. There's one step of the chain. Is it dragging us down, or setting us free?"

"Free—free from the perplexities of property," cried Dolores. "Free to carve out a life."

"Certainly I have wished I was a younger son. Only if it could have come in some other way!"

Dolores had to go to luncheon at Miss Vincent's, and then to deliver her lecture. It was well that she had given it so often as almost to know it by heart, for the volcano of anxiety was surging high within her.

As she went out she saw Gerald waiting for her, and his whole mien spoke of failure.

"Failed! Yes," he said. "The poor child is regularly bound to that Jellicoe, the master of the concern, for twenty-five pounds, the fine that my uncle brought on the mother, as O'Leary said with a grin, and she is still under sixteen."

"Is there no hope till then?"

"He and O'Leary declare there would be breach of contract if she left them even then. I don't know whether they are right, but any amount of mischief might be done before her birthday. They talk of sending her to Belgium to be trained, and that is fatal."

"Can't she be bought off?"

"Of course I tried, but I can't raise more than seventy pounds at the utmost just now."

"I could help. I have twenty-three pounds. I could give up my term."

"No use. They know that I shall not be of age till January, besides the other matter. I assured them that however that might end, my uncles would honour any order I might give for the sake of rescuing her, but they laughed the idea to scorn. O'Leary had the impudence to intimate, however, that if I chose to accept the terms expressed, 'his wife might be amenable.'"

"They are?"

"Five hundred for evidence on the previous marriage in my favour; but I am past believing a word that she says, at least under O'Leary's dictation. She might produce a forgery. So I told him that my uncle was investigating the matter with the consul in Sicily; and the intolerable brutes sneered more than over at the idea of the question being in the hands of the interested party, when they could upset that meddling parson in a moment."

"Can nothing be done?"

"I thought of asking one of your old ladies whether there is a lawyer or Prevention of Cruelty man who could tell me whether the agreement holds, but I am afraid she is too old. You saw no mark of ill-usage?"

"Oh no. They would be too cunning."

"If we could help her to escape what a lark it would be!"

"I do believe we could" cried Dolores. "If I could only get a note to her! And this red ulster! I wonder if Miss Hackett would help!"

Dolores waited for Miss Hackett, who had lingered behind, and told her as much of the facts as was expedient. There was a spice of romance in the Hackett soul, and the idea of a poor girl, a G. F. S. maiden, in the hands of these cruel and unscrupulous people was so dreadful that she was actually persuaded to bethink herself of means of assistance.

"Where did you meet the girl?" she said. Dolores told her the street.

"Ah! depend upon it the things were with Mrs. Crachett, who I know has done washing for people about on fair-days, when they can't do it themselves. She has a daughter in my G. F. S. class; I wonder if we could get any help from her."

It was a very odd device for a respectable associate and member of G. F. S. to undertake, but if ever the end might justify the means it was on the present occasion. Fortune favoured them, for Melinda Crachett was alone in the house, ironing out some pale pink garments.

"Are you washing for those people on the common, Melinda?" asked Miss Hackett.

"Yes, Miss Hackett. They want them by seven o'clock to-night very particular, and they promised me a seat to see the performance, miss, if I brought them in good time, and I wondered, miss, if you would object."

"Only tell me, Melinda, whom you saw."

"I saw the lady herself, ma'am, the old lady, when I took the things."

"No young person?"

"Yes, ma'am. It was a very nice young lady indeed that brought me down this pink tunic, because it got stained last night, and she said her orders was to promise me a ticket if it came in time; but, oh my! ma'am, she looked as if she wanted to tell me not to come."

"Poor girl! She is a G. F. S. member, Melinda, and I do believe you would be doing a very good deed if you could help us to get her away from those people."

Melinda's eyes grew round with eagerness. She had no doubts respecting what Miss Hackett advised her to do, and there was nothing for it but to take the risk. Then and there Dolores sat down and pencilled a note, directing

Ludmilla to put on the red ulster after her performance, if possible, when people were going away, and slip out among them, joining Melinda, who would convey her to Miss Hackett's. This was safer than for Gerald to be nearer, since he was liable to be recognized. Still it was a desperate risk, and Dolores had great doubts whether she should ever see her red Maori again.

So in intense anxiety the two waited in Miss Hackett's parlour, where the good lady left them, as she said, to attend to her accounts, but really with an inkling or more of the state of affairs between them. Each had heard from New Zealand, and knew that Maurice Mohun was suspending his consent till he had heard farther from home, both as to Gerald's character and prospects, and there was no such absolute refusal, even in view of his overthrow of the young man's position, as to make it incumbent on them to break off intercourse. Colonial habits modified opinion, and to know that the loss was neither the youth's own fault nor that of his father, would make the acceptance a question of only prudence, provided his personal character were satisfactory. Thus they felt free to hold themselves engaged, though Gerald had further to tell that his letters from Messina purported that an old priest had been traced out who had married the impresario, Giovanni Benista, a native of Piedmont, to Zoraya Prebel, Hungarian, in the year 1859, when ecclesiastical marriages were still valid without the civil ceremony.

"Another step in my descent," said Gerald. "Still, it does not prove whether this first husband was alive. No; and Piedmont, though a small country, is a wide field in which to seek one who may have cut all connection with it. However, these undaunted people of mine are resolved to pursue their quest, and, as perhaps you have heard, are invited to stay at Rocca Marina for the purpose."

"I should think that was a good measure; Mr. White gets quarry-men from all the country round, and would be able to find out about the villages."

"But how unlikely it is that one of these wanderers would have kept up intercourse with his family! They may do their best to satisfy the general conscience, but I see no end to it."

"And a more immediate question—what are we to do with your sister if she escapes to-night? Shall I take her to Mrs. Henderson?"

"She would not be safe there. No, I must carry her straight to America, the only way to choke off pursuit."

"You! Your term!"

"Never mind that. I shall write to the Warden pleading urgent private business. I have enough in hand for our passage, and the 'Censor' will take my articles and give me an introduction. I shall be able to keep myself and her. I have a real longing to see Fiddler's Ranch."

"But can you rough it?" asked Dolores, anxiously looking at his delicate girlish complexion and slight figure.

"Oh yes! I was born to it. I know what it was when Fiddler's Ranch was far from the civilization of Violinia, as they call it now. I don't mean to make a secret of it, and grieve your heart or Cherie's. She has had enough of that, but I must make the plunge to save my sister, and if things come round it will be all the better to have some practical knowledge of the masses and the social problems by living among them."

"Oh that I could make the experiment with you!"

"You will be my inspiration and encouragement, and come to me in due time."

He came round to her, and she let him give her his first kiss.

"God will help us," she said reverently; "it is the cause of uprightness and deliverance from cruel bondage."

The plans had been settled; Gerald had arranged with a cab which was to take him and his sister to a house five miles out in the country, of which Miss Hackett had given the name, so that they might seem to have been spending the evening with her. Thence it was but a step to the station of a different railway from that which went through Silverton, and they would go by the mail train to London, where Ludmilla could be deposited at Mrs. Grinstead's house at Brompton, where Martha could provide her with an outfit, while Gerald saw the editor of the 'Censor', got some money from the bank, telegraphed to Oxford for his baggage, and made ready to start the next morning for Liverpool, whither he had telegraphed to secure a second-class passage to New York for G. F. Wood and Lydia Wood, the names which he meant to be called by.

"The first name I knew," he said, "the name of Tom Wood, is far more real to me or my father than Edgar Underwood ever could be."

He promised that Dolores should have a telegram at Clipstone by the time she reached it, for she had to give her second lecture the next day, and was to return afterwards. All this had been discussed over and over again, and there had been many quakings and declarations that the scheme had failed, and that neither girl could have had courage, nor perhaps adroitness, and that the poor prisoner had been re-captured. Gerald had made more than one expedition into the little garden to listen, and had filled the house with cold air before he returned, sat down in a resigned fashion, and declared—

"It is all up! That comes of trusting to fools of girls."

"Hark!"

He sprang up and out into the vestibule. Miss Hackett opened the door into the back passage. There stood the "red mantle" and Melinda Crachett. Gerald took the trembling figure in his arms with a brotherly kiss.

"My little sister," he said, "look to me," then gave her to Dolores, who led her into the drawing-room, and put her into an arm-chair.

She could hardly stand, but tried to jump up as Miss Hackett entered.

"No, no, my poor child," she said, "sit still! Rest. Were you followed?"

"No; I don't think they had missed me."

She was so breathless that Miss Hackett would have given her a glass of wine, but she shook her head,

"Oh no, thank you! I've kept the pledge."

The tea-things were there, waiting for her arrival. Dolores would have helped her take off the red garment, but she shrank from it. She had only her gaudy theatrical dress beneath. How was she to go to London in it? However, Miss Hackett devised that she should borrow the little maid-servant's clothes, and Gerald undertook to send them back when Martha should have fitted her out at Brompton. The theatrical costume Miss Hackett would return by a messenger without implicating Melinda Crachett. They took the girl up-stairs to effect the change, and restore her as much as they could, and she came down with her rouge washed off, and very pale, but looking like herself, as, poor thing, she always did look more or less frightened, and now with tears about her eyelids, tears that broke forth as Gerald went up to her, took her by the hand, and said—

"Brighten up, little sister; you have given yourself to me, and I must take care of you now."

"Ah, I do beg your pardon, but my poor mother—I didn't know—"

"You don't want to go back?"

"Oh no, no," and she shuddered again; "but I am sorry for her. She has such a hard master, and she used to be good to me."

Miss Hackett had come opportunely to make her drink some tea, and then made both take food enough to sustain them through the night journey. Then, and afterwards, they gathered what had been Ludmilla's sad little story. Her father, in spite of his marriage, which was according to the lax notions of German Protestants, had been a fairly respectable man, very fond of his little daughter, and exceedingly careful of her, though even as a tiny child he had made her useful, trained her to singing and dancing, and brought her forward as a charming little fairy, when it was all play to her.

"Oh, we were so happy in those days," she said tearfully.

When he died it was with an injunction to his wife not to bring up Ludmilla to the stage now that he was not there to take care of her. With the means he had left she had set up her shop at Rockquay, and though she had never been an affectionate mother, Ludmilla had been fairly happy, and had been a favourite with Mr. Flight and the school authorities, and had been thoroughly imbued with their spirit. A change had, however, come over her mother ever since an expedition to Avoncester, when she had met O'Leary. She had probably always contrived a certain amount of illicit trade in tobacco and spirits by means of the sailors in the foreign traders who put into the little harbour of Rockquay; but her daughter was scarcely cognizant of this, and would not have understood the evil if she had done so, nor did it affect her life. O'Leary had, however, been the clown in Mr. Schnetterling's troupe, and had become partner with Jellicoe. The sight of him revived all Zoraya's Bohemian inclinations, and on his side he knew her to have still great capabilities, and recollected enough of her little daughter to be sure that she would be a valuable possession. Moreover, Mrs. Schnetterling had carriedher contraband traffic a little too far, especially where the boys of the preparatory school were concerned. She began to fear the gauger and the policeman, and she had consented to marry O'Leary at the Avoncester register office, meaning to keep the matter a secret until she could wind up her affairs at Rockquay. Even her daughter was kept in ignorance.

Two occurrences had, however, precipitated matters. One was the stir that Clement had made about the school-boys' festival, ending in the fine being imposed; the other, the discovery that the graceful, well-endowed young esquire was the child who had been left to probable beggary with a dying father twenty years previously.

Jellicoe, the principal owner of the circus, advanced the money for thefine, on condition of the girl and her mother becoming attached to the circus; and the object of O'Leary was to make as much profit as possible out of the mystery that hung over the young heir of Vale Leston. His refusal to attend to the claim on him, together with spite at his uncle, as having brought about the prosecution, and to Mr. Flight for hesitating to remunerate the girl for the performance that was to have been free; perhaps too certain debts and difficulties, all conspired to occasion the midnight flitting in such a manner as to prevent the circus from being pursued.

Thenceforth poor Lida's life had been hopeless misery, with all her womanly and religious instincts outraged, and the probability of worse in future. Jellicoe, his wife, and O'Leary had no pity, and her mother very little, and no principle; and she had no hope, except that release might come by some crippling accident. Workhouse or hospital would be deliverance, since thence she could write to Mrs. Henderson.

She shook and trembled still lest she should be pursued, though Miss Hackett assured her that this was the last place to be suspected, and it was not easy to make her eat. Presently Gerald stood ready to take her to the cab.

Dolores came to the gate with them. There was only space for a fervent embrace and "God bless you!" and then she stood watching as they went away into the night.

CHAPTER XXVIII. — ROCCA MARINA

It was a late autumn or winter day, according to the calendar, when The Morning Star steamed up to the quay of Rocca Marina, but it was hard to believe it, for all the slope of one of the Maritime Alps lay stretched out basking in the noonday sunshine, green and lovely, wherever not broken by the houses below, or the rocks quarried out on the mountain side. Some snow lay on the further heights, enough to mark their forms, and contrast with the soft sweetness of the lap of the hills and the glorious Mediterranean blue.

Anna and Franceska stood watching and exclaiming in a trance of delight, as one beauty after another revealed itself—the castellated remnant of the old tower, the gabled house with stone balconies and terraces, with parapets and vases below, the little white spire of the church tower of the English colony, looking out of the chestnut and olive groves above, and the three noble stone pines that sheltered the approach.

Mr. White, in his launch, came out with exulting and hearty welcome to bring them ashore, through the crowd of feluccas, fishing-vessels, and one or two steamers that filled the tiny bay, and on landing, the party found an English wagonette drawn by four stout mules waiting to receive them— mules, as being better for the heights than horses.

Anna and Franceska insisted on walking with Mr. White and Sir Robert, and they fairly frisked in the delicious air of sea and mountain after being so long cramped on board ship, stopping continually with screams of delight over violets or anemones, or the views that unfolded themselves as they went higher and higher. The path Mr. White chose was a good deal steeper than the winding carriage road cut out of the mountain side, and they arrived before the mules with Mrs. Grinstead and her brother, at the Italian garden, with a succession of broad terraces protected and adorned with open balustrades, with vases of late blooming flowers at intervals, and broad stone steps, guarded by carved figures, leading from one to another.

"It is like Beauty's palace," sighed out in delight Francie to her sister.

"There's Beauty," laughed Anna, as at the open window upon the highest verandah-shaded balcony appeared the darkly handsome Maura and Mrs. White, her small features as pretty as ever, but her figure a good deal more embonpoint than in Rockquay times.

Hers was a very warm welcome to the two sisters and their friend, and to the others who reached the front door a few minutes later. Such an arrival was very pleasant to her, for it must be confessed that, save for the English visitors, who were always gladly received, the life at Rocca Marina was a dull one, in spite of its being near enough to San Remo by the railway for expeditions for a day.

Within, the dwelling was a combination of the old Italian palace with English comforts. Mr. White, in his joy at possessing his graceful lady wife, had spared no expense in making it a meet bower for her, and Geraldine was as much amused as fascinated by the exquisiteness of all around her; as she sat, in a most luxurious chair, looking out through the open window at the blue sea, yet with a lively wood fire burning under a beauteous mantelpiece; statues, pictures, all that was recherche around, while they drank their English tea out of almost transparently delicate cups, filled by Maura out of a beautifully chased service of plate on a marble mosaic table.

"And now you must let me show you your rooms," said Mrs. White. "I thought you would like to have them en suite, for I am such a poor creature that I cannot breakfast down-stairs, and Mr. White is obliged to be out early."

So she led the way through a marble hall, pillared in different colours, rich and rare, with portraits of ancient Contes and Contessas on the walls, up a magnificent stone stair with a carved balustrade, to a suite indeed, where, at the entrance, Sibby was found very happy at her welcome from Mrs. Mount, who was equally glad to receive a countrywoman.

There was a sitting-room with a balcony looking out on the bay, a study and bedroom beyond for Clement on one side, and on the other charmingly fitted rooms for Geraldine, for her nieces, and her maid; and Mrs. White left them, telling them the dinner hour, and begging them to call freely and without scruple for all and everything they could wish for. Nothing would be any trouble.

"We have even an English doctor below there," she said, pointing to the roofs of the village. "There are so many accidents that Mr. White thought it better to be provided, so we have a little hospital with a trained nurse."

It was all very good, very kind, yet the very family likeness to Lilias Merrifield and Jane Mohun made Geraldine think how much more simple in manner one of them would have been without that nouveau riche tone of exultation.

"Here is a whole packet of letters," ended Mrs. White, "that came for you these last two or three days."

She pointed to a writing-table and went away, while the first letters so amazed Geraldine that she could think of nothing else, and hastened to summon Clement.

It was from Gerald, posted by the pilot from on board the steamer, very short, and only saying—

"DEAREST CHERIE,

"I know you will forgive me, or rather see that I do not need pardon for rescuing my sister. Anywhere in England she would be in danger of being reclaimed to worse than death. Dolores will tell you all the situation, and I will send a letter as soon as we arrive at New York. No time for more, except that I am as much as ever

"Your own, my Cherie's own,

"GERALD."

There followed directions how to send letters to him through the office of the 'Censor'.

Then she opened, written on the same day, a letter from Dolores Mohun, sent in obedience to his telegram, when he found that time for details failed him. It began—

"DEAR MRS. GRINSTEAD,

"I know you will be shocked and grieved at the step that your nephew has taken, but when you understand the circumstances, I think you will see that it was unavoidable for one of so generous and self-sacrificing a nature. I may add, that my aunt Lily is much touched, and thoroughly approves, and my uncle Jasper says imprudence is better than selfishness."

After this little preamble ensued a full and sensible account of Ludmilla's situation and sufferings at the circus, and the history of her escape, demonstrating (to the writer's own satisfaction) that there was no other means of securing the poor child.

Of course the blow to Geraldine was a terrible one.

"We have lost him," she said.

"That does not follow," said Clement. "It is quite plain that he does not mean to cut himself off from us, and America is not out of reach."

"It is just the restless impatience that you warned him against. As if he could not have taken her to the Hendersons."

"She would not have been safe there, unless acts of cruelty could have been proved.”

“Or to us, out here.”

“My dear Cherry, imagine his sudden arrival with such an appendage! I really think the boy has acted for the best.”

“Giving up Oxford too!”

“That can be resumed.”

“And most likely that wretched little girl will run off in a month’s time. It is in the blood.”

“Come, come, Cherry. I can’t have you in this uncharitable mood.”

“Then I mustn’t say what I think of that Dolores abetting him.”

“No, I like her letter.”

It fell hard upon Geraldine to keep all to herself, while entertained in full state by her hosts. Perhaps Adeline would have liked something on a smaller scale, for she knew what was ostentatious; but though Mr. White had once lived in a corner of the castle, almost like an artisan; since he had married, it had become his pride to treat his guests on the grandest London scale, and the presence of Sir Robert Audley for one night evoked all his splendours. He made excuses for having no one to meet the party but the chaplain and his wife and the young doctor, who he patronizingly assured them was “quite the gentleman,” and Theodore White—“Just to fill up a corner and amuse the young ladies.” Theodore had been lately sent out, now a clerk, soon to be a partner; but he was very shy, and did not amuse the young ladies at all! Indeed, he was soon so smitten with admiration for Franceska, that he could do nothing but sit rapt, looking at her under his eyelids.

The chaplain had received an offer of preferment in England, and was anxious to go home as soon as possible. Clement was now so well, that after assisting the next day in the week’s duties among the people, and at the pretty little church that Mr. White had built, he ventured to accept the proposal of becoming a substitute until the decision was made or another chaplain found. He was very happy to be employed once more in his vocation.

The climate suited him exactly, and the loan of the chaplain’s house would relieve him and Geraldine from the rather oppressive hospitality of the castle. The search for Benista’s antecedents would of course go on with the assistance of Mr. White and his Italian foreman, but both assured him that the inquiry might be protracted, as winter was likely to cut off the communications with many parts of the interior, and many of the men would be at their distant homes till the spring advanced.

Meantime, Geraldine and her nieces had a home life, reading, studying Italian, drawing with endless pleasure, and the young ones walking about the chestnut-covered slopes. She sat in the gardens or drove with Mrs. White in her donkey-chaise, and would have been full of enjoyment but for the abiding anxiety about Gerald. It was rather a relief not to be living in the same house with the Whites, whose hospitality and magnificence were rather oppressive. Mr. White wanted to have everything admired, and its cost appreciated; and Adeline, though clever enough, had provoking similarities and dissimilarities to her sisters. The same might be said of Maura, to whom Francie at first took a great fancy, but Anna, who had seen more of the world, had a sense of distrust.

"There's something fawning about her ways," said she, "and I don't know whether she is quite sincere."

"Perhaps it is only being half Greek," said Geraldine.

However, the two families met every day, and Mrs. White called their intercourse "such a boon, such a charming friendship," all unaware that there was no real confidence or affection.

They had not long been seated when the little Italian messenger boy brought them a budget of letters. Of course the first that Geraldine opened was in her nephew's writing. It had been written at intervals throughout the voyage, and finished on landing at New York.

Passing over the expressions of unabated affection, and explanation of the need of removing Ludmilla out of reach of her natural guardians, with the date on the second day of the voyage, the diary continued:

"Whom, as the fates would have it, should I have encountered but the Cacique! Yes, old Fernan and Marilda have the stateliest of staterooms in this same liner, and he was as much taken aback as I was when we ran against one another over a destitute and disconsolate Irish family in the steerage. Marilda is as yet invisible, as is my poor little Lida. It is unlucky, for the good man is profuse in his offers of patronage, and I don't mean to be patronized."

Then, after some clever descriptions of the fellow second-class passengers in his own lively vein, perhaps a little forced, so as not to betray more than he intended, that he felt them uncongenial, there came—

"Lida is up again; she is a sweet little patient person, and I cannot withstand Fernan's wish to present her to his wife, who remains prostrate at present, and will till we get out of the present stiff breeze and its influences.

"12th.—The presentation is over, and it has ended in Lida devoting herself to the succour of Marilda, and likewise of her maid, who is a good deal worse than herself.

<hr>

"16th.—These amiable folks want to take Lida off with them, not to say myself, to their 'Underwood' in the Rockies; but I don't intend her to be semi-lady's-maid, semi-companion, as she is becoming, but to let her stand on her own legs, or mine, and put her to a good school at New York. I have finished an article on 'Transatlantic Travellers' for the 'Censor', also some reviews, and another paper that may pave my way to work in New York or elsewhere. My craving is for the work of hard hands, but I look at mine, and fear I run more to the brain than the hands. My father must have been of finer physique than the Sioux bullet left to me; but I have no fears."

"No, indeed," sighed Geraldine; "he has not the fine athletic strength of his dear father, but still—still I think there is that in him which Edgar had not."

"Force of character," said Clement, "even if he is wrong-headed. Here is Fernan's letter—

"'Imagine my amazement at finding Gerald on board with us. He tells me that you are aware of his escapade, so I need not explain it. He is not very gracious to either of us, and absolutely refuses all offers of assistance either for himself or his sister. However, I hope to be able to keep a certain watch over him without offending him, and to obviate some of the difficulties in his way, perhaps unknown to him. Marilda has, as usual, suffered greatly on the voyage, but the little Lida, as he calls her, has been most attentive and useful both to her and her maid, who was quite helpless, and much the worst of the two. My wife was much prejudiced against Lida at first, but has become very fond of her, and is sure that she is a thoroughly good girl—worth the sacrifice Gerald has made for her. In his independent mood, he will not hear of our offering a home to the poor child; but if, as I hope, your researches turn out in his favour, he may consent to let us find suitable education for her. At any rate, I promise Geraldine not to leave these two young things to their fate, though I may have to act secretly. I can never forget how I took him from his father's side, and the baptism almost in blood. We go to New Orleans first, and after the cold weather home, but letters to the Bank will find us.'"

"Good, dear old Fernan and Marilda!" cried Geraldine, "I can see their kindness, and how, with all their goodness, it must jar on Gerald's nerves."

"I hope he won't be an ass," returned Clement. "Such patient goodness ought not to be snubbed by—" He caught his sister's eye, and made his last words "youthful theorists."

Mrs. Henderson too forwarded a letter from Lida, being sure that it would be a great pleasure to Mrs. Grinstead. It went into many more particulars about the miseries of the circus training than had been known before, and the fears and hints which made it plain that it had been quite right to avail herself of the means of escape; after which was added—

"I never thought to be so happy as I am here. My brother is the noblest, most generous, most kind of creatures, and that he should do all this for me, after all the harm he has suffered from my poor mother! It quite overpowers me when I think of it. I see a tear has dropped, but it is such a happy one. Please tell Mr. Flight what peace and joy this is to me, after all my prayers and trying to mind what he said. There are such a gentleman and lady here, cousins to my brother, Sir Ferdinand and Lady Travis Underwood. She has been more or less ill all through the voyage, and her maid worse, and she has let me do what I could for her, and has been kindness itself. They were at the bazaar. Did you see Sir Ferdinand? He is the very grandest and handsomest man I ever did see, and so good to all the poor emigrants in the steerage. He is very kind to me; but I see that my brother will not have me presume. They have bidden me write to them in any need. I never thought there could be so many good people out of Rockquay. Please give my duty to Mr. Flight and Lady Flight, good Miss Mohun, and dear Miss Dolores. I wear her ulster, and bless the thought of her."

CHAPTER XXIX. — ROWENA AND HER RIVAL

Letters continued to come with fair regularity; and it was understood that Gerald, with Lida, had taken up his quarters in an "inexpensive" boarding-house at New York, where he had sent Lida to a highly-recommended day-school, and he was looking out for employment. His articles had been accepted, he said; but the accounts of his adventures and of his fellow-inmates gave the sense that there was more humour in the retrospect than in the society, and that they were better to write about than to live with. He never confessed it, but to his aunt, who understood him, it was plain that he found it a different thing to talk philanthropic socialism, or even to work among the poor, and to live in the society of the unrefined equals.

Then he wrote that Lida had come one day and told him that one of the girls, with whom she had made friends, had a bad attack of cough and bronchitis, and could not fulfil an engagement that she had made to come and sing for a person who was giving lectures upon national music. "'I looked at some of her songs,' little Lida said in her humble way, 'and I know them. Don't you think, brother, I might take her part?' Well, not to put too fine a point upon it, it was not an unwelcome notion, for my articles, though accepted, don't bring in the speedy remuneration with which fiction beguiles the aspirant. Only one of them, which I send you, has seen the light, and the 'Censor' is slow, though sure, so dollars for immediate expenses run short. I called on the fellow, Mr. Gracchus B. Van Tromp, to see whether he were fit company for my sister, and I found him much superior to his name— gentlemanlike and intelligent, not ill-read, and pretty safe, like most Yankees, to know how to behave to a young girl. When he found I could accompany my sister on piano or violin he was transported. Moreover, he could endure to be enlightened by a Britisher on such little facts as the true history of Auld Robin Gray and the Wacht am Rhein. The lecture was a marked success. We have another tonight, 16th. It has resulted in a proposal to these two interesting performers to accompany the great Gracchus on a tour through the leading 'cities,' lecturing by turns with him and assisting. He has hitherto picked up as he could 'local talent,' but is glad of less uncertain help, and so far as appears, he is superior to jealousy, though he sees that I'm better read, 'and of the cut that takes the ladies.' It is no harm for Lida; she was not learning much, and I can cultivate her better when I have her to myself, and get her not to regard me so much like a lion, to be honoured with distant respect and obedience. We shall get dollars enough to keep us going till my talents break upon the world, and obtain stunning experiences for the 'Censor'. My father's dear old violin is coming to the front. Our first start will be at Boston; but continue to write to Gerald F. Wood, care of Editor of 'Cole's Weekly'."

"How like his father!" was the natural exclamation; but the details that followed in another week were fairly satisfactory, and the spirit of independence was a sound one, which had stood harder proofs than perhaps his home was allowed to know, though these were early days.

February was beginning to open the buds and to fill the slopes with delicate anemones, as well as to bring back Mr. White's workmen, among whom Clement could make inquiries. One young man knew the name of Benista as belonging to a family in a valley beyond his own, but it was not an easily accessible one, and a fresh fall of snow had choked the ravine, and would do so for weeks to come.

Yet all was lovely on the coast, and Mr. White having occasion to go to San Remo, offered to take the three girls with him.

"Young ladies always have a turn for shops," said he.

"I want to see the coast," said Franceska, with a little dignity.

"But I do want some gloves—and some blue embroidery silk, thank you, Mr. White," said Anna, more courteously.

"And I want some handkerchiefs, if Mr. White will take me too!" returned Uncle Clement in the same tone.

"I know so well what you mean, dear," observed Maura, sotto voce to Francie. "It is so trying to be supposed mere common-place, when one's thoughts are on the beautiful and romantic."

It was just one of the sayings that had begun to go against Francie's taste, and she answered—

"Mr. White is very good-natured."

"Ah, yes, but so—so—you know."

Francie was called, and left Mr. White's description to be unutterable.

The two elder ladies spent the day together, and Mrs. Grinstead then heard that Jane Mohun had written, that both Lord Ivinghoe and Lady Phyllis Devereux were recovering from the influenza, and that Lord Rotherwood had had a slight touch of the complaint.

"It is a very serious thing in our family," said Adeline, with all the satisfaction of having a family, especially with a complaint, and she began to enumerate the victims of the Devereux house and her own, only breaking off to exclaim, "I really shall write at once to beg them all to come here for the rest of the winter, March winds and all. My cousin Rotherwood has never been here, and they might be quite quiet among relations. So unlike a common health resort."

Mrs. White's hospitable anticipations were forestalled. The party came home from San Remo in high spirits. They had met Lord Rotherwood and his son in the street, they had been greeted most warmly, and brought to luncheon at the villa, where they found not only Lady Rotherwood and Phyllis, but Mysie Merrifield.

It was explained that their London doctor had strongly advised immediate transplantation before there was time to catch fresh colds, and a friend of the Marchioness, who permanently possessed a charming house at San Remo, had offered it just as it was for the spring. The journey had been made at once, with one deviation on Lord Rotherwood's part, to beg for Mysie, as an essential requisite to his "Fly's" perfect recovery. A visit had been due before, only deferred by the general illness, and no difficulty was made in letting it be paid in these new and delightful scenes. Phyllis had been there before. She was weak and languid, and would much rather have stayed at home, except for seeing Mysie's delight in the mountains and the blue Mediterranean, which she dimly remembered from her infancy at Malta. Only she made it a point of honour not to allow that the sea was bluer than the bay of Rockquay.

Ivinghoe was looking ill and disgusted, but brightened up at the sight of the visitors, and his mother, who thought Monte Carlo too near, though she had kept as far from it as possible, accepted the more willingly Mr. White's cordial invitation to come and spend a day or two at Rocca Marina. Trifles were so much out of the good lady's focus of vision that the possible dangers in that quarter never occurred to her, though Maura was demurely bridling, and Francie, all unawakened, but prettier than ever, was actually wearing a scarlet anemone that Ivinghoe had given to her.

In the intervening days, Rocca Marina was in a wonderful state of preparation. The master of it was genuinely and honestly kindly and simple-hearted, and had entertained noble travellers before, who had been attracted by his extensive and artistic works; but no words can describe the satisfaction of his wife. In part there was the heartfelt pleasure of receiving the cousin who had been like one of her brothers in the home of her childhood; but to this was added the glory of knowing that this same cousin was a marquis, and that the society of San Remo, nay of all the Riviera and the Italian papers to boot, would know that she was a good deal more than the quarry-owner's wife. Moreover, like all her family, there was a sense of Lady Rotherwood's coming from a different sphere, and treating them with condescension. Jane and Lily might laugh, but to Adeline it was matter of a sort of aggressive awe, half as asserting herself as "Victoria's" equal and relation, half as protecting her from inferior people.

Geraldine perceived and was secretly amused. Of course all the party dined at the castle on Saturday night, and heard some lamentations that there was no one else to meet the distinguished guests, for the young doctor was not thought worthy.

"But I knew you would like a family party best, and the Underwoods are— almost connections, though—"

In that "though" was conveyed their vast inferiority to the house of Mohun.

"I always understood that it was a very good old family," said Lady Rotherwood.

"Clement Underwood is one of the most valuable clergy in London," said her lord; "I am glad he is recovering. I shall be delighted to hear him again."

Maura was standing under the pergola with Lord Ivinghoe.

"And is not it sad for poor Franceska Vanderkist?—Oh! you know about poor Mr. Gerald Underwood?" said Maura, blushing a little at the awkward subject.

"Of course," said Ivinghoe impatiently. "He is in America, is he not? But what has she to do with it?"

"Oh, you know, after being his Mona, and all. It can't go any further till it is cleared up."

Phyllis and Mysie came up, asking Maura to tell them the name of a mountain peak with a white cap. The party came up to dinner, which was as genial and easy as the host and Lord Rotherwood could make it, and as stiff and grand as the hostess could accomplish, aided by the deftness and grace of her Italian servants. In the evening Theodore came up to assist in the singing of glees, and Clement's voice was a delightful and welcome sound in his sister's ears. Ivinghoe stood among the circle at the piano, and enjoyed. He and his sister were not particularly musical, but enough to enjoy those remarkable Underwood voices. After that Maura never promoted musical evenings.

An odd little Sunday-school for the children of the English workmen had been instituted at Rocca Marina, where Maura had always assisted the chaplain's wife, and Anna and Francie shared the work. Mysie heard of it with enthusiasm, for, as Ivinghoe told her, she was pining for a breath of the atmosphere, but she came down to enjoy the delights thereof alone, taking Maura's small class. Maura was supposed to be doing the polite to Lady Phyllis, but in point of fact Phyllis was lying down in the balcony of her mother's dressing-room, and Maura was gracefully fanning herself under a great cork tree, while Lord Ivinghoe was lying on the grass.

Francie looked languid, and said it was getting dreadfully hot, but Mrs. Grinstead took no notice, trusting that the cessation of attentions would hinder any feeling from going deeper, so that—as she could not help saying to herself—she might not have brought the poor child out of the frying-pan into the fire—not an elegant proverb, but expressing her feeling!

More especially did it do so, when she found that Lord Rotherwood was so much delighted with the beauty and variety of the marbles of Rocca Marina as to order a font to be made of them for the church that was being restored at Clarebridge, and he, and still more his son, found constant diversion in running over by train from San Remo to superintend the design, and to select the different colours and patterns of the stones as they were quarried out and bits polished so as to show their beauty. Their ladies often accompanied them, and these expeditions generally involved luncheon at the castle, and often tea at the parsonage, but it might be gradually observed, as time went on, that there was a shade of annoyance on the part of the great house at the preference sometimes unconsciously shown for the society of the smaller one.

Mysie openly claimed Anna as her own friend of some standing, and both she and Phyllis had books to discuss, botanical or geological discoveries to communicate or puzzle out, with Mrs. Grinstead or her nieces. Lord Rotherwood had many more interests in common with Clement Underwood than with Mr. White, and even the Marchioness, though more impartial and on her guard, was sensible to Mrs. Grinstead's charm of manner and depth of comprehension. She patronized Adeline, but respected Mrs. Grinstead as incapable of and insensible to patronage.

That her gentlemen should have found such safe and absorbing occupation in the opposite direction to Monte Carlo was an abiding satisfaction to her, and she did not analyze the charms of the place as regarded her son. She had seen him amused by other young ladies, as he certainly was now by that Miss White, who was very handsome and very obliging.

She knew and he knew all the antecedents too well for alarm, till one day she saw Maura's face, as she made him pull down a spray of banksia from the side of a stone wall, and watched the air of gallant courtesy with which he presented it.

Francie watched it too, as she had watched the like before, and said nothing, but there was an odd, dull sense of disappointment, and the glory had faded away from sea and sky, spring though it was. Yet there were pressures of the hand in greeting and parting, and kind, wistful looks, as if of sympathy, little services and little attentions, that set her foolish little heart bounding, in a way she was much ashamed to feel, and would have been more utterly ashamed to speak of, or to suppose observed. She only avowed to Anna that it was very warm, weary weather, and that she was tired of absence, and felt homesick, but Aunt Cherry was so kind that she must not be told.

Lady Rotherwood proposed moving away, but her husband and son would not hear of it till their font was finished.

It was not unwelcome to any one of the elder ladies that the young officer's leave would be over in another week. Geraldine was glad that Francie should be freed from the trial of seeing attention absorbed by Maura, and herself so often left in the lurch, so far as that young lady could contrive it, for though not a word was said, the brightened eye and glowing cheek, whenever Lord Ivinghoe brought her forward, or paid her any deference or civility, were dangerous symptoms. Peace of mind in so modest and innocent a maiden would probably come back when the excitement was once over.

As to Adeline, there was nothing she dreaded so much as the commotion that would be excited if Ivinghoe's flirtation came to any crisis. His mother would never forgive her, his father would hardly do so; she would feel like a traitor to the whole family, and all her attempts to put a check on endeavours on Maura's part to draw him on—an endeavour that began to be visible to her —were met by apparent unconsciousness or by tears. And when she ventured a word to her husband, he gruffly answered that his niece's father had been an officer in the army, and he could make it worth any one's while to take her! Young lords were glad enough in these days to have something to put into their pockets.

CHAPTER XXX. — DREAMS AND NIGHTINGALES

"Office of 'Lacustrian Intelligencer,'

"Jonesville, Ohio,

"March 20.

"DEAREST CHERIE,

"I told you in my last that the chief boss in the office at New York had written to me that he had been asked to send an intelligent young man to sub- edit the Lacustrian Intelligencer at Jonesville, a rising city on Lake Erie. I thought it would be worth while to look at it, especially as we were booked to give a lecture at Sandusky, and moreover our relations to Gracchus have been growing rather strained, and I do not think this wandering life good for Lida in the long run; nor are my articles paid enough for to be a dependence. So after holding forth at Sandusky, we took our passage in a little steamer which crosses the little bay in the Lake to Jonesville—one of those steamers just like a Noah's Ark.

"Presently Lida came up and touched me, saying in her little awestruck whisper (which has never been conquered), 'Brother, I am sure I saw one of mother's cigarettes.' I said 'Bosh!' thinking it an utter delusion; but she was so decided and so frightened, that I told her to go into the saloon, and went forward. A woman was going about the deck, offering the passengers a basket of candies, lights, cigarettes, and cigars. Saving for Lida's words, I never should have recognized her; she was thin to the last degree, haggard, yellow, excessively shabby and forlorn-looking, and with a hollow cough; but as her eyes met mine (those eyes that you say are our water-mark) both of us made a sort of leap as if to go overboard, and I went up to her at once, and would have spoken, but she cried out, 'What have you done with Lida?' I answered that she was safe, and demanded in my turn where were O'Leary and Jellicoe. 'Drowned, drowned,' she said, 'in the wreck of the Sirius. They'll never trouble you more. But Lida!' I thought that it was safe to take her into the saloon to see Lida, when they fell into each other's arms, and afforded the spectators a romantic spectacle. Don't think I am making a joke of it, for it was tragic enough in the result of the agitation. Blood was choking the poor woman. We could only lay her down on the couch, and happily there were lemons on board. There was a good-natured Irishman who gave me all the help he could, even to the carrying her to his house, where his wife was equally kind. He fetched the priest, a French Canadian, and the doctor, and Lida has been watching over her most tenderly; poor things—they seem really to have cared for one another, and Lida will be the happier for having done these last duties.

"21st. She is a little better. So far as we have gathered from one who must not talk nor be agitated, the circus had got into difficulties and debt to Bast, the van proprietor. I believe Lida's voice was their last hope, and they had some ghastly scheme of disposing of her in Belgium. When they lost her, their chances were over, and with the proceeds of their last exhibition, Jellicoe and the O'Leary pair left the elephant, etc., to take care of themselves and make their excuses to Mr. Bast, and started for Liverpool and the U. S. in the Sirius. Storms overtook them, the women were put into the first boat, those which followed were swamped. Poor fellows, I own I can't sing a pious dirge for them. There were three days of hunger and exposure before the boat was picked up, and she was finally landed at Quebec, where she was laid up with pleurisy in the hospital. And there was a subscription for the wrecked when she came out, which enabled her to set up this reminiscence of her old trade, drifting from one pier or boat to another till she came to this one, but all the time with this awful cough. The doctor thinks it her knell; her lungs are far gone, but she may probably rally in some degree for the summer, though hardly so as to be moved.

"That being the case, I have been to the Lacustrian office, and engaged myself to be its hack, since I must have some fixed pay while she lives. Perhaps I shall be able to do a little extra writing and lecturing, especially if she gets better, enough to spare Lida to help me. Her voice really is a lovely soprano, and draws wonderfully, but I don't want it to be strained too early. Our good Irishwoman, Mrs. Macbride, is willing to let us have her two rooms, left empty by her sons going west, and her daughter marrying, on fair terms, Lida promising to be a sort of help and to teach the children. We shall eat with them. I shall be at the office all day and half the night, so I don't need a sitting-room. Don't be anxious, dear old Cherie. We shall do very well, and it is only for a time. Lida is like a little angel, and as thankful for a smile from her mother as if she had been the reprobate runaway.

"Your ever-loving

"GERALD."

This was the letter that came to Mrs. Grinstead, and one with similar information went to Dolores Mohun at her college at Cambridge. Dolores, who had found Mysie much more sympathetic than Gillian, could not but write the intelligence to her, and Mysie was so much struck with the beauty of the much-injured brother and sister devoting themselves to their mother, that she could not help telling the family party at breakfast.

"That's right," said Lord Rotherwood. "The mother can clear up the doubt if any one can. Is there nothing about it?"

"No," replied Mysie; "I should think the poor woman was too ill to be asked."

"They must not let her slip through their fingers without telling," added Ivinghoe.

"I have a mind to run over to Rocca Marina and see what more they have heard there," said Lord Rotherwood. "I suppose your letter is from one of the girls there?"

"Oh no, it is from Dolores."

"Dolores! She is at Cambridge. Then this news must have been round by Clipstone! They must have known it for days past at Rocca!" exclaimed Lord Rotherwood.

"No," said Mysie, "this came direct to Dolores from Gerald Underwood himself.—Oh, didn't you know? I forgot, nobody was to know till Uncle Maurice gave his consent."

"Consent to what?" exclaimed Ivinghoe.

"To Dolores and Gerald! Oh dear, mamma said so much to me about not telling, but I did think Cousin Rotherwood knew everything. Please—"

Whatever she was going to ask was cut short by Ivinghoe's suddenly striking on the table so as to make all the cups and saucers ring as he exclaimed—

"If ever there lived a treacherous Greek minx!" Then, "I beg your pardon, mother."

He was off: they saw him dash out of the house. There was a train due nearly at this time, as all recollected.

"Papa, had not you better go with him?" said Lady Rotherwood.

"He will get on much better by himself, my dear," and Lord Rotherwood threw himself back in his chair and laughed heartily and merrily, to the amazement and mystification of the two girls. "You will have a beauty on your hands, my lady."

"Well, as long as it is not that horrid White girl—" said her ladyship, breaking off there.

"A very sorry Rebecca," said her lord, laughing the more.

But the Marchioness rose up, and the two cousins had to accept the signal.

The train, after the leisurely fashion of continental railways, kept Ivinghoe fuming at the station, and rattled along so as to give travellers a full view of the coast, more delightful to them than to the youth, who had rushed off with intentions, he scarce knew what, of setting right the consequences of Maura's —was it deception, or only a thought, of which the wish was father?

He reached the station that led to the works at Rocca Marina. The sun was high, the heat of the day coming on, and as he strode along, the workmen were leaving off to take their siesta at noontide. On he went, across the private walks in the terraced garden, not up the broad stone steps that led to the house, but to a little group of olive trees which cut off the chaplain's house from the castle gardens, and where stood a great cork tree, to whose branches a hammock had been fastened, and seats placed under it. As he opened the gate a little dog's bark was heard, and he was aware of a broad hat under the tree. Simultaneously a small Maltese dog sprang forward, and Francie's head rose from leaning over the little table with a start, her cheeks deeper rose than usual, having evidently gone to sleep over the thin book and big dictionary that lay before her.

"Oh!" she said, "it is you. Was I dreaming?"

"I am afraid I startled you."

"No—only"—she still seemed only half awake—"it seemed to come out of my dream."

"Then you were dreaming of me?"

"Oh no. At, least I don't know," she said, the colour flushing into her face, as she sat upright, now quite awake and alive to the question, between truthfulness and maidenly modesty.

"You were—you were; you don't deny it!" And as she hung her head and grew more distressfully redder and redder, "You know what that means."

"Indeed—indeed—I couldn't help—I never meant! Oh—"

It was an exclamation indeed, for Uncle Clement's head appeared above the hammock, where he too had been dozing over his book, with the words—

"Halloo, young people, I'm here!"

Franceska would have fled, but Ivinghoe held her hand so tight that she could not wrench it away. He held it, while Clement struggled to the ground, and then said—

"Sir, there is no reason you or all the world should not know how I love this dearest, loveliest one. I came here this morning hoping that she may grant me leave to try to win her to be my own."

He looked at Francie. Her head drooped, but she had not taken her hand away, and the look on her face was not all embarrassment, but there was a rosy sunrise dawning on it.

All Clement could say was something of "Your father."

"He knows, he understands; I saw it in his eyes," said Ivinghoe.

To Clement the surprise was far greater than it would have been to his sister, and the experience was almost new to him, but he could read Francie's face well enough to say—

"My dear, I think we had better let you run in and compose yourself, or go to your aunt, while I talk to Lord Ivinghoe."

Trembling, frightened, Francie was really glad to be released, as her lover with one pressure said—

"I shall see you again, sweetest."

She darted away, and Clement signed to Ivinghoe to sit down with him on the bench under the tree.

"I should like this better if you had brought your father's full assent," he said.

"There was no time. I only read his face; he will come to-morrow."

"No time?"

"Yes, to catch the train. I hurried away the moment I learnt that—that her affections were not otherwise engaged. I never saw any one like her. She has haunted me ever since those days at Rockquay; but—but I was told that she cared for your nephew, and I could not take advantage of him in his absence. And now I have but three days more."

"Whoever told you was under a great error," said Clement gravely, "and you have shown very generous self-command; but the advantages of this affair are so much the greatest on one side, that you cannot wonder if there is hesitation on our part, till we explicitly know that our poor little girl would not be unwelcome to your parents."

"I know that no one can compare with her for—for everything and anything," stammered Ivinghoe, breaking from his mother's language into his father's, "and my father admires her as much as I do—almost."

"But what will he and your mother say to her being absolutely penniless?"

"Pish!"

"And worse—child to a spendthrift, a man of no connection, except on his mother's side."

"She is your niece, your family have bred her up, made her so much more than exquisitely lovely."

"She is a good little girl," said Clement, "but what are we? No, Ivinghoe, I do not blame you for speaking out, and she will be the happier for the knowledge of your affection, but it will not be right of us to give free consent, without being fully assured of that of Lord and Lady Rotherwood."

Ivinghoe could only protest, but Clement rose to walk to the house, where his sister was sitting under the pergola in the agitation of answering Gerald's letter, and had only seen Francie flit by, calling to her sister in a voice that now struck her as having been strange and suppressed.

Clement trusted a good deal to his sister's quicker perceptions and habit of observation to guide his opinion in the affair that had burst on him, and was relieved that when Ivinghoe, like the well-bred young man that he was, went up to her, and taking her hand said, "I have been venturing to put my fate into the hands of your niece," she did not seem astonished or overwhelmed, but said—

"She is a dear good girl; I do hope it will be for her happiness—for both."

"Thank you," he said fervently. "It will be the most earnest desire of my life."

Geraldine thought it best to go in quest of Francie, whom she found with Anna, incoherent and happy in the glory of the certainty that she was loved, after the long trial of suppressed, unacknowledged suspense. No fears of parents, no thought of inequalities had occurred to trouble her—everything was absorbed in the one thought—"he really did love her." How should she thank God enough, or pray enough to be worthy of such joy? There was no room for vexation or wonder at the delay, nor the attentions paid to Maura. She hushed Anna, who was inclined to be indignant, and who was obliged afterwards to pour out to her aunt all her wonder, though she allowed that on his side there was nothing to be really called flirtation, it was all Maura—"she was sure Maura was at the bottom of it."

"My dear, don't let us be uncharitable; there is no need to think about it. Let us try to be like Francie, and swallow all up in gladness. Your mother—"

"Oh, I can't think what she will do for joy. It will almost make her well again."

"But remember, we don't know what his parents will say."

And with that sobering thought they had to go down to luncheon, where Francie sat blushing and entranced, too happy to speak, and Ivinghoe apparently contented to look at her. Afterwards he was allowed to take possession of her for the afternoon, so as to be able to tease her about what she was dreaming about him. After all it had probably been evoked by the dog's bark and his step; for she had thought a wolf was pursuing her, and that he had come to save her. It was quite enough to be food for a lover.

Clement would have wished to keep all to themselves, at least till the paternal visit was over, but Ivinghoe's days were few, and he made sure of bringing his parents on the morrow. An expedition had been arranged to the valley where some of the Benista family were reported to live, since the snows had departed enough for safety; but this must needs be deferred, and there was no doubt that the "reason why" would be sought out.

Indeed, so close was the great house, and so minute a watch was kept, that the fact of Lord Ivinghoe's spending the whole day at the parsonage was known, and conclusions were arrived at. Maura stole down in the late evening among the olive trees, ostensibly to ask Anna and Francie to come and listen to the nightingales.

But thereby she was witness to a scene that showed that there was another nightingale for Franceska than the one who was singing with such energy among the olive boughs. In fact, she saw the evening farewell, and had not the discretion, like Anna, to withdraw herself and her eyes, but beheld, what had ever been sacred to both those young things, the first kiss.

Poor Maura, she had none of the reticent pride and shame of an English gentlewoman. She believed herself cruelly treated, and rushing away, fell on Anna, who was hovering near, watching to prevent any arrival such as was always probable.

It would not be well to relate the angry, foolish words that Anna had to hear, nor how Maura betrayed herself and her own manoeuvre. It is enough to say that she went home, weeping demonstratively, perhaps uncontrollably; and that Anna, after her trying scene, was able to exalt more than ever Ivinghoe's generosity towards the absent Gerald, and forbearance towards Franceska. If he had ever passed the line, it was more Maura's doing than his own.

CHAPTER XXXI. — THE COLD SHOULDER

A telegram early the next day announced that the Rotherwood family were on their way, and they came in due time, the kind embrace that Francie received from each in turn being such as to set doubts at rest.

In fact, the dread, first of Monte Carlo, and secondly of Maura White, had done much to prepare the way with Lady Rotherwood. If she had first heard of her son's attachment to the pretty child who acted Mona, daughter to the upstart Vanderkists, and with a ruined father of no good repute, she would have held it a foolish delusion to be crushed without delay; but when this same attachment had lasted eight or nine months, and had only found avowal on the removal of a supposed rival; when, moreover, her darling had been ill, had revived at the aspect of the young lady, and had conducted himself in a place of temptation so as to calm an anxious mother's heart, she could see with his eyes, not only that Franceska was really beautiful, graceful, and a true lady, but likely to develop still more under favourable circumstances; that she had improved in looks, air, and manner on her travels, also that she had never been injured by any contact with undesirable persons, but had been trained by the excellent Underwoods, whose gentle blood and breeding were undeniable. Nor would "the daughter of the late Sir Adrian Vanderkist, Baronet, of Ironbeam Park," sound much amiss. He was so late, that his racing doings might be forgotten.

Indeed, as the Marchioness looked up to the castle, she felt that she could forgive a good deal to the damsel who had saved the family from the "sorry Rebecca," who had cried all night, and was still crying, whenever any more tears would come, and not getting much pity from any of her relatives. Mr. White told her that she was a little fool to have expected anything from a young swell; her brother said she might have known that it was absurd to expect that any one could look at her when Miss Franceska was by; and Mrs. White observed that it was wonderful to her to see so little respect shown for maiden dignity, as to endure to manifest disappointment. Adeline might speak from ample experience, and certainly her words had a salutary effect.

However, the Whites en famille were not quite the same externally. When Lord Rotherwood, after luncheon, went to see old White at the works, and look after his font, he met with a reception as stiff and cold as could well be paid to a distinguished customer who was not at all in fault; and for the first time Mr. White was too busy to walk back with him to the castle to see Adeline, whom he found, as usual, on a couch on the terrace in the shade of the house, a pretty picture among the flowers and vines. She was much more open with him, as became one who understood more of his point of view.

"Well, Rotherwood, I suppose I am to congratulate you, though it is scarcely a fair match in a worldly point of view."

"For which I care not a rap. She is a good, simple girl, and a perfect lady."

"And Victoria? May I ask, does not she think it a misalliance, considering what these Vanderkists are—and the Underwoods?"

"There's no one I respect more than Lancelot Underwood. As to Victoria, she is thankful that it is no worse."

"Ah! I know what you mean, but you can't wonder that my husband should feel it hard that there should have been some kind of flirtation. He is fond of Maura, you know, and he does feel that there must have been some slyness in some one to cause this affair to have been so suddenly sprung on us."

"Slyness—aye, I believe there was. Tell me, Ada, had you any notion that that lad, Gerald Underwood, was engaged to Dolores Mohun?"

"No; who told you?"

"Mysie let it out. She had been warned not to mention it till his position was ascertained, Maurice's consent and all."

"I must say Mysie should have spoken. It was not fair towards me to keep it back."

"Still less fair of Maura, if that's her name, to hint at attachment between Franceska and the boy. That was the embargo upon my poor fellow. He rushed off to have it out the moment he saw how matters stood."

"Well, it was a great shame; but girls are girls, especially with those antecedents, and Maura did not know to the contrary. You will believe me, Rotherwood, I never had any desire that she should succeed. I would have sent her away if I could; but you can't wonder that Mr. White is vexed, and feels as if there had been underhand dealing."

"I see he is. But you will not let him make it unpleasant for the Underwoods."

"Oh no, no! They have not much longer to stay. They are in correspondence about a rheumatic clergyman."

Mrs. White, however, determined not to expose Maura to her husband, though she reproached her, and was rather shocked by the young lady's self-defence. It was a natural idea, and no one had ever told her to the contrary. It was all spite in Mysie Merrifield to proclaim it after having kept it back so long.

She really was in such a state of mind that Mrs. White was rather relieved that the Rotherwoods had taken Franceska to San Remo to stay till Ivinghoe had to depart. Anna was left to send off the little felicitous note that she had written to her mother.

Each and all were writing letters that would be received with rapture almost incredulous, for no one but Sophia could have had any preparation.

"It is pleasant to think of poor Alda's delight," said Geraldine, over her writing-case. "After all her troubles, to have her utmost ambition fulfilled at last; and yet—and yet it does seem turning that pretty creature over to a life of temptation."

"In good hands," said Clement. "The youth himself is a nice honest fellow, a mere boy as yet; but it is something to have no harm in him at two-and-twenty and in the Guards; and his parents are evidently ready to watch over and guide them."

"If her head does not get turned," sighed Geraldine.

"Just as likely in any other station," replied Clement. "The protection must come from within, not from the externals; and I do think that she—yes, and he too—have that Guard within them."

"I think the sooner we are away from this place the better," said Geraldine. "There are such things as cold shoulders, and perhaps displeasure is in human nature, though it is not our fault."

"Which is the worse for us," laughed her brother, "since we can't beg pardon."

The cold shoulder was manifested by a note of apology the next morning from Mr. White. He was too busy to go with Mr. Underwood to Santa Carmela on this day, but had sent the young quarry-man to act as guide, and his foreman as interpreter. So Clement had his long ride on mule-back mostly in silence, though this he scarcely lamented, for he could better enjoy the mountain peaks and the valleys bright with rich grass, with anemones of all colours, hyacinths, strange primulas and gentians, without having to make talk to Mr. White. But his journey was without result. He did find an exceedingly old woman keeping sheep and spinning wool with a distaff, who owned to the name of Cecca Benista. She once had a brother. Yes, Gian was his name, but he went away, as they all did. He had a voice bellissima, si bellissima; and some one told her long, long ago, that he had made his fortune, and formed a company, but he had never come home—no, no, and was probably dead, though she had never heard; and he had sent nothing—no, no!

Then Clement tried the priest of the curious little church on the hill-side, a memory of Elijah and the convents on Mount Carmel. The Parrocco was a courteous man, quite a peasant, and too young to know much about the past generation. He gave Clement a refection of white bread, goats' milk cheese, and coffee, and held up his hands on the declining of his thin wine. There was a kind of register of baptisms, and Giovanni Batista Benista was hunted out, and it was found that if alive he would be over seventy years old. But no more was known, and there was no proof that he was dead twenty-two years before!

That long day had convinced Geraldine that the pleasantness of intercourse with the Whites was over, and she was not sorry that a letter was waiting for Clement to say that the rheumatic clergyman would arrive, if desired, in another week. This was gladly accepted, and the question remained, whither should they go? Clement's year of absence would be over in June, and he was anxious to get home; besides that, it was desirable to take Francie to her mother as soon as possible. The only cause for delay was the possibility of Gerald's extracting something further from his mother, which might lead to further researches on the Continent; but as most places were readily accessible from London, this was decided against, and it was determined to go back to Brompton at the same time as the Rotherwoods returned from San Remo.

On the last Sunday Mr. White showed himself much more cordial than he had been since the crisis. He waited in the porch to say—

"Well, sir, you have given us some very excellent sermons, and I am sure we are much obliged to you. If I can help you any more in investigating that unlucky affair of your nephew, do not hesitate to write to me. I shall be delighted to assist you in coming to your rights."

"Thank you; though I sincerely hope they are not my rights."

"Ah, well. You are not so advanced in life but that if you came into anything good, you might marry and start on a new lease! You are pounds better than when you came here."

Which last clause was so true that Clement could only own it, with thanks to his good-humoured host, who lingered a little still to say—

"I am sorry any vexation arose about those foolish young people, but you see young women will wish to do the best they can for themselves, and will make mischief too if one listens to them. A sensible man won't. That's what I say."

Clement quite agreed, though he was not sensible of having listened to any of the mischief-making, but he heartily shook hands with Mr. White, and went away, glad to be at peace.

CHAPTER XXXII. — THE TEST OF DAY-DREAMS

Faith's meanest deed more favour bears,
  Where hearts and wills are weighed,
 Than brightest transports, choicest prayers,
  That bloom their hour and fade.—J. H. NEWMAN.

That return to Brompton was the signal for the numerous worries awaiting Clement. First, the doctors thought him much improved, but declared that a return to full work at St. Matthew's would overthrow all the benefit of his long rest, and would not hear of his going back, even with another curate, for an experiment.

Then all went down to Vale Leston together. Mr. Ed'dard was welcomed with rapture by his old flock. Alda had been almost ill with excitement and delight, and had not words enough to show her ecstasy over her beautiful daughter, nor her gratitude to Geraldine, to whose management she insisted on attributing the glorious result. In vain did Geraldine disclaim all diplomacy, Lady Vanderkist was sure that all came of her savoir faire. At any rate, it was really comfortable to be better beloved by Alda than ever in the course of her life! Alda even intimated that she should be well enough to come to Brompton to assist in the choice of the trousseau, and the first annoyance was with Clement for not allotting a disproportioned sum for the purpose. He declared that Francie ought not to have more spent on her than was reserved for her sisters, especially as it would be easy for her to supply all deficiencies, while Alda could not endure that the future Lady Ivinghoe should have an outfit unworthy of her rank, even though both Wilmet and Geraldine undertook to assist.

There were other difficulties, for which the sojourn at Vale Leston was to be dreaded. Gerald had been of age for two months, and there were leases to be signed and arrangements made most difficult to determine in the present state of things. Major and Mrs. Harewood wanted to wind up their residence in the Priory, and to be able to move as soon as the wedding was over, since Franceska begged that it might be at the only home she remembered, and her elders put aside their painful recollections to gratify her; so that it was fixed for early August, just a year since her unprepared appearance as Mona.

After all, Alda was really too ill to go to London, and Franceska had to be sent in charge of her aunt Cherry and of her sister Mary. Lady Rotherwood would be in town, and might be trusted to have no unreasonable expectations.

Poor Sophy! Penbeacon's destiny was one of the affairs that could not be settled, and therewith her own, though her mother could not succeed in penetrating any of the family with the horror of giving Lord Ivinghoe such a brother-in-law.

In the midst of the preparations came a letter from Gerald. He did indeed write every Sunday, but of late his had been hurried letters: he was so fully occupied and had so much writing on hand that he could not indulge in more length.

"You have been urging me," he said, "to find out what my mother knows. I have not liked to press the subject while she was so ill, as she always met every hint of it with tears and agitation. However, at last, Lida brought her to it, and we really believe she knows no more than we do what became of her first husband. She never heard of him after she fled from him. She was almost a child, and he had been very cruel to her. But she did tell us where we may be nearly certain of finding out, namely from Signor Menotti, Via San Giacomo, Genoa, or his successors, a man who trained singers and performers, and moreover took charge of Benista's money, and she thinks he had considerable savings. Poor woman, I believe she had no idea of the harm she might be doing me, though it was scarcely in human nature to see prosperity look so aggressive without trying to profit thereby; and when she had put herself into O'Leary's power, the notion was to make an income out of me by private threats and holding their tongues. That I should have any objection to such an arrangement, except on economical principles, never entered their heads, and they tried to make as much as possible out of either me or Clement, by withholding all the information possible till it was paid for, and our simultaneous refusal to be blackmailed entirely disconcerted them, and made them furious. Lida said the man was violent with her mother for letting out even what she did to trousseau, and the first annoyance was with Clement for not allotting a disproportioned sum for the purpose. He declared that Francie ought not to have more spent on her than was reserved for her sisters, especially as it would be easy for her to supply all deficiencies, while Alda could not endure that the future Lady Ivinghoe should have an outfit unworthy of her rank, even though both Wilmet and Geraldine undertook to assist.

There were other difficulties, for which the sojourn at Vale Leston was to be dreaded. Gerald had been of age for two months, and there were leases to be signed and arrangements made most difficult to determine in the present state of things. Major and Mrs. Harewood wanted to wind up their residence in the Priory, and to be able to move as soon as the wedding was over, since Franceska begged that it might be at the only home she remembered, and her elders put aside their painful recollections to gratify her; so that it was fixed for early August, just a year since her unprepared appearance as Mona.

After all, Alda was really too ill to go to London, and Franceska had to be sent in charge of her aunt Cherry and of her sister Mary. Lady Rotherwood would be in town, and might be trusted to have no unreasonable expectations.

Poor Sophy! Penbeacon's destiny was one of the affairs that could not be settled, and therewith her own, though her mother could not succeed in penetrating any of the family with the horror of giving Lord Ivinghoe such a brother-in-law.

In the midst of the preparations came a letter from Gerald. He did indeed write every Sunday, but of late his had been hurried letters: he was so fully occupied and had so much writing on hand that he could not indulge in more length.

"You have been urging me," he said, "to find out what my mother knows. I have not liked to press the subject while she was so ill, as she always met every hint of it with tears and agitation. However, at last, Lida brought her to it, and we really believe she knows no more than we do what became of her first husband. She never heard of him after she fled from him. She was almost a child, and he had been very cruel to her. But she did tell us where we may be nearly certain of finding out, namely from Signor Menotti, Via San Giacomo, Genoa, or his successors, a man who trained singers and performers, and moreover took charge of Benista's money, and she thinks he had considerable savings. Poor woman, I believe she had no idea of the harm she might be doing me, though it was scarcely in human nature to see prosperity look so aggressive without trying to profit thereby; and when she had put herself into O'Leary's power, the notion was to make an income out of me by private threats and holding their tongues. That I should have any objection to such an arrangement, except on economical principles, never entered their heads, and they tried to make as much as possible out of either me or Clement, by withholding all the information possible till it was paid for, and our simultaneous refusal to be blackmailed entirely disconcerted them, and made them furious. Lida said the man was violent with her mother for letting out even what she did to Lance, and he meant to put a heavy price even on the final disclosure, in the trust (which I share) that it may prove the key to the mystery. She had no notion that the doubt was upsetting my position. Poor thing, she never had a chance in her life—gipsy breeding at first, then Benista's tender mercies and the wandering life. She could not fail to love my father till his requirements piqued her, and it was a quarrel, exasperated perhaps by the commencement of his illness, over her neglect of my unlucky self, and her acceptance of Schnetterling's attentions, that led to her abandoning him. I really do not think she ever realized that it was a sin. That good Pere Duchamps is the first priest of any kind she ever listened to, and he has had a great effect upon her. He would like to extend it to Lida and me, but Lida is staunch to her well-beloved Mr. Flight as well as to me, and there is a church on the other side the bay to which I take her when our patient is well enough to spare her to walk, or we can afford the crossing. Easter was a comfort there.

"The warm weather has revived the patient, and she may live some months longer, though she is a mere skeleton. Lida tends her in the most affectionate manner, and is really a little angel in her way. She has got some private pupils in music, and is delighted to bring in grist to the mill, which grinds hard enough to make me realize the old days you are so fond of recollecting.

"Don't ask me to send you the Lacustrian. I am ashamed of it, and of my own articles. Nothing will go down here but the most highly spiced, and it is matter of life and death to us, as long as my mother lives, to keep on the swaying top of the poplar tree of popularity. You would despise the need, and talk of Felix, but it is daily bread, and I cannot let my mother and sister starve for opinions of mine. One comfort for you is that if I ever do come home again to reign at Vale Leston, I shall have seen the outcome of various theories of last year, and proved what is the effect of having no class to raise a standard or to look up to. I don't think I shall be quite so bumptious, and I am quite sure I shall value my Cherie's tenderness much better than I have ever done, more shame for me! Love to the bride and all at Vale Leston. There is an old age of novelty about these eastern states, quite disgusting in comparison with the reverend dignity of such a place as Vale Leston. You never thought that I appreciated it! You will find no fault with me on that score now. The lake is beautiful enough, but I begin to hate the sight of it, especially when a Yankee insists on my telling him whether we have in all Europe anything better than a duck-pond in comparison. Little Lida is my drop of comfort, since she has ceased to be mortally afraid of 'Brother.' Love to all and sundry again.

"Your loving G."

There was a consultation over this letter, which ended in John Harewood's volunteering to go to Genoa, and find out this Menotti or his representative, returning in time for the wedding, and hoping that the uncertainty would thus be over in time for the enjoyment of a truly prosperous event.

A letter that came before his departure rendered Geraldine doubly anxious for the decision. Mrs. Henderson sent it to her to read, saying that it was by Lady Merrifield's advice, since she thought that it should be known how it was with Gerald, for even to Dolores he had not told half what Ludmilla related.

"It is a long time since I received your dearest, kindest of letters, and if I did not answer it sooner, it was not from want of gratitude, but attendance on my poor dear mother and assistance to our landlady occupies me at every minute that I can spare from giving music lessons to some private families, and an evening class. I am very thankful to be able to earn something, so as to take off something of the burthen on my dear brother's shoulders. For, alas! the care and support of my mother and me weigh very heavily upon him. The proprietor of the Lacustrian has parted with his other clerk, and my brother has the entire business of not only writing, extracting for, and editing the paper, but of correcting the press, and he dares not remonstrate or demand better payment, as we live from week to week, and he could not afford to be dismissed. He is at the office all day, beginning at six in the morning to meet the central intelligence, he only rushes home for his meals, and goes back to work till twelve or one o'clock at night. Even then he cannot sleep. I hear him tossing about with the pain in his back that sitting at his desk brings on, and his hands are so tired by writing, and with the heat, which has been dreadful for the last few weeks, and has taken away all the appetite he ever had. You would be shocked to see him, he is so thin and altered; I cannot think how he is to continue this, but he will not hear of my writing to Lady Travis Underwood. He is never angry, except when I try to persuade him, and you never saw anything like his patience and gentleness to my poor mother. She never did either, she cannot understand it at all. At first she thought he wanted to coax the confession out of her, and when she found that it made no difference, she could not recover from her wonder—he, whom she had deserted in his babyhood, and so cruelly injured in his manhood, to devote himself to toiling for her sake, and never to speak harshly to her for one moment. She knew I loved her, and she had always been good to me, except when O'Leary forced her to be otherwise, but his behaviour has done more to touch her heart than anything, and I am sure she is, as Pere Duchamps says, a sincere penitent. She is revived by the summer heat, and can sit under the stoop and enjoy the sweet air of the lake; but she is very weak, and coughs dreadfully in the morning, just when it is cooler, and my brother might get some sleep. She tries to be good and patient with us both, and it really does soothe her when my brother can sit by her, and talk in his cheerful droll way; but he can stay but a very short time. He has to rush back to his horrid stuffy office, and then she frets after him and says, 'But what right have I to such a son?' and she begins to cry and cough."

"Ah!" said Clement, as Geraldine, unable to speak for tears, gave him the letter. "This is a furnace of real heroism."

"Christian heroism, I am sure," said Geraldine. "Oh, my boy, I am proud of him. He will be all the better for his brave experiment."

"Yes, he had an instinct that it would be wholesome, besides the impelling cause. Real hardship is sound training."

"If it is not too hard," said she.

"'Let not their precious balms break my head,'" said Clement.

"I do not like that pain in the back. Remember how he dragged his limbs when first we had him at home, and how delicate he was up to thirteen—only eight years ago!"

"Probably it will not last long enough to do him much harm."

"And how nobly uncomplaining he is!"

"This has brought out all the good we always trusted was in reserve."

"Better than Emilia's experiment," sighed Geraldine.

For Emilia Vanderkist, before her year was over, was at home, having broken down, and having spent most of her holidays with Mrs. Peter Brown, the wife of Sir Ferdinand's partner. She had come back, not looking much the worse for her hospital experience, but with an immense deal to say of the tyranny of the matron, the rudeness of the nurses to probationers, the hardness and tedium of the work to which she had been put, and the hatefulness of patients and of doctors.

Anna sympathized with all the vehemence of her sisterly affection, and could hardly believe her aunts, who told her that things must have changed in a wonderful manner since the time of Angela's experiences, for she had been very happy in the same place, and made no complaints.

Emilia had written to her cousin Marilda to express her willingness to return so soon as the Travis Underwoods should come home, and in the meantime she remained at Vale Leston, not showing quite as much tolerance as might be expected of the somewhat narrow way of life of her sisters. She did not like being a lodger, as it were, in Sophy's bedroom; she found fault with the parlour-maid's waiting, complained of the noise of the practising of the three little sisters, and altogether reminded Geraldine of Alda in penance at home.

Major Harewood was detained longer than he expected, for on arriving at Genoa he found that Menotti had migrated, and had to follow him to his villa on the Apennines, where, in the first place, he had to overcome the old man's suspicions that he was come to recover Benista's means on behalf of his family, and then at last was assured that the man had been dead long before

1870. Still John Harewood thought it well to obtain positive evidence, and pursued the quest to Innspruck, where Menotti averred that the man had been left by his companions dying in the care of some Sisters of Charity.

So it proved. At Innspruck, the record of the burial of Giovanni Benista, a native of Piedmont, was at length produced, dated the 12th of February, 1868, happily and incontestably before Zoraya's marriage to Edgar Underwood!

John Harewood made haste to telegraph the tidings to Vale Leston and to Jonesville, and came home exultant, having dispelled the cloud that had brooded over the family for nearly a year, and given them freely to enjoy the wedding.

Would they do so the more or the less for Emilia's announcement that she had a letter from Mr. Ferdinand Brown, eldest son of Sir Ferdinand's partner, offering her marriage, and that she had accepted him? He was, of course, a rich man, but oh! how Emily, Annie, and Gerald had been wont to make fun of him, and his parents.

"But, my dear Nan," said she, "I shall be able to do much more good in that way."

"Oh!"

"And really I cannot go back to those intolerable backgammon evenings at Kensington Palace Gardens."

CHAPTER XXXIII. — A MISSIONARY WEDDING

The neighbourhood said that nothing was ever done at Vale Leston according to the conventionalities, and the Devereux wedding was an instance.

Lancelot had brought word that Bishop Norman May had actually arrived from New Zealand for a half-year's visit, bringing with him the younger missionary Leonard Ward, and that Dr. May's happiness was unspeakable. "A renewed youth, if he needed to have it renewed."

Clement and William Harewood went over to see them, and returned greatly impressed, and resolved on convoking the neighbourhood to be stirred in the cause of the Pacific islands. At the same time, one of the many letters from Lady Rotherwood about arrangements ended with—"My husband hopes you will be able to arrange for us to be introduced to your connections of the May family, the Bishop, Mr. Ward, and the good old doctor of whom we have heard so much."

"We must invite them all to the wedding," said Mrs. Harewood, who, as still inhabiting the Priory, would be the hostess.

"Certainly," returned William Harewood, "but I don't think Mr. Ward would come. He looks like an ancient hermit."

"The best way," said Mrs. Grinstead, "would be to finish up the wedding-day with a missionary garden-party."

"Geraldine!" said Lady Vanderkist from her sofa, in feeble accents of dismay; but Mrs. William Harewood hardly heard, and did not notice.

"It would be the most admirable plan. It would give people something to do, and make a reason for having ever so many more."

"Baits cleverly disposed," said William. "The S.P.G. to attract Ward, Ward to attract the Marquis, and the Marquis to attract the herd."

"Everybody throngs to the extremest outskirts of a wedding," said Geraldine.

"They may have the presents on view in the long room," said Wilmet.

"Provided they don't have the list of them printed," said Geraldine. "Lance won't put them into the 'Pursuivant'; it is disgusting!"

"So I have always thought," said Robina; "but you hardly make allowances for the old ladies who love to spell them out."

"The Marquis of Rotherwood—a gold-topped dressing-case; Miss Keren Happuch Tripp—a pincushion," said Geraldine. "It is the idlest gossip, and should not be encouraged."

"And," added Robina, "as we go out through the cloister there will happily be no rice. Will has stopped it in the churchyard."

"And fortunately we have no school-boys to reckon with, except Adrian and Fely, who will be quite amenable."

For Kester Harewood was in India, and Edward on the Mediterranean; Adrian was at home, doing credit to Miss Mohun, and so vehemently collecting stamps, that he was said to wish to banish all his friends to the most remote corners of the earth to send them home.

Francie's elder sisters declined being bridesmaids, so that Phyllis and Mysie were the chief, and the three young sisters, Wilmet, Alda, and Joan, with two little Underwoods and two small Harewoods, all in white frocks and sashes, were to attend and make a half-circle round the bride.

All took effect as had been purposed, each party being equally desirous that it should be truly a Christian wedding, such as might be a fit emblem of the great Marriage Feast, and bring a blessing—joyous and happy, yet avoiding the empty pomp and foolish mirth that might destroy the higher thoughts.

How beautiful Vale Leston church looked, decked with white roses, lilies, and myrtle! The bride, tall and stately in her flowing veil and glistening satin train, had her own sweet individuality, not too closely recalling the former little bride. She came on her uncle Clement's arm, as most nearly representing a father to her, and the marriage blessing was given by the majestic-looking Bishop, with the two chief local clergy, Mr. William Harewood and Mr. Charles Audley, taking part of the service. It was a beautiful and impressive scene, and there was a great peace on all. It was good to see the intense bliss on Ivinghoe's face as he led his bride down the aisle, and along the cloister; and as they came into the drawing-room, after she had received an earnest kiss, and "my pretty one" from his father, it was to Dr. May that he first led her. Dr. May, his figure still erect, his face bright and cheery, his brow entirely bare, and his soft white locks flowing over his collar. He held out his hands, "Ah, young things! You are come for the old man's blessing! Truly you have it, my lady fair. You are fair indeed, as fair within as without. You have a great deal in the power of those little hands, and you—oh yes, both of you, believe, that a true, faithful, loving, elevating wife is the blessing of all one's days, whether it be only for a few years, or, as I trust and pray it may be with you, for a long—long, good, and prosperous life together."

The two young things bent their heads, and he blessed them with his blessing of eighty years. Lord Rotherwood's eyes were full of tears, as he said in a choked voice—

"Thank you, sir," while Franceska murmured to Mysie—

"I do like that he should have been the first to call me 'my lady.'"

The luncheon included only the two families, and the actual assistants at the wedding, and it was really very merry. Lady Rotherwood did inspire a little awe, but then Alda, sitting near, knew exactly how to talk to her, and Alda, who, like Geraldine, had dressed herself in soft greys and whites, with her delicate cheeks flushed with pleasure and triumph, looked as beautiful as ever, and far outshone her twin, whose complexion and figure both had become those of the portly housewife.

Meta, otherwise Mrs. Norman May, had eyes as bright and lively as ever, though face and form had both grown smaller, and she was more like a fairy godmother than the Titania she had been in times of old. She had got into the middle of all the varieties of children, dragged thither by Gertrude's Pearl and Audrey, and was making them happy.

Ethel and Geraldine never could come to the end of what they had to say to one another, except that Ethel could but be delighted to make her friend know the brother of her early youth; and show her the grave, earnest-looking man who had suffered so much, and whose hair was as white as the doctor's, his face showing the sunburn of the tropics; and the crow's-feet round his eyes, the sailor's habit of searching gaze. He did not speak much, but watched the merry young groups as if they were a sort of comedy in his eyes.

They were very merry, especially when the doctor had proposed the health of the bride, and her brother, Sir Adrian, was called on to return thanks for her.

"Gentlemen and ladies," he said, "no, I mean ladies and gentlemen, I am very much obliged to you all for the honour you have done my sister. I can tell Lord Ivinghoe she is a very good girl, and very nice, and all that, when she is not cocky, and doesn't try to keep one in order."

The speech was drowned in laughter, and calls to Ivinghoe to mind what he was about, and beware of the "new woman."

So the young couple were seen off to spend their honeymoon in Scotland,

and the rest of the party could pair off to enjoy their respective friends, except that Mary and Sophy had to exhibit the wedding presents to all and sundry of the visitors of all degrees who began to flock in.

Seats were ranged on the lawn, and when every one had had time to wonder at everything, from Lady Rotherwood's set of emeralds, down to the choirboys' carved bracket, the house-bell was rung, and all had to take their places on the lawn, fairly shaded by house, cloister, and cedar tree, and facing the conservatory, whose steps, with the terrace, formed a kind of platform. It is not needful to go through all, or how John Harewood, as host, explained that they had thought that it would be well to allow their guests to have the advantage of hearing their distinguished visitors tell of their experiences. And so they did, the Bishop pleading the cause of missions with his wonderful native eloquence, as he stood by the chair where his father sat listening to him, as to a strain of sweet music long out of reach. Then Leonard Ward simply and bluntly told facts about the Pacific islands and islanders, that set hearts throbbing, and impelled more than one young heart to long to tread in the like course.

Then Lord Rotherwood thanked and bungled as usual, so that Gustave Tanneguy would have a hard matter to reduce what he called the "aristocratic tongue" to plain English, or rather reporter's English. The listeners were refreshed with tea, coffee, and lemonade, and there was a final service in the church, which many gladly attended, and thus ended what had been a true holiday.

CHAPTER XXXIV. — RIGHTED

"No. 14, Huron St., Jonesville, Ohio,

"July 19.

"MY DEAR MADAM,

"You were so kind as to tell me to write to your ladyship if we were in any difficulty or distress, and I have often longed to do so, but my brother always said that we had no right to trespass on your goodness. Now, however, things are at such a pass that I think you will hear of us with true compassion. I do not know whether he told you that we met my poor mother on board a steamer upon this lake. Her husband had been drowned in a wreck while crossing, and she was reduced to great poverty, and had also, from exposure, contracted disease of the lungs, which, the doctor said, must terminate fatally in a few months. My brother took charge of her, and has supported us ever since, now four months, by working at the editorship of the Lacustrian Intelligencer, with such small assistance as I could give by music lessons. It involved severe labour at desk work and late hours, and his health has latterly given way, his back and lower limbs being gradually affected, and last Monday even his hands proved helpless. My poor mother broke another blood-vessel on Sunday, and died ten minutes later. My brother desired me to sell his dear violin and his watch to pay the funeral expenses, but after that I know not what we can do, as he is quite helpless, and can hardly be left even for the sake of my small earnings. Dear Lady Travis Underwood, pray help us, as I know you and Sir Ferdinand love my poor dear generous brother, and will not think him ungrateful for having declined your kindness while he could support himself and us. No doubt we shall get help from England, but not for some time, so I dare to ask you.

"I remain, your humble servant,

"LUDMILLA.

"P.S.—Everybody knows him as Jerry Wood. We are at Mr. MacMahon's, 14 Huron Street."

This sad letter, in Lida's neat pupil-teacher's hand, came enclosed within a longer letter from Marilda.

"Grand National Hotel, Jonesville.

"July 23rd.

"MY DEAR GERALDINE,

"You will believe that this letter from poor Lydia made Fernan telegraph at once to her, and hurry off as soon as we could reach the train. We found things quite as bad or worse than we expected. The poor children were living in two rooms in a wretched little house of an Irish collier, who with his wife happily has been very kind to them, and says that nothing could surpass their goodness to that poor mother of theirs, who, she tells me, 'made a real Christian end' at last. I am sure she had need to do so.

"The burial was happily over, conducted by the French priest, as the woman was a Roman Catholic to the last. Gerald was sitting up by the window, so changed that we should not have known him, except for the wonderful likeness to Felix that has come upon him. It seems that he had not only all the writing of that horrid paper to do, but all the compositor's work, or whatever you call it. The people put upon him when they saw how well he could do it, and he could not refuse because his mother needed comforts, and he durst not get thrown out of employment. He went on, first with aching back, then his legs got stiff and staggering, but still he went on, and now it has gone into his hands; he cannot hold a pen, and can hardly lift a tea-cup. But he is so cheerful, almost merry. The doctor says it is a paralytic affection, and that overwork has developed the former disease from the old injury to the spine, which seemed to have passed off, and there is intermittent fever about him too, a not uncommon thing in these low-lying lake districts. We have moved him to this Grand National Hotel, a big, half-inhabited place, but better than the MacMahons' house, though the good woman cried over him and Lydia at their farewells, and said she never should see such a young gentleman and lady again with hearts so like ould Ireland. She would hardly take the money that Fernan offered her; she said they had brought a blessing on her house with their tender, loving ways.

"Fernan is gone to Milwaukee to get further advice and more comforts for Gerald, and we mean, as soon as he can be moved, to take him home with us, since the air of the Rockies will revive him if anything will. This place is fearfully hot and oppressive; the bay seems to shut out air from Lake Erie, and I cannot bear to think what that poor boy must have gone through in that close little den, with the printing-press humming and stamping away close to him; but he says it is his native element, and that when he is better he must go to Fiddler's Ranch. He sends his love, and fears that you have missed his letters, but he could hardly write them, and thought Lydia might alarm you. He is a very dear boy, and I do hope we make him comfortable; he is so thankful for the little we can do for him, and so patient. He tells me to give special love to Francie, and say he is glad that Mona's game of chess was played out with a good substitute for Ferdinand. These are his words, which no doubt she will understand. We think of moving next week, but much depends on the doctor's verdict. My love too to the dear Francie; she will be a great lady, quite beyond our sphere. Perhaps she may be able to give Emily some amusements, though I fear they will only make her more discontented with our humdrum ways. I never thought hospital work would suit her. Gerald says there is nothing like trying one's theories, and that having to exaggerate his own has made him sick of a good deal of them, though not of all. Poor dear boy, I hope he will live to show the benefits he says he has derived from this sad time. It shall not be for want of anything we can do. He is as near our hearts as ever his dear father was, and Lydia is a dear little girl.

"Your ever affectionate cousin,

"MARY ALDA TRAVIS UNDERWOOD."

It was a great shock, though mitigated by hearing that Gerald was in such hands as those of his first friend, and kind Marilda; but there was great surprise at no notice being taken of the tidings that secured Gerald's position. John Harewood had telegraphed them, but it only now fully broke on him that he ought to have sent them to Jerry Wood instead of Gerald Underwood, so that Italian telegrams were not to blame.

On one thing Clement ventured, being nearly certain that the reaction of Gerald's mind would not include the preventing of all Penbeacon works. He encouraged young Bramshaw to set about the plans so as to make the washings as innocuous as possible, being persuaded that this was the only way to prevent more obnoxious erections on ground just beyond. Moreover, this gave the lovers hope, and Alda had, under Clement's persuasion and rebukes, withdrawn her opposition to the engagement, so that Sophy was free to wander about Penbeacon with her Philip, and help to set up his theodolite, and hold the end of his measuring-tape.

Her mother could not well stand out on the score of unequal birth, when Mr. Ferdinand Brown, whose father had swept out the office, came down and was accepted with calm civility, it could not be called delight, even by Emilia.

But he was a worthy young man, and well educated, and it was for his sake that Clement and Geraldine had stayed on at the Priory, giving the Harewoods and their curates holidays in turn; though even this amount of work was enough to leave with Clement a dread conviction that his full share of St. Matthew's would be fatal to him, insomuch that he had written to the patron, the Bishop of Albertstown, seriously to propose resignation.

Fresh letters arrived from America, the first slightly more cheery, but the next was dated from Violinia, to the general surprise, and it was very short, from Sir Ferdinand.

"DEAR CLEMENT,

"We have the telegram, a relief to the poor lad's mind, but he has not spoken much since. It came just as we were starting in an invalid Pullman, fitted with every comfort; but the jars of these lines are unavoidable and unspeakable, and he suffered so terribly, as well as so patiently, that we had to give up our intention of taking him to Underwood. The one thing he begged for was that we would take him to Fiddler's Ranch. You know there is a mission-station here, so we have him in the clergyman's house, and the place is so advanced that he has every comfort. But I doubt whether the dear boy will ever move again. He is perfectly helpless, but his brain quite clear, and his spirits good.

"Ever yours,

"F. A. TRAVIS UNDERWOOD."

There followed a long letter, dictated by Gerald himself, and partly written by Lida, partly by Marilda, at several different times.

"DEAREST, MOST DEAREST CHERIE, AND ALL—

"I should like to be able to sign my name to my thanks to all, if only to feel that I have a name, and one so honoured, but these fingers of mine will not obey me, so you must take the will for the deed, and believe that you have made me very happy, and completed all I could wish. I fear you never will believe how jolly it is to lie here, the pain all gone, since having done with that terrific train, and the three tenderest, most watchful of slaves always round me, while my Cherie is spared the sight of the wreck.—(L.)

"You know that good old Fernan established a missionary station here, building a church, and getting the ground consecrated where my father lies. I can just see the top of the cross, and there he promises that I shall lie. You will be able to put my name in the cloister under my father's, as no impostor.

"Don't grieve, my Cherie, it is best as it is; my brains were full of more notions than you ever quite guessed, and of which I have seen the seamy side out here, though there is much that I should feel bound to work out, and that might have grieved you. I was not tough enough for the discipline that was needed to strike the balance. (He is thinking aloud, dear fellow.—M. A.) I am afraid I have often vexed you in my crudeness and conceit, but I know you forgive. I am very thankful for this year, and for the way in which my poor mother was given into my hands at last. Fernan has helped me to make a short will, to save confusion and difficulty.

"I have left everything to Clement, knowing that you and he will provide for all. Fernan and Marilda will care for Lida. (That we will.—M. A.) I cannot leave her to be a tax on Vale Leston. Give my books and MSS. to Dolores, and please be kind to her. My violin, which Fernan redeemed for me, the eponym (How do you spell it?—M. A.), by the way, of this place, my father's own fiddle, give to Lance for his pretty Ariel; Anna, my good sister, should have my music, which will be a memory of happy evenings. Emmie may like the portfolio of drawings that I made for the mission-house; dear old Sibby the photograph in my room of the 'Ecce Homo.' I have it in my eye now.— (M. A.)

"Everything is such a comfort, Fernan and Marilda are the best of nurses and helpers, and I mourn for the folly that chaffed about them and boredom. Tell Emmie so. Fernan has made this place a little oasis round my father's grave, and his parson, who has a mission among the remains of the Sioux, is with me every other day, and does all that Clement could desire for me. So do —do believe that it is all for the best, dear people.—(L.)

"One thing good is, that I shall not bring any bad blood into the Underwood inheritance. By the bye, tell them—(Continued by Marilda) Mr. Gracchus Van ———— suddenly arrived here, greatly shocked at Gerald's state, and actually wanting to marry Lydia on the spot—which of course she declined. But Fernan was pleased with him, and he told him he had never met any one to hold a candle to 'Jerry Wood,' so 'smart' and 'chipper,' as he saw at first, and then cheerful, good-humoured, and kindly, whatever happened. None of your Britisher's airs, but ready to make the best of any fixings. I don't think dear Gerald meant me to tell all this, but think of the difference from the fastidious fine gentleman he used to be! He is dozing now, I fear he is getting weaker; but he is ever so sweet and good, and I quite long to beg his pardon for having called him your spoilt boy. Mr. Fraser, the clergyman here, is very much struck with him, and Fernan remembers the time when he baptized him as he lay unconscious. Dear Cherry, it will grieve you, but I think there will be comfort in the grief.

"Your affectionate cousin,

"M. A. T. U."

There were long letters to Dolores, dictated to Lida—all in the same spirit. One of them said, "Go bravely on, my Dolores; though we do not live together in our bicycle-roving castles. You will do good work if you uphold the glory of God and the improvement of man, all through creation and science. I should like to talk it over with you. Things are plainer to me than in the days of my inexperience and cocksureness. Short as the time was, in months, it showed me much more, especially my own inefficiency to deal with the great problems of these times, perhaps of all times. Remember this, but go on—if we do but put grains of sand into the great Edifice."

More was written, but these were the most memorable extracts, before the letter that told that something like a fresh stroke had come, and taken away the power of distinct speech, then that the throat had failed, and there was only one foreboding more to be told, and soon realized. The young ardent spirit, trained by so short a discipline, had passed away in peace. And they laid him beside his father, whose better spirit he had unconsciously evoked, and whom he had loved so deeply. The doctors said that the real cause of his death had been the Indian bullet, inflicting injury on the spine, which the elasticity of youth had for the time overcome, but which manifested itself again under overstrain. Ferdinand, when he awoke the child back to life, had given him years not spent in vain for himself or for others.

It would have been utter desolation to the little sister save for the motherly tenderness of Marilda, who took her to the home in the Rocky Mountains, and would fain have adopted her, but that Lida, acting perhaps on advice from her brother, only begged to be so educated as to fit her to be independent, and to be given a start in life. It would be shown in a year or two whether her vocation should be musical or scholastic.

Gerald had his meed of tears at home, but not bitter ones. Nay, those that had the most quality of bitterness were Emilia's, shed in secret lest interpretations should be put on those that had the quality of remorse, as she recollected the high aspirations that had ended so differently in the two cousins.

Dolores dried hers, to feel a consecration on her studies and her labours as she grew forward to the fulfilment of her purpose of being a leading woman in the instruction and formation of young minds, working all the better for the inspiriting words and example, and the more gently and sympathizingly for the love that was laid up in her heart.

She and his "Cherie" came to have a great affection and understanding of each other, and discussed what Dolores called "ethics" with warm interest, the elder lady bringing the old and sacred lights to bear on the newer theories.

Clement was the undoubted owner of Vale Leston, and the John Harewoods had decided on leaving the Priory. Just at the same time, when the acceptance of Clement's resignation of St. Matthew's had arrived, William Harewood was offered a canonry at Minsterham, with the headship of the theological college. The canonry had been the summit of his ambition when a boy, and there was no one fitter than he for the care of a theological college. He was pre-eminently a scholar, and his fifteen years of parish experience made good preparation for training young clergy.

So Clement could decide on presenting himself to the living of Vale Leston, with a staff of curates, and Geraldine to be his home sister, making the Priory a resting-place for overworked people, whether clergy, governesses, or poor, or mission-folk at home. It was a trust to be kept for Lancelot and his boy, who would make the summer home of the family there, to Dr. May's great content. It was a peaceful home, and to every one's surprise, Alda decided to remain at hand, chiefly to keep her boy under his uncle's influence, which thus far was keeping him well in hand, and as he would go to a public school with little Felix, might be prolonged.

It was a comfort and encouragement to feel that hereditary dangers and temperament could be subdued and conquered in Gerald; and if the sins of parents had their consequence in the children, the scourge might become a palm. When the commemorative brass in the cloister was to be put up, Geraldine said—

"I should like to put 'Rejoice with me, for I have found the piece that was lost.'"

"He never was lost."

"Oh no, no, my dear boy. But his work was so like the finding the stained, tarnished piece of silver, cast aside, defaced, dust-marked, and by simple duty and affection bringing her back."

"I see! Let us have the inscription in Greek. Then none can apply it to himself! It was a wonderful work, and it is strange that having fulfilled it, he who brought the child from his father's arms should lay him to his rest beside his father."

THE END